STORM of
SHADOWS

Other Books by Christina Dodd

Christina Dodd's The Chosen Ones series
Storm of Visions
Storm of Shadows

Christina Dodd's Darkness Chosen series
Scent of Darkness
Touch of Darkness
Into the Shadow
Into the Flame

Christina Dodd's Romantic Suspense
Trouble in High Heels
Tongue in Chic
Thigh High
Danger in a Red Dress

CHRISTINA
DODD

STORM of
SHADOWS

THE
CHOSEN
ONES

A SIGNET BOOK

SIGNET
Published by New American Library, a division of
Penguin Group (USA) Inc., 375 Hudson Street,
New York, New York 10014, USA
Penguin Group (Canada), 90 Eglinton Avenue East, Suite 700, Toronto,
Ontario M4P 2Y3, Canada (a division of Pearson Penguin Canada Inc.)
Penguin Books Ltd., 80 Strand, London WC2R 0RL, England
Penguin Ireland, 25 St. Stephen's Green, Dublin 2,
Ireland (a division of Penguin Books Ltd.)
Penguin Group (Australia), 250 Camberwell Road, Camberwell, Victoria 3124,
Australia (a division of Pearson Australia Group Pty. Ltd.)
Penguin Books India Pvt. Ltd., 11 Community Centre, Panchsheel Park,
New Delhi - 110 017, India
Penguin Group (NZ), 67 Apollo Drive, Rosedale, North Shore 0632,
New Zealand (a division of Pearson New Zealand Ltd.)
Penguin Books (South Africa) (Pty.) Ltd., 24 Sturdee Avenue,
Rosebank, Johannesburg 2196, South Africa

Penguin Books Ltd., Registered Offices:
80 Strand, London WC2R 0RL, England

ISBN-13: 978-1-61523-605-3

Copyright © Christina Dodd, 2009
All rights reserved

 REGISTERED TRADEMARK—MARCA REGISTRADA

Printed in the United States of America

Happy anniversary, Scott.
Lots of years, lots of memories,
two kids, and true love.
Thank God I found you.

ACKNOWLEDGMENTS

Thank you to the wonderful team at NAL who have been so enthusiastic about this story—Kara Welsh, Lindsay Nouis (who I know does all the real work), the brilliant art department led by Anthony Ramondo, the publicity department with Craig Burke and Michele Langley, and of course, the spectacular Penguin sales department. A heartfelt thank-you to my editor, Kara Cesare, who contributes so much to my work with her discerning eye and tactful suggestions.

Prologue

Thirty-two years ago
High in the Idaho Mountains

As the sunrise tinged the sky, the Indian stood naked outside the Sacred Cave. He shivered in the frigid air, resisting the call to enter. It was not an honorable resistance; as the chief of his tribe, it was his duty to go to the gods when they called. But always he was afraid of the small, dark hole, of the hard, black rock, of the ancient paintings in the stone.

His ragged all-weather coat lay at his feet, the tear in the green nylon mended with a wide strip of silver duct tape. He had flung his jeans, white with age, and his long johns, pink from a washing with his red flannel shirt, across a rock. His boots and socks were stacked below. He looked longingly at the clothes, the footwear, and the warmth they represented.

Did the gods care about his old age? About his duties on the reservation? About the difficulties of coming up to this high, bleak spot when winter himself stalked the land?

No. They cared only about themselves. He didn't know much about them. The old traditions and stories had faded from their small tribe, but he knew one thing for sure; they were very human gods.

So Bitter Eagle lay on his belly, groaning as the mountain's cold bones stripped the warmth from his flesh. Arms outstretched, he worked his way into the tiny crack in the stone, pushing the leather bag before him and wishing he had grown too fat to cross the threshold, yet knowing that was impossible. The Bear Creek tribe was small and poor, easily dismissed by the US government and, some said, too proud for their own good. But they had learned early on that to depend on anyone besides themselves meant giving up their freedoms. So they lived in their small houses, hunted the lofty peaks of the Sawtooth Wilderness, raised gardens and children, and slowly faded from the modern world's memory.

Never had one of the Bear Creek tribe grown fat on life.

As Bitter Eagle entered the womb of Mother Earth, he sniffed. Usually the cave smelled like molten rock and broken dreams.

Now the air was smoky, with the bitter tang of blood.

No wonder the gods had called him.

Someone had violated their sanctuary.

He knelt in the entrance. Sun leaked through the crack in the rock behind him, but at this time of the year, when the sun was low in the south, and this time of the day, at first light, it cast only a feeble illumination. It was the Sacred Cave itself that glowed with an unearthly light, a dim phosphorescence that seemed to seep from the living rocks. The ceiling above his head was low, but gradually it sloped up and back, extending so far that it ended in the home of darkness. Messages danced across the walls in drawings and words, some so faded with age as to be less than a thought, some as fresh and new as this morning's sunrise.

He didn't know who had written them. Wise men, cruel witches, women who saw portents and men of power. He didn't try to read them. Didn't try to understand the cries of grief, didn't dare repeat the spells of magic, didn't want to fall under an enchantment that would lead him farther and farther into the cave until he stumbled on the bones of the others who had succumbed to the fascination and died, sacrifices to the gods.

Instead, he looked for the cause of the smoke and blood.

There. In a pit built where the floor took its first downward slant into the earth, the embers of a fire still glowed red. He crawled forward, his eyes darting back and forth, looking for the lifeless body he thought must be sprawled on the hard floor. For why else would he smell blood, except that some foolish soul had broken the law and entered the Sacred Cave . . . and there had lost his life?

Yet he saw nothing. Whoever had come here was now gone, leaving no stain on the floor.

Should he revive the fire, or extinguish it? Which would please the fickle gods?

Standing, he walked to the pit and knelt beside the shallow depression in the rock. From his bag, he withdrew kindling and logs of dry, aromatic cedar, and laid them carefully on the embers. He leaned forward to blow on the infant flames, and from within the cave, a puff of wind performed the service for him.

So. He had guessed right. The gods wished him to cleanse the air with his offerings. He fed the fire bit by bit, building the flames, waving his arms in great circles to spread the fragrant smoke throughout the massive cave. The scent of pine retreated, but the tang of blood grew stronger, strong enough to taste it on his tongue. He got to his feet and scanned the area, trying to locate the source, then picked up a flaming torch from the fire and followed his nose into the depths of the cave, farther than he had ever been before.

The blood-soaked stench guided his footsteps, leading him on until at last he found it, a dark mass just over the edge of a two-foot drop.

It took a moment for him to realize what it was—a human female had given birth in this cave, and recently enough that the placenta was fresh.

The gods would be displeased.

His horror made him stumble backward, off another step and into the darkness.

He landed awkwardly, going down on one knee, and dropped his torch. The branch rolled away and vanished over the edge. The little flame disappeared. Terrified he was going to follow it, plunge into the chasm and disappear into the black depths, Bitter Eagle put his hand out to catch himself. He touched something sticky, cool, and soft, and . . . the thing moved beneath his fingers.

Alive. It was alive.

He snatched his hand back and cradled it against his chest over his pounding heart. He stood carefully and backed up, feeling his way with his bare feet, up the jagged rocks toward the entrance, never taking his gaze away from that place where the thing had wiggled under his touch. The scent of woman's blood from his hand made him halt in his tracks.

The silence pounded in his ears.

What was that thing?

Was it . . . the baby?

No. No. It was cool. There was no human warmth in it.

But a newborn who had been abandoned by its mother would cool as its body heat dissipated, as its heart slowed and its breath failed.

What did it matter? A baby born in this cave was forfeit to the gods. The mother, whoever she was, had known the law, and had done this deliberately to dispose of her baby.

But the gods had never given Bitter Eagle the gift of a child. Three wives, and while they were with him, all had been barren. The world called him Bitter Eagle, a name given while he watched the village children at play.

Perhaps the cruel gods had called him here to give him a gift . . . and perhaps they had called him to finish the sacrifice.

He should leave the infant to its fate.

He took a step toward the entrance.

And the baby gave forth one small, newborn mewl of anguish.

The sound flew to his heart, to the center of his pain.

The infant was tiny. It was dying. It needed warmth and food and comfort.

It needed him.

Swiftly, knowing he was breaking one of the most ancient and sacred commandments, he turned back to the tiny being.

He laid his hand on it. It was indeed a human baby.

Lifting it into his arms, he cradled it against his chest and walked toward the entrance.

Wind ripped through the cave, pushing him back.

The gods were not pleased.

But a lifetime of obeying their desires had not made him complicit with this . . . this murder.

He fought his way forward, leaning against the wind that blasted him toward the chasm.

The baby hung limp in his grasp. Dead? Was Bitter Eagle displeasing the gods for a child who had already passed on?

Yet he struggled toward the entrance, toward that narrow glimpse of pale sunlight. Sand whipped into his eyes, blinding him, searing his lungs.

If he put the baby down, the wind would stop. He knew it would.

Still he moved inch by inch, one foot in front of the other. The entrance came closer and closer.

Above him, the black granite groaned, threatening him with immolation. If he didn't get out *now*, he, too, would be a sacrifice.

He made a rush toward the narrow crack in the rock, dropped to his belly and shoved the child out into the cool sunlight. From the heights, he heard the wind scream with fury, heard the shift as stones broke free and roared toward the cave floor. He dove toward the entrance, wiggled his head out, his shoulders out, his chest out—and something slammed onto his foot, trapping him in place.

Skin ripped. Bones crunched. Pain ripped into his gut and brain. He writhed with torment, wanting to beg the gods' pardon, knowing it was too late. He was trapped forever. He would die here, and the child with him.

The child . . .

He fought his way out of the fog of agony and looked at the child.

The infant lay on its side facing him, and it looked back.

It was a boy, a tiny newborn covered with afterbirth. The umbilical cord had been severed close to his body, so close the knife had nicked his leg. His skin was red-tinged, his chest moved up and down with each breath, and he shivered in minuscule convulsions.

But his eyes were open, and he stared gravely at Bitter Eagle, waiting for him to finish his rescue.

Bitter Eagle could not die now. He could not fail his first test as a father.

Shutting his pain inside his formidable will, he stretched himself toward the pile of clothes he had shed before entering the cave. His fingertips could not quite touch . . . He strained forward. . . .

In his foot, something tore—some ligament, some bone, some muscle. New waves of pain escaped their confinement to batter him, dimming his eyes and shortening his breath.

The child struggled as if trying to reach him . . . or as if death leaned too close.

With his suffering, Bitter Eagle had bought himself one vital inch.

He caught the edge of his old nylon coat between two fingers and pulled it toward him. With one hand he scooped the infant off the cold stone; with the other he slid the coat beneath the child, placed him onto the material, and enclosed him in the warmth.

Then he set to work. He dragged his jeans toward him and pulled his hunting knife from its leather sheath. He held it for a minute, allowing his body temperature to warm the plastic handle, allowing himself a moment of rebellion against what he must do.

Then he struggled to fit his arm back into the cave.

That must have amused the gods, for they sent no more missiles to break his body or his spirit. Or perhaps they simply waited in anticipation for a fresh gush of blood to appease their anger. Certainly they laughed as he set the blade in his own flesh, as close to the boulder as he could, and started cutting. His writhing, the moans that broke from him, the way he used knowledge gleaned from cutting up chickens . . . all that must have satisfied their malice.

When he was done, he eased himself out of the cave and back to the real world—a real world that would no longer call him Bitter Eagle, but Cripple Eagle.

Very well. He had paid the price for his son.

He lifted the jacket.

It was so light, for a moment he wondered if the child had vanished, stolen from him by the gods while he hacked at his own flesh.

But no. The baby was still there, no longer blue with cold, moving his arms and legs, and starting to squawk in hunger as a healthy child should.

Perhaps the gods had been placated.

And as soon as he had finished the thought, the first flakes of snow trickled out of the lowering sky.

Placated? No. They were determined to mock Bitter Eagle's struggles, and kill him and his child.

Now Bitter Eagle set to work to make sure he and his child lived long enough to make it down the mountain. He wrapped his long johns around the bleeding stump where his foot had been, fumbled his way into his flannel shirt, painfully pulled his jeans over his legs, and put both socks over his one remaining foot. He unwrapped the baby from his jacket and placed him so they rested together, chest to chest, heart to heart. Swiftly, he buttoned the flannel over them both—then, catching a glimpse of the child's back, he stopped.

Lifting the baby, he wiped his thumb down the fragile spine, and stared with wonder and with dread. For there, etched in black and spreading toward the baby's shoulder blades, was the mark of crumpled angel wings.

Bitter Eagle knew of a legend told among his people for generations, of children abandoned by their parents, deprived of their love and care, and instead given by the great Creator gifts of power and magic. Yet never had Bitter Eagle seen the mark that set one of those children apart.

Now he held one such child against his heart.

No wonder the evil gods had punished him for stealing their sacrifice.

This child was special. This child was one of the Abandoned Ones.

Chapter 1

———————◆———————

"**I**'m looking for the antiquities librarian. I have an appointment. I'm Aaron Eagle."

"Yes, Mr. Eagle, I've got you on the schedule." The library's administrative assistant was gorgeous, lush, and fully aware of his eligibility. She smiled into his eyes as she pushed the book toward him. "If you would sign in here." She pointed, handed him a pen, and managed to brush his fingers with hers. "And here." She pointed again. "Then if you don't mind, we'd like your fingerprint. Just your left thumb."

"I'm always amazed at the security required to visit antiquities." Aaron smiled at her as he pressed his thumb onto the glass set into the desk. A light from beneath scanned his thumb.

"The Arthur W. Nelson Fine Arts Library antiquities department contains some extremely rare manuscripts and scrolls, and we take security very seriously because of it."

"So if I made my living stealing antiquities, you'd know."

"Exactly."

"If I'd been caught."

"Thieves always eventually get caught." She had him stand on the line and took his photograph.

"I would certainly hope so." He stepped onto a grate that shook him hard, then through an explosives screener that puffed air around him.

She riffled through the piles of paper on her desk, compared them to the information on her computer screen, and smiled with satisfaction. "But you seem to be exactly who you say you are."

"I do seem to be, don't I?" He leaned back over the grate. "Perhaps we could discuss who you are tonight over drinks"—he glanced down at the nameplate on the desk—"Jessica?"

"I'd like that"—she glanced down at the form on her desk—"Aaron."

"Great. I'll get your number on the way out, and we can arrange a time and place."

She nodded and smiled.

He smiled back and headed down the corridor, and as he walked, he peeled off his thumbprint and slipped the micromillimeter-thin plastic into his pocket.

"Just take the elevator down to the bottom floor," she called after him.

"Thank you, I will. I've been here before."

"That's right. You have." Her voice faded.

The corridor was plain, painted industrial gray, while the elevator was stainless steel on the outside and pure mid-twentieth-century technology on the inside. The wood paneling was obviously plastic, the button covers were cracked, the numbers worn to near invisibility, and the mechanism creaked as it descended at a stately rate.

But this was the Arthur W. Nelson Fine Arts Library, and their funding didn't include upkeep on nonessentials like a new elevator for the seldom-visited antiquities department. They were lucky to have updated security in the last ten years, and that only occurred when it was discovered one of the librarians had been systematically removing pages from medieval manuscripts and selling them for a fortune to collectors. If he hadn't decided to get greedy and remove a Persian scroll, he might still be in business, but Dr. Hall had been the antiquities librarian for about a hundred and fifty years and he caught on to that right away.

In fact, it was Dr. Hall that Aaron was on his way to see now. When it came to ancient languages, the old guy was a genius, and he knew a hell of a lot about prophecies, religious and otherwise. Which was exactly the kind of expertise Aaron needed right now.

The elevator door opened, and he strode along another short, industrial gray corridor that led to a metal door at the end. He rang the doorbell at the side. The lock clicked, he turned the handle, and he walked in.

Nobody was there. Whoever had let him in had done so remotely.

The place smelled like a library: dust, old paper, cracking glue, broken linoleum, and more dust. Gray metal shelving extended from one end of the basement to the other, clustered in rows, filled to capacity with books.

No one was in sight.

"Hello?" he called. "Dr. Hall? It's Aaron Eagle."

"Back here!" A voice floated over and through the shelves. A woman's voice.

They must have finally dug up the funding to get Dr. Hall another assistant. Good thing. The old guy could croak down here and no one would notice for days.

Aaron headed back between a shelf marked MEDI-EVAL STUDIES and one marked BABYLONIAN GODS. He broke out from among the shelves into the work area where wide library tables were covered with manu-scripts, scrolls, and a giant stone tablet.

A girl leaned over the stone tablet, mink brush in hand. "Put it on the table over there." She waved the brush vaguely toward the corner.

Aaron glanced over at the table piled with Styro-foam containers and fast-food bags wadded up into little balls. He looked back at the girl.

Her skin was creamy, fine-grained and perfect, and that was a good thing, since she did not wear a single drop of makeup. No foundation, no blush, no pow-der, no lipstick. She was of medium height, perhaps a little skinny, but with what she was wearing, who could tell? Her blue dress drooped where it should fit and hung unevenly at the hem. He supposed she wore it for comfort. He didn't know any other reason any woman would be caught dead in it. The neckline hung off one shoulder, revealing a dingy bra strap, the elastic stretched and frayed. She had thin latex gloves stretched over her hands—nothing killed a man's amo-rous intentions like latex gloves—and she wore brown leather clogs. Birkenstocks. Antiques. As the crowning touch, she wore plastic-rimmed tortoiseshell glasses that looked like an extension of the frizzy carrot red hair trapped at the back of her neck by a scrunchie that had seen better days . . . about five years ago.

Yet for all that she was not in any way attractive, she paid him no heed, and he wasn't used to that treatment from a woman. "Who do you think I am?"

"Lunch. Or"—her glasses had slid down her nose—"did I miss lunch? Is it time for dinner already? What time is it?"

"It's three."

"Rats. I did miss lunch." Lifting her head, she looked at him.

He did a double take violent enough to give him whiplash.

Beneath the glasses, dense, dark lashes surrounded the biggest, most emphatically violet eyes he'd ever seen.

Like a newly wakened owl, she blinked at him. "Who are you?"

"I'm. Aaron. Eagle." He emphasized each word, giving time between for the village idiot to absorb the name. "Who are *you*?"

"I'm Dr. Hall."

Aaron was immediately pissed. "I've met Dr. Hall. You are most definitely not Dr. Hall."

"Oh." A silly smile curved her pale pink lips. "You knew Father."

"Father?"

"Dr. Elijah Hall. He retired a year ago." Her smile died. "I'm sorry to tell you, but he, um, died a few months ago."

"Dr. Elijah Hall was your father?" Aaron didn't believe that for a minute. Her "mentor," maybe, but Dr. Hall was way too old to have a daughter this girl's age.

Aaron frowned. Of course, Dr. Hall was way too old to be a "mentor," too.

"Where did he die? How?"

"On the Yucatan Peninsula. Of a heart attack."

"You were there with him?"

"No, he . . . After he retired and had settled me into this job, he went off adventuring. Alone."

The girl was grieved. Aaron could see that.

She was also irked at being left behind.

The cynical part of him observed, "He left you in a good job."

"Nepotism. It's true." She lifted her chin. "It's also true I'm qualified for the job. I'm not as good with the ancient languages as my father was, but really, with a brain like his, how is that even possible? What cinched it for the library, of course, is that I'm cheap."

"Yes. I see that." He also saw she wasn't as unattractive as he'd first thought. Hidden under that dress, she had boobs, B, maybe C cups, some kind of waist, and curvy hips. She had good bones, like a racehorse, and of course those amazing eyes. But her lips were good, too, lush and sensual, the kind a man would like to have wrapped around his— "So let me get this straight. You are Dr. Elijah Hall's granddaughter?"

"No. I'm. His. Daughter." Now she spoke like *he* was the village idiot. "He married late in life."

"To somebody much younger."

"Not *much* younger. Ten years isn't much younger, would you say? Mama was forty-two when she had me."

"And you're twenty now?"

"I'm twenty-five. I've got a BS in archeology from

Oxford and a graduate degree and PhD in linguistics from Stanford, not to mention some extras like a stint teaching vanished languages at MIT." She waved at a desk overflowing with papers, artifacts and, atop it all, a new Apple laptop. Her voice got louder and more aggravated as she spoke. "I've got all the papers in there if you need to see them. I've had to keep track of all that stuff because everyone thinks I'm twenty!"

"Obviously, we're all dolts."

"Yes."

He could tell it never occurred to her to deny it, or flatter him in any way. The girl was clueless about the most basic social niceties, and worse, she didn't seem to notice he was a man.

Why did he care?

"When I was seven, my mother died in a cenote in Guatemala retrieving this stela." The girl waved her hand at the table.

He glanced at the stone tablet engraved with hieroglyphic-like characters, then did his second double take of the day. He leaned over it, studied it with intense interest. "Central American. Pre-Columbian. Logosyllabic. Epi-Olmec script. Perhaps a Rosetta stone for the transition between the Olmec and Mayan languages . . ."

"Very good." For the first time, she looked at him, noticed him, and viewed him with respect. Not interest, but respect.

"I had no idea this existed." His fingers itched to touch the stela, and he carefully tucked his hands into his pockets.

"No one did. After Mama died, Father brought it

here and shut it in the vault. I think he blamed himself for letting her go down there." As she spoke, Aaron glimpsed a hint of something more beneath the open artlessness he'd so condescendingly diagnosed. In the depths of her soul, she had carefully constructed a wall of sadness, and with it, she kept the world out.

But when he looked again, she blinked at him as if she had trouble recalling the year.

Was there more to the girl than what first met the eye? Surely not.

He couldn't keep calling her "the girl," not even in his mind. "What's your name?"

"Dr. Hall . . . Oh, you mean my first name." She smiled at him, those amazing eyes lavishing him with happiness. "I'm Rosamund."

Didn't that just figure?

"My parents named me after Rosamund Clifford—"

"The Fair Rosamund, King Henry the Second's mistress, reputedly the most beautiful woman in the world." Could this Rosamund be any more unlike her? "Henry built Rosamund a bower and surrounded it by a maze to protect and keep her, yet somehow the wildly jealous Eleanor of Aquitaine poisoned her and she died for love."

"Most of that is romantic fantasy, of course, but you do know your history. And your linguistics." This Rosamund, plain, unkempt, and appallingly dressed, viewed him with approval.

"History. Yes. That's actually why I'm here." He might as well give her a shot at his question. "I wanted to talk to Dr. Hall about a prophecy—"

"My goodness." Rosamund blinked at him again. "You're the second one today to ask me about that."

Chapter 2

A aron went on alert. Not that he gave any indication of it. He put one hip up on the table and posed like a *GQ* model during a photo shoot: one hand slipped into his jacket pocket, the other casually at his side, a relaxed smile on his face. "The second one what?"

She fluttered like a hen disturbed from its nest.

Good. She was responding to his best James Bond sophistication.

Then she said, "Please be careful leaning against that table. If you jiggle it, the stela could fall, the stone could break, and the tablet is priceless. Irreplaceable."

He straightened, and with a great deal more sternness, he asked, "The second one *what*?"

"The second man to ask about a prophecy. Of course, I'm not the expert my mother was. Prophecies and legends were her specialty, but you can't live and travel with a divination specialist without having some of it rub off on you. Of course my father knew an incredible amount, too, but he scoffed at any revelations that might have come true. He was a professional disbeliever." She adjusted her glasses more firmly on her nose. "What did you want to know?"

Aaron tamped down his impatience and in that slow voice he had reserved just for her, he asked, "Who was the other man who inquired about prophecies?"

"He wasn't like you."

Aaron relaxed a little.

"He didn't know anything about antiquities. Do you know he tried to touch a medieval manuscript with his bare hands?" Her horror was palpable.

Score one for our side.

Her eyes got wide, her frown faded, and her horror melted like cold ice cream covered with hot fudge. "But I imagine he gets away with that kind of arrogance all the time."

"Why's that?" Aaron did *not* like what was going on here.

"Because he is the most gorgeous man I've ever met in my life." She clasped her latex-gloved hands above her heart and stared into space like a zombie.

Man, this girl annoyed him. He cleared his throat. "You know, I'm accounted to be quite handsome myself."

She glanced at him. "Oh, you are. I noticed that right away. Very handsome." Somewhere in the lost depths of her femininity, she seemed to recognize that she'd insulted him. Then she made matters worse. "But *he* is most glorious thing I've ever seen. I mean, in person. Well, no, actually I've never even seen an actor as good-looking as *Lance Mathews*." She breathed his name as if it were a holy incantation.

"You have to be kidding. His name is Lance?"

"Yes." She seemed unaware of Aaron's disgust. "As in . . . Sir Lancelot."

"I'll bet."

"He has the most amazing blue eyes and smooth tan, and golden hair that curls around his head like a statue of Apollo Belvedere."

"Tough competition," Aaron acknowledged.

"He's tall and has broad shoulders, and his jeans fit his gluteus maximus in a way I could not fail to notice. He wore a"—she apparently had to search for the word—"a golf shirt with an alligator on the pocket, and the cuff that surrounded his biceps brachii and triceps brachii emphasized their extraordinary formation."

It figured that she could rip out the Latin names for the muscles, but was uncertain about what to call a *golf shirt*. "I had no idea Sir Lancelot wore Polo," Aaron said dryly.

"Like a warrior serving his chosen maiden, he brought me an offering."

"What offering?" Aaron looked around in alarm. Had this Lance Mathews brought explosives into the library?

"An espresso and a lemon scone." She sighed with such pleasure, Aaron wondered what she would do for a lobster and a glass of chenin blanc.

His gaze dropped to those pink, full lips and imagined them opening to welcome a bite of shellfish, dripping with butter, and then expressing her appreciation with lavish kisses placed on his cheeks, his lips, his . . . *okay*. This gig had ruined his sex life, and obviously it

was starting to affect his mind. "Did he have any identifying features? A tattoo, a birthmark . . . ?"

She turned amazed violet eyes on him. "Yes."

Crap.

"How did you know?" she asked.

"I'm psychic that way." He wasn't psychic, just
logical.

"His shirt was open down to the third button, and
high over his sternum, he had a flame tattooed in blue
and red and gold." She placed her hand, palm down,
on her breastbone just below her throat as if remembering the exact position of the mark that had so thrilled
her.

"Nasty habit, tattooing. One always worries about
whether it was done in a sterile environment free of in-
fection or disease." Not that Aaron didn't have plenty
of friends who had plenty of marks, both natural and
artificial, and he wouldn't bare his back to anyone he
deemed suspicious. But he really needed to jerk Dr.
Hall out of her obviously delightful memories of Lance
and back to the present . . . with him.

"Yes. So true. But my mother had a tattoo. Actually,
two. They looked like pre-alphabetic symbols, and she
had one on each of her index fingers."

"Fascinating." More fascinating than Rosamund
realized.

She prattled on, oblivious to his interest. "I have
one, too. Just a tiny one. On my—"

Intrigued and surprised, Aaron stepped closer.

Seeing his interest, she hastily backtracked. "Well,
that doesn't matter."

"It did. It does! What is it? Where is it? And why did

you have it done?" He couldn't help smiling at her, all buttoned-up and clueless.

"It was a ritual tattooing done on an island in the South Pacific. A fascinating culture. I passed through puberty while in their care, so they initiated me into their society. It was a great honor." She had answered his last question, but not the first two.

"You've got hidden depths."

"I do, don't I?" She looked up at him without seeming to notice he had shifted his charm into high gear. "Why do you think you need the prophecy?" she asked. "What do you think it's going to do for you?"

One of the reasons Aaron was so good at what he did was his ability to think on his feet, and he did so now. "I work for the Gypsy Travel Agency. Have you heard of them?"

A small frown puckered her forehead as she thought. "The Gypsy Travel Agency advertises that it's the oldest travel agency in New York City, specializing in trips to the wild places of the world under the auspices of Romany experts. Right?"

"Absolutely correct. Did you happen to hear on the news what happened this past week?"

"I'm sorry. I've been working almost nonstop . . ." Her longing gaze strayed toward the stone tablet.

With brutal bluntness, he said, "The Gypsy Travel Agency's building in SoHo was obliterated in a blast that took everything—all the books, all the knowledge, and most important and tragic, all of the experienced agents."

Her attention returned to him in a rush. "How

horrible for you! Do the demolitions experts know who did it?"

"There are a lot of theories, but no certainties." At least, no certainties among the officials combing the site for evidence. Aaron and his friends knew all too well what had happened. "All the experts know is that the blast was tightly contained; nothing inside survived intact, yet the buildings around the Gypsy Travel Agency are untouched. The blast vaporized the agency."

"I'm so sorry to hear this." Her voice grew thick. "You must be devastated."

"It's difficult." More difficult than he could explain.

"So you want the prophecy to see if this tragedy was predicted?"

"Exactly."

"And you're looking for answers about the future?"

"If possible."

"I'll try and help." Plucking a tissue from the box, she wiped her eyes and blew her nose.

She was a woman easily touched by sorrow, and almost too easy to manipulate. "You say your mother taught you about prophecies, and your father scoffed at them," he said.

"My mother was an expert linguist, and she used that skill to translate prophecies. She believed certain prophecies were the work of accomplished seers. While she was alive, my father seemed to honor that belief, but once she had gone, my father taught me the hard truth. It is impossible to perceive which are genuine."

"Why?"

"Because there's a prophecy for everything. Everything that happens was predicted by someone."

"So all we need to do is go to the prophecy for *today* and we'll know what's going to happen *tomorrow*."

"Exactly. But if you would follow me into the stacks . . ." She led him into the rows of metal shelving. She stopped halfway between the door and her workstation, and gestured from one far end to the other. "These are the prophecies for this millennium. Look." She took down a book, blew off the dust, and flipped it open to page twenty-seven. "In this manuscript, written in the Aramaic script, there is a prophecy that claims that today is the first day of the Apocalypse." She looked up at him. "Somewhere in the stacks, there is a prophecy that says yesterday was the first day of the Apocalypse, and one that says tomorrow will be the first day of the Apocalypse. Every day of every year has a prophecy that claims the Apocalypse starts on that day. One of them is probably right—can you tell me which one?"

He had understood the odds against success, but seeing it illustrated so graphically ripped the scales from his eyes. "Yet some prophecies have more value than others." He argued because he had to. Because he and his friends desperately needed that prophecy.

"If the prophet has a track record of success, yes. Or if the manuscript was created on rare media or by monks or etched into the walls of . . . of . . ." She waved her hands, looking for inspiration.

"The Sacred Cave?" he suggested.

"Exactly!"

"Or if you can pinpoint the subject of the prophecy as being in the right place at the right time."

She thought about that, then nodded. "That would work. Or at least help."

"How did your mother decide which prophecies were real?"

Rosamund smiled a fond smile, picked up a fine brush, and whisked it over the stone tablet. "She said it was important to look at all the real factors, but in the end . . . she said it came down to her gut feeling."

Yes, he understood that. "Do you ever get gut feelings?"

"When I get the flu." She laughed too long at her own joke, then grew uncomfortable under his steady regard, and confessed, "I used to. Sometimes. But my father said gut feelings were nothing but wishful thinking, and I might as well depend on a fortune-teller's crystal ball as on my intuition."

"He wanted you to stay in the real world." And why? When Aaron had come down to the library basement with antiquities that needed to be authenticated or manuscripts that required translation, Dr. Hall had been brilliant, stiff-necked, and grim, yet unwillingly fascinated by the variety of Aaron's interests and keenly interested in prophecies and the paranormal. Most important in Aaron's mind was his sharp instinct for the genuine above the counterfeit.

Never, ever had he mentioned that he had a daughter.

Why had he so emphatically quashed Rosamund's curiosity?

Why had he kept her a secret?

Had Dr. Hall foreseen a dread prophecy for her?

"Are you familiar with the legend of the Chosen?" Aaron asked.

"The Chosen . . ." He could almost see Rosamund flipping through the encyclopedia of her mind. "Yes. The Chosen and the Others. When the world was young, a beautiful woman gave birth to twins, each marked as something set apart from average people. Repulsed by their difference, she took them into the darkest woods—in these fairy tales, it always is the darkest woods—and left the babies for the wild animals to devour." She looked at him inquiringly. "Is that the legend you mean?"

"That's it. Do you know the rest?" He did. He'd been doing his reading—*When the World Was Young: A History of the Chosen*, the textbook of choice among his peers.

Rosamund continued. "Those two children were the first Abandoned Ones, babies left by their parents without love or care, and to compensate, given a gift of power. The babies survived. The girl was a seer. The boy was a fire-giver. They gathered others like them and formed two gangs, one for good—the Chosen Ones—and one for evil—the Others—and they fought for the hearts and souls of the Abandoned Ones."

"A battle that goes on today," he finished.

"Yes." Her brow knit. "It's not a very comforting fairy tale."

"How many are?"

"Most have endings of some kind. The witch is tipped into the oven. The evil stepmother falls from a cliff—" She caught sight of his face. "All right, not very happy endings, but still, there's none of that 'the battle goes on today' stuff."

"Yet it's so much more realistic to know there can never be an end, or at least not until the"—he could scarcely stand to say the words—"until the Apocalypse."

"If the legend of the Chosen Ones were true, which it's not."

Aaron wished that she was right.

But unfortunately for her and her future peace of mind, she was staring right into the eyes of one of the Chosen Ones.

Chapter 3

"What I find of interest is the persistence of the story." Rosamund warmed to her topic. "Do you know that the Chosen Ones are discussed in European and Arabic medieval texts, given credence in Chinese scrolls, and portrayed in Native American cave art?"

"I did know about the Native American cave art," Aaron acknowledged.

"You're Native American. Have you seen the cave art?" she asked eagerly.

"Once. Briefly."

"Oh, I would love to view it in the original." She clasped her hands at her chest and looked at him, bright-eyed and appealing.

"It was obliterated by a collapse." At least he thought it must have been. He'd been too busy getting the hell out to look back and make sure.

"Oh." She sagged in disappointment, then straightened. "I've read the details of the myth in the original

Latin, drafted during Julius Caesar's reign. I theorize that the reason the Chosen Ones is such a successful legend is because there's a sense of continuity. Do you know that every seven years, a new seven Chosen are drafted to become protectors of the innocent?"

"I did know that." He had not been happy about it, either.

In the throes of relentless enthusiasm, she said, "I've got a book that tells all about it. Wait here."

A month ago, Aaron had been called to the Gypsy Travel Agency, a casual invitation he'd found odd in the extreme. Yet in his line of work, he found it best not to let oddities go uninvestigated. Once there in the cast-iron building that housed the agency, he'd been called before the board of directors, a bunch of white, business-suited, humorless men who laid the facts on the line.

They knew what he did for a living, they knew how he did it, and if he hadn't signed the contract agreeing to go to work for them as one of this cycle's Chosen Ones, they would have betrayed him to a certain Japanese businessman, a businessman with a grudge and the money to carry that grudge to its most extreme. It was blackmail, pure and simple, and if Aaron had not agreed to their terms, he would be dead by now.

But frankly, he'd signed their contract, then barely escaped the blast at the Gypsy Travel Agency when he and six others, strangers to one another, had been taken to be confirmed as the Chosen Ones. In the days since, their seer had been almost killed by one of her visions, he himself had been far too close to death for his own comfort, and his prospects weren't looking any too cheery for the immediate future. Just getting to the Arthur W. Nelson Fine Arts Library had been an exercise in caution.

Yet for all their travails, the remaining six Chosen had bonded together, swearing fealty to one another and to their mission.

Now, if only Rosamund and her prophecies could help guide them in the right direction.

Rosamund returned with a leather-bound book, blew the dust off the top, and showed him the cover.

Taken aback, he said, "You've got a copy of *When the World Was Young: A History of the Chosen.*"

"It was published by some obscure press in the early sixties as the definitive story of the Chosen Ones, and best of all, it's in English."

"Yeah, that is helpful."

Flipping to the table of contents, she found what she was looking for, then opened to the right page and read, " 'For seven years, the Chosen Ones are required to work tirelessly under the one they elect as leader to save abandoned children like themselves from the clutches of the Others. Then if they wish, they're allowed to retire, as another group is brought in and trained to help the innocent.' "

"Does this book, or any of the texts or paintings you spoke of, indicate what happens when a tragedy occurs, and all the Chosen are killed?" *Or blown up the way the Gypsy Travel Agency had been blown up?*

"Oh!" She lifted a finger. "Interesting that you should mention that. According to the Greeks, the Chosen Ones made Athens their home for centuries, and in 430 BC, at the height of their power, a plague of some vicious disease swept through the city. Of course, there continues to be debate as to the exact nature of the plague, and how it came to the city, but according to the historian for the Chosen Ones, it was introduced by the Others. The resulting misery and death killed almost a third of the populace and most of the Chosen, and caused Athens to lose the Peloponnesian War. Athens never recovered her former glory, and eventually passed her dominance to Rome."

"So when the Chosen Ones fail in their efforts—"

"Death, suffering, and disaster result." Rosamund sounded cheerful enough, but then, she didn't believe in the Chosen.

He had the gift and the mark of the Chosen. *He* was looking disaster right in the face.

In the five days since the blast, they had lost one of their own new members, and been forced to face the chance that they—and the world as they knew it— were doomed.

Worse for Aaron, and so much worse for Rosamund, her Sir Lancelot was no fair knight. He was one of the Others, and whatever he wanted with Rosamund and her prophecies, Aaron knew it could not be good.

Rosamund Hall had become a leading performer in a legend unfolding before her very eyes, and she didn't even realize it.

"So *you're* not superstitious?" Aaron asked.

"My father was a man concerned with facts."

"I asked about *you*, not your father."

"I've never seen any reason to believe the prophecies were anything but humbug." Rosamund sounded regretful.

"Is that what your father called them? Humbug?" Aaron could hear old Dr. Hall saying that.

"The delusions of a weak and pitiful mind."

Aaron could hear Dr. Hall saying that, too. "Your father didn't believe the Chosen Ones had ever existed?"

"He never discussed that particular legend with me, but no." She glanced at the tablet on the table. "Did I answer your question?"

"Not exactly."

"That's good." She adjusted the lighted magnifying glass over a glyph.

He'd lost her interest. "Listen—"

She glanced up, clearly startled to see him there. "Oh. Did I answer your question?"

"You already asked . . . Never mind. Listen, about Lance Mathews—"

Rosamund jumped like he'd stuck a pin in her. "That reminds me! On your way out, would you ask Jessica to make sure she calls me at five? I have to leave early."

Something about her mushy smile put him on alert. "Five isn't early."

"I forget to leave sometimes."

"Don't you get locked in?"

"Sometimes. But my father left a lot of work unfinished, and this . . . this is . . . just think, my mother's work, just waiting for me to delve into . . ." She waved a hand over the tablet, and as if they'd caught her, she leaned toward them again, spellbound.

This girl was a wreck. "Why do you need to leave early?"

"To get ready for my date."

Shit. "Tonight. With Lance Mathews."

She straightened her shoulders and stared at him . . . through her glasses, which were perched on the end of her nose. "Why not?"

"Tonight I was hoping you could come with me to see my friend's library. Irving is ninety-three years old and has this incredibly impressive collection of antique manuscripts and artifacts. But he needs someone who understands what he's got, someone who can help him out."

"I don't do appraisals." She managed to sound snooty and insulted.

"It's been appraised—world-class stuff." He baited the hook. "The Smithsonian would be proud to add his collection to theirs."

"Really." Clearly, she didn't believe him.

"I'm not an authority like you, or him"—a lie; he knew more about valuable antiquities than almost anyone in the world—"but Irving has had the money and the contacts to build his collection. I've seen Egyptian scrolls, European illuminated prayer books, Tibetan prayer wheels, early Incan quipu—"

Her eyes narrowed in suspicion.

He finished with the assurance, "All bought legitimately or given to him by friends."

She was right to be skeptical. The market for finding, stealing, and selling antiquities was huge and lucrative, and the scholars who actually worked in the field lamented the loss of important data. The pieces couldn't be studied if they were moved from the excavation sites in the jungle or the desert into private libraries and personal museums by thieves willing to risk danger and death for a profit.

And some collectors would do anything to complete their collections, including stealing from each other, from public museums, or even from the Arthur W. Nelson Fine Arts Library. . . .

"Actually, Irving is the one who was wondering about the prophecies, and since I knew Dr. Hall was one of the world's foremost experts . . . and he passed his torch to you. . . ." Aaron hoped the combination of temptation, guilt, and competition would work on Rosamund.

But she stood with her arms crossed.

"But you can't come; you've got a date." He hoped he disarmed her with his sad resignation, because he didn't have any intention of failing.

"That's right. I've got a date." She sounded fiercely determined.

He turned away, dragging his feet a little, then snapped his fingers and turned back. "I've got an idea. Why not go with me now?"

"These are still working hours." She looked so horrified, he might have suggested scribbling in crayon on the Magna Carta.

"You said yourself you frequently stay all night. You're obviously your own supervisor. Irving *is* ninety-three, he's got no family, and I know the Arthur W. Nelson Fine Arts Library would be thrilled if he made it the heir to his collection. For that reason alone, you could be forgiven for leaving two hours early." Aaron's dashing charm hadn't impressed her at all, but that didn't stop him from trying. With an appealing smile, he said, "Irving's house is a quick cab ride away." It was actually in the Upper East Side, and in Manhattan, that translated to miles of start-and-stop traffic.

No need to bring that up, either.

He picked up the cover for her worktable and carefully placed it over the stone tablet and the pile of notes. "If you'll grab your stuff, we'll run up there, you can talk to him and decide if you're interested in working with him on this prophecy he's after, and I'll personally deliver you to your home in time to get ready for that date. I mean, heck, if you wanted, you could go as you are!"

He may have oversold that one, because she pushed her glasses up on her nose and stared at him coldly.

He lifted his hands as if to stop her from charging him. "Or you can change your dress first." Glancing at his watch, he said, "If we go now, we'll be done in a jiffy."

"Well . . ." She visibly wavered.

"It'll be fun." He offered his hand—and enjoyed incredible satisfaction when she placed her hand in his.

"All right," she said. "Let's go."

Chapter 4

———— ✦ ————

Rosamund let Aaron tow her toward the door. She shouldn't let him push her around.

But he was that kind of man.

He exuded presence and authority from the top of his well-cut black hair to the tips of his well-shined black shoes. His dark eyes watched her with a hint of patronizing impatience, and his outfit—black suit, starched white shirt, and red tie—made her think of Mr. Perez, the wealthy, honorary head of the library board, and how he was always pushing her around. *Explain this expense on your report, Dr. Hall. Speak at the annual fund-raiser, Dr. Hall.* Except Mr. Perez was middle-aged and rotund, and Aaron Eagle was too tall, too strong, and too stern.

That was why she liked Lance Mathews better. He was like her—not concerned with worldly matters like designer watches and expensive shirts.

Although she vaguely remembered reading something one time when she was stuck on a plane without a decent book . . . something about the golf shirt with the alligator being expensive . . .

This man, this Aaron Eagle, was corporate America and high society . . . except he wasn't. His tanned skin held a hint of red, and he had the proud, high cheekbones, narrow nose, and broad, stubborn chin of a North Plains Indian warrior. His body was whipcord strong. His hands were broad-palmed and long-fingered, with the dexterity of a man who handled weapons and horses and women. . . .

Scrub that thought.

The point was, he wore the clothes well, but although they'd been tailored to a perfect fit, somehow, they didn't . . . *fit* him.

Aaron pushed her into the elevator and punched the button for the main floor, and still he held her hand as if she were a rebellious child.

And as a matter of fact, he did make her feel rebellious. He just looked so . . . so superior.

"Where did you say this Irving's house was?" She twisted her hand.

At once he freed it. "Have you heard of Irving Shea?"

"I've done more than hear of him. I've met him!" At one of the incredibly boring, stuffy, scholarly get-togethers her father had attended in the name of raising funds. Irving Shea was tall, dark-skinned, white-haired, very old and bent with the constantly increasing burden of years, yet he had given off an air of vitality that charmed her. "Irving Shea is *your* Irving?"

"He's the one."

Her father had told her Irving was the head of

some successful corporation, one of the first African-American men to take such a position, and obviously Daddy had respected him for both his achievements and his knowledge of antiquities. "He is the ex-CEO of that company that blew up."

"That's right. The Gypsy Travel Agency."

"Wow. I'll bet Mr. Shea is upset."

"Upset, yes. He's also determined to get to the bottom of the matter."

She could add two and two and get four. "So you want the prophecy for more than just yourself? You want it for Mr. Shea."

"He'll want to personally fill you in on any details." The elevator doors opened and Aaron walked ahead, totally unconcerned whether she followed him. "I am surprised Irving hadn't heard of your father's death."

"I haven't placed the obituary or planned the memorial service or anything because . . . because I still don't know if I *believe* it." Now why had she confessed that to, of all people, this man?

He stopped so fast she ran into the back of him. "Why not?"

She rubbed her bruised nose. "Because Father texted me and said . . . It was this weird message."

"Then perhaps we should talk about it when we're out of here." Aaron gestured around the short corridor and down toward the desk where Jessica's head bobbed out to observe them.

"Why? Because of *Jessica*? Jessica's harmless."

"Perhaps. But this is a secure area. Someone might be listening, someone more than just me."

"Right." There. Such a thought had never occurred

to her. And that comment—it was exactly the type of thing that made her think her hunch was right. Beneath his debonair sophistication, this gentleman hid a predator's instincts.

They exited through the electronic gate, and while Aaron signed out, Jessica said, "You're leaving early today, Rosamund. I didn't know you could ever tear yourself away from your research long enough to play hooky. So I guess you've got some antiquities emergency, huh?" And she smiled at Aaron as if they would obviously consider funny little Rosamund a diversion.

Normally Rosamund didn't care; Jessica and Rosamund were about the same age, but there the similarities stopped. Jessica was pretty and popular. Rosamund was . . . not. Jessica was always kind in her own way, inviting Rosamund to the after-work outings, bringing her lunch and scolding her for neglecting herself, and most recently, making Rosamund sew the sagging hem on her skirt. Rosamund barely noticed Jessica because Jessica's main area of expertise seemed to be what she learned from beauty magazines.

But with Aaron by her side, Jessica's amused assumption that Rosamund must be leaving, not because of him, but because of work . . . Well, that irked her, especially since it was true.

An almost unrecognizable impulse made Rosamund lean across the desk. "Guess what I'm doing tonight?"

Jessica's amusement deepened. "I don't know. What?"

"I'm going on a date." Vaguely, Rosamund realized she sounded like a high school sophomore who'd been invited to the senior prom.

"With who?" Jessica's smile faltered, and she looked between Rosamund and Aaron disbelievingly. "Not . . . ?"

Aaron scowled.

"No, silly. Not him."

Jessica relaxed and smiled. "No, I didn't think so."

"Do you remember my first appointment?" Rosamund heard that giggly, breathless tone in her own voice, and wondered at herself. Not that she cared, but she did wonder.

"Lance Mathews?" Jessica's smile disappeared again, this time for good. "You're kidding. *You're* going out with Lance Mathews?"

"Yes!" Rosamund knew she was grinning like a madwoman. "Can you believe it? He asked me out and I gave him my number and he gave me his and he's got his own car and he's going to pick me up for drinks and dinner and—"

Aaron hooked his hand under her arm and jerked.

As he towed Rosamund toward the door, she yelled, "And he told me to dress up and I'm even going to try that anti-frizz stuff you gave me for my hair." Rosamund's last, satisfying glimpse of the library was a snapshot of a dozen older, low-voiced, academic library patrons scowling at her, and Jessica, gaping like a big-breasted fish.

"Happy now?" Aaron hailed a cab and stuffed her inside.

"Yes," Rosamund replied to the back of his head as he leaned forward to give the driver directions.

"Central Park. Drop us off by the zoo. Double the fare if you hurry."

Chapter 5

———◆———

Aaron settled into the cab beside Rosamund, and in a tone that clearly expressed his disgust, asked, "Is there anyone else you want to tell about Lance Mathews? Would you like me to roll down the window so you can stick your head out and yell his name while we ride?"

"No! Head and arms inside!" the East Asian driver said, and put his foot on the gas pedal all the way to the floor.

Rosamund drew her dignity around her. "I'm perfectly happy now." Then she ruined the picture by grinning. "Did you see her? She was so jealous."

The tires squealed as the kamikaze driver rounded a corner. Horns honked as other cabs slammed to a halt to let them pass.

"I can't wait to see this Lance Mathews," Aaron said. She wasn't sure, but she thought he added, "To punch his face in."

Conversation stopped as the cab careened north on

Madison Avenue, crossed three lanes of traffic to take a left along East Sixty-sixth, cut another left to travel south on Fifth, and parked at the curb by the entrance to the zoo.

Aaron tossed the cabbie the money, pulled her across the seat and out the door, and told the driver, "Now leave as fast as you came."

Rosamund watched the cab zoom back across the oncoming traffic, and said, "Wow. He seriously wanted the double fare."

"Greed makes the world go 'round." Aaron hustled her toward the park. "Come on. If we hurry we can get a good view of the four o'clock sea lion feeding and presentation."

"How do you know there's a sea lion feeding and presentation at four?"

"I like the zoo." He tossed a crumpled twenty at the cashier, got their tickets, and hauled her toward the gates.

Rosamund ogled him. "You do? You don't seem the type to . . ."

He turned his head and looked down at her.

"To . . . to, um . . ." Under his dark gaze, she was having trouble remembering what she meant to say.

"I like watching families together, human and animal."

And just like that, it occurred to her that, before she let him drag her around to any more places, she should ask a few questions. "Are you married? Do you have children?"

"Do you even know the meaning of the word subtlety?" But he chuckled, a nice sound, deep in his chest. "No. And no."

"Oh. That's weird." Because she didn't need her glasses to figure out that he probably had to fight off the opposite sex, and possibly some of the same sex. "Have you ever been married?"

"Never. Why?" He still held her arm, but he slowed down, strolling along as if they were a couple.

"I don't know. It seems that when people—men—like to watch families, it's because they miss their own family."

"Good observation." Now he was watching her as if she interested him . . . sort of like a bug under the microscope. "So you're *not* oblivious."

"Of course not," she huffed. What kind of comment was that? "I am a woman."

"I'm glad you've realized that, at least." She thought he was going to end on an insult, but in a cool, conversational tone, he said, "I was abandoned as a baby, and adopted by a single father. He was the chief of our . . . his tribe. There were only a few of the Bear Creek left in the world, and fewer still living a traditional life."

She heard the delicate way he distanced himself from the tribe. "You aren't Bear Creek?"

"No. I'm American Indian, obviously, but my father's tribe knew I was not one of them, and no one ever came looking for me or my mother."

"Do you know what happened to your mother?"

"After she gave birth to me, she flung herself off a cliff."

Rosamund sucked in a breath, so shocked she didn't have words to speak.

"My foster father's tribe lived in the mountains in Idaho, in circumstances so poverty-stricken they were hanging on by their toenails, so when he died they wandered off toward a less difficult lifestyle."

With the curiosity that made her the premier researcher of ancient manuscripts, she asked, "What did you do?"

"I learned to take care of myself."

"How old were you?"

"Fourteen."

Note to self—don't whine to Aaron Eagle about my upbringing.

"Did you go into a foster home?" she asked.

"No, I stayed in the mountains." He led them into the Temperate Zone exhibit, stopped and looked at the swan geese. "It was a good way to learn what it takes to survive."

"But what about high school? What about college?" She couldn't imagine a life without classes.

"I didn't graduate." One of the huge geese lifted its head and looked at Aaron, then rose and paced toward him.

"From college, you mean."

"From high school."

Lifting itself on its toes, the goose spread its wings wide and flung itself at Aaron, honking wildly.

Rosamund took an involuntary step backward. "What is he doing?"

"Challenging me." Aaron bowed his head to the imprisoned bird, and backed away as if in respect.

He understood the wild, captive bird far too well. He yielded dominance far too gracefully.

She didn't understand him, but if she simply did a little more research into his background, she would comprehend his inner workings. Once that occurred, he would cease to be interesting to her. "So at the age of fourteen you dropped out of society, disappeared into the American wilderness, survived by yourself for . . . ?"

"Five years."

"And when you came out, you were"—she waved a hand up and down his well-groomed self—"this?"

He adjusted his already perfect tie. "*This* is who I am."

He had intrigued her, given her something to ponder . . . about him. No matter what he claimed, the parts of Aaron Eagle did not add up to the image he so successfully projected. She needed to decide what she thought about wandering around New York City with a stranger and an enigma.

Taking her arm, he led her through the garden to the sea lion pool. The railing was lined with people. The sea lions were barking in anticipation of a feeding. The people were talking and pointing and barking back. Aaron stopped Rosamund a few feet away, and in a voice pitched to reach her ears only, he asked, "You said your father texted you. What did he say?"

Rosamund looked around at the crowd. "You brought me here so if someone is listening, they won't hear what we say."

"If someone is listening with the right kind of equipment, it will filter out the background noise and we would have no secrets." He smiled, a slash of amusement. "But I doubt if anyone is that interested in us."

She hoped he was right, because his words sent a chill up her spine.

"What did your father say?" Aaron asked again.

"The text said, 'You were right, Elizabeth.' Then, 'Study hard, Elizabeth.' Then about five minutes later, another text came through." She shuffled her feet, suddenly all too aware how insignificant this sounded. "It said, 'Run.'"

But Aaron didn't seem to think the messages insignificant. Instead, his face grew cool and considering. "Elizabeth is your mother's name."

"Yes. Not many people remember that, which is why I think . . . I think he was giving me a signal it really was him."

"Yes . . ." Aaron stood completely still, listening to some inner logic. "'Study hard.' What does that mean?"

"I don't know, but I started looking around for my mother's things, and found a notebook and that stone tablet."

"Anything of interest there?"

"The notebook is fascinating!" She could scarcely contain her excitement. "She was a master at translating pre-Columbian languages. I could have learned so much from her. . . ." Her voice faltered. The pain of her mother's death would subside at times, but it never faded.

"I wish I'd known this. I would have recommended we bring the notebook," Aaron said.

"It'll be there when I return. No one goes down there except me."

"No one except Lance Mathews."

She stiffened at Aaron's tone. "He's hardly going to break in, and even if he did, he'd be hard-pressed to comprehend the contents of my mother's notebook!"

"Right." That seemed to cheer Aaron no end. "Lance Mathews is a philistine when it comes to understanding your work."

She bristled. "I wouldn't say he was a philistine. He's simply . . . unschooled."

"Ha." But Aaron really paid no heed to her denial. "You were told your father died of a heart attack, so perhaps it was preceded by a stroke, or he was confused by pain."

He wasn't saying anything she hadn't thought herself. "True."

"Yet I knew Dr. Hall. It's hard to imagine him suffering from dementia."

"Also true. Daddy was so exact, so precise in his thoughts and his speech. Yet as a rule, he didn't text. He said he didn't understand why it was better than e-mail or a call."

"Typical old guy."

"Yes. So I can't imagine how a man who was confused by a stroke could figure out how to text, or why he would text my mother."

"Or why he would tell her to run." Aaron wandered toward the pool and pointed at the largest sea lion, which was barking at the zookeeper.

She looked, and nodded as if she were interested, when actually, right now, she didn't care about the sea lions.

Aaron moved them to the other end of the pool, about two feet away from the press of the crowd. After surveying the people around them, he asked, "At the time of his death, was anyone with Dr. Hall?"

"I received a phone call from a police officer telling

me of the death. I asked what had happened. He told me a heart attack. I asked what Daddy was doing, where he was, who was with him. The officer seemed suddenly unable to speak English." Her hand rested on Aaron's arm. "My Spanish is good, so I asked him in Spanish. The call was cut off. I prepared to fly down to retrieve the body and question him face-to-face, but the next day, I got a call from the head of the library board. They'd received an urn with his ashes." She was proud of herself. She'd recited the horrible litany without flinching.

Yet, for all his cold eyes and inscrutable demeanor, Aaron seemed to see something in her resolute gaze that roused his compassion. Carefully he uncurled her fingers from his arm and held her hand between both of his. "You believe there is a possibility that the ashes aren't your father's."

"I even opened up the urn and looked at them." She felt more and more foolish, but something about Aaron brought the words bubbling out of her. "They're white and . . . ashy. I thought there would be some pieces that were vaguely human, but it looks like fireplace ash."

"And yet as you looked, there was such a sense of loss." Aaron slid his arm around her and gathered her into his body, under his jacket.

He was hugging her.

For a long moment, she stood with her arms between them, her fists clutched tightly, not knowing what to do.

When he didn't move, she relaxed, inch by inch, loosening her fists, sliding her arms around him, burying her nose in his chest. . . . She closed her eyes. He was warm.

Did he understand how abandoned she had felt when her mother died? When she looked back on the child she had been, all unknowing as they brought her mother's limp body up from the cenote, she felt sorry for that girl. Because she had waited for someone to tell her it was all right, that her mother would come back to her, hold her in her arms again, be with her. She hadn't understood what that loss meant, or the anguish that would tear at her, or what it would mean in the future.

She hadn't understood that on that same day, she would lose her father, too, or at least the father he had been. For the Elijah Hall she had known was gone, replaced by a strict teacher who kept her at a distance, taught her only what he thought she should know, occasionally disparaged her natural abilities. In all the years since, he had hugged her only once, right before he left to go back to Central America, and even then he had been stern, warning her to take care in a way that made it clear he had his doubts she could manage to tie her shoes. And she wasn't *that* inept. Not usually.

Rosamund turned her head and spoke, and revealed the tiniest bit of her pain to a man she barely knew . . . yet he would understand. This man knew loss. "I remember when my mother would translate languages—she was so good, it was like magic—and my father would look at her with such delight and love in his eyes. Her death broke something in him, and I don't know what, or why."

"Maybe he blamed himself." Aaron's voice was a rumble in his chest under her ear.

"No, she was always the one who decided where we would go and what we would do. Father and I both rode along on the floodwaters of her passion for learning . . . and for life."

"Yes, and maybe he knew of the danger and let her go because he couldn't bear to tell her no."

Rosamund laughed a little. "No one could tell my mother no. She was like a hurricane of enthusiasm, sweeping everything away before her."

"He was her husband. He was responsible for her safety."

She looked up at Aaron. He looked completely serious. "That's archaic!"

"Men are archaic." Aaron sounded very sure. "To see the one you love killed, knowing you didn't protect her . . . that will break any man's spirit."

She didn't agree with him. Not really. Why would her father feel responsible for her mother's death? It wasn't *his* fault.

"It's hard to be alone in the world," Aaron said.

She didn't know if he was talking about her father or her . . . or himself. She only knew he smelled good. Very manly, with hints of spice—cloves?—and citrus. Soap and clean human skin . . . nice . . .

He was nice, cradling her and giving her comfort as no one had since . . . since her mother's death.

That was why she was so startled when, without warning, he pushed her away.

Chapter 6

Give Irving my regards.

G A woman's voice, clear and husky, whispered the words—*into Aaron's mind.*

Aaron stood stiff and still, breathing deeply.

Nothing panicked him. He prided himself on his cool analysis of any situation, on his quick thinking, and those qualities had saved his life in more than one tough situation. Yet this . . . this violation of his being made him want to run, to hide, to vanish in broad daylight.

Where had those words come from?

He scanned the crowd around the sea lion pool.

A handsome woman in her sixties sat on a wooden bench in the shade in the Central Garden. She was watching him, a knowing smile on her lips.

He had never seen her before.

Who was she?

One of *them*. One of the Others. One who knew Irving, who wanted to send him a message.

So she found one of the Chosen Ones—she found Aaron—and spoke in his mind. How did she know he was one of the Chosen Ones? Could she read his thoughts, too? Because if that was the case, he needed to clear his head, and *observe*.

The woman was short. Well-built. Dark hair. Dark, dark eyes. Tanned skin. She turned her head, lifted a cigarette to her lips, and took a long, slow pull, and a look at her profile made him sharply aware that she'd been a pretty woman once. Still was, but—

Rosamund put her arm around his back and said firmly, "Let's walk."

He stumbled along with her. The Chosen Ones had already confronted one mind speaker, and although in the end they had survived, it had been a disaster.

Was the older woman going to say something else? Had she taken possession of his brain? *Could she control him?*

And Rosamund said, "I know you weren't raised in normal circumstances, but didn't anyone ever tell you not to stare at people who are scarred?"

"What?"

"You don't stare at people who are scarred." Rosamund sounded exasperated and a little angry. "I mean, that poor woman. Isn't it enough that someone slit her nose down the middle, without having some guy in a suit staring at her?"

"What?" Aaron searched his brain. He seemed alone, but then, he hadn't been aware of anyone in there until the words had whispered through his head.

"Aaron!" Rosamund let go of his arm. "Are you really so insensitive?"

He looked down at her.

She looked flushed and indignant, her violet eyes narrowed behind dark-rimmed glasses, her carroty hair almost sparking. "You really are that insensitive!" With a huff, she stalked away.

Nothing else could have yanked him out of his stupor. After all that had happened in the last five days, and now *this*, he was not letting Rosamund escape him. Lengthening his stride, he caught up with her, took her arm, and hustled her toward the street. "I'm not being insensitive. I recognized her, and she could cause problems." It was sort of true, and he needed to soothe Rosamund, get her to Irving's, and in a hurry.

"You know her? I take it she's not a friend."

"No."

"Did her husband do that to her?"

"Why do you think that?"

"In old Spain, a husband would slit his wife's nose down the middle as a punishment for infidelity."

Rosamund would know something like that. He suspected she was a repository of odd facts. . . . "I don't know who did it."

"I hope she got her revenge." Rosamund stalked along beside him. "You wouldn't think that kind of barbaric behavior was possible today, but husbands still have too much power over their wives. She looks Romany—"

"Gypsy. Of course. She's a gypsy!" He couldn't believe it took Rosamund to point that out. Where was his brain?

Maybe the gypsy was blocking his thoughts. Or maybe he was just petrified.

"Romany, maybe from another country. The injury must have happened when she was young. I think she's had plastic surgery, but probably it had healed so it was too late to really fix it. How could you recognize her and not know this? What do you mean, she could cause problems?" Rosamund pulled her arm free. "And would you stop shoving me around?"

"I'm sorry. I saw a cab. On the street. I wanted to catch it. Rush hour, you know? Are you hungry? Irving has two cooks now, good ones, and I make a point of being there for dinner." He was babbling, trying to distract her, herding her through the exit from the zoo.

"You're not answering any of my questions." The girl was too smart for her own good.

"I will. When we get to Irving's, you can ask anything you want." Not that she was going to get any real answers, but she could certainly ask. He flung his arm up at the oncoming cab and the driver swerved to the curb.

As she climbed in, Rosamund said grudgingly, "You're really good at that."

"What?"

"Making the cabs stop."

Certainly it made sense that, looking like she did, like an incredibly intelligent bag lady, she would have trouble getting a cab.

Irving's mansion was less than a mile away, a nineteenth-century, perfectly preserved behemoth complete with dozens of bedrooms, a library with shelves that rose from floor to ceiling, a cavernous dining room that would seat thirty, and at least a dozen bedrooms. Usually Irving, the ninety-three-year-old former CEO of the Gypsy Travel Agency and protector of the Chosen Ones, lived alone with his butler, went to work in the mornings, and went home at noon for his nap. That nap had saved his life, for he had been sleeping when the explosion occurred.

McKenna, the butler, and Martha, the dedicated servant of the Gypsy Travel Agency, rounded out their beleaguered group.

As Aaron paid the cab, Rosamund stood admiring the mansion's exterior, talking about neo-French Classic style and finials until he took a long breath to stave off boredom. Then he hustled her up the stairs to the front door. As he reached up to ring the bell, the door was flung open and Aleksandr Wilder rushed out. The twenty-one-year-old was tall, rail-thin, with big bones and the facial features of a Cossack. He was also as clumsy as a puppy, smacking into Rosamund's shoulder. If Aaron hadn't had his arm around her waist, she would have tumbled down the stairs.

"Take it easy!" Aaron snapped, and when Aleksandr would have steadied her, Aaron pushed his hands away.

"I'm sorry!" Aleksandr looked into her eyes and blushed bright red. "I'm just . . . I tutor calculus at Fordham in the summer and I haven't been there because of . . . you know . . . so they called home and talked to my grandmother, who is a scary woman when she's mad. She called and spoke to Irving, so now I get to go out, but I'm late. So . . . sorry!"

"Be careful out there." Aleksandr scanned the exclusive neighborhood, hoping not to see that woman, never to experience that mind-speaking again.

"I am careful," Aleksandr assured him. "My grandfather taught me *careful* before I could walk."

Aaron supposed that was true. The boy was related to the famous Wilders. Nineteen years ago they had broken their pact with the devil—the pact that gave them infamous powers—and in doing so, had freed everyone in their extended family, too, even the Varinski branch of the Ukraine. Apparently, not all of them had taken the downfall with any grace, and while no one knew for certain, Aaron suspected the devil was none too pleased, either.

But while Aleksandr claimed he had been trained to watch for danger, he showed no signs of caution now. Instead, he backed down the stairs, stumbling over every other step, and all the while, he stared at Rosamund. "Hi." He waved a hand malformed by fire. "You must be the librarian. Will I see you later?"

Obviously, he didn't give a damn about seeing Aaron later.

"She's got a date tonight." Aaron hadn't thought he would be glad to say it, but he was.

Aleksandr slumped. "Man, Aaron. You move fast." Turning, he galloped down the steps.

"Not with Aaron," Rosamund called after him.

"He's out of earshot." A fact Aaron felt great satisfaction in telling her.

"How did he know I was a librarian?"

Aaron guided her through the open door. "Because I went out to find the world's foremost expert on prophecies."

"I'm sorry you didn't get my father, but I really am awfully good with prophecies and languages." Abruptly, she stopped walking, stopped talking.

Shutting the door behind them, he could see her absorbing the marble floor, the soaring gilded ceiling, the matching Chippendale tables, the original Chagall hanging on the wall. He saw the moment when she made her decision about the decorating.

Her quiet face lit up with pleasure; she clutched Aaron's arm, and turned those warm violet eyes on him. "You were right. The ambience is a stunning mix of nineteenth-century glamour and mid-twentieth-century modernism. Did Mr. Shea put this together himself? Because if he did, he has a discerning eye."

A form moved out of the shadows, took the shape of Irving's man of all trades, and bore down on them. "Actually, Dr. Hall— I assume you are Dr. Hall?"

Aaron said, "Dr. Rosamund Hall, this is McKenna, Mr. Shea's butler."

She shook McKenna's hand.

"I did the decorating, using original antiques from the mansion and adding the best of the twentieth and twenty-first centuries, taking care to imbue this area with wealth and quiet elegance to match Mr. Shea's image." McKenna, a middle-aged, conservatively suited hobbit of a man, had a ponderous way of speaking that could possibly go on forever.

Aaron was preparing to intervene when, across the foyer, one of the doors slammed open.

A young woman walked out. Her hair was jet-black with purple highlights, her eyes were rimmed in black kohl, and she wore a plaid skirt, gold lamé platform heels, a studded dog collar, and matching leather bracelets that covered the tattoos Aaron knew were there. Holding an empty paper tube aloft, Charisma stalked toward the library and bellowed, "All right! Who left the toilet paper for me to change *again*?"

Chapter 7

"It's a miracle." Dr. Campbell slipped his stethoscope into the pocket of his white coat and beamed. "In this place, it's not often I get to say that. Mr. White, *you* are a miracle."

"I appreciate that." Gary restrained his impatience, using the controls on the hospital bed to move himself into a sitting position. "Now, please, I've been asking for food and I'm getting no cooperation at all."

The doctor's tired face grew serious. "You have to realize, Mr. White, you've been in a coma for four years. You've been fed through an IV."

Like Gary didn't know that. Days and weeks and months and years of that eternal drip, drip, drip landing in his veins and echoing through his head, and every time, his rage and frustration—and fear—grew.

But Dr. Campbell was still babbling. "Until we do some testing, we'd like you to keep eating through a tube—"

"I want some food."

The floor nurse moved restively. "I told you, doctor, he's been very insistent and not at all cooperative. He *tore* the IV tubes out of his arm."

The doctor, the nurses, the technicians lined the little private room in this cold, dim mausoleum of a nursing home where Gary's living body had been stored, out of sight and out of mind, for the last four years. They stared at him as if he were the freak in a sideshow, and acted as if he should be happy to look on their faces.

Instead, he wanted to rant and rage.

But he didn't. He kept his voice low and in a reasonable tone said, "I am the patient. You're the medical staff. My insurance is paying you to take care of me. I don't need to cooperate with you; you need to cooperate with me." Then his voice changed, grew deep and commanding. *"And I want to eat."*

Slowly, with great patience, as if Gary were simpleminded, Dr. Campbell said, "Mr. White, your muscles are atrophied, your digestive system is compromised, and until last night, when you woke up so unexpectedly, your brain showed little activity. We believed you were on the verge of death. Please let us revel in the miracle of your recovery while we do the necessary tests to determine how—"

Gary interrupted. "Let me make myself clear. I don't want anyone to know that I've come out of the coma."

"But your relatives!" the nurse said.

"I don't have any relatives."

"Just two days ago we had inquiries about your condition!" she insisted.

God, she was a stupid cow. "My employer who hopes I will die, no doubt."

"No." Nurse McStupid sent an appealing glance toward the doctor. "No, not your employer."

Dr. Campbell shook his head at her.

Gary pounced on that. "What about my employer?"

Dr. Campbell said, "Mr. White, you really should focus on your recovery—"

At the same time, Nurse McStupid said, "There's been an accident."

He looked back and forth between them, then saw the technicians were watching the television, eternally turned on and now muted.

The Gypsy Travel Agency building, a sight Gary knew all too well, flashed across the screen.

Gary reached for the remote, turned up the sound, and got the last of the story.

The Gypsy Travel Agency had exploded five days ago in a still unexplained demolition that left the building and everyone in it vaporized.

The technicians and nurses were shaking their heads as if it was a tragedy.

Nurse McStupid was watching Gary anxiously, as if expecting him to dissolve in surprised tears.

But he felt nothing but a bone-deep satisfaction.

Dr. Campbell took the remote out of Gary's hand and turned off the television. "The world has changed while you were asleep."

"So true. It appears I'm no longer employed."

"But you *do* have at least one relative," McStupid said. "The very night of the explosion, you had two visitors, a woman named Martha—I thought she was your aunt—and an elderly man who escorted her. He was tall and black; I don't remember his name."

"Irving," Gary said with loathing.

"Yes, that was it. Your aunt said you used to be a hero."

"I *am* a hero." Being a hero was how Gary got in that coma, and without help from any of his "relatives," he had gotten himself out.

"You've been one of our favorite patients. The story of the blast that caused your head injuries indicated that you tried to save six lives at great risk to your own. It's that kind of behavior that has won you the admiration of everyone here." Gary could see through the doctor's machinations. He was trying to make Gary be a good guy and live up to his reputation.

Gary had spent his life living up to that reputation, and look what it got him. Four damned lost years. "I am not going to hang around here, being a human guinea pig so you can get published in the *New England Journal of Medicine*." The doctor wanted to speak, but Gary had no intention of yielding the floor. "So bring me food, help me get on my feet, and get me out of here as fast as you can."

The festive atmosphere in the room faded as the medical staff grew quiet, hostile.

"Well," Dr. Campbell said stiffly, "I'm sorry to hear you feel that way, especially about the nurses who have worked so vigilantly to care for you for so many years."

The doctor wanted Gary to feel guilty.

He didn't.

The doctor straightened his skinny shoulders and prepared to throw his weight around. "Nevertheless, your best interests are at the heart of my concern, and I intend to personally supervise your recovery. Until you can stand up and walk out of this room, this is where you will stay."

"Walk out of this room? Is that all I need to do?" Shoving the covers aside, Gary sat up and swung his legs over the edge of the bed.

The floor nurse, Miss McStupid Cow, rushed to his side. "Mr. White, you shouldn't do this."

"Let him go." Dr. Campbell watched with the grim satisfaction of a man who expected to be momentarily vindicated. "He wants to prove something to us. He's going to prove something to himself, instead."

Gary wanted to laugh, but he saved his breath for the effort of getting his feet on the floor.

The linoleum was cold. So was the bed rail he used to steady himself. He leaned against the mattress until the muscles in his legs were once again used to holding his own weight; then slowly he pushed off.

The nurse hovered there, hands outstretched.

He snorted. Lifting his foot, he took a shuffling step.

The whole room took a collective breath of surprise.

He balanced again, and took another step. He let go of the railing, steadied himself, and took another step. And another.

His hips ached from the unaccustomed weight, his knees creaked, the legs that stuck out from beneath the flowered hospital gown were emaciated and stringy with sinew. Yet with each step, he could feel his strength returning.

Yes. This was what he had bargained for. This was what he'd been promised.

He got to the door, took two steps outside, then returned to step across the threshold. Staring at Dr. Campbell in cold triumph, he said, "So as you can see, I can leave whenever I want. But first—*I want a god-damn meal!*"

Dr. Campbell turned to Nurse McStupid. "Start him on clear liquids, and as soon as he holds them down and passes fluids—"

"I know the routine," she said.

Turning back to Gary, the doctor said, "Mr. White, I don't know how it is possible for you to wake from such a debilitating coma and be alert and strong enough to move, much less walk, but I can assure you we'll do everything we can to get you out of here in a hurry. In the meantime, you should be thanking God for bringing you back from the brink of death."

"Thank God? I assure you, God had nothing to do with it." Gary grinned savagely as he made his way back to the bed. "Rather—I'll pay the devil his due."

Chapter 8

McKenna gave a pained sigh. "I'm sorry you had to witness that, Dr. Hall. I'm afraid our little group is growing impatient with each other's foibles."

Aaron watched Rosamund, interested to see how Miss Prissy Librarian would react to Charisma and her domestic drama.

Rosamund blinked, pushed her glasses up on her nose, and said, "The other women tell me it's my job to replace the toilet paper in the women's bathroom at the library because I don't make coffee. But I don't drink coffee, so I don't think that makes sense, do you?"

"Sounds like they're taking advantage of you to me," Aaron said bluntly.

"But they're so forceful."

"And you don't care enough about real life to object."

She thought about that as if it were a new concept to her. "I do care about real life. It's just not as interesting as what's in my books."

He laughed shortly. "That's about to change. McKenna, is everybody in the library?"

"Miss Charisma, Miss Isabelle, and Mr. Samuel are in the library," McKenna answered with obvious intention to continue.

But Aaron didn't have time to let McKenna carry on in the way he liked to. He had about an hour to make Rosamund forget Lance Mathews, and he needed to get cracking. Taking Rosamund's hand, he walked away. "Great. If you'll notify Irving that Dr. Hall is here to look at his private library"—he looked meaningfully at McKenna—"I'll take her to meet . . . our little group."

McKenna always read between the lines, and he could hurry when needed, without ever breaking a sweat. He did so now, starting up the stairs. "I'll notify Mr. Shea immediately, sir."

Rosamund dragged along behind Aaron. "I'm not dressed for company."

At least she knew that.

"Who am I meeting?" she asked.

"Friends of mine. You'll like them." Aaron hoped, because if everything worked out as he had planned, they would be her constant companions.

As they reached the door, Sam came striding out, carrying the toilet paper tube and grumbling, "It's not like I'm the only one around here who has annoying habits." Seeing them, he stopped. "Hey, Aaron, I thought you went after an old guy who reads prophecies."

"I got his daughter instead."

"Good work. I'll take a beautiful young lady rather than an old duffer any day." He offered his hand to Rosamund. "Samuel Faa. I'm an attorney and apparently the most annoying man in the world."

"I'm Rosamund Hall. I'm a librarian." She stared up at Sam as if spellbound by his black eyes and hair. Sam started to preen, and Aaron was getting ready to rein her in, when she said, "Are you Romany? Because we saw this woman in the park, and I noted she had many of the same features."

Sam stiffened and said briefly, "I am adopted, but yes, I'm Rom."

"How fascinating to run into two people of the same rare genetic background in the same day!"

Tactless, Aaron mouthed to him, then aloud, "Come on, Rosamund." He put his arm around her waist and pushed her toward the door.

Sam twirled the empty paper roll around his index finger. "Be right back."

"But really," she said to Aaron, "don't you think it's fascinating that we met two Romany in one day?"

"Since we work for the Gypsy Travel Agency, possibly it's not a coincidence." Charisma rose from her seat in front of the computer. "I'm Charisma Fangorn."

Isabelle sat on the sofa surrounded by paperwork. She shuffled it into a pile, put a book on top, rose, and extended her hand. "I'm Isabelle Mason."

"I'm Rosamund Hall." But Rosamund walked right past the two women, all her attention on the massive room. "*This* is the library you told me about, Aaron? It's gorgeous!"

The library was the jewel of the mansion, with walls painted the color of mustard, heavy blue velvet curtains, and wide sweeps of antique Aubusson rugs on the floor. The tall, wide, medieval-style fireplace was set with logs, and large, soft chairs and a leather sofa clustered around it. A gaming table and two pool tables dominated the center of the room.

But what clearly had captured Rosamund's attention were the mahogany shelves filled with leather-bound books and dotted with antiques.

Aaron grinned as he watched the mesmerized Rosamund wander deeper into the room. His plan was working.

He moved close to Isabelle and Charisma, and said in a quick, quiet voice, "I was the second man to come to the library and ask her about prophecies today."

Isabelle gave a murmur of dismay. "One of the Others was there before you?"

"Exactly, and she's got a date with him tonight."

"Are they ahead of us on everything?" Charisma complained.

"I suppose, but she's distractible. We just have to offer the right bait." He glanced at Rosamund's face, enraptured as she pulled a book from the shelf. He had only a few seconds to ask about the woman who had spoken in his mind. "Have either of you met a Rom woman with a nose that's been cut who is a—"

"Aaron, look!" Rosamund rushed to his side. "A first edition of Dickens's *Christmas Carol* with illustrations by John Leech!"

"That's only the beginning," he assured her. "It's the contents of Irving's *private* library that will truly interest you."

She looked down at the book in her hand, then up at him, her eyes wide with excitement.

An answering excitement kicked at his gut.

His first impression had been wrong. There was something endearing about a woman who flushed over a first edition Dickens, yet remained so oblivious to her own appearance she hadn't noticed that the material at the neckline of her dress formed a ragged fringe. "McKenna has gone to get Irving. He'll want to take you up himself."

"That will be wonderful! But . . . oh. I don't have much time." She glanced at her utilitarian watch. "I have that date with Lance Mathews."

His warm response to her abruptly faded. "How could we forget that?"

She took the Dickens back, placed it carefully on the shelf where she'd found it, then returned to the little group.

Charisma fixed her emerald green eyes on Rosamund and enunciated clearly, "I'm Charisma Fangorn."

Rosamund heard her this time. "Hello. I'm Rosamund." Her smile blossomed. "Fangorn? As in Fangorn Forest from *Lord of the Rings*?"

"My mother's an aging hippie, among other things, and after she divorced her husband, she chose her own last name, and mine." Charisma took Rosamund's hand and led her to one of the sofas. "You'd better sit. This could be a long wait."

Rosamund looked at her watch again. "I have a date. With Lance Mathews. I really need to get ready early because . . . um, I don't usually use makeup and stuff and I don't do a very good job."

"Don't worry about the makeup," Charisma said. "I'll help, and when I'm done, you'll look great."

Rosamund looked at her in alarm.

From the top of her black and purple dyed hair to her purple-painted toenails, Charisma was an original. Her black eyeliner and dark red lipstick had been tattooed on, and another tattoo curled along her spine to bloom by her left ear. Yet for all the artifice, she was smart and strong and determined. If any of them survived the challenges ahead, it would be Charisma.

"Don't worry," Charisma said in a soothing tone. "I can do librarian makeup, too. But really, you'd better sit down." Charisma plopped down on the couch. "At his age, Irving doesn't move any too quickly."

"Of course." Rosamund sat beside Charisma. She reached for the nearest book, the one Isabelle had so carefully placed on top of the stacked papers.

Isabelle jumped a little.

Rosamund didn't notice, of course. Instead she picked up the book and asked, "What are you reading?"

"*The Historian.*" Isabelle smoothly picked up the stack of papers. "It's one of my favorites. Have you read it?"

Aaron took them, glanced at the top one, read *Chosen Procedures* written in scrawled, old-fashioned handwriting, and placed them on the computer desk away from Rosamund's easy reach.

"No. I think it's about vampires, right?" Rosamund decisively shook her head. "I don't believe in the occult."

Charisma's eyebrows lifted. "Sucks to be you," she muttered.

Aaron put a brotherly arm around her and squeezed—hard. "Charisma's our comedian."

Charisma elbowed him in the ribs.

"Really, who does believe in the occult?" Isabelle laughed indulgently, and met Aaron's gaze. "Yet that doesn't stop me from enjoying the story."

"I suppose not." Rosamund smoothed her hand across the dark cover. "But my father so strongly disapproved of anything involving the paranormal, he even yelled at me when I read *Dracula*." She shuddered as if at a horrible memory.

"If you want to borrow *The Historian*, I won't yell at you," Isabelle said gently. She was beautiful in an exotic way, with delicate bones and faintly slanted eyes. She'd been adopted and raised by one of the best families in Boston, and Aaron speculated that somewhere in her unknown bloodlines, she boasted an Asian ancestor. She spoke in a high-class, Boston accent and wore platinum-set, one-carat diamond studs, a classic Chanel watch, and a three-carat platinum-set diamond ring. Sometime while Aaron had been out of the house, she had received replacements for the clothes that had been destroyed in the Gypsy Travel Agency explosion, for instead of jeans and a T-shirt, she wore what Aaron's expert eye identified as a Tory Burch blue linen dress.

In his business, it paid to recognize the difference between a designer and a knockoff.

Yet Isabelle was barefoot; apparently, Charisma was not without her influence.

And neither was Isabelle.

Charisma must have plundered Isabelle's wardrobe. Seeing Aaron eye her kilt-style pleated skirt, she bobbed up and into a little curtsy. "Like it?"

"Very nice," he said. "Burberry, right?"

She sighed. "You know the weirdest things for a straight guy."

"Isn't that the truth?" Sam stood in the doorway, examining Aaron in overdone masculine horror.

Aaron flipped him the bird.

Charisma plucked at her blue stretch camisole. "Can you guess this?"

"Armani's spring collection." He'd been at the showing, stalking Mrs. Malay and her stolen cache of pre-Columbian art.

"And the heels?" Charisma stuck out her foot and turned it from side to side, admiring the tacky gold sandal.

"I can't begin to guess."

"Ha! They're Zappo's! Since no one will let the womenfolk leave the house"—she was getting sarcastic about their enforced confinement—"we've been hitting the Internet with Irving's credit card. It's all about overnight shipping."

"But what brand are they?" He was guessing something cheap.

"I dunno." She shrugged. "But this outfit needed some pop."

"Clearly." The Chosen Ones had known each other for five days—five strife-ridden, challenging days—and from the first moment, Charisma had been his favorite. She made him laugh.

Aaron looked around. "We're missing Jacqueline and Caleb."

Samuel thumped his fists together.

"In bed again?" Jacqueline was their seer. Caleb was her bodyguard. In the days since the Gypsy Travel

Agency had blown up, they had gone through hell. Now desperately in love, they seized every available moment to be together.

"They're celebrating." Charisma took off one of her heels and rubbed her foot. "They went down and got their marriage license."

"I knew they were going to get married, but . . . their marriage license? Already? I was only gone a few hours." Although the last few days had been life on fast-forward.

"That's the plan," Sam said. "He's so freaked out because Jacqueline was kicked around and he wasn't there to save her, and she's so freaked out because of her mother, they want to be married in the eyes of God. They're looking for a chapel or nondenominational church."

"Okay." Aaron supposed that made sense. "Wow."

Irving appeared in the doorway, tall and thin, looking every day of his ninety-three years, and at the same time hale and hearty. He had recovered from the shock of losing so many friends and associates in the blast of the Gypsy Travel Agency building, and now showed the steel that had made him one of the pioneering CEOs of the twentieth century. He extended his hand to Rosamund. "Dr. Hall, how good to see you again. I'm so glad you managed to carve some time out of your busy schedule to visit me." He was obviously unsure exactly what to say, so he cleverly said little.

"I knew she would enjoy your library," Aaron said, "and I hoped we could convince her to return to help us find our prophecy."

Irving frowned. "She can't stay?"

"She has a date tonight," Charisma said.

"With Lance Mathews," Isabelle said.

Aaron looked right at Irving and said with meaning in his voice, "He's the *other* guy."

Chapter 9

R osamund looked from Charisma to Isabelle to Irving to Samuel to Aaron.

They were talking in code. She could tell they were, but for all her talent at translation, she could only comprehend the actual words.

And really, why was this diverse group of men and women living together in Irving Shea's mansion? Even she knew that was odd.

She needed to leave, and she had the perfect excuse. Standing, she said, "I probably ought to go now and get ready for my date."

"My dear, you've come to see my private library, which I would love to show you. Furthermore, it has come to my attention your father has passed on. You must allow me to offer refreshments and my sympathies. You can't refuse an old man who is feeling very, very guilty about his neglect." Irving offered his arm. "This will take only a few minutes, and of course, as soon as you're ready to go, McKenna will drive you home."

Irving was right. She couldn't refuse him, not when he was being so kind and thoughtful. Taking his arm, she walked with him toward the stairway, but she couldn't resist looking back at Aaron.

He was following close on their heels, an Indian warrior stalking his prey.

Yet his presence reassured her.

Funny. She didn't know if she liked him, and she was almost sure he didn't like her, yet something about his presence comforted her. She knew, without a word from him, that he would never let anything happen to her. And not just because he wanted her to translate a prophecy, either. He seemed to understand her father had felt guilty about her mother's death, and in a weird way, he'd almost seemed to think her father should feel guilty. Because Aaron was the kind of man who, regardless of the odds, would protect his woman from harm.

Not that she was his woman, of course, but . . .

"Here we are." Irving guided her along the upstairs corridor to a tall, wide, hardwood door. He opened it and said with self-deprecating humor, "My private library is attached to my bedroom with a connecting door. At night, when I can't sleep, I enjoy being able to rise and sit among the detritus of the ages."

She stepped inside and realized Irving's private library was more than a library; it was a repository of relics. Leather-bound texts and parchment scrolls shared the shelves with ornate antique fans and pottery. A complete and yellowed human skeleton hung on a stand in the corner. An African war mask grinned at her from one wall. A gracefully rendered copy of some unknown da Vinci painting hung on another. A worn leather chair sat between an illuminated world globe in a tall maple stand and a long library table stacked with books, scrolls, a Mesopotamian fertility goddess, and a crystal ball—a beautifully rounded glass ball sitting on a primitive carved wood base.

"Do you like it?" Irving was as eager as a boy.

"How spectacular! And peculiar." She prowled deeper into the room. "It reminds me of a medieval alchemist's library." She sank down into one of the three leather office chairs located by the library table. "Only comfortable."

"Thank you! When the Cho—children"—Irving stammered over the word—"came to live with me, I ordered some comfortable seating for them in case they wished to study the history of their . . . of the Gypsy Travel Agency." He swallowed, and his brown eyes glistened with tears.

His grief broke her heart. "I was sorry to hear about the devastation of the company. I know how much that must have grieved you."

In this she struck a chord, for the old man looked both fierce and anguished. "So many friends and associates gone, killed by an ancient enmity. When I think of the knowledge and experience destroyed in that blast—"

Aaron put his hand on Irving's shoulder. "It was a tragedy, but we've got to look to the future."

A woman's voice spoke. "Isn't that why Rosamund is here?"

In unison, Irving, Aaron, and Rosamund turned toward the door. A buff, handsome, grim-faced man stood there, but it was the tall, gorgeous, platinum blonde beside him who drew Rosamund's gaze. The blonde wore leather gloves with the fingers exposed, and had the most peculiar amber brown eyes. . . .

She walked in slowly, holding her ribs as if she was in pain, and Rosamund saw a ring of bruises around her throat. Sometime in the very recent past, she had been attacked and hurt badly. Yet she scrutinized Rosamund so acutely, Rosamund was mesmerized.

Aaron said, "Rosamund Hall, this is Jacqueline Vargha and her fiancé, Caleb D'Angelo."

"How do you do?" Jacqueline stripped off her gloves, then offered her bared hand. When Rosamund took it, Jacqueline placed her other hand on the crystal ball.

Rosamund felt a warmth flow to her from Jacqueline, a comfort, a confirmation. Without volition, she relaxed back into the chair.

In a tone of surprise, Jacqueline said, "Rosamund! You have come to find the prophetess."

"Has she?" Irving seated himself in his leather easy chair and smirked at Aaron in ill-concealed satisfaction.

"She has," Jacqueline assured him.

"The prophetess? The prophet is a woman?" Rosamund looked at Aaron in reproach. "You didn't tell me that."

"I . . . didn't know it mattered." He had a twist on his lips that looked like pained amusement.

She didn't have time for pained amusement. "Of course it matters. If the prophet is a woman, that greatly cuts down on the research. Traditionally, female prophets don't get as much respect as male prophets, for in the great span of history they were frequently illiterate, so their prophecies are mentioned as mere footnotes by the men who recorded the divinations. Even if they were literate, they were usually a lot less verbose than men. The men always had to brag about themselves and give their credentials. The women said what they had to say and shut up."

Jacqueline listened, still watching Rosamund as if she were the most interesting woman in the world. "That's all true. The prophetess knew what she wanted to say, but she refused to say it until she was free."

"Until she was free? What does that mean?" Caleb moved closer, standing behind Jacqueline with an air of protectiveness Rosamund found endearing in such a tough-looking guy.

"The prophetess was black, a slave, and there's a"— Jacqueline's eyes narrowed—"there's a white house."

"A white house? Like *the* White House?" Aaron asked.

"I don't know." Jacqueline looked back at Caleb and shrugged.

"George Washington owned slaves. Maybe she lived in his household?" Aaron looked between the women.

"George Washington didn't live in the White House. It wasn't yet built when he was president," Irving told him.

"The facts of history trip me up again." Aaron's mouth quirked in self-mockery.

Rosamund remembered what he had told her. He hadn't even finished high school. For all his obvious wealth and sophistication, he would of course have gaps in his education. "A southern plantation house, perhaps?" she asked.

"I wish I could tell you more, but that's all I was told. We'll have to discover the rest ourselves." Taking her hand off the crystal ball, Jacqueline gave Rosamund's hand a final, kind squeeze, then released it.

Rosamund looked at her hand, then at Jacqueline. Either this woman had an odd way of being kind, or Rosamund just didn't understand human relationships. Ruefully, she admitted it was probably the latter.

Caleb gave a sigh that sounded like relief. Wrapping his arms around Jacqueline, he pulled her against him, her back to his front, and held her loosely.

She relaxed against him with a weary smile, and pulled on her gloves.

"Who told *you*? Perhaps I could trace their sources and discover more," Rosamund said.

"My mother helps me with my . . . research." Jacqueline closed her eyes in pain. "And I'm afraid she has recently died."

"I'm sorry. I'm so sorry." Rosamund remembered her own scorching grief of losing her mother, and touched Jacqueline's arm.

Jacqueline's eyes sprang open. "I am sorry for your losses, too. Please. Consider us your family now."

Rosamund felt the warmth, muted this time, and a concern that made her want to relax and just be in this world at this time.

But she couldn't. If she stopped working and thinking and seeking the truths of other times, she would have to face the truths her emotions had presented her. And she didn't dare do that.

So she turned to Aaron. "Why didn't you tell me the details about the prophetess? That narrows the search parameters."

He spread his hands. "Silly me."

"I can help. I have some texts that I believe would greatly interest you," Irving said eagerly.

She looked hungrily at the books he stacked at her elbow. "I would love to." She glanced at her watch and half rose. "But I have to get ready for my date."

"Of course you do." Irving was everything that was amiable. "But first, here's Martha with a special after-noon tea she made just for you."

A woman, dressed all in black, pushed a laden tea cart into the room.

"Martha escaped the blast that destroyed the Gypsy Travel Agency building, and we are very grateful that she transferred her loyalty and service to us." Irving's fingers trembled.

Martha did not smile. She didn't look as if she knew how. The woman was anywhere between sixty and ninety; the braids in her gray hair were wrapped around her head in a traditional European manner. She looked serious and grieved and . . . Romany.

Trapped by empathy and guilt, Rosamund sank back into her chair.

Aaron pulled up a seat next to her. "Martha is a su-perb cook, and remember, you didn't eat lunch."

"Martha, did you make the chutney and cheese sandwiches?" Irving asked. "Those are my favorites."

"And the watercress and roast beef sandwiches." Martha indicated the three-tiered, flowered platter. "Of course there's scones and clotted cream, with pumpkin and mandarin orange marmalade."

The scent of the tea and the fresh bread wafted toward Rosamund, and her stomach growled. Aaron was right. She *was* hungry. And really, it was better if she didn't go to dinner with Lance Mathews when she was starving. If she ate now, she could concentrate on his glorious self. "I surrender. The aromas are too compelling. I must give in to temptation."

As Martha poured tea into dainty cups and placed food on the flowered china, Irving moved to a seat close to Rosamund. "This is a piece that fascinates me, called Bala's Glass." He held a rounded clear dome about two inches wide, with a flat bottom, and he stroked it with his fragile, warped, old fingers. "By good fortune, I brought it here from the Gypsy Travel Agency to study on the very day of the explosion."

She looked up at Aaron.

He watched her with cool eyes, making her think once again that the moment of communion in the park could never have happened. This man, this Aaron, was sophisticated, offhand, impersonal, without feeling . . . but he had friends who seemed to cherish him.

Today at the zoo, he had told her a lot about himself and his past. He had comforted her in a way no one ever had. Yet something about him made her skin prickle with wariness. When she glanced up and caught his dark eyes gazing at her, some primitive instinct told her to hide herself.

He hunted too well. He observed too much. If she weren't careful, he would see who she really was.

"Would you like to hold it?" Irving asked.

She stared at him blankly, then recovered. "Oh! Bala's Glass. Yes, please." She took the ornament from him. It was heavy for its size, gloriously smooth, almost warm to the touch, and deep in its core, all the colors of the rainbow glowed as if captured by the shiny surface. "From India?"

"Or Sri Lanka. Have you heard the legend of Bala of the Danavas?" Irving accepted a plate of artfully made little sandwiches from Martha.

"I have. Bala of the Danavas was a great warrior who defeated the gods, so in the guise of a favor, they asked him to sacrifice himself." She placed the flat side of the glass on her palm, turning it from side to side as she pulled the tale from the depths of her memory. "So pure was his courage, he agreed, and to humiliate him, they bound him with thirteen strings and killed him in slow agony. Because of his pure birth and his deed, his bones became the seeds of diamonds and had the power of the gods in them."

"Very good! Not many know that story." As if he couldn't resist touching the reading glass, Irving slid his hand over the smooth dome. "This is old, very old, and if the legend is to be believed, was created from Bala's bones."

"Irving." Aaron was in shock. "This is a *diamond*?"

Chapter 10

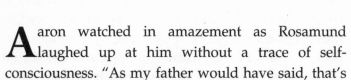

Aaron watched in amazement as Rosamund laughed up at him without a trace of self-consciousness. "As my father would have said, that's the problem with legends. When they come up against facts, they fail to pass the test."

"Why would you say that?" he asked cautiously.

"Because this"—she held the artifact out—"has no faults or inclusions. It's too big to be a perfect jewel, so it's just glass." She chuckled.

"Oh." Aaron chuckled along with her, and fought the urge to cup his hands underneath the glass. Diamond. Whatever it was. "I should have realized."

"Of course, if it is ancient, a piece of glass this size and weight and clarity is an extraordinary accomplishment and nothing to be mocked." She gently placed it back on the table.

Aaron said, "Right. Even if it's nothing but a magnifying glass, it deserves respect for its age."

"As I said, I didn't have the chance to study the, er, glass. But I'm sure, Dr. Hall, that you're right." Irving waited while Martha set a plate in front of Rosamund, and she took her first bite of a cream scone.

She licked her lips, took another bite, exclaimed in ecstasy and thanked Martha, and Aaron saw her focus shift from leaving Irving's mansion to eating and translation.

For the first time since Aaron had met Rosamund, he relaxed.

Lance Mathews had been forgotten.

Irving continued talking, working to keep her busy. "What I know is that Bala's Glass is a reading glass. In the hands of the right person, it can translate languages so ancient or obscure they're indecipherable."

"That's absurd!" She took a bite of sandwich and a sip of tea, pulled a manuscript and Bala's Glass toward her, and went to work. "I can read this with Bala's Glass." She took it away from the text. "But of course it's early Latin, no reason why I couldn't."

With a conspiratorial smile at Aaron, Jacqueline took Caleb's hand and they slipped out of the room.

Martha poured more tea, refilled the plates, and quietly left.

"Here, Rosamund." Irving rose and rummaged in his bookshelves. "I've got an exact copy of an Ethiopian first-century scroll, Egyptian hieroglyphics . . . with a twist. See whether you can work your way through this without the glass, and then with it."

Rosamund noted the language. Her eyes lit up. "I wish I had my personal notebook. It's got my mother's interpretations and my father's and mine, but I left it at the library. I really need it before I can properly dig into this."

Aaron surged to his feet. Here was something he could do. Something besides study the young woman opposite. His instincts were stirring. He had seen the signs. She hid herself from the world for a reason.

She hid herself from him. And why should he care? She was a mess from head to toe, without any obvious womanly impulse. She could barely practice the merest of social niceties. Nothing here should intrigue him.

But she did.

He needed to get away. "I'll get your notebook for you."

She blinked at him as if she couldn't quite remember who he was. "Can you get through the security without an appointment?"

Without a bit of a problem. "I can try."

"Thank you."

She was so polite, as if they'd just met, and yet at the zoo, he'd shared his past with her. Something about Rosamund invited confidences. Perhaps because she was so guileless, he knew she wouldn't make judgments. Or perhaps something about her pulled the poison from the memories. He never told anyone about his birth, his early life in the mountains, his lack of education; yet within hours of meeting her, he had confessed everything to her.

The woman seemed so open, so naïve, even immature. Yet when she told him about her father, he had caught a glimpse of something in her eyes—fear and anguish long denied and now freshly exposed.

He hadn't been able to resist. He had taken her into

his arms, held her, experienced a moment of communion between two wounded souls. . . .

And right now, he wasn't sure she remembered.

She irritated him like a grain of sand irritated an
oyster.

"Irving, if I could speak to you for a minute?" Aaron
stepped into the corridor and waited for Irving to join
him. With a glance, he verified that Rosamund was busy,
and shut the door behind them. Looking directly into
the old man's rheumy eyes, he said, "I saw a woman in
Central Park, and she said, 'Give Irving my regards.'"

Irving lifted his eyebrows inquiringly. Butter
wouldn't melt in his mouth. "How nice. Did she give
you her name?"

"No. Apparently she thought you would recognize
her, since she didn't speak with her mouth—she spoke
in my mind." Aaron cut off Irving with a harsh gesture.
"Who is she, Irving? What is she?"

"Obviously she's a mind speaker. Not a very good
one, apparently. The good ones influence you and you
never realize it." Irving was telling Aaron stuff he already knew.

"I think she's good. I think she's powerful. I think
she wanted me to realize what she was doing, and to
see her so I could describe her to you."

"Why would she do that?" Irving was being deliberately obtuse.

Aaron wanted to shake him. "She *knows* you."

"My career has spanned seventy years . . . so far.
I've met a lot of people—"

"She feels so strongly about you she hunted me
down to pass on a message."

"I wish I could see her." Irving tapped his forehead. "That might jog something loose. This is the curse of being an old man. My memory isn't what it used to be."

Aaron wasn't buying it. Not Irving's professed ignorance or his pretend innocence. He'd seen the old guy use his age to manipulate circumstances before. He knew he was doing it now. But it didn't matter; if Irving wouldn't talk, Aaron couldn't make him. "All right. You've got the message."

"Is that all?"

"That's all. No! Wait." Aaron stopped Irving with a touch. "Was Rosamund's mother one of the Chosen?"

"No. What makes you think that?"

"According to Rosamund, Elizabeth Hall had tattoos on her fingers that looked like a primitive alphabet, she was a miracle at translation, and it sounds as if she was murdered. Maybe by an Other."

Irving hesitated.

Aaron exploded with frustration. "Oh, for God's sake, Irving. What difference does it make if I know Elizabeth Hall was Chosen?"

The closemouthed old man weighed how much information to release before he admitted, "She wasn't Chosen. At that time, we didn't need someone who could translate old texts. But she was one of the Abandoned Ones, and yes, she had a gift."

"Was she murdered by the Others?" Aaron insisted.

"I don't know that. If it's true, then the Others have been seeking this prophecy—or a prophecy—for years."

"Good to know." Aaron was playing catch-up, seeking their prophecy with a girl who, although not gifted, was the translator they needed. Or at least, Jacqueline said so, and so far, as their seer, she had been eerily accurate. "How many more people are like Elizabeth Hall, out in the world with gifts, and we know nothing about them?"

"Too many, and every day there are more."

"Can't we get them? To help us?" Aaron gestured wildly. "In case you haven't noticed, Irving, we're in dire straits!"

"I didn't make the rules. I'm old, but not old enough to have anything to do with the rules!" Irving was exasperated. "We're allowed seven every seven years. We can replace one who is lost, but we can't have more than seven official Chosen in one cycle. We base . . . that is, the board of directors based their decisions about whom to choose on what our upcoming needs appeared to be, and according to the strength of the talents and gifts given."

"The strength of the talents and gifts *that you know about.*"

"Exactly. Because we don't find all the Abandoned Ones. Some of them escape detection altogether and die. Some of them are taken by the Others to be raised in evil. And some are raised in orphanages or by foster parents, and we never know who they are."

"It's a lousy world."

"It's your job to make it better."

"I know that!" Aaron's frustration with their lack of action—everyone's frustration at their lack of action—chewed at his composure. Knowing that their fate currently rested in the hands of a girl with no belief in the Chosen Ones or their mission made him tense and snappish. And the pressure Irving so skillfully applied made Aaron say, "I didn't ask to make the world better, but I'm in now, Irving. I'm sticking with my compatriots—except, gee, we've already been betrayed by one Chosen and we're down to six. We need someone else. What are we going to do about *that*, Irving?"

"I don't know." Irving sagged against the wall. "The number of gifted has been steadily dwindling in past years. That's why we pulled in Aleksandr, although he hasn't a gift that we know of and he's young. Very young. We hope his gift will appear. Worse, the records were destroyed in the explosion, so I haven't a clue of the Abandoned Ones available to us."

This time, the old guy was so obviously distressed, Aaron believed him. "Don't worry. We'll figure it out."

Irving's eyes narrowed as he thought. "Except . . . well, no."

"You have someone?"

"A previous Chosen, but he . . . he's not stable."

"What does 'not stable' mean?"

"He can't control his gift. Last time he used it, he created disaster."

"That doesn't sound too good." Because the only disaster Aaron had experienced so far had been the destruction of the Gypsy Travel Agency, and that was a biggie. "You keep thinking. In the meantime, I'm off to do my job."

"Don't get caught," Irving warned.

Fury at being trapped in these circumstances grabbed at Aaron, and he snarled, "I was only caught once, and I suspect I had help from the Gypsy Travel Agency."

"Yes," Irving agreed, "and if we can hook you, so can the Others. So be careful. Be very, very careful."

Chapter 11

───── ❦ ─────

It was after six p.m. when Aaron walked into the Arthur W. Nelson Fine Arts Library and up to Jessica's desk. The main room was quiet; two elderly women sat together, a heavy art tome spread out before them on the table. A student with papers placed haphazardly around him snored peacefully on the carpet. Unfortunately for Aaron, Jessica's shift was over and she'd been replaced by some guy, and not even a gay guy, which might have worked to Aaron's advantage. The boy was just some kid working his way through college.

Aaron put on his best stuffy official act and said, "I'm Aaron Eagle. I was here earlier to meet with Dr. Hall. I took her to examine some manuscripts owned by my employer, and she asked me to return for her notebook."

The kid—his nameplate said he was Dylan—studied Aaron. "I heard she had a date with some really hot stud. I take it it's not you."

Damn. Jessica had talked to him before she left. "Apparently the date fell through. Disappointing for her." Aaron shrugged the tiniest bit. "But not surprising, you know?"

Dylan's eyes grew cold. "I like Rosamund, and I don't think she's nearly the dog everyone else thinks she is."

Great. Aaron had just set the kid's back up.

"Anyway," Dylan said, "I can't let anyone into Rosamund's area without an appointment."

"She needs that notebook." Aaron pulled out his cell phone. "What if I call her and she can tell you what she needs and you go down and get it?"

"No one goes in Rosamund's area unless she's there. Those are the rules." The kid was not about to back down.

Part of Aaron's job was recognizing when to admit defeat. He never made a scene; a scene attracted attention, and he didn't really want anyone to remember he'd been here at all. "You're right. I know you're right. I was just hoping . . . oh, well." He nodded. "Have a good evening!"

"You, too." Dylan watched him walk away, and Aaron didn't have to see him to know he smiled. Nothing made a college kid as happy as making an overbearing adult toe the line.

As Aaron walked, he glanced at the security cameras, located them, then picked out a dark, empty, unsurveyed corner and made his way there. Standing quietly among the stacks, he perused the books, made sure he was alone . . . then dissolved into a dark mist that disappeared into the shadows.

Next, he did what he did best.

He made his way unseen to the antiquities department. He located Rosamund's worn leather notebook, stuffed with papers. He surrounded it with himself, making it as much a part of the shadows as he himself was. Then the dark mist that was Aaron wafted like smoke through the cracks in the doors, down the corridors, and when he knew himself to be safe, out of the Arthur W. Nelson Fine Arts Library.

"Rosamund." Aaron's warm, deep voice spoke close to her ear. "I have your notebook for you."

She turned her head. Her neck popped. Her eyes felt square, like they'd shaped themselves into pages. Aaron's face swam before her tired gaze, and she said the first thing that came to her head. "Do you realize it is a crime that Irving hasn't allowed these manuscripts to be scanned and uploaded to the public domain?"

He straightened. "You're welcome."

"Oh." She looked down at the notebook he had handed her. "Thank you. They didn't give you trouble about going down to the antiquities when I wasn't there?"

"Since I'd been there earlier . . ."

"Good." She'd been sitting for too long. She needed to get up, stretch, go to the bathroom. "This will be very helpful. Now if you'll excuse me . . ." She pushed away from the table and scrambled to her feet.

"When you come back, I'll have a glass of warm milk ready for you." Martha stood up out of Irving's big leather easy chair. "That will help relax you so you can sleep."

"That would be lovely, but I really need to—" Horrified remembrance flashed through Rosamund. She clapped her hands over her mouth. "Oh, *no*. I forgot my date with Lance Mathews!"

"Oh, dear," Martha said.

"What time is it?" Rosamund looked around wildly. A clock. She needed a clock. Irving had jars of teeth in here, but he didn't have a clock?

Aaron glanced at his watch. "Ten twenty."

"I need to call him, to explain. . . ." She felt sick.

"If he works from eight to five, it's a little late. You might wake him up." Martha's voice was low and gravelly, as if she smoked when she could sneak away. Cigarettes or maybe, as rough as she looked, cigars.

"But I . . . He was supposed to pick me up and take me to dinner!" Rosamund flushed hot and then cold as she imagined Lance Mathews standing on her doorstep, dressed in a suit like Aaron's—no, in casual clothes like the ones he had worn earlier—and thinking she had stood him up.

Charisma wandered through the door, her black and purple hair in Pippi Longstocking braids. She wore pajamas, huge fluffy slippers, and a tattered robe, and was unwrapping an ice-cream sandwich and holding another one. "Hey, Rosamund, I thought about saying something to you about that date, but you were so absorbed I thought you must have cancelled."

"I never have dates that aren't blind dates, and then the guys never call back. The one time I actually have a guy look at me and like me and ask me out—and he's *gorgeous*—and I forgot. How big a loser am I? I want to jump off a cliff."

"I don't care how gorgeous he is. He isn't worth that," Aaron said.

"It's okay, Rosamund. A real man . . ." Charisma began. Then she bit into the ice-cream sandwich, and her face lit up. "Good," she said. "Better than good."

With some vaguely deep meaning in his voice, Aaron asked, "What were you saying before you started eating, Charisma?"

"Oh! Right." Charisma coughed. "A real man totally gets when a woman gets involved in her work. I'm sure Lance Mathews will get how important your work is to you, too."

"Really?" Rosamund looked from Charisma to Martha to Aaron.

They all nodded.

"Sure." Charisma handed Rosamund the second ice-cream sandwich. "Here, eat this. It will make you feel better."

Rosamund peeled back the paper.

"Aren't I right about guys understanding how important a woman's work is, Aaron?" Charisma asked.

"Heavens, yes. If Lance Mathews is half the man I think he is, he will understand completely." Aaron turned to Martha. "Has anyone told Rosamund that Irving called the library?"

Rosamund paused, the ice-cream sandwich halfway to her mouth. "The library? You mean the Arthur W. Nelson Fine Arts Library? Why? What did he call for?"

"He convinced the board to give you a leave of absence to work for him," Martha said.

"Irving's a wily old thing," Charisma said. "He insinuated that he wanted you to assess his collection because he was deciding who was going to get it. The head of the board, some snooty guy in a suit—"

"Mr. Perez." Rosamund bit into the ice-cream sandwich, chewed and swallowed. "This is tremendous."

"A gourmet ice-cream sandwich, orange ice cream between two oatmeal cookies." Charisma polished hers off.

Rosamund took another bite, and closed her eyes as she chewed. "Bliss."

When she opened them, Aaron was watching her so intently she figured she must have a crumb on her face, and dabbed at her mouth.

"Apparently Mr. Perez bowed and scraped and let Irving have his way. You're on loan to Irving as long as he wants you." Charisma flung herself back into a chair, and declared, "That sandwich was *sick*. Now I can die happy."

Rosamund didn't know if she could die happy, but she had to admit, the infusion of flavors and sugars did wonders to decrease her anxiety about Lance Mathews. "So you really think he won't be mad that I forgot him?"

Charisma made an amused face. "No. Geez, only a guy with an immense, silly ego would notice."

"So true." Aaron captured Rosamund's hand, brought it to his mouth, and took a bite of her ice-cream sandwich.

"Hey!" she said.

"You're right—it is good." Still holding her hand, he looked into her eyes.

Her breath caught in her throat. That sculpted,

strong, and bronzed face . . . that curious, intent expression . . .

What was wrong with her? She was interested in Lance Mathews, not Aaron Eagle, but when Aaron looked at her like that, he made her breath sing in her chest.

He let go of her hand.

She looked away.

No one seemed to notice the brief moment of chest-singing . . . except her.

"Irving's bedroom is right through that door. But let me lock it on this side." Martha went over and turned the key.

"Irving had a cot brought in here for you." Charisma waved at the twin-sized folding bed. "And Isabelle and I put together clothes we thought would fit you. Irving wants you to be comfortable while you look for the prophecy."

When Rosamund glanced back at Aaron, he was looking at Charisma with the kind of affectionate smile she never saw him use when he looked at her.

Nope. She was right. He didn't even like her.

"Hey, Rosamund, probably you want to sleep now," Charisma said.

"I'll get your warm milk," Martha said.

"No, that's not necessary. I'll sleep. Now . . . I need to use the facilities." She edged toward the corridor, far too aware of three pairs of eyes keenly watching her. "I'm tired. I know I'll sleep well. I really will." She made it into the bathroom, shut the door behind her, locked it and leaned against it.

She understood the situation. She really did. They

desperately wanted an explanation about the explosion at the Gypsy Travel Agency, what it meant and what would happen next. They thought she could find that explanation . . . and when she was engrossed in her research, she believed she could provide it, too.

But her father had been so angry whenever she showed him her stories about fairies and dragons, witches and magicians. He had been so insistent that she forget all the things her mother had taught her about the Chosen Ones and their enemies.

How did she dare to imagine she could find a true prophecy among the multitude of farcical ones? Irving had gone to great lengths to keep her here, but she *had* to find a life to live that did not include research.

If she could only get it started.

Remembering the way Aaron looked at her, as if she were the village idiot . . . remembering the way Lance Mathews looked at her, as if she were the first course of a meal . . . she knew what she had to do.

Pulling her cell phone from her pocket, she texted Lance Mathews.

sorry missed r date. try again?

Chapter 12

———❖———

Lance Mathews threw his phone across the office and hissed in annoyance. "The stupid little—"

From the desk in the shadows, a smooth, quiet voice spoke. "Mr. Mathews, you know I don't appreciate inappropriate language."

The sound of Osgood's rebuke was enough to calm Lance's fury. Or rather, his rebuke was enough to *freeze* Lance's fury.

Because no one knew better than Lance just who, and what, Osgood was.

"It is bad enough that the Chosen recruits escaped the blast at the Gypsy Travel Agency."

"That wasn't my fault!"

"No. The people whose fault it is have been punished."

"Are they dead?" If Osgood had taken his irritation out on them, it might go better for Lance.

"No. They were lucky that I always find it amusing

to hunt inexperienced Chosen Ones. It adds a piquancy to eternity."

"Right." Lance's mouth grew dry.

"But as for you—you should have secured the girl when you first made contact." Osgood's tranquil voice held a hint of a Southern accent.

"I thought it would be better if she anticipated our date." When actually, Lance had been intent on putting off his painful duty as long as he could.

"Excuses, Mr. Mathews?"

"No." Excuses were a waste of time. Osgood had a way of always knowing the truth.

On the surface, Osgood was nothing more than a New York City businessman, a very successful one, with nightclubs and bars all over the city, the East Coast, and beyond. He owned whorehouses, too, and single-handedly had gained the monopoly on prostitution, illegal gambling, and drugs. If there was money to be made on immorality, he made it.

Yet no one—not the media, not the government, not the man on the street—really knew anything about him. He owned enough police officials and politicians to make sure of that.

Osgood had no family. He had no friends. He had come up from nowhere and no one knew where he slept—or if he slept.

Lance could have sold the story on Osgood for a lot of money, but he wasn't fool enough to try. No one rolled on Osgood and lived. In fact, it was a fast and easy way to die in agony—and that wasn't the end of it.

The problem was what happened after death.

Because Osgood owned the monopoly on suffering in the afterlife, too.

At some point, Osgood had invited the devil into his soul.

Together, they made one hell of a team.

Now Lance stood in Osgood's bare, dim office in his high-rise in midtown, and asked, "Who the h— Who knew that homely thing would go off with another man?"

"This kind of disappointment, especially coming from you, frustrates me. And you know how much I dislike frustration."

Lance risked a glance toward the gray metal desk.

Osgood hadn't moved, so maybe Lance would come out all right this time.

"It won't happen again," he said fervently.

"I trust not, but I like to give guidance when I can."

A chill ran up Lance's spine.

"Take off your shirt and come here."

Lance didn't dare move. Didn't dare not.

"Oh, come, Mr. Mathews," Osgood's voice cajoled. "Surely you know I'm not going to eliminate you at this point. I own seven Others, each capable in his or her own way. You are the one best qualified for this job, and I would have a difficult time replacing you."

"I know." Driven by terror and pulled by hope, Lance pulled off his shirt. Holding it in tight fists, he stumbled toward the desk.

"You shouldn't be so afraid." Now Osgood sounded reproachful. "I realize how very much you cherish that pretty face of yours. That perfect hair. The body, so perfectly created for sin. And this youthful beauty is so useful to me. I wouldn't hurt that tender outer surface."

"Thank you." Lance knelt before Osgood and stared up toward his face.

There was nothing remarkable about Osgood's looks. He was past middle age, small-boned and not tall, bald and descended from some unmemorable branch of the white European populace. What hair he had was wispy brunet, his eyes were an indistinctive brown, and he was lightly tanned. He wore good clothes and expensive shoes, and was always formally dressed. He seldom showed expression; he looked the same when he was working, when he was fucking, when he was piloting his plane or threatening a debtor.

Right now, he wore that same serene face—and he scared Lance half to death.

"Half to death." Osgood plucked the thought from Lance's mind, and mused aloud. "Exactly. Half to death would work very well."

"What are you going to do?" Lance's voice quavered.

Osgood traced the mark of the flame on Lance's chest. "Do you know, on the day your mother tossed you in the garbage, you received this mark as part of your gift, a compensation for the lack of a family's love." He held up a hand. "I had nothing to do with it, I assure you. I don't share power. But I do harness it."

"I know." Lance thought of the Others, going about Osgood's business all over the night-clad city.

"The thing about marks like this is—once the flesh and the spirit have been ripped apart, a weakness forever remains. And for someone like me, that's opportunity, golden opportunity. It would be a shame not to take advantage of that weakness, now wouldn't it?" Osgood warmed to his subject. "For instance, Mr.

Mathews, I can feel your heart thumping beneath the flame. Racing, really. Are you frightened?"

Lance nodded, too scared to look away from that incredibly calm face.

"You should be." Osgood flattened his hand on Lance's chest. A blue flame lit in his eyes, burning like the hottest embers of hell.

And pain slashed like a knife into Lance's heart.

He collapsed on the floor, writhing as agony tightened his shoulders and spread up his neck.

Osgood pushed back his chair and watched. "It appears you have a previously unrecognized heart defect. Probably it runs in your family—maybe you got it from your whore of a mother, or from the abusive sot she married."

Sweat broke out on Lance's forehead, trickled down his spine. He couldn't breathe; his skin turned cold. He wanted to vomit; he couldn't unlock his jaw.

"Death from a heart attack can take several minutes, and as I understand it, those minutes of torture seem to go on forever. That's what makes a heart attack so interesting to view. The victim struggles so much—well, if he can."

Lance could barely hear Osgood's voice through the buzzing in his ears.

"Actually, the usual first sign of a heart attack is death. Did you know that, Mr. Mathews?"

Red spots paraded before Lance's eyes. His struggles were growing more convulsive, less constant.

"But in your case, if you perform well and don't make any more silly mistakes, your heart defect might remain unnoticed for the rest of your very long, long life."

Suddenly, the pain was gone. Lance could breathe again. And he did, lying on the floor, gasping in the sweet, warm air of life.

"Mr. Mathews, I don't want you to think that I've punished you unduly. After all, it was only this one little tiny failure." Osgood waited for a response, then gently prompted, "Right?"

Lance gathered all his strength, and wheezed, "Right."

"But nor do I want the Others to think I've favored you unduly. That would cause dissension in the ranks, and worse, it might encourage sloppiness with their work."

This time, Lance knew to agree right away. "I understand."

"So should you contemplate failing me again, please remember this hitherto undetected heart defect, the agony involved in dying of a heart attack, and how very long it can take."

"I will." The memory would hang like a knife above Lance's head every day of his life.

"Now, I suggest you make your plans to take command of Dr. Hall and her knowledge so that when she finds that prophecy, it is ours."

"I will. I swear I will."

Osgood flicked his fingers in Lance's direction. "Get out."

Lance crawled toward the door.

When he reached it, Osgood called, "Mr. Mathews."

Lance looked back.

Osgood touched his own chest, and once again, his eyes glowed blue. "Remember."

Chapter 13

"And here he is. Mr. I-Can't-Stand-the-Librarian-Upstairs." Samuel chalked his pool cue and sneered as Aaron strode toward the bar in the downstairs library.

"Shut up, Samuel." As he poured himself two fingers of tequila, Aaron didn't look at the Chosen sprawled on the sofas. "I have my reasons."

"Yes. I know. You tell us every evening." Samuel numbered the reasons on his fingers. "She doesn't pay attention to her clothes. She doesn't pay attention to her grooming. She can't carry on a conversation because she's always thinking about what she just read, or what she read years ago, or what she's going to read next. Personally, I think you're jealous because she doesn't pay attention to you."

"Asshole." Aaron swallowed the tequila neat.

It wasn't what Rosamund did that made him watch like a cat at a mousehole. It was who she was . . . and no matter how much time he spent with her, he couldn't quite figure that out.

Charisma stepped away from the pool table. "Shut up, Samuel. You're no sweet dream yourself."

"I changed your damned toilet paper the other day."

Charisma shot back sarcastically, "What do you want? A cookie?"

Turning back to the game, Samuel stumbled, and when Aaron laughed, Samuel picked up a gold platform sandal. "Damn it, Charisma. At least I pick up my shoes."

"Sorry about that." Charisma started to take it.

But he threw it, and then the second one, across the room at the fireplace.

Hands on her hips, Charisma got in his face. "You are the biggest jerk!"

He glanced at Isabelle, sitting with her feet tucked under her, sorting through stacks of papers. "So I've been told. Many times."

The inactivity was getting on everyone's nerves.

When the explosion had first taken out the Gypsy Travel Agency, everyone had been willing to hole up in Irving's home and be safe. But days and days of enforced confinement had cured that. They had quickly realized that, yes, the Others were powerful and ruthless, and planned to eliminate them all, but they had to do something to fight them.

More important, they had discovered that living with strangers in a restricted space, while being deprived of their belongings and their freedoms, made everyone want to crawl the walls. The guys went out occasionally on the theory that men were less vulnerable than women, but then something happened like Aaron's mind speaker, and they all went back into a huddle waiting for a sign, or a prophecy, or some direction.

Waiting for the prophecy was the sensible thing to do. They all knew it. But Samuel paced like a caged lion. Charisma's Internet orders poured in, everything from clothes to gourmet ice-cream sandwiches to jigsaw puzzles. Isabelle obsessively took notes from papers gleaned in forays through Irving's notebooks and the historical documents he'd kept at the house, trying to get a sense of previous Chosen methods and procedures. Aleksandr ran off to school every chance he got. Only Jacqueline and Caleb were still calm and pleasant, but they weren't here this evening. Aaron didn't have to ask where they were or what they were doing. As Samuel said, *I'd be happy, too, if I was getting laid all the time.*

Aaron brooded over Rosamund, who barely noticed him, and when he wasn't brooding, he researched Dr. Elijah Hall's death. According to every record he could find, it had occurred exactly as Rosamund had been told. Yet . . . how to explain that text he had sent?

Run.

Samuel took his shot, flubbed it, then turned on Aaron. "I'll tell you why *I* don't like your Dr. Hall. It's not because she doesn't pay attention to anything. It's because she hasn't found that rotten prophecy yet. What kind of librarian did you bring us, Aaron? Because I am sick and tired of being stuck in this house."

"At least you're doing something." Charisma leaned

on her cue. "Legal research on the computer has got to be more interesting than just sitting here. I mean, I know you're using the computer, because you can't stand to leave Safari as the default browser."

"I'm not using a stupid Apple browser," he shot back.

"It's a lot less buggy than your Microsoft browser," she snapped.

"Come on, guys." Aleksandr pulled one of his earphones out of his ear. "I'm listening to music."

"You're a kid," Samuel said.

Aleksandr pulled the other earphone out. "*I'm* a kid? *I'm* not having a big fat tantrum and throwing people's shoes."

Aaron, already pissed off, got more pissed off about Aleksandr. The youngest member of their group, and he had the most freedom. Aaron poured himself a second drink, and said, "You're not bored because you get to go to the university every day while the rest of us are stuck in this house waiting for the Librarian Upstairs to find us a prophecy."

"I wish I could *sleep* at the university. Instead I have to sleep across the hall from Mr. I'm-Going-to-Get-Up-and-Exercise"—Aleksandr glared at Aaron—"but you can't stand to actually get up, so you hit your snooze alarm over and over and everyone within earshot has to wake up every eight minutes for the next forty-five minutes until you finally manage to roll your lazy ass out of bed."

Isabelle slammed her notebook closed, and in a voice that carried over and through their arguments, she said, "Would you all just shut up?"

Silence fell.

They had elected Isabelle to be their leader because of her serene good grace and intelligent, balanced decisions. In all the trouble they'd already had, she had kept her head and directed them fairly.

Now they all stared at her, at her angry eyes and tightly folded lips.

Then Samuel said, "Do you want to fight, Isabelle? Because if you do, I'm your man."

She flushed. "You make this whole ordeal even more unbearable. *You* are unbearable."

"You do want to fight. C'mon, Isabelle." Samuel danced toward her, fists up. "Just once, forget who you are, and let's fight."

She half lifted her notebook as if she wanted to throw it at his head, and the only thing stopping her was her upbringing.

Aaron glanced between them. Her upbringing, and that light in Samuel's eyes that clearly relished the thought of breaking through Isabelle's reserve.

Those two had known each other before they came to be Chosen. Something had happened between them, something that wasn't yet finished. But it wasn't going to get finished now, because Isabelle put her book down, rose, and started for the door.

"Coward," Samuel taunted.

Isabelle swung on him, fists clenched.

"All right." Martha stood in the doorway, frowning darkly at them. Her voice carried over Samuel's stupid jeers, drowned out the click of Charisma's cue against the balls, and made them all straighten up and pay attention. "There's no choice. I'm taking you all down to Davidov's Brew Pub."

Samuel got that look on his face, the one that said Martha had interrupted just when he had Isabelle where he wanted her. "Gee, Martha, thanks. We can go outside, as long as you lead us yourself? What are we going to do, walk single file, Indian style?" Samuel turned to Aaron. "You ought to be good at that, Tonto."

"My God, Samuel." Isabelle sounded as if she were in despair. "Do you have to be as offensive as you know how?"

"Someone has to counterbalance all that gentility of yours," he answered.

Aaron didn't care whether Samuel tried to insult him. Not when he could brush close to him and, sotto voce, say, "You missed your chance again, champ. She's never going to care." Then he smirked.

He could almost hear Samuel's teeth grind.

Charisma grabbed her shoes off the fireplace and hopped around as she put them on.

Martha stood straight and stiff, her hands clasped before her. "Mr. Faa, the pub is underground. It's connected to the mansion through one of the tunnels that honeycomb the city."

Isabelle picked up her sweater off the back of the sofa.

Martha continued. "I would send you on your own, but you'd get lost in the dark and cry like a baby, and I'd hate to see you so mortified." Clearly, that was a lie. She would love to see Samuel mortified. "Now if you're done complaining, I'll escort you to the pub."

Aaron started to dump his drink in the bar sink, then paused and looked up toward Irving's private library.

Samuel took his turn to whomp on Aaron's ego. "Don't worry, Tonto. Your librarian won't notice you're gone. She doesn't even know you're alive."

"To hell with you," Aaron muttered. But Samuel was right, so he poured out the tequila and put down his glass.

He looked up in time to see Martha turn.

McKenna stood directly behind her, quivering with Celtic outrage. "Martha. Mr. Shea expressly forbade that we take them out, and you know what he thinks of Vidar Davidov!"

Martha considered the butler for a long moment. She turned back to the Chosen Ones clustered behind her. "In the interest of fairness, I should tell you that while you will be perfectly safe in Davidov's Pub, Mr. Shea is concerned that during the trip there, you might be attacked by the Others and captured or killed. The danger is real, and one you might want to take into account."

The Chosen Ones looked at each other, then looked at her.

"I'm not the leader of the Chosen, but I feel as if I can speak for us all." Charisma looked around.

Everyone nodded.

"If I don't get out of this house pretty soon, I'm going to throw myself screaming out the window." Her voice rose with every word.

Martha turned back to McKenna. "There you have it. If Mr. Shea wishes to complain, he can come to me."

McKenna scuttled off toward the stairs.

"What a tattletale," Samuel said.

"No, Mr. Faa," Martha said. "He is loyal to Mr. Shea. There is a difference."

"What about you? What are you loyal to?" Samuel was still being snotty.

She looked at him without expression in those calm, dark eyes. "I am loyal to the Chosen Ones. I am loyal to you, Mr. Faa."

Chapter 14

⎯⎯⎯⎯⎯⎯ ❦ ⎯⎯⎯⎯⎯⎯

The tunnel was dim and cool, lit by occasional shafts of sunlight from grates twenty-five feet above in the New York City sidewalks. For the first half mile, the tunnel was wrapped in gray concrete, and the Chosen Ones exclaimed and pointed, awed and amazed at the network that connected the city.

Abruptly, the smooth surface quit. Gravel and dirt crunched beneath Aaron's shoes, the air grew dank, and once, pebbles from the ceiling fell like a patter of hail behind them. It got darker until they came to what looked like a crossroads, where passage after passage stretched into the gloom. Here Martha switched on her flashlight and continued steadily on. As they passed one passage, Aaron caught a whiff of fetid air. He looked; it plunged downward, and the hair stood up on the back of his neck.

They were being watched.

The Chosen Ones moved closer to each other, and to Martha.

"Martha, who built this labyrinth?" Samuel asked.

Unlike the Chosen, Martha seemed impervious to the atmosphere. "Some of the tunnels were dug during Prohibition to move liquor. Some were dug during the World Wars as safety measures. Some were dug by the railroad or the subway commission and used and abandoned, or never used at all. And others . . ." She shrugged.

"Why don't we hear about these?" Isabelle asked.

Martha looked sideways at her. "Do you think the city of New York wants a bunch of tourists stumbling around down here?"

"I was afraid it was because vagrants or escaped criminals lived down here." Isabelle looked at a filthy sleeping bag discarded among a fall of tin cans.

Martha said nothing.

"They don't, do they?" Aleksandr sounded hopeful.

"I would ask that you not come down without an escort," Martha said.

"It gives me an ooky feeling to know the tunnels have been here, and I've been oblivious." Charisma shivered.

"Are there levels below this?" Aaron suspected he already knew the answer.

But without a bit of expression in her voice, Martha said, "I couldn't say. If there are, I have no desire to go there."

Although she had no gift, she had obviously held a position of importance in the Gypsy Travel Agency. She had created magic for their induction. She had gained the respect of Zusane, their previous seer, and of Irving and McKenna. Yet in the last nine days they had faced tragedy and danger, and sworn to stand at each other's backs, and the Romany woman was still a mystery.

Behind them, they heard running; they turned and saw Caleb and Jacqueline holding hands and sprinting across the rough ground toward them. Caleb had that look on his face, the one that said he was not happy with the level of safety here.

"You okay?" Charisma asked.

Jacqueline stopped, panting. "There was something back there."

"Someone," Caleb said. "There was someone back there."

Aaron looked into the twilight behind, and saw the quick scuttle of a very large someone . . . but he knew what Jacqueline meant. The someone looked like a walking pile of filthy rags, and when he glanced toward the Chosen, his face—or hers—gleamed with pallid resentment.

Martha didn't look back. "We're almost there."

True to her prediction, Aaron stumbled on a curb as the ground suddenly became concrete again. They made a hairpin turn, and the tunnel came to a precipitous end in a rough rock wall and a short, wide steel door with a tiny nameplate that said DAVIDOV'S.

Martha tapped on the metal.

The sound barely carried, but at once the weighty door opened, the rich, yeasty smell of brewing beer rolled out on a wave, and a warm, pleasant, male voice said, "Martha, I heard you were coming. And you brought the new Chosen Ones."

Aaron squinted into the dim pub, trying to get a bead on the guy, whoever he was.

"I'm Vidar Davidov," he said. "Welcome to my pub."
He stepped back into one of those squares of light from
above, and Aaron heard the women suck in a collective
breath.

Put him on the deck of a longship with a sword in
his hand, and Vidar Davidov was the poster boy for a
medieval Viking raider. He was easily six and a half
feet tall, probably thirty years old. His electric blue
eyes lit up his long, square, chiseled face. His wavy,
white blond hair brushed his wide shoulders. His
T-shirt hugged his hewn chest. His arms were muscled
strongholds, his wrists brawny, his palms broad, his
fingers tapered. His legs were long and clad in old, soft
denim that molded his lower body like a worn leather
glove. "Come in. Come in!" He smiled at Isabelle,
Charisma, and Jacqueline, white teeth gleaming like a
toothpaste commercial, and in a trance, they followed
him as if he were the pied piper and they were the children of Hamlin.

The guys exchanged glances.

With a fair amount of dark humor, Caleb muttered,
"If I swung that way, he'd be the one I'd date."

Vidar proved that his hearing was better than they
might have liked when he said, "You should be so
lucky."

The women laughed and settled at the round table
in the middle of the empty pub.

The guys followed more cautiously.

Martha wandered in, shut the door behind her, went
to the bar, and perched on a stool.

The place had the kind of woodland atmosphere
that warmed like an embrace, with oak-paneled walls

that reached up to a fifteen-foot ceiling decorated with leaves and branches so artfully done they resembled the forest canopy. The bar was a slab of granite, with huge round tapped kegs set into the wall behind. Worn wood tables dotted the floor, with padded leather benches and deep cushioned chairs gathered around them. The lighting was just right, not too bright, not too dark, and dappled like a sunny day beneath a giant oak tree in a European woods a thousand years ago.

Aaron liked the pub.

He wasn't so sure about Vidar. He couldn't put his finger on it, but something about the guy was off. Just . . . off. Vidar should have acted like a brewmaster, a pub owner, and a business owner. Instead he acted like royalty. Very hospitable royalty, but royalty nevertheless.

"Would you beautiful women allow me to pick your brew?" Vidar leaned forward, hands on the table, and smiled.

Jacqueline and Charisma nodded.

Isabelle bit her lip. "To tell you the truth, I'm not a beer drinker."

"I know. You like a chardonnay, not too dry, and you sip one glass all night long."

Aaron was unwillingly impressed. Vidar had pegged Isabelle with a single glance.

"I'll pick out a brew I think you'll like, pour you a small glass, and after you've given it a fair try, I'll pour your one glass of chardonnay." Vidar lifted a querying eyebrow. "All right?"

"All right." Isabelle blushed under his gaze.

Samuel grabbed a chair and, with a loud, harsh scraping, dragged it beside Isabelle and seated himself.

"A good, dark beer for me, the darker the better." Samuel gave the order as if Vidar were nothing more than a waiter.

"That won't do any good, Mr. Faa. Nothing will wipe that bitter taste from your mouth." With a flare of his aristocratic nostrils, Vidar dismissed Samuel, turned away, and headed behind the bar. He tapped one of the small kegs for Martha, making a low comment as he set a pint in front of her. She laughed, a low, amused, liquid sound that made everyone turn their heads to look, and they found her looking back at them with the knowing gaze of an affectionate mother for her foolish children.

Aleksandr, Caleb and Aaron pulled up chairs at the round table.

"Why did you guys leave Irving's without us?" Jacqueline glared at them all, torn between indignation and fright.

"We didn't think you'd even notice we were gone," Samuel said sarcastically.

"We're a team!" Jacqueline answered.

"You and Caleb are a team within the team." Isabelle hugged her.

Jacqueline dropped her head onto Isabelle's shoulder in a brief moment of appreciation, and smiled at Charisma.

Jacqueline's ascension to the role of seer had been pain- and sorrow-filled, and the ordeal had bonded the women in a way that Aaron and the guys knew they couldn't comprehend. Women just had this thing about friendship—they told each other everything, they comforted each other, they groomed each other, they gave each other constant approval and clothing advice, and commiserated over each other's foster mothers.

Aaron was grateful that these women cared for Rosamund, too—but in a different way. They made sure she washed, dressed, and brushed her teeth. They insisted she brush her hair and gave her a curfew, telling her she couldn't work past ten at night. They treated her as if she were their dumb younger sister, or maybe a sister who had not yet been tested by fire. Without Jacqueline, Isabelle, and Charisma, Aaron knew Rosamund would be a wreck—and so would he.

Vidar served frothy pints to each of them. Each beer looked a little different, with varying levels of froth and diverse shades of brown, amber, and gold, and for Isabelle, a pale, sparkling beer with a faint rosy tinge. She stared at the glass, and everyone at the table could see her struggle between her good manners and her good taste.

"Try it," Vidar murmured. "A woman so exquisite could never offend me, not even if you don't like my beer."

She looked up at him with cautious eyes, and Aaron realized that for all her poise and beauty, something sometime had deeply wounded her.

His gaze shifted to Samuel, who was glowering into his dark beer.

The bastard had done his part, no doubt, but beneath that sting lurked a sorrow Aaron couldn't comprehend. But then . . . they all had their secrets. They hid their pain.

Isabelle lifted the glass and took a sip, and her eyes widened in surprise. "This is good."

"You don't have to say it if it's not true," Samuel said.

"But it is true. This tastes fresh and . . . I don't know . . . like spring." She smiled at Vidar. "Thank you. I will enjoy this."

As if he couldn't resist, Vidar slid his hand over her shining head.

Then in an abrupt change of attitude, he pulled up a chair next to Aleksandr. Staring right into his face, he said, "You remind me of someone I knew years ago."

"He's a Wilder. Perhaps you've heard of them?" Charisma took a sip of her beer and gave him a thumbs-up.

"Wilder?" Vidar balanced his chair on two legs. "No, that's not the name . . ." He snapped his fingers. "Varinski. Konstantine Varinski! It has to be the same family. You're the spitting image!"

"Konstantine Varinski is my grandfather." Pride radiated from Aleksandr.

"Is that ruffian still around? When I knew him, he was the scourge of the steppes, Lucifer was none too happy with the attention he was getting, and the first thing I knew Konstantine had made a deal with the devil and all hell broke loose—"

Martha cleared her throat.

Vidar looked toward the bar.

Martha shook her head.

"Oh." Vidar dropped his chair legs back down. "His grandfather is one of that Konstantine's descendants, and so is young Aleksandr. I see."

Aaron tasted his pint and found the ale precisely to his taste—smooth, crisp, and brown. All around the table, the Chosen were tasting, nodding. Even Samuel relaxed in his chair. Aaron had to hand it to him; Vidar had a flare for brewing, for creating the right atmosphere, and for making the right choice.

As they unwound from the tension of the past week, Samuel tapped the table with his fingers. "I've been wanting to talk to you guys, because I'm pretty sure we've got more trouble with the Gypsy Travel Agency than Irving has told us."

Chapter 15

———⟨◆⟩———

Everybody looked at Samuel warily.

Charisma groaned and dropped her head into her hands.

Vidar stood up and eased away.

"Yes, I know. I'm a bastard to bring this up now. But we're away from the mansion, and I've been reading up on some of the things the Gypsy Travel Agency was doing after Irving incorporated." Samuel shook his head. "Very questionable stuff, legally and ethically."

"Like what?" Isabelle sipped her beer, then dabbed the froth off her upper lip.

"Infiltrating rival travel agencies and stealing their itineraries and clients. Collecting antiquities from archeological sites they 'discovered'"—Samuel used air quotes for "discovered"—"bringing them into the States and selling them to collectors for a tidy profit."

"Why 'discovered'?" Caleb repeated the air quotes.

"I'm reading between the lines, but I suspect they used their powers to convince native peoples to reveal

sites holy to them that they'd been hiding for generations, looted the most valuable stuff, announced the
find, alerted the National Geographic Society and secured themselves exclusive tour rights, then whipped
up a bunch of excitement among the press and led
eager tourists on expeditions." As Samuel recited the
list of misdeeds, he looked as if he'd eaten something
rancid.

"And to think I've just been stealing the stuff,"
Aaron said ironically.

"That's not all. I think the Powers That Be used the
Chosen Ones and their gifts to get themselves named
as beneficiaries in wills." Samuel grimaced. "I'm pretty
sure that's how Irving acquired his mansion."

Isabelle, the ever doubtful, asked, "Why do you
think that?"

"Because the family of the deceased brought a law-
suit claiming Irving was a con artist who had fooled
their grandfather into believing in the occult." Samuel
took a long draw on his beer. "What's that sound like
to you?"

"It doesn't sound good," she admitted.

"None of what I'm telling you is certain, but there's
a great deal of evidence, and among New York City
lawyers, the Gypsy Travel Agency has a sort of stench."
Samuel lifted a hand. "Before you say it, yes, yes, that's
like the garbage complaining the garbagemen stink."

"He appears to be a little sensitive about lawyer
jokes," Aaron said to Caleb out of the corner of his
mouth loudly enough for Samuel to hear.

Samuel sent him a withering glance.

Aaron clutched his chest and pretended to die.

For one moment, the atmosphere at the table lightened.

Samuel sighed. "Sorry about that Tonto thing earlier, man."

"It really was so wrong. I'm not from Tonto's tribe." Aaron's ale was tasting better all the time.

"I'll try to remember that." Deliberately, Samuel steered them back to their troubles. "So what do you guys think of all these charges against the Gypsy Travel Agency?"

"According to the contract we signed, the Chosen Ones were supposed to be the defenders of the weak and abandoned, and the warriors against evil. So I don't understand why they did this stuff." Aaron turned to Charisma. "You're the Chosen Ones expert. Was the corporation involved in questionable activity?"

Charisma looked down at the table. "I think so. You have to understand, I'm extrapolating here."

"Extrapolate away." Isabelle thanked Vidar as he set another beer in front of her.

"Okay." Charisma took a breath. "The Gypsy Travel Agency is and has been the cover for the Chosen Ones for over a century."

"And a great cover it was," Jacqueline said.

"What do you know about it?" Aaron asked.

"She was practically raised in the organization," Caleb told him.

"Having a mother who was the seer for the Chosen Ones put me right in the middle of the action," Jacqueline agreed.

"Right." Aaron should have remembered—the rest of them had been recently chosen on the merits of their gifts . . . well, except Aleksandr, who had been chosen because of his family background and because they needed a seventh person to complete their number. But Jacqueline had been chosen from the moment her foster mother, Zusane, had fished the abandoned infant out of a Dumpster, verified that she had the mark of the eye on her palm, and pronounced her her successor.

"I saw some of the sleazy stuff they did, and the older Chosen taught me the history with a reverence that bordered on evangelical." Jacqueline spun her icy glass on the table. "In the nineteenth century, the Chosen Ones lost three of their team in an attack by the Others, so they immigrated to New York City and looked for replacements. The city was a rough place then—"

Vidar set more glasses on the table, and proved he'd been listening. "Don't fool yourself. It's a rough place now."

"Yes, but there's more help now," Jacqueline said. "Not as many desperate, angry women throw their babies away."

He inclined his head in agreement.

Jacqueline continued. "In those days, there were so many Abandoned Ones to choose from, they set up the Gypsy Travel Agency to pay for expenses—food, clothes, travel expenses, incidentals."

"A travel agency. That is so weird," Aleksandr said.

"Not true. It makes sense," Charisma answered. "Having a travel agency made it easy to move the Chosen Ones wherever they were needed in the world, and the people who worked for the agency—people like Martha, who had no gifts but traveled with the job, and the guides themselves—would watch for children who had been abandoned and for trouble created by the Others."

"Why the *Gypsy* Travel Agency?" Aleksandr asked.

"Because in the beginning, when the world was young, the first man who was Chosen—"

"One of the twins?" Samuel had steadfastly refused to read *When the World Was Young: A History of the Chosen*, and since Aaron was none too clear on the background of the Chosen Ones, he was glad Samuel had asked.

"Yes, one of the twins," Charisma said impatiently. "The boy-infant was picked up by a wandering tribe of Romany. He traveled with them, creating fire in the palm of his hand—that was his gift—and always thereafter the Romany featured strongly in the myth and the reality of the Chosen Ones."

"My grandmother is Rom, but I never knew all this stuff." That explained Aleksandr's intense interest.

"There are different tribes," Vidar said.

"Next time I talk to my grandmother . . ." Aleksandr's voice trailed off. His eyes got wide. He looked like he'd had a slap on the back of his head.

"What's wrong?" Charisma asked.

"My grandmother. My tutoring. She'll kill me." He looked at his watch and leaped to his feet. "I'm late!"

Aaron grinned. The kid always said his grandmother was scary when she got mad. He must not be joking.

"Come on." Vidar turned toward the far corner of the room. "I'll let you out this door. It'll put you up on street level right away."

"Thank you!" Aleksandr was slavishly appreciative.

"Let me know how it all comes out!" he yelled over his shoulder at the Chosen.

Their group affection for the young man who had no gift except a wonderful upbringing and a cheerful nature had them calling,

"Have fun, kid."

"Don't take any wooden nickels."

"Study hard."

"He's the tutor."

"Oh, that's right. Well, teach him a lot."

"Teach *her*," Aleksandr corrected. "My student today is a girl." His expression was blasé—but he blushed.

"You stay here, Vidar. I'll walk him up." Martha slid off the barstool, grabbed Aleksandr by the arm, and walked him out the door.

At the table, they exchanged glances.

"Our young Aleksandr has found himself a flame." Jacqueline's eyes glowed with the fervor of a recent convert to love.

"I hope he doesn't get burned." As thrilled as Jacqueline was, Samuel was the opposite, looking at Isabelle with angry eyes.

She looked angry, too . . . and guilty. She took another sip from her glass, and said, "This really is very tasty. I see I've been hasty in condemning beer."

"Thank you," Vidar called from behind the bar.

The guy really did have good hearing.

"Back to the subject at hand. During World War Two, travel was necessarily curtailed and the need for help throughout the world increased." Jacqueline mechanically recited stuff she'd known for years. "So the Chosen Ones were assisting more people than ever, drawing on their cash reserves, and at the end of the war, the whole association was broke."

Aaron noticed that Vidar was nodding. Aaron watched him, and drank, and wondered how this guy who wasn't one of the Chosen and looked like he was about thirty could know enough to agree with Jacqueline's analysis. Had he been raised in the Gypsy Travel Agency, also?

"Here's where it gets a little fuzzy." Jacqueline looked around the table. "I think Irving was ambitious, a young black man of education and intelligence, and in the Gypsy Travel Agency, he saw an opportunity to shine. By the end of the fifties, when the agency was in total chaos, he somehow managed to convince the board to hire him as the CEO. Once in the position, he was the best thing the organization had ever seen. He turned them around, made them profitable again, did whatever it took to allow the Chosen Ones to rescue abandoned babies or help the helpless."

"He did whatever it took," Aaron repeated thoughtfully. "So he did all that stuff Samuel talked about?"

"Yes." Vidar brought another round.

Isabelle looked at him. She was slightly tipsy, a loss of control Aaron had never seen from her. In a voice a little louder than normal, she asked, "For the sake of the Chosen Ones and their mission, he made immoral decisions?"

"Yes." Vidar placed a new ale in front of Aaron and whisked the old glass away.

"And we're paying for them now?" Isabelle asked.

"Yes." Vidar walked around the table, a blond Viking god with eyes that looked . . . well, in this light, they looked knowing . . . and ancient.

Aaron watched the interchange. He wasn't so much tipsy as buzzed, and very interested that Vidar answered questions for Isabelle, and with such certainty. "So you know Irving?"

"Sure. Why?" Vidar asked.

"Because I had an encounter with a mind speaker who said—"

Caleb jerked around to stare at Aaron. "The woman with the cut nose?"

"Yes."

"Send Irving my regards?"

"Yes!"

"Irving claimed to know nothing." Caleb leaned back in his chair, disgusted and obviously not believing a word of it.

"He told me that, too." Aaron leaned back, too, relieved to know it hadn't been just him.

"So, Vidar, who's the woman?" Caleb asked.

"An old flame of Irving's," Vidar said. "She didn't take the breakup well."

Hunched over the bar, Martha snorted.

Aaron's feeling that this guy was *wrong* grew stronger. He was like someone out of an Indian legend, a being of unimaginable age and wisdom. And power? Cautiously, he asked, "Can you tell us everything we need to know?"

"No," Vidar said.

"Do you know everything we need to know?" Isabelle's eyes were slightly heavy, her words slightly slurred, but Aaron looked at her with respect. That was a good question.

"Yes," Vidar said.

"Why can't you tell us?" Right now, with his eyes narrowed and his voice cold, Samuel seemed every inch the successful lawyer.

Vidar didn't answer. Instead he stood quietly, his tray balanced on his hand.

But Martha turned around on her barstool. "He can, but you have to ask the right questions."

Vidar frowned at her.

"Have you seen the mess they're in? We've got to give them some clues. They need all the help they can get," she snapped.

"What's the most important thing we need to know right now?" Isabelle asked.

"Good question," Aaron approved. She wasn't as inebriated as she seemed.

"You need a seventh Chosen," Vidar answered.

"Does anybody else ever come to your pub?" Samuel asked.

"Only if I want them to," Vidar said. "Only if I want them to."

So Aaron was right. Vidar was more than a brewmaster and this place was more than a pub. And Aaron and the Chosen Ones carried the fate of the world on their shoulders.

He looked around at the inexperienced, irritated, confused, inebriated, and uncertain group and said in a solemn voice, "The world is so screwed."

Chapter 16

———◆———

A thought percolated through Rosamund's consciousness.

Aaron wasn't here.

Of course, when he was here, she didn't really notice him. Sometimes when she tore her attention from her work in Irving's private library, Aaron wasn't sitting in the chair across the way. When that happened, it was someone else—Irving, or Charisma, or Isabelle, and once it had been a scowling Samuel.

But usually by the next time she looked up, Aaron had appeared, and he'd ask whether she'd made any progress in finding the prophecy and whether there was anything he could bring her that would help. Only he didn't say it like he wanted to help. He said it like . . . like he wanted her to look at him.

She got nervous when she looked at him. Handsome, clean, well-dressed, with an edge of primal intensity that made her want to cross her legs, lean back in her chair, and give him a sultry smile.

Or do as her father's text had commanded, and *run*.

Who *was* Aaron Eagle, really?

An ardent lover concealed behind an impassive facade? A primitive warrior clad in the skin of a debonair James Bond?

To her, he was a book that wouldn't open its pages.

As the afternoon drifted into evening, she found herself looking up more and more often, wondering when he was going to materialize and tell her she should eat or drink or shower or change her clothes.

But he was just gone.

Finally she gave up the attempt to concentrate, stood and stretched, and wandered over to the window to look out on the street. It was an August evening on the Upper East Side. Pedestrians hurried along the sidewalk, looking hot and grumpy. Cars and cabs cruised along the broad street. She was standing there, idly watching, wondering how many days she'd been here . . . three? four? . . . and looking for Aaron, when she thought she saw a familiar face.

But what would *he* be doing here? He hadn't answered her text, so she had figured he was like all the rest of the guys she'd ever met—sorry he'd accidentally asked her on a date, glad she'd not shown up. Plus it was stretching coincidence that in a city of eight million people he would happen to walk by the place she was working when he didn't know where she was, and at precisely the moment when she looked out. . . .

Idly she watched him stride down the sidewalk, shoulders broad, hair blond and crisp, and that face . . . that face!

She stiffened. She stared. She slammed herself against the window. "Lance!" she yelled. "Lance!"

He walked on.

"Lance!" She tried to open the window, fumbled with the lock, couldn't budge it. "Lance!"

She pounded on the glass.

He didn't turn. He was going to be gone if she didn't *do* something.

She ran out of the room and down the stairs, through the foyer and out the front door. She raced down the sidewalk, turned the corner, and saw his glorious self walking away from her. "Lance!" she yelled.

He started. Turned. Saw her. Smiled in wonder. "Rosamund!" He hurried toward her, caught her by the arms, pulled her against the wrought-iron fence in the shadow of the building. "What are you doing here?"

"I work here. I mean, today, now I work here. For a while. I'm helping them translate some texts for their library."

"That's wonderful." He glanced doubtfully at Irving's mansion.

"What are *you* doing here?" she asked.

"I'm on my way to visit the Met." He smiled, abashed. "I know it's nerdy, but I love to stroll through the museum."

"Oh, me, too!" She could hardly believe this. "What's your favorite part?"

"I couldn't begin to choose."

"The marbles, especially the Greek and Roman art."

"I love the marbles."

"There's that wood room. I can't remember what it's

called, but imagine a whole room where everything, even the stuff you look at through the windows, is wood!"

"I know. Isn't it great?"

"And the art."

"My favorite is the ... Gosh, let's talk about the nineteenth century!"

"The early Impressionists. I know. Me, too." She stood with her hands clasped before her chest, staring at him. She knew she was babbling, but he looked even better than he had in the library basement, with the wonderful physique and the fabulous face with the eyes. What eyes! Not to mention that he sort of glowed from within, as if he had a lamp of goodness lit inside him.

She had to stop staring. So she glanced around. "I think you're going the wrong way."

"The wrong way?"

"To the Met." She pointed. "It's back that way."

"This is so embarrassing." Although he looked annoyed. "I have no sense of direction. But listen—after we didn't have our date—"

"I know. I'm so embarrassed, too. I had to work. I lost track of time and forgot to call." Remembering everything Charisma and Aaron had said, about how a real man would understand, she waited anxiously for Lance's reaction.

"The first time I met you, I knew you were that kind of girl, the kind who is so dedicated to her work she would lose herself in it." He smiled, and the glow within him got stronger.

She melted. "I texted you."

"I know, and the next day I went back to the library to find you and they said you were on loan to someone else, and my heart broke. I thought about texting *you*, but I was afraid to interrupt your work."

He was so perfect, so thoughtful. "I hoped it was something like that."

"I kept your text."

"Really?"

"I was hoping you'd have a minute to send me another one, maybe tell me about your work."

"Really?" She remembered what he'd been asking about when he came to the library. "I got wrapped up in what I'm doing here, but actually, my research should be of interest to you, too."

"What a coincidence!"

"I thought that, too. I'm searching for a prophecy that relates to a prophetess who was a black slave in a white house."

Although Lance still smiled, his eyes sharpened discerningly. "How fascinating. That was exactly what I was looking for. I don't want you to break a confidence, of course, but could you tell me how you're doing?"

"It's a fascinating quest, and I think I'm getting close." She thought of the books and papers scattered across the table upstairs. "Would you like me to let you know when I succeed?"

"That would be absolutely marvelous." He looked up at the mansion, scanning the windows. "Since we've run into each other, maybe we could go get a coffee."

She shouldn't go. She should go back to work. "I'd love to!"

He took her arm. "I know this great little place not far away—"

"Hey, Rosamund! What are you doing out here in your socks?" Aleksandr stood at the corner, holding a book and looking at her, a puzzled, concerned expression on his face.

She looked down at herself. She was wearing a loose gathered skirt, a plaid flannel pajama top, and Aaron's big fuzzy gray socks. One heel was twisted sideways and pouched out on her ankle. The other one had lost its elastic and slouched on the top of her foot. She put her hand up to her hair. It hadn't been combed today. The curls clung around her face in 1980s exuberance. She couldn't remember when her face had been washed, and . . . "Oh, no."

Lance was so beautiful.

She was so not.

Catching her hand, he smiled into her face. "You are charmingly disheveled, a woman who is dedicated to her work."

"Wow." He liked her like she was.

"Rosamund?" Aleksandr started toward them.

"I understand we'll have to take a rain check. You have to stay here and work," Lance said. "But promise me you'll keep me updated with what's happening with you. Text me?"

"Yes."

"Promise?"

"I promise."

He chucked her under the chin, then started down the sidewalk.

"Wait!" she said.

"I really need to leave." He glanced toward Aleksandr.

"But you're going the wrong way!" She pointed back toward Central Park. "It's that way to the Met."

"I've been talking too long. I'm going to have to go. . . ." He picked up speed. "Remember!" he called.

"I will!" She waved even though he never looked back.

"Who was that guy?" Aleksandr stared after Lance.

"I was supposed to have a date with him, but I came here instead." She huffed in disgust. "He happened to walk by, and I saw him, and . . . oh, I like him so much!" Suddenly anxious, she said, "You won't tell Aaron I saw him, will you? I don't think Aaron wants me to do anything except find the prophecy."

"I won't tell him," Aleksandr promised. "You can have a boyfriend if you want. We should all be able to . . . to fall in love if we want to."

He sounded a little more fervent than she expected.

She cast a final longing glance toward Lance's disappearing figure, then tucked her hand into Aleksandr's arm. They started toward the front door. "Why do you say it like that?" Her mind made the logical leap. "Have you met someone?"

"Yes, and she's so cool." Aleksandr sounded awed. "I'm tutoring her. She needs my help in calculus, but she's completely brilliant and pretty, and today she took my hand and told me that in two lessons I had helped her more than all the professors in the world. And she's just so . . . you know . . ."

"I do know." She completely understood. Aleksandr loved a girl who was like Lance, only female.

"I wanted to kiss her," he said, "but she's not like the other girls. She's younger than me, and shy. I didn't want to scare her away, you know?"

She looked at Aleksandr. He was handsome, twenty-one, with the assurance of a much older man. He was obviously experienced and knew his way around women, yet with this girl, he was awed and careful. "She's special," Rosamund said.

"She sure is."

They rounded the corner, and the front door of the mansion was hanging open. "Uh-oh." She tugged at Aleksandr. "Come on, hurry! If McKenna finds out I left the door open, he'll kill me, and if Aaron finds out I left my work, he'll be cranky."

They rushed up the steps, tiptoed into the foyer, and looked around.

No one was there.

She gave a sigh of relief, and started to trudge toward the stairs. "Listen, Aleksandr, about your girlfriend—I won't tell on you if you won't tell on me."

"Thank you. Yes." He put out his hand, and she shook it. "Agreed."

Chapter 17

The door of Irving's private study slammed open, smacking the wall behind it.

Rosamund jumped, and looked up from her scroll to see Aaron posed in the doorway, jacket over his shoulder and hooked to one finger, tie loosened, hair rakishly askew, a half smile crooking his mouth.

She hadn't seen him smile since that time in the basement of the Arthur W. Nelson Fine Arts Library when he was trying to convince her to tell him about Lance. She glanced out the window. It was dark now. He'd been gone all day. When she thought about Lance, she was glad of that, but . . . where had Aaron been?

And why did she care?

He swaggered in. "Rosamund. Hello." His voice sounded very deep, very suave, very sure.

"Hello." She waited for him to say something else, but he stood there staring at her, that crooked smile on his lips, so she ventured, "Did you need something?"

He took a long breath. Tossed his jacket on Irving's

leather chair. Turned to face her. "How would you know if I did?"

"You'd . . . tell me?"

"I'd have to, wouldn't I? Because you wouldn't recognize a signal if it was blinking on an oncoming semi."

"Since I've lived in New York City most of my life, I don't drive, but as a pedestrian, I certainly know to avoid a, um . . ."

His nostrils flared. His eyes narrowed. He looked as if he were restraining a vast annoyance. "I didn't mean that about the signal literally."

"Right." Talking to him was like trying to decipher a lost language. But she was a linguist of no small talent. If she questioned him, she would surely get him figured out. "Did you want to discuss the prophecy?"

"Why would you think that?"

"B-because that's all you ever ask me about?"

Perching his hip on the table, he slid close to her. "But that's not what I'm *really* saying, is it?"

"I'm trying to ascertain what you're *really* saying right now."

Cupping her chin in his hand, he smiled into her face. "You should listen . . . with your womanly instincts."

"My womanly instincts?" Occasionally, someone— Jessica—would make fun of her for being a nerd. Rosamund didn't like it, yet she didn't usually care much, either. But she was pretty sure Aaron was making fun of her right now, and for some reason, that made her mad. "I don't know what I've done to you to make you be so rude to me."

He drew back. "Rude? I'm not being rude."

"You just said to listen with my womanly instincts. I suppose you don't think I have any."

"They could use a little polishing, because I'm trying to tell you . . . oh, let's try it this way." With his hand still under her chin, he removed her glasses and placed them off to the side. Leaning over, he put his lips on hers. And kissed her.

She didn't know what to do. Was he making fun of her again? It seemed an odd way to do it. Yet for all that she didn't believe he really wanted to kiss her—after all, he spent all his time scowling at her and asking how the translations were going—it was a nice kiss. His lips had a soft, smooth texture, and at the same time, he moved them firmly on hers, taking the time to explore the outline of her mouth and the seam where her lips met.

So what was the harm?

On the other hand, Jessica had told her men weren't discriminating in their attentions—*can't walk past a knothole in a tree* were her exact words.

But Aaron didn't seem the type who would be indiscriminating. He seemed like the kind of guy who could have any woman he wanted. So why—

He lifted his head. He looked down at her. "Close your eyes."

She did.

"Pay attention."

How had he known she hadn't been . . . ?

He swept her out of her seat and into his arms. Thrust his tongue into her mouth and tasted her as if she were an hors d'oeuvre and he a starving man. Kissed her. Really kissed her.

She didn't know what to do.

She groped at his shirt, managed to grab handfuls in her fists, then walked her fingers up to his shoulders and dug them into the muscles, trying to hold on while his passion buffeted her, then swept her along like a great storm. Everything about this kiss was bigger than any- thing she'd experienced before—the way he strained her body against his, the passion with which he devoured her, his groan when she responded, the dancelike move he used to turn her so her back was to the table.

He lifted her until her bottom rested on the wooden surface, then bent her until she was prone, the cool wood surface against her back.

She stiffened.

Lifting his head, he whispered, "Don't worry. No valuable manuscripts in the way."

"Right." She stared into his face. His straight, blue- black hair glistened in the light. His dark eyes were shadowy with desire. Strain stretched the skin across his broad cheekbones, and his mouth was damp from hers.

He was as different from Lance as it was possible for a man to be . . . yet when he bent his head to hers again, she opened her mouth to him.

As he licked at her, sucked her tongue, used his to arouse her, her blood pulsed warm and fast in her veins. She was breathing so fast, her chest felt as if it would burst, and when he slid his hands under her plaid flannel pajama top and held her rib cage, she groaned. "Please. Oh, please." She didn't recognize her own voice. She sounded so vibrant, so strong and yet so needy.

He looked into her eyes. "Do you want me to do this?" His thumbs caressed the lower curves of her breasts.

"Yes." She lifted one knee, rubbed the table with her stockinged foot.

"Or this?" His hands moved up to cup her, and those wicked, knowing thumbs moved in slow, light, constant circles on her nipples.

Her back snapped into an arch, and she pressed herself into his palms.

He laughed shortly, triumphantly. Then he kissed her again, leaning so his chest pressed against hers, his hands were between their two bodies, and all she could feel was . . . everything. The table beneath her back, his muscles beneath her grip, the caress of his hands on her breasts, the need to demand more, to beg for him to lift her skirt, to press himself between her legs, to relieve this awful, wonderful *yearning* . . .

With a sigh that sounded as if it had been dragged from his depths, he pulled his lips away from hers. He straightened, slipped his hands from underneath her shirt, and helped her to sit up. Taking her by the waist, he lifted her off the table and propelled her toward her cot. Throwing back her covers, he put his hands on her shoulders and seated her.

For one moment, her imagination went wild. He was going to take her clothes off. Take his clothes off. Get under the covers with her and satisfy her in a way only Aaron Eagle could do.

He did lift her feet onto the mattress. . . . Then he tucked her arms by her side, covered her, and leaned against the blankets so she couldn't move. "Go to sleep,

Rosamund, and maybe after this, you won't look at me like you can't quite place my name."

"I know your name!" He wasn't making sense again, and she struggled to free herself.

He let go and stepped away. He gathered up his coat. He walked to the door, turned, and in that deep, suave voice said, "Watch out for signals."

And he left.

She sat up, her crossness swamping all those lovely feelings he had created with his kiss, his touch.

What had gotten into him?

She licked her lower lip and realized—he tasted like ale. Good, rich, yeasty, dark ale.

Aaron had kissed her because he was drunk.

Aaron woke the next morning and lay there with his eyes closed, waiting for the pounding headache to begin.

No headache.

In fact, considering how much he'd had to drink yesterday, he didn't feel too bad. The Chosen Ones had sat in Davidov's Pub all afternoon, drinking whatever beer or ale or weird pink liquor Vidar had placed in front of them. By the time they'd left that evening, every one of them had been so sozzled they had barely noticed the scuttling roaches and rats and people in the tunnels, although Aaron retained enough sense to be grateful for Martha, who had returned to lead them back to the mansion.

There they had faced an irritated Irving, who spoke to them severely about their duty to the traditions of the Chosen Ones, and when he was done lecturing them, they had nodded, tiptoed off, and broken into embarrassed giggles as soon as they were out of sight. Then Aaron had gone to check on Rosamund and—

"Oh, my God!" He sat straight up in bed.

He'd kissed her. French-kissed her. On the library table.

He looked down at his hand, cupped in the shape of her breast. He had more than kissed her; he'd groped her. Groped her until her nipple had thrust its way into his palm and made him realize, even in his drunken state, that if he didn't stop, he wasn't going to stop.

"Shit." He pressed his hands on his eyes.

His little librarian was probably indignant, and who could blame her? She hadn't said no, but he hadn't given her the chance, either. If she was mad enough . . . oh, no. If she was mad enough, she was probably out the door right now. Or getting ready to leave.

He had to stop her.

He flung the covers back, grabbed pants and a shirt, and dressed so fast he pulled a button off his shirt. He started to sprint for Irving's library, did an abrupt about-face, headed for the bathroom, and brushed his teeth.

Then he was back out the door, running down the corridor, hoping and praying Rosamund was still there, still working on the prophecy. If she was, he would beg her pardon, promise never to kiss her again. . . .

Well, never to kiss her again without her permission. Because her mouth had been sweet and warm and surprised, and as he heated up the space between them, she had responded with charming passion.

He stopped, leaned his hand against the wall, and took a long breath.

If he didn't stop thinking about that, he was going to pop a boner, and that wouldn't be reassuring to a frightened, angry woman.

He started off again.

If she would just be in the library, he would promise to behave like a gentleman and not like the basically uncivilized Indian he knew himself to be. Because she might not realize it, but beneath his Armani suits, he was every inch the savage of legend. He prided himself on controlling that side of himself, but somehow, with her rosy lips, large violet eyes, and absolute cluelessness, Rosamund Hall slipped under his guard.

Because he'd seen what hid behind her eyes. Because he recognized that well of guilt and sadness; he'd found the same well within himself. But while he understood what events drove him to transform himself from a young mountain-dwelling savage into a man at home with the finest society, a man who could talk about fashion and antiquities with the same panache, he didn't know what had happened in Rosamund's life to frighten her enough to hide in the depths of a research library.

He stopped before the door of her current hiding place. Checked himself to make sure he was zipped and buttoned, mostly, then raised his hand to knock. Just a little knock so he didn't startle her.

Before he made contact, the door flung open, and Rosamund walked out.

Her cheeks were bright with color, her eyes sparkled, and she smiled with vivacious joy. She was alive as he had never seen her, irresistible as he had never imagined.

With a glance at him, she said, "What are you doing standing there? Get ready!" She brushed past him and hurried toward the stairway.

"Get ready?" He watched her turn and walk backward. "For what?"

"I found the prophetess. She was a black slave in Casablanca." Rosamund grinned at him without a shred of self-consciousness. "Do you know what Casablanca means in Spanish?"

Of course he did. "White house. *White house!*" That was it—that was what Jacqueline had said—that their prophecy would come from a black female slave in a white house.

"Are you sure that's it?"

"I'm sure."

Rosamund had done it—but she didn't act as if she even remembered they'd shared a kiss.

"Pack your bags," she said. "We're going to Casablanca."

Lance Mathews sat in his tiny apartment and trembled. If he were a praying man, he would pray that his carefully planned encounter yesterday would bear fruit. But in his situation, praying seemed hypocritical and frankly useless. Yet as he'd told Osgood, he hadn't gotten to remove Rosamund from the Chosen Ones, but this was even better. He'd extracted her promise to keep him apprised of her progress in finding the prophecy. He'd already received one text last evening: *Hi. Glad u're u.*

He had supposed she imagined she was flirting, so he wrote back, *U're funny n sweet.*

They might as well be exchanging those Valentine candy hearts, and he felt vaguely nauseated.

Then she'd asked, *U drink?*

He'd looked down at the thin line of cocaine he'd lined up to take the edge off his fear and texted back, *No. Why?*

Good, came back from her. Then nothing.

Then his fear of Osgood fought with his instincts about Rosamund. He had set the bait well yesterday afternoon. If he left her alone, she'd keep coming back.

But it had been twenty-four hours since their last encounter. Osgood would want a report. . . . Lance's hand hovered over his phone.

No. If he bugged her about the research, she might get suspicious, might have second thoughts.

A pain stabbed at his chest. "Wait," he said. "Damn you, wait. I know I'm right."

He'd better be right.

Then the phone sang out the rap lyrics, *"Lucifer ripped my soul from my body and I smiled because I knew. . . ."*

Lance grabbed his cell and looked.

It was from Rosamund. *Off 2 Casablanca. Prophetess found!*

Throwing back his head, he laughed long and hard.

The bitch fell for it. She fell for it! She was reporting her every movement, her every success, to him.

Leaning over, he snorted the first line of coke, and for the first time in days, relaxed.

Osgood would be pleased.

Chapter 18

———◆◇◆———

Aaron had visited Casablanca before, and knew it to be a cosmopolitan city of bright lights, broad boulevards, and stylish shops.

Unfortunately, Rosamund needed to go into the old town.

So they checked into their hotel, and headed out into the walled medina constructed long ago by the Bedouins who founded the city.

"The prophetess came here when she was sold by the chief of her tribe for predicting his violent death. Of course, he did die when his tribe killed him for selling her, but it was too late. She was far away, destined to live out her life in a place far from her small village." Rosamund plunged through the dark, twisting streets filled with secrets of the long-ago slave trade.

He followed, wondering how a woman who was so awkward in New York City could be so relaxed in exotic Casablanca. Morocco had been a French protectorate,

French was heard in their hotel and on the streets, and while Rosamund spoke the language, she spoke haltingly and with rusty awkwardness. She was red-haired and freckled in a place where women had dark hair and clear complexions. She dressed carefully in a long-sleeved ankle-length gown, and tied a scarf around her hair, but she stood out in a land of women dressed in modest abayas and high-necked, hair-covering hijabs.

Yet she confidently walked along the narrow street of squat antique shops, her travel pack fastened to her waist, with Bala's Glass inside. By some random process he didn't understand, she picked a store, and plunged inside.

Aaron followed on her heels.

The place reeked of spices and Moroccan coffee and hashish, and the only light seeped through the front windows grimy with the dirt of the street.

Rosamund didn't seem worried. She walked to the back where the light was faintest. She said to a pile of rags, "I want to buy a prophecy."

The pile of rags coalesced into the owner, clad in a hooded robe called a djellaba. He rose from the dark corner, and smiled with a flash of white teeth. "Of course, most generous of patronesses. You have chosen the right place. I am Hamidallah, and I have many fine prophecies. Are you looking for one in particular?"

"I'm looking for the work of the prophetess of Casablanca."

Hamidallah faltered. Only for a second, but he did falter, and Aaron's sharp eyes noted that well. "The prophetess? Ah, yes, I know her. She is very nice."

"She's been dead for two hundred years," Rosamund corrected.

"Come on." Aaron took her arm. "He doesn't know what he's talking about."

Aaron didn't understand how Hamidallah moved so fast, but he was suddenly between them and the door. "I have much knowledge, most honorable and impatient of gentlemen. But these things take time. Come. Sit. Drink coffee with me, and let me show you my wares."

Aaron would have refused.

Rosamund didn't give him a chance. "We are honored by your invitation, most knowledgeable of shopkeepers."

As they seated themselves on the floor, Aaron felt like they were in a forties black-and-white movie, complete with the mysterious, dark-eyed Bedouin spy who would smile as he sliced their heads off with a scimitar.

Well, except that Hamidallah was seventy years old and one hundred and twenty pounds soaking wet.

Probably Aaron should be more worried about poison in the coffee.

Hamidallah offered them hashish, and Aaron's mind veered to poison in the hookah.

Rosamund politely declined the hashish, and together they drank the coffee, which was so strong Aaron knew he'd be awake for days, and nibbled on some candy made of sesame seeds, almonds, raisins and spices.

When the polite preliminaries were over, Hamidallah got down to business. "I have only one document that is from the prophetess, and her language was mysterious and twisted. She was a powerful enchantress, famous for her curses, and so I bring this out only for you, miss, and would sell it only for a great price." He opened a gray metal file cabinet—Aaron thought that took a lot of the woo-woo out of the transfer—and with great ceremony, produced a frayed sheet of paper.

Rosamund accepted it, and looked it over, her glasses perched on the end of her nose.

Aaron had seen a lot of fakes in his time. This was a good one. The paper was old and worn; the handwriting was done with a quill and india ink, in ornate, indecipherable script. He waited with interest to see if Rosamund would recognize the con, and she didn't disappoint him.

With a long disappointed sigh, she handed the paper back to Hamidallah. She folded her hands in her lap, and asked reproachfully, "What have I done to make you have such contempt for me? Why would you insult me with this sad imitation of an old and revered writing?"

"I don't understand." Hamidallah spread his hands in an impersonation of bewilderment.

"This paper has been tumbled in a dryer to look old, and the ink was applied no more than a week ago. The writing is a combination of Arabic script and hieroglyphics, put together in a mishmash of styles." She looked right at Hamidallah. "I am the daughter of Elizabeth and Elijah, and I know of these things."

With a sigh as weighty as hers had been, Hamidallah returned the paper to his file cabinet and shut it inside. "My apologies, Dr. Hall, I thought you no more than a foolish tourist looking for adventure."

Aaron almost fell over in surprise. How was this possible? Hamidallah knew who she was, or at least who her parents were. Moreover, his entire demeanor changed, becoming respectful and almost embarrassed.

She stood, dusted off her skirt, and sadly moved toward the door.

Hamidallah bustled forward and pressed something into her hands. "Dr. Hall, please accept this gift as a token of my esteem, and for luck."

She looked down at the small figurine. "Thank you. I am honored by your esteem."

"I cannot speak with certainty, but my uncle Mubeen is very old and has collected many treasures in his lifetime. You can perhaps visit his shop, and tell him I sent you." Hamidallah's directions were confusing, involving twists and turns that would take them deep into the old city.

Aaron could almost feel the knife against his throat.

But as Rosamund left the shop, Hamidallah caught Aaron by the shoulder. "Listen, young friend, the daughter of Elizabeth and Elijah will need more than my small token to keep her safe. The prophetess was powerful and evil, a trickster and a witch. Hunting her, even so long after her death, invites bad luck. Stay at Dr. Hall's back. Don't let her out of your sight."

"She's probably already halfway to your uncle's," Aaron said in exasperation. Then as Hamidallah's hand tightened on his shoulder, he nodded. "I am not a foolish tourist, either, old friend, and Rosamund is a gem that I greatly treasure. I promise to die rather than allow her to be hurt."

"Before this quest is over, she will need that," Hamidallah said.

That was exactly what Aaron did not need to hear. "Are you a seer to know this?"

"No, young friend; not *I*." Before Aaron could grab Hamidallah by the throat and shake the truth out of him, the old man bowed and vanished into the back of the shop.

Aaron stood staring after him, wondering how Hamidallah had done that, and why his own head was spinning.

Rosamund stepped back inside. "Aaron, are you coming?"

He looked at her, feeling slightly unsteady on his feet.

Had the old man poisoned him?

Rosamund stepped close and looked deep into Aaron's eyes, then took his hand and dragged him into the street. "This has started very well, but be careful how much of the candy you eat. Sometimes it contains marijuana."

"What?" As soon as she said it, he knew it was true, because he wanted to giggle.

She looked left and right, then set out like a bloodhound on the scent. "In Morocco, cannabis is nothing more than an ingredient, and considered a love potion—or in Hamidallah's case, a little something to persuade the client to accept a counterfeit."

Aaron wasn't so stoned he couldn't figure out the other option. "Or possibly put the client to sleep to be robbed and kidnapped . . . or murdered."

She didn't answer—which was an answer in itself.

He had a knife in his boot and one up his sleeve, and a pistol strapped to his chest, and already his head was clearing. He knew all the weapons he could carry and all his vigilance were not nearly enough, not against a battalion of ruffians on the Casablanca streets, the ill will of a malevolent prophetess, and the Others. Yet Aaron and Rosamund couldn't retreat. The Chosen Ones needed that prophecy. So he had to depend on Rosamund's knowledge of antiquities and his own nose for trouble to protect them.

"Have you been in Casablanca before?" The streets narrowed as they walked, the women vanished from sight, and the men looked like Hollywood villains.

"Not here, exactly, but in other cities like this. When I was young, and my mother was alive, we traveled extensively."

"If you haven't been here, how could Hamidallah know your parents?"

"The world of antiques, real and fake, is very small, and even in this part of the world, they have cell phones and e-mail." She grinned at him, mocking his perceptions of the primitive conditions. "My parents were well-respected because they in turn respected the cultures with which they dealt. They said if you want to know the truth about the past, you have to talk to the people who care."

"And the people who care are the ones still living in that culture."

"Exactly. The West has a habit of dismissing that link, much to its own detriment." She stopped, looked at the grimy white, two-story building with the narrow green door that looked exactly like all the other grimy white, two-story buildings with narrow green doors, and said, "Here we are!"

Mubeen clearly knew they were coming, for he welcomed them and at once explained he didn't have the prophecy. But he thought perhaps, if Dr. Hall would permit, he would call to find out what happened to the documents found in the attic of the most honorable Jedidi family.

The call took fully an hour, during which time Mubeen's wife served them some of the most wonderful food Aaron had ever put in his mouth. The salad was fresh, the tagine rich with spices, lamb and apricots, and Faeqa made the bread in the kitchen and brought it out to them while they ate. They finished with more coffee—Aaron now thought he wouldn't sleep for weeks—and fresh fruit and yogurt.

Mubeen came back, seated himself, and with a serious face, he said, "The Jedidi family was wealthy and influential in old Casablanca, and to their great misfortune, it was they who held the prophetess while she was imprisoned here. The years since have not been good to them, and upon finding documents written by the prophetess, they sold them to the Hassan II Ain Chok University in the hopes that by that action they would end the bad luck she visited upon their family. The book is now in the university collection, and available for viewing, but until it has been properly studied by Dr. Al-Ruwaili, it can be seen only in a display case and from a distance."

"I'm an antiquities librarian," Rosamund said. "Perhaps I can convince Dr. Al-Ruwaili to let me examine the book."

Even before she finished, Mubeen was shaking his head. "Forgive me, but you are a woman from an esteemed family, and the professor is young and suspicious. He believes that with these papers, it is possible for him to make a name for himself."

"Nevertheless, I would like to speak with him," Rosamund said firmly.

"What's in these papers?" Aaron asked.

"While the prophetess remained in Casablanca, waiting to be sold, she foretold deaths and births and destinies, making all fear her and at the same time, driving her own price up. For many men wanted to own a creature with such gifts." Mubeen took a cup of coffee from his wife. "The ill will of the prophetess lingers in the Jedidi family and now I fear for our young professor. In the name of your parents, Dr. Hall, please be careful that the prophetess does not taint your life."

"I search for her final prophecy, my friend, but I do not believe she has powers that can reach across the ages." Rosamund was very polite, but very firm.

Mubeen looked at Aaron, and Aaron could see the warning he wanted to issue hovering on his lips. Aaron leaned toward the merchant. "I am here to make sure that Dr. Hall remains unharmed by the old malevolence of the prophetess or the current dangers posed by those who would harm her for her knowledge."

"Good," Mubeen said. But his face was troubled, and after he showed them out, he locked and bolted the narrow green door.

Rosamund, of course, was oblivious. "I want to go to the university."

"Of course you do," Aaron said, and led the way. But until they reached the broad streets of the new city, he kept his hand on the pistol under his coat.

Chapter 19

"I don't understand how Dr. Al-Ruwaili could be so rude. What did he think I was going to do, steal the prophetess's manuscript right out from under his nose?" In a rage, Rosamund threw her travel pack on the floor and flung herself on the bed in her hotel room, arm over her eyes.

Aaron lingered by the door. "Mubeen told you what Al-Ruwaili feared—that if the daughter of famous archeological explorers looked closely at the book, everyone would dismiss his accomplishments as hers."

"That is so absurd."

"Men's egos are never absurd. Pitiful, perhaps, but not absurd."

She lifted her head and stared at him in confusion, then laughed. "You're being ironic."

"Very good." Coming to the bed, he placed his hands at her sides on the frayed bedspread, trapping her between his arms. "I'm going to go out and see what I can find. I want you to promise me you'll lock the door behind me and open it to no one. Not room service, not a messenger, not the manager of the hotel."

"But if I'm hungry—"

"Before I brought you back to the hotel, I fed you for just that reason. Now, promise you'll do as you're told, or I can't leave."

Having him lean over her like this and act concerned rather pleased her. She wanted to squirm closer, rub herself against his chest, see if he would kiss her again.

Of course, that was impossible. He wasn't drunk.

She scooted away. "Why would someone hurt me?"

"Some people are threatened by women who are intelligent. Some people are threatened by women who are beautiful. You are both."

"Right." Sitting up, she looked into his eyes, expecting to see expanded pupils or bloodshot whites. "You don't look as if you're drugged."

He sighed. "I'm not drugged. I'm concerned. Now—promise."

"I promise."

"Fine." He actually did kiss her. Lightly. Like someone indulging a child. "Now lock the door behind me, then go to sleep. I'll be back before morning."

"Wake up." Aaron shook Rosamund out of a sound sleep. "Wake up. I have the book."

She dragged herself into a sitting position, blinked and rubbed her eyes, then grabbed her glasses and shoved them on her nose. His face came into focus: excited, dynamic, vibrant. "How did you get in here?"

"I got a copy of your key from the front desk." He held a small package wrapped in cheesecloth. "Look. This is it!"

She looked at the clock. It was one thirty in the morning. "What were the people who work the front desk thinking? You could be a murderer or a rapist."

He straightened in obvious annoyance. "Yes, I could, but we came in together. This is a male-dominated society, and you're a woman alone. As far as they're concerned, I'm in charge of you."

Annoyed in her turn, she said, "That is so politically incorrect. And I put the security bar on. How did you get around that?"

"There are ways. Now—pay attention. Look!" He handed her gloves and placed the package in her lap.

She unwrapped the cloth, and her exasperation evaporated.

This was the slim, leather-bound volume she'd seen from afar in the university library.

Awed, she carefully touched the binding. "This is the prophetess's book. But Al-Ruwaili was so adamant. How did you convince him to let me examine it? Not just let me examine it, but take it out of the university library?"

"I am a very persuasive soul," Aaron said.

She opened the book to the fly page, where in ornate French penmanship, a woman had written *The Works of Sacmis, prophetess of Casablanca, as scribed by Rasheeda Jedidi.* Rosamund leafed through the first few pages. The book had been a journal, blank pages meant to be filled with a girl's dreams. Instead, it was a recitation of dread prophecies suggested by the prophetess and at first recorded with some excitement by Rasheeda.

But something about this situation with Aaron niggled at Rosamund's brain, some memory of a similar incident involving her, and a library, and Aaron. "You got my notebook out of the Arthur W. Nelson Fine Arts Library, too."

"So I did." He seated himself on a chair nearby, a broad, tall, dynamic man with dark, sharp eyes and strong hands capable of loving a woman . . . or killing a man.

She said, "You shouldn't have been able to get to the antiquities department without me."

"As I said, I'm very persuasive."

She leafed on, looking at the way the precise handwriting began to change, to become a scrawl of worry and then panic as Sacmis's prophecies began to come true. "Is there something you should tell me?" she asked politely.

With equal civility, he said, "I can't imagine what."

She met his gaze with a fierce impatience. "Do you think I'm an idiot?"

"That is the last thing I think." But he had the guts to pretend he didn't know what she was going to say.

"You came up from the most dire poverty, yet now you live with a bunch of people in a huge mansion in New York City. You apparently have no job, but you dress in designer clothes. You get people to give me texts when they should not. . . ." She hated to say it, but she was morally obliged to confront him. "I know what you do for a living!"

"*What?*"

"You make people an offer they can't refuse."

Aaron's mouth moved, but nothing came out.

"I'm right, aren't I?" she demanded. "You threaten people so they give you what you want!"

He appeared to be thinking before he spoke. "I do not threaten anyone, but I do what is necessary in the performance of my duty."

"I can't believe it." She stared at him accusingly. "You're the Godfather!"

The corner of his mouth twitched over and over, as if he were fighting profanity—or a smile. "Are you willing to study this text regardless of how I obtained it?"

She shouldn't consent to work with Aaron. She knew she shouldn't. He was immoral, and if she collaborated with him, then by extension, she was immoral, too.

But . . . she looked down at the carefully bound book with its yellowed paper, felt the desperation and worry that leeched from the increasingly hurried writing, and knew the intense curiosity of a researcher who held a precious manuscript within her hands. "Will you return it when I'm done?"

"I promise I will."

"Give me a half hour, and I'll tell you what we need to know."

Chapter 20

———⬥———

Rosamund sat propped against the pillows on her bed and read the last page of the journal aloud. "'Sacmis is gone, sold to the French king's agent. May the curse upon us now lift.'"

At those words, the hair rose on the back of Aaron's neck, the warnings from Hamidallah and Mubeen echoed in his mind, and he knew they needed to get out of here.

"The French king." She absentmindedly rubbed the binding with one gloved finger. "I wonder which one?"

"Louis the Sixteenth." He snatched the book away from Rosamund, wrapping it in the cheesecloth and taking care not to touch it with his bare hands.

"If you believe in the curse, I suppose that's right." Laughing quietly, she pulled off her gloves. "But you can hardly blame the French Revolution on the prophetess."

"I can blame his beheading on her. The royal family

should have fled France. What prophecy did she give them that they stayed?"

Rosamund grew serious. "You don't like Sacmis very much, do you?"

"I don't have to believe in witches to know there are people in this world who enjoy making other people suffer." He didn't know what was making his instincts riot. Maybe Dr. Al-Ruwaili had realized his book was gone. Maybe their activities today in the medina had attracted the attention of the Casablanca police. Or maybe Sacmis was everything she claimed to be—a witch, a seer, and a hovering and constantly malicious spirit. And one of the Others? "I think a prophetess who produces only evil visions is dabbling in the occult."

"There's no such thing as the occult," she said automatically.

"There's no such thing as a prophetess, either, but we're busting our butts chasing her. Now." He took Rosamund's hands. "I'm taking the text back. It's two ten in the morning. Make sure you put the security bar on the door after I leave."

"I will, although if you can get in, I don't really un-derstand the point." She rubbed her eyes like a tired, cranky child.

"I'm a very special person." That feeling of urgency increased. "Promise you won't let anyone but me through that door." When she would have answered smartly, he put his finger on her lips. "Promise."

She pushed his hand away. "I promise."

He kissed her, a swift, warm kiss that tasted of surprise on her part. "I wish I could linger, but this cursed thing has to go back." He smoothed his fingers across her lips.

For one moment, she looked at him as if he were a god of the Indian nations. Then her interest withered. "Any knothole in a tree," she said.

"What?" What did that mean?

She lay down, pulled the covers up to her chin, and turned her back to him.

He did not understand her.

Hell, he didn't understand women in general, but he didn't understand Rosamund in particular, and no matter how warmly tempting she looked, her eyes heavy and her hair rumpled from sleep, right now he didn't have time to figure her out.

He checked his weapons, the knives and the pistol, then took the stairway down to the lobby, took a taxi to within five blocks of Hassan II Ain Chok University. There he stepped onto the lonely streets and assumed the dark mist of his other self. He wrapped himself around the book, shielding it from anyone who might be watching. Driven by that awareness of looming trouble, he hurried to the university. Slipping into the library, he returned the blighted book.

The security alarm never went off. The cameras never caught sight of him. Dr. Al-Ruwaili would never be any the wiser.

Next he hit the night-clad streets, intent on getting back to the hotel and Rosamund. It was three in the morning, no time to be wandering around a strange city alone. Yet he had no choice; a taxi was nowhere in sight.

He was tired. After three city blocks, his gift failed him, returning him to normal form. He gathered his strength, once again became a mist in the night, and walked another block before his disguise wavered and collapsed. But surely by now he was far enough away from the scene of the crime.

But the smell of danger grew stronger.

Rosamund. Was Rosamund secure? He needed to return to Rosamund.

Taking a breath, he hurried through a market filled with shuttered stalls, toward the heart of Casablanca where the lights still shone and he could catch a ride.

He and Rosamund both felt certain they were on the track of the right prophecy. He, especially, noted the prophetess's oblique references to the Chosen Ones and the Others, to a battle that would begin in the New World with an explosion and could be averted . . . somehow.

But they hadn't found the right text yet, so the trip to Casablanca had been both a success and a failure. When he got back to the hotel, he would have to e-mail the Chosen Ones and tell them. . . . Footsteps. He heard footsteps behind him. A man's tread.

His heart picked up speed. He picked up speed.

The footsteps followed at his exact pace.

He slowed.

The footsteps slowed.

He came to a corner, stopped, and turned.

In the light of the stars, he saw a man—young, wiry, dressed in jeans and a T-shirt. He held a knife loosely in his right hand, and continued steadily toward Aaron.

Aaron looked to the left.

Two men in djellabas, their eyes fixed on him, walked toward him. Both were holding clubs.

Not good, Aaron. Not good at all.

He turned to walk the direction he had been going.

Another man, in jeans and a T-shirt, moved toward him, fists clenched, smiling with the pleasure of the kill.

A trap. But why? Who had set it up? More important, how had they set it up? He'd left the hotel in a cab, then disappeared onto the streets. How had anyone managed to track him?

Were these men the Others?

Perhaps. But the Others had gifts of stealth and violence. They didn't have to depend on knives, clubs, and fists.

Aaron could use his pistol, try to bully his way past these guys, but the use of firearms in a foreign country could land him in more trouble than he now faced. Or he could allow them to herd him down the dark, quiet street.

For most men, that would be a bad choice.

For him, it could be his salvation.

Pulling his pistol, he kept it close to his body and walked toward the line of small booths, closed for the night. When he heard the footsteps behind him close in, he sprinted toward a pile of a dozen black plastic garbage bags and the black hole of an alley beyond. He leaped to clear the bags, prepared to assume the form of darkness—and a blast of pain slammed into his right thigh.

That bastard with the knife had nailed him.

He landed on his feet. His right leg crumpled.

And they were on him. One club made contact with his cheek. His face broke open. The other smacked his chest. His breastbone cracked.

He fired the pistol, aiming toward the guy with the smile.

The guy screamed and spun backward.

Aaron caught a glimpse of him holding his uselessly swinging arm.

Another blow to the right thigh made Aaron scream as the knife in his thigh spiraled and tore flesh.

He fired again, knew he had missed when a bag of garbage blew, spewing rotting vegetables through the air.

Lights came on in the shop behind them.

The guy in the T-shirt kicked the pistol out of Aaron's hand. Aaron's trigger finger snapped.

In the distance, sirens shrieked.

"Hurry," Aaron heard one mugger say. "Kill him. Get the book."

How did they know?

"Then we'll take the woman."

No. Rosamund.

One of the thugs lifted his club to smash Aaron's skull.

Pulling the knife from his sleeve, Aaron lunged and gutted him.

More lights lit in more windows.

Aaron got his feet under him, rose and slashed at the remaining attackers with the bloody knife and ran toward the alley, concentrating on staying conscious long enough to get away and . . . vanish.

Rosamund woke as soon as the door to her room opened. Sleepily she sat up, groped for her glasses, put them on. Aaron stood in the doorway, a dark silhouette against the light in the corridor. "Did you return it?" she asked.

"I did." His voice sounded funny. Strained, and he wasn't enunciating as clearly as usual.

"Are you all right?"

"I'm fine. Why?"

"Just checking."

"We'll leave for Paris in the morning. Good night, Rosamund."

"Good night, Aaron."

He shut the door, and she stared at it.

Weird. He'd managed to get the security bar off again—from the outside. The man was obviously an enforcer, and if she had any sense, she'd be frightened of him.

But for some reason, she wasn't. Because he was on her team. And he kissed well. And—Rosamund hugged herself with the pleasure of one more piece of the puzzle solved—he was taking her to Paris.

Paris! She was so excited, she wanted to celebrate. To sing or dance or . . .

Lance! She could text Lance! She was so excited, she could barely type the message into her cell phone.

On the path of the prophetess. Next, Paris!

Chapter 21

—————◆◈◆—————

"When my mother was alive, we lived abroad, and we used to travel all the time. We visited the pyramids of Egypt, bathed in the River Ganges, went on a dig in Guatemala, but never have I set foot in Paris." Rosamund hung out the window, chattering every minute as the cab whipped from their hotel toward the fashion houses on the rue du Faubourg Saint-Honoré. "This is everything I ever imagined. It even smells like Paris!"

"Does it?" Aaron couldn't smell anything. His nose was swollen. His eyes were blackened. His jaw felt dislocated. He'd cut up the tablecloth in the Casablanca hotel room to tie around his thigh and staunch the bleeding, but the knife wound still really sucked. His chest hurt like a son of a bitch, and each breath slashed him with pain.

But . . . considering what had happened last night, he felt pretty good. Something weird was happening to him. Something he didn't understand.

"When I was little, before my mother died, she would come in from the dig and say, 'Elijah, let's take Rosamund to Alaska'—or Hong Kong or Auckland—and off we'd go for a couple of weeks, or a month, or two months. Sometimes we'd stay in a hotel, sometimes we'd camp out, and sometimes we'd take the train. I was homeschooled, of course, so I studied every day, but I studied hard so I could go off with my parents and learn rock climbing or photography or scuba diving." As the taxi cut a U-turn, Aaron hung on to her blouse to keep her from flying out of the cab. "It was a great life. In those days, my father taught me everything I could learn. He was happy then. He adored my mother so much, and when she died, he didn't want me to know too much because I think he was afraid that I . . . Have I ever shown you a picture of my mother?"

"No, but I'd like to see one."

Rosamund zipped open her travel pack, handed him her cell phone, a pen from the hotel in Casablanca, and Bala's Glass, then finally reached her wallet. Flipping it open, she showed him a worn photo of her parents, standing in front of the Coliseum in Rome.

He almost didn't recognize old Dr. Hall. The guy was younger, of course, but more important, he looked positively pleasant, which was quite a change from all the times Aaron had met with him.

Elizabeth Hall he easily recognized, although he'd never met her—she looked like a slightly older, more tanned version of Rosamund.

"Isn't she beautiful?" Rosamund asked wistfully.

"She certainly is." Obviously, Rosamund didn't have a clue how much they resembled each other.

As Rosamund loaded her stuff back in her pack, she asked, "Where are we going?"

"To meet my friend Philippe."

"You've got friends here? Great! He can tell us the best places to eat."

"You're in Paris," Aaron told her. "All the places are the best places to eat."

"I'm so happy!" She flung her arms around his neck.

The cab careened to the curb and slammed to a stop.

At the impact, Aaron grunted.

"I'm sorry." Pulling back, Rosamund touched his bruised cheek. "Are you sure you're all right? You really hurt yourself running to catch that bus. You should go to a doctor."

He kept his arms around her. "Yes, and you should kiss me and make me better." Because he didn't understand it, yet as long as he was close to her, he could almost feel his bones knitting, his flesh healing.

He thought she would laugh at his teasing.

She didn't. Instead, with almost injured dignity, she pulled herself free.

"*Ici!*" the cabbie said, and stuck out his hand for the fare.

As Aaron paid, Rosamund climbed out of the taxi and stood on the sidewalk, staring up and down the street. He joined her, and she asked, "Does your friend work around here? Because this is where Paris haute couture originates."

"I know." Taking her arm, he limped with her toward the tall brass and glass doors. Two uniformed doormen held them open, and Aaron and Rosamund entered the grand lobby of Philippe's Salon.

The lobby was bold whites and pale pinks, velvet cushions and polished woods. The air was cool and fresh with Philippe's signature perfume. Tall models with long legs, dressed in black tops, minuscule black skirts, and five-inch spike heels, strode up to them to offer refreshments, to take their coats, and to show them to seats before a fake fire made of red silk strips fluttering in a fan's breeze.

Rosamund refused coffee, tea, and champagne, huddled in a chair, and looked miserable. When the models disappeared behind the gauzy curtains that separated the dressing area from the lobby, she whispered, "What are we doing here?"

"Philippe is the biggest gossip and snoop in Paris, and he has a photographic memory." Aaron eyed Rosamund and wondered what Philippe would do when he caught sight of her in the dress she'd bought in Casablanca, the one that looked like the upholstery on his couch at home, and her Birkenstocks. "He'll know who has whatever memoirs the prophetess left behind in her sojourn here."

"Oh." Rosamund went limp with relief. "So we can find out and get out of here."

Rosamund Hall was the only woman Aaron knew who could sit in a Paris salon and talk about leaving as soon as possible.

"Aaron. *Mon ami!*" Philippe rushed from the back room, arms spread wide, straight pins stuck in his blue cotton shirt and a pair of scissors in a holster on his belt.

"Philippe. You old fraud!" Aaron embraced him with affection. "Knock it off with the French. You know you're from Boise, Idaho."

"*Oui*, but Boise is from the French *les bois*, meaning the woods," Philippe trilled, "so I am French by birth."

"If that made any sense, you'd be a tree by birth, too."

"You were always too smart for me." Philippe cupped his hands around Aaron's head and looked into his eyes. In a totally different tone, one that only carried to Aaron's ears, he asked, "Who kicked the shit out of you?"

"Four guys jumped me last night in Casablanca and tried to kill me."

"I wish I'd been there."

"I wish you had been, too." Because a gay man growing up in Boise, Idaho, learned to fight, and fight dirty.

"Did you make them sorry?"

"A couple of them."

"How about some first aid?"

"I could use a sterile gauze wrap for my leg."

"I can get you that. And maybe some antibiotics?"

"*Bon*."

Philippe laughed, as Aaron intended.

Then Aaron said, "But first, let me introduce you to my partner, Dr. Rosamund Hall."

Philippe turned, and magically he was the gay fashion designer once more. "Darling, you have come to the right place. We will be everything you ever wanted from a Paris salon!"

"I never wanted to be in a Paris salon," Rosamund said, eyes wide.

"Oh, dear, dear, dear, dear. That's awful!" Philippe threw his arms up into the air in an excess of horror. "You'll give me a complex!"

If possible, Rosamund looked even more dismayed.

"Come back to my office and we'll talk." With a swish, he led the way to the back.

Aaron took Rosamund's hand and helped her to her feet. "It's okay," he said soothingly. "He does the drama queen act for effect, but he's a genius, a top-notch designer, and rich as Hades."

"And I'm cute as all get-out, too!" Philippe called. Leading them through the pink and white showroom and into his office, he shut the door behind them. Contrary to every other part of the salon, his office was dark paneled walls, a serviceable desk, a killer computer, and rows of file cabinets.

"Sit down." He waved them toward chairs in front of his desk. "After you called, Aaron, I did a little checking around. The man you want is Louis Fournier."

Aaron groaned. "No, I really don't."

"Yes, you really do. He's a fanatical collector of pre–World War One manuscripts, scrolls, and codices, and just a few weeks ago he acquired the journal of one Sacmis, the prophetess of Casablanca."

Rosamund clasped her hands in delight. "You're sure of this?"

In a tone that was a direct contrast to hers, Aaron said, "You're absolutely sure?"

Philippe leaned against his desk, crossed his arms,

and viewed them both with amusement. "Of course I am sure."

"Can we ask him if we can look at the text?" Rosamund turned to Aaron. "Honestly, Dr. Al-Ruwaili is not typical of collectors. Most of them like to show off their acquisitions."

"I do know quite a bit about collectors. Some of them are quite uncooperative. Fournier has that reputation. He's also wealthy beyond belief and a lecherous old beast." Aaron lifted his eyebrows at Philippe. "Where does he keep his collection?"

"In his home."

"Can we somehow get in?"

"I anticipated your wish." Philippe lifted two embossed cards off his desk. "Voilà! Invitations to his party tomorrow night."

"Society party?" Aaron asked.

"The highest," Philippe answered.

"I'll need a tuxedo. And . . ." Aaron waved a hand at Rosamund.

She sat frozen in alarm as the two men turned and looked her over from head to toe.

"Can you do it in one day?" Aaron looked worried.

"Do what?" She looked from Aaron to Philippe and to Aaron again.

"It will take a lot of effort, but I think so." Philippe stroked his chin.

"Do what?" They were making her very nervous.

Philippe plucked the glasses off her nose.

"What are you doing?" She blindly made a grab for them—and missed.

"Do you have contact lenses?" Philippe asked.

"No," she answered.

"Have you considered laser eye surgery?" he asked.

"No," she said more emphatically.

"Why not? Dorothy Parker said, 'Men seldom make passes at girls who wear glasses.' "

Tartly, Rosamund replied, "Letty Cottin Pogrebin said, 'Men who never make passes at women with glasses are asses.' "

Philippe turned to Aaron. "I like this one. You've done well, my friend. Now—let's get to work."

Chapter 22

Early the next evening, Aaron sat in the lobby of Philippe's polished Paris salon, drinking coffee, flipping through French fashion magazines, and waiting impatiently for Philippe to finish transforming Rosamund into a society beauty. Aaron was pretty sure it could be done; he'd seen enough loveliness peek through that clueless, uninterested facade to make him want to kiss her senseless. Or maybe it wasn't so much the loveliness that made him want to kiss her, but her continued cluelessness to his interest.

He glanced toward the gauze curtains where occasionally squeaks of dismay made him think Philippe was either torturing a kitten or waxing Rosamund's brows.

How could a woman live with a man, travel with him, spend every minute of the day in his presence, and not pick up on any of the lures he sent out? She liked men. Obviously. She was enamored of that limp prick Lance Mathews.

Aaron clearly heard Rosamund's panicked voice say, "But I've only had those glasses for five years!" followed by Philippe's reassuring murmur.

Even after Aaron had kissed her, Rosamund looked at him blankly when he smiled at her, stared at him in confusion when he scowled at her, let him take her hand but left it limp in his, let him guide her with his hand at the small of her back, yet never turned into his embrace—

One of the tall, leggy models dressed in black walked out, leaned over Aaron, and in a voice no louder than a whisper said, "Philippe asked that I assure you we're almost done."

"Great," he said absently, and picked up another magazine.

When he looked up again, she was gone. Behind the curtain, he supposed, to work on Rosamund . . .

Rosamund. Did the woman not know how to flirt? At all?

Or was she just not interested in him?

He found himself staring at a fashion layout and scowling. He needed to relax. Philippe knew what Aaron wanted. All Aaron had to do was have a little patience. . . .

He caught sight of himself in the mirrors that stretched from one wall to the other.

For a guy who'd been beaten and stabbed two nights ago, he looked pretty good. Most of the bruising had faded to yellow, he had full range of motion in his jaw, his finger hurt, but it was knitting, his breastbone only ached when he took a big breath or when he twisted wrong, and his thigh . . . his thigh was ugly. The site of the stab wound still ached and burned, even with the antibiotics Philippe had procured. If healing quickly was the benefit for being one of the Chosen Ones, then he was all for it.

Two of Philippe's tallest, most fashionable models stepped out from behind the gauzy curtain at the back of the showroom, parted it in the middle, and held it in an expectant hush.

Aaron put his coffee aside, flung the magazine on the table, and stood.

Philippe stepped out with a flourish. "I am a genius," he proclaimed.

"I know." Aaron was willing to give him his due. "That's why I brought Rosamund here."

"But no. You don't understand. I am a *genius*."

By that, Aaron concluded Philippe had been wildly creative and extravagant, and Aaron would have a huge bill with which to contend. Aaron could only hope his bank account held up under this continued drought of income. "So . . . you used the raw material that is Rosamund and made . . . ?"

Philippe turned back toward the curtained entrance and spread his arms wide. "I give you . . . the librarian!" Turning back to Aaron he added in an undertone, "The librarian everyone wants to fuck."

Aaron did a double take.

The woman who walked into the waiting room was not at all what Aaron had envisioned. Instead of glamour, instead of silk and velvet, Rosamund was . . . she was . . .

She wore a suit of gray wool, with a long-sleeved, formfitting jacket that buttoned up the front, tucked in at the waist, and showed just a hint of creamy cleavage. The knee-length hem of the pencil-thin skirt was right-wing conservative, as were the gray patent pumps with the two-inch heels.

Her curly, carroty hair had been cut to shoulder length and tamed into a smooth wave that flowed around her face and over one eye. Her makeup was so discreet as to be almost invisible, doing nothing more than accenting the lines and curves of her face.

Most important, her tortoiseshell glasses had been replaced with a square, black, severe style that made her violet eyes the focus of the whole package. Her eyes . . . and her lips, which were a glorious, bright red.

Wordless, Aaron gestured for her to turn.

The back of the gray wool suit cupped her rear like a glove, and a gathered kick pleat pointed like an arrow at the crack of her ass.

Philippe was right. She was the librarian everybody wanted to fuck—and Aaron wanted to fuck her.

Now.

"That is not what I told you to do," Aaron said furiously. With her dressed like that, how were they supposed to fit in at Louis Fournier's party? More important, how the hell was he supposed to keep it in his pants? "That's not high society party wear!"

"I told you so." Rosamund stood, wringing her hands, looking wretched. "Philippe, I told you this was a mistake."

"Oh, honey." Philippe patted her cheek. "This is not a mistake. This is the most glorious creation of my career, and Aaron, I have you and the fair Rosamund to thank for it. Relax. You'll see what a success this will be. All I ask in payment is that you tell every woman who asks that Philippe designed the outfit."

"She's going to stand out in the crowd." Which was the last thing Aaron had wanted. He wanted to blend in, to be invisible, to be like everyone else at the party.

"*Mais oui*! I'm already calling in extra staff to deal with the rush." Philippe gestured to his models, who at once rushed behind the curtains. "As for you"—Philippe turned to Rosamund—"you stroll into that party and *be yourself*. These people are so bored, they never meet an original, and you are going to be the most popular woman there."

"Aaron doesn't like it," Rosamund said.

"Trust me." Philippe's gaze dropped to Aaron's groin. "He does. Now, Cinderella"—he clapped his hands—"my limousine is here to take you to the ball. Let's go!"

Philippe talked all the way to the limo, holding her hand, reassuring her, while Aaron stalked behind them and the models, laden with paraphernalia, walked behind him.

The chauffeur stood in uniform beside the open door, and one glance from him proved Philippe was even more correct than Aaron had feared.

The chauffeur wanted to fuck her.

Aaron was tempted to swear viciously and with all the languages at his disposal. But he was afraid that if he opened his mouth, he would give a roar like a wild beast defending his mate. So he contented himself with glaring at the chauffeur with such malicious intent that the man paled and stepped away.

Philippe, of course, saw it all. "Stop frightening Claude. He can't help it if he's heterosexual."

Aaron bared his teeth at the hapless Claude.

"There we go." Philippe handed Rosamund into the limo, then slid in beside her. "Zelda!" he called.

The first tall model leaned into the limo, offering a silver tray laden with fashion trappings.

"Here's your purse." Philippe handed Rosamund a small gray patent clutch. He opened it and showed her the inside. "See? There's your magnifying glass, just as I promised."

Rosamund plucked Bala's Glass from its depths, looked at it, looked at Aaron, nodded, and put it back.

"The purse has a chain handle in case you want to sling it over your shoulder." Philippe extracted the chain from the interior of the purse and showed it to her. "Please try not to do that. It will ruin the line of your jacket."

"Don't use the chain. It'll ruin the line of my jacket," Rosamund repeated obediently.

Pulling a red ceramic compact out of his pocket, Philippe opened it and showed her the contents. "Here's your powder foundation for touch-ups. Here's your lipstick. I showed you how to put them on. Make sure you refresh before you go into the party." He tucked it in the purse with the glass. Without looking away from Rosamund, he snapped his fingers and called, "Nadia!"

Zelda backed out, and the second tall model leaned in and offered her silver tray.

"Here's your champagne." Philippe expertly popped the cork. "Here's your glass." He poured two crystal stems, handed one to Rosamund and placed the other in the built-in bar. He buried the champagne bottle in the ice bucket in the side of the car, then kissed Rosamund on both cheeks. "Have fun, and remember, Cinderella, try not to lose your shoe!" He laughed merrily, then got out of the limo and clapped his hand to Aaron's shoulder. In a low voice, he said, "Although from the look on your face, I really ought to warn her about losing her panties. You're giving off pheromones enough to bring every woman in Paris to orgasm."

"Apparently . . . not." Aaron looked into the luxurious interior of the limo.

Rosamund sat stiff and still, staring at the champagne flute held between her beautifully manicured fingers.

Philippe chuckled. "You're closer than you think. Just in case you're wondering, it's an hour drive to Louis's château. The glass between the driver and the backseat is soundproof and completely opaque. I have tested it myself. But do be careful with the fair Rosamund, Aaron. If she's not a virgin, she's the closest thing to it, and to top it all off, she's clueless."

"That I do know." Aaron started to get in, then turned back to Philippe. "I ought to kill you for this."

"Just name the first baby after me!" Philippe evaded Aaron's grab for his shirtfront, stepped back, and waved as Claude shut the door and drove them into the rainy Paris streets.

Chapter 23

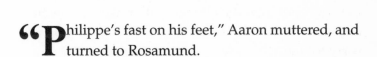

"**P**hilippe's fast on his feet," Aaron muttered, and turned to Rosamund.

She looked on the verge of tears. "I told him you'd hate this. I told him I wasn't pretty like this. I begged him to do something different, but he insisted that this was exactly me. But I don't want it to be me. I wanted to be pretty. For once in my life, I wanted to be pretty."

While she talked, Aaron leaned forward and pressed the button to close the window between the driver and the backseat. When they were sealed inside, surrounded by black leather and dim light, with the sound of the motor purring in the front and the rainy Paris streets passing outside, he turned to her. Grasping the champagne flute, he placed it beside his in the bar. Removing her glasses, he carefully slid them into the door pocket. He took her into his arms, and in a fury of frustration and desire, he said, "You are so much more than pretty."

And he kissed her. Kissed her with all the pent-up anguish of a man who had seen and touched and traveled with the woman he wanted. Ruthlessly, he opened her lips, tasting mint toothpaste and all the while wondering what that soft, red mouth would feel like wrapped around his dick. He thrust his tongue inside, pretending he had entered her body with his. He handled her struggles impatiently, moving her hands off his chest and up around his shoulders.

He couldn't bear for her to push him away. Not now. Not when she had just become everything he had never dared to imagine she could be—a sensual creature living in this moment and aware of her own self.

When he pulled his lips away—the girl needed to breathe, after all—she clutched her fingers in his hair and held him still. "Don't kiss me because you feel sorry for me."

He wanted to laugh, but it would have hurt his still-sore ribs. "Pull down my fly and tell me if that feels like pity to you."

"Your fly? You mean, the zipper in your trousers?" Rosamund twisted in his arms.

Aaron knew what she was trying to do. She was trying to regain her equilibrium, be the rational, sensible, unyielding librarian.

It was way too late for that.

He held her off-balance, looked into her shocked eyes, and got right to the heart of his interest. "What are you wearing under that skirt?"

"*What?*" She sounded so shocked.

Was Philippe right? Was she a virgin? If she was, her first time shouldn't be in the backseat of a limo, not even when Philippe had assured him they were as good as alone.

On the other hand, lots of girls had their first time in the back of a car, and the world was well-populated, so Aaron assumed they weren't scarred by the experience.

Now, if he came too soon, that might scar her—and as horny as he was, coming too soon was a real possibility.

"Tell me what kind of panties you're wearing." He couldn't wait for the answer. Instead he at once slid his hand up her outer thigh, relished the silk of her stockings, finding the lace at the top and the clasp of a sleek garter. Then the smooth gloss of her skin, the bare globe of her ass, the fragment of lace between her cheeks . . .

A thong. She was wearing a garter belt and the smallest wisp of a thong ever created.

"I'm going to kill Philippe." Somewhere, in the depths of his mind, Aaron knew his voice sounded tortured. He pushed her skirt up around her waist, and said, "Next time I see him, I'm going to kill him."

Her fingers combed through the hair at the back of his neck, over and over, driving him mad with the pleasure of her touch. How had she so unerringly found one of his pleasure zones?

Why, when he inhaled, did he smell the scent of leather warmed from their bodies? The spicy perfume at her throat? Why did each bump of the road make him imagine how it would feel if he put her on his lap and let her ride him like a stallion?

The skin between her thighs felt like silk, yet his thumb found a small, raised area. "What's this?" It felt like . . . like a pattern . . .

"It's my tattoo." As he stroked her, her voice grew sultry.

He had forgotten . . . no, he had tried to forget about her tattoo. "This is the one you got on a South Sea island?"

"Yes. It's a ritual. All the girls who pass through puberty there are tattooed with a . . . with a . . . oh, Aaron . . ."

"Tell me what it is." He nipped her earlobe to get her attention, then sucked it into his mouth and laved it with his tongue.

"An orchid."

"Of course. What else would it be?" A honeyed orchid, smooth to the touch, and resembling a woman's—

"What color is it?"

"Pink."

"Of course," he said again. He never doubted it for a minute.

"Specifically, it's a moth orchid, phalaenopsis, said to resemble a moth in flight and native to"—she struggled to speak—"Southeast Asia."

She seemed to think he required more information, which he did, but not about the flower. "Rosamund."

"Hm?"

"You research everything. Did you research sex?" He hoped to hell she had.

She grew warm in his arms.

God. She was blushing.

"Yes." She sounded stoutly defiant. "I was curious, and I thought there was a chance that someday I might . . . get to . . . you know . . ."

Shit. She'd just admitted it. *Virgin. Virgin. Virgin.*

"Darling, I promise. Today's your lucky day." What a stupid thing to say. He sounded like a guy flubbing his pickup lines in a bar.

She didn't seem to care, especially not when he used his hand to spread her legs, and ran his fingers under the lacy elastic, up and down, touching everything that had never been touched before.

He was exploring untouched territory, and the mere thought made him harder.

Primitive and brutish? Undoubtedly. Uncivilized? Completely. Politically incorrect? You bet. A big fat disadvantage when it came to having the kind of sex he wanted to have? Oh, yeah. But none of that made any difference to the primitive, brutish, uncivilized, and politically incorrect virile beast that hid in his brain and heart.

Rosamund was a virgin. She was his, all his, only his. And he was going to keep it that way.

He placed the heel of his hand at the front over her mound, and pressed it once. She jumped, caught her breath, looked frightened and . . . excited.

Excited. Thank God.

He did it again and again, a slow, warm pump of pressure. "Feel that?" he whispered. "That's what it'll feel like when I'm between your legs. It's good, isn't it?"

She nodded, wide-eyed.

"Then there's this." He slid his fingers under the thong, separated her nether lips, found her clit, and stroked it between his thumb and fingers. "I can do this while we're screwing, and you'll orgasm. Over and over. You'll be clawing with need and then limp with relief, and then clawing with need again."

She trembled in his arms, digging her fingers into his shoulders, moving her hips in tiny, uncertain circles.

"I'm not sure, but I think you'll scream while you come. Do you know? What kind of sounds you make?"

"No, I . . . Sounds? Like moaning and . . . I can't imagine I'll make any sounds."

"Really?" If he could have, he would have laughed. "Do you use a vibrator?"

She tensed. She wet her lips, trying to concentrate on answering the question while below, he stroked her, over and over. "I do. The vibrator. They say . . . um, religions say . . . that you'll go crazy if you use one, but I think I'll go crazy if I . . ."

"Don't?"

"Right. If I don't. The vibrator. It's good." Her lips parted as she tried to catch her breath. "That's good, too. What you're doing. Really good."

As the needs of her body overcame the cautions of her mind, her hip movements were becoming more insistent.

He was seeing, bringing about, the blossoming of a warm, sensual, demanding creature.

That blossoming made him feel like a god.

As he touched Rosamund, she grew damp, and that was all the permission he needed. With one smooth motion, he thrust his finger inside her.

His own audacity was almost his undoing.

She was tight and hot, and his dick suddenly developed an imagination, one that claimed *it*, not his finger, was inside her. Aaron trembled on the verge of coming in his shorts, something he had not done since his early teens. He strained to hold himself back.

Then he realized . . . she'd stopped moving and was barely breathing. . . .

"What's wrong?" He kissed her ear, her throat. "Did I hurt you?"

"No. No, but this is too . . ."

She hesitated for so long, he found himself doing what he had sworn he would never do—trying to comprehend a woman's mind. "It's too . . . deep? Public? Distasteful?"

She shook her head after each guess.

"Intimate?"

"Yes." She hid her face in his shirt. "Yes."

"Do you want me to stop?" Merely asking the question almost killed him.

She shook her head.

No, stupid. She wants you to slow down. To seduce her. Because she is a virgin, and this is the price you have to pay.

Be careful what you ask for, Aaron Eagle.

Carefully, slowly, he slid his finger out of her.

She whimpered in distress.

Apparently, the intimacy was too soon and too intense, but at the same time, she liked having him fill her.

He took the tiniest bit of comfort from that. Soon he would fill her with himself, breach her virginity, and she would gasp and hold him in her arms, and he would bring them both to climax.

Soon. Damn it. *Soon.*

He wedged himself in the corner between the door and the leather back, then pulled her into his lap, discarding her panties on the way. He cradled her shoulders with one arm, her bare bottom against his closed fly, a taunt to his control, and let her legs sprawl across the seat.

He leaned around to reach for the champagne flute.

She chose that moment to squirm in his lap, trying to adjust her skirt over her thighs to some instinctive female predetermined decent level halfway down her thighs.

Her butt wiggled against the hardest erection he'd ever experienced, an erection so big King Kong could have climbed it holding Fay Wray in his palm. Aaron could almost see an atomic blue glow coming from his balls, and it was a miracle the damned crystal flute didn't crack in his grip.

When she finally subsided, he ungritted his teeth long enough to ask, "Satisfied?" Because he sure as hell wasn't.

Something of his agony must have sounded in his voice, for she cast him a look of cautious horror. "Am I too heavy?" She tried to spring free.

"No." He caught her around the waist. "You are not too heavy. I simply want you to enjoy a sip of champagne. I know Philippe, and I'm sure this is no less than Dom Perignon." He held the glass to her lips, and watched her profile as she took her first sip.

She closed her eyes as if the taste was ecstasy, and that worshipful expression made him want to pull her under him and show her another way to ecstasy.

In a dreamy voice, she said, "Do you know Dom Perignon is famous for tasting champagne and saying, 'I am drinking the stars'?"

"I've heard that." Of course, she knew more about it

than he did. The woman was a plethora of both useless and useful information.

"Actually, while the good monk was responsible for increasing the quality of the Benedictine wines, he didn't make bubbly champagne, and the quote came from late nineteenth-century advertising." She cupped his hand with hers to bring the glass to her mouth again. "But it really *is* like drinking stars."

"Yes." He leaned his mouth close to her ear, and suggested, "If you would like, I can show you other ways to taste the stars."

Rosamund audibly swallowed her wine. "Really?" Her voice squeaked.

The clean scent of her hair filled his head, intoxicating him as surely as the champagne intoxicated her. "Finish your glass," he said, and immersed his fingers into his own champagne flute.

The champagne bubbled against his skin, and he almost laughed at her expression—amazed and rapt as he slipped his hand under her skirt, shocked by the cool touch of his champagne-dipped fingers in the warmth between her legs. "Darling, open for me. A little more . . ."

She did. Gradually, with reluctant fascination.

He dipped his fingers again, and this time when he slid his fingers along her clit, she whimpered. "Do you like that?" he whispered in her ear. "Can you feel the bubbles?"

"It feels like it tastes. Cool and sort of—"

He repeated his actions—the dip into the glass, the caress between her legs, over her clit, around the entrance to her body, and back to the glass. "Sort of what?" he asked.

"Intoxicating. I feel as if the world is spinning away from me. Is it possible to get tipsy from champagne . . . there?"

"I don't know. Let me see." In one easy motion, he slid out from underneath her, leaving her wedged into the warm place in the leather that he had just vacated. He spread her legs wider, pushed his arm under her bottom, tilted her hips up, and leaned forward to taste her.

And there it was, on the pale skin of her inner thigh—an orchid, genus phalaenopsis, opening its pink petals just for him.

"Aaron. No!" She tried to push him away.

But this time he wouldn't allow her to escape. "Shh," he whispered against her skin. "I'm getting tipsy on champagne. And you." He tasted her, controlling her struggles, then pressed his tongue inside, long, slow, damp thrusts of his tongue that matched the ancient, primitive rhythm of sex. Dimly he heard her moans, small and quiet at first; then as she lost control, they grew deeper, longer, more desperate.

Taking his glass, he took a sip of champagne; then with the cool liquid still on his tongue, he kissed her nether lips again.

Never had champagne tasted so much like an aphrodisiac.

Her legs moved restlessly around him. She put one foot flat on the seat, the other against the floor. With one hand, she held his head in place, while the other dug divots into the leather seat. She lifted herself to his mouth, over and over, demanding, without words, that he give her what he had promised. That he give her satisfaction.

He took another sip of champagne, held it in his mouth, and lavished the bubbly wine into the most intimate places of her body.

She hovered on the brink for a long, long minute. Then he took her clit and sucked the champagne, and her clit, and at the same time thrust his finger inside her—

Just as he had known she would, she screamed, screamed and arched as if he'd branded her with his tongue.

And maybe he had.

Her orgasmic spasms went on and on, clutching at his finger, filling his mouth, feeding his need to make her happy and his desperate desire to make her his own.

And he would. Now. Here. On the seat. He wanted to wrap her in his arms, to feel her buck against him. He wanted to thrust his knee between her legs to prolong her pleasure. He wanted to know how it would be for him when he pressed his cock inside her. And why not? She was ripe, ready, damp and halfway to another climax.

He pulled her down on the seat and under him. He reached for his fly and—

That dumb son of a bitch Claude tapped on the window between the seats.

Chapter 24

"**W**hat the hell?" Aaron lifted his head.

The car was slowing.

"What is it?" Rosamund's voice sounded blurred, uncertain.

He lifted himself on one elbow.

They had turned into the long, lighted driveway that led to the château.

They were here. At the party. *Now.*

"That liar Philippe said it would take an hour." Aaron looked at his watch and swore viciously. "It's been an hour and fifteen minutes."

"Oh, no." Rosamund pushed her hair out of her eyes. "We've been doing, um, this for over an hour?"

"Time flies when you're having fun." He was ten minutes away from his own satisfaction, and the château was two minutes away. Hell, he could get off in two minutes, but— He looked down at Rosamund.

She had barely finished the kind of orgasm that made him want to polish his good lover merit badge.

If he jumped her and finished in two minutes, he'd deserve to lose that badge forever. She needed more than a quickie and a pat on the butt. She needed a chance to find herself again. And she obviously didn't have a clue how to do that because virgins didn't know how to play at sophistication, pretend sex was nothing more than a game, recover from a quick romp and go on to another.

That's what he liked about her being a virgin. Right? *Right?*

Somehow, his own pep talk wasn't convincing him at all.

But the lights along the length of the drive were shining in the windows, the evening was fading into night, and they had a job to do.

The manuscript. They needed that manuscript.

Focus, Aaron.

Somehow, he needed to forget the demands of his libido and concentrate on a prophecy that would save his life, and hers, and maybe every one of the Chosen.

"Come on, darling, let's help you up." With his hands under her arms, he slid Rosamund into the seated position. "That wasn't the best way to end lovemaking, was it?" He found her tiny excuse for a pair of panties on the floor and slid them up her legs, trying desperately to ignore the garter belt and the scent of champagne and willing woman that wafted to his nose. "Lift up so we can put these on."

She pressed herself more firmly into the seat and whispered, "I'm . . . wet."

Well, of course she was. He'd been using champagne on her and she'd been coming into his mouth. . . .

No! Don't think of that.

Because if he did, when Claude opened the door, Aaron would be on her and in her, and wouldn't give a damn who saw his bare butt pumping away. . . .

"Is there a napkin or something I could use to . . . ?" She looked so humiliated he had to kiss her again. Just a quick, soft kiss to her lips.

Pulling his handkerchief from his pocket, he pressed it between her legs.

Her swift intake of breath told him she hadn't quite finished her climax, and he was torn between regret and triumph. Regret that she would be frustrated; triumph that she would be helpless to resist him when he made his way to her bedroom later.

For now, he tried for matter-of-fact and kind, drying her with tender touches that he kept strictly dispassionate. "How's that?"

"I can get dressed now." She waited until he withdrew his hands, then in a flurry pulled up her panties and pulled down her skirt.

He tucked his handkerchief back into his pocket, located her glasses in the door pocket, and slid them on her nose. "Is that better?"

"I can see. But my hair. How's my hair?" She raked her fingers through it. "Philippe will kill me if my hair doesn't fall correctly."

"He must have done something right, because it looks just like it did when we left the salon." He found the mirror on the ceiling and flipped it down so she could see.

Her hand flew to her swollen mouth. "My lipstick! Where—"

Aaron unclicked the latch and handed her the purse, and watched as she got out the compact. But when she tried to apply the lipstick, her hands were shaking. "I don't know how to do this even when I haven't been—" She hung up on the word.

"Coming?" He took the lipstick out of her fingers, knelt in front of her, carefully applied the color, and tried to find the right words to help her face the ordeal ahead. "I want you to promise me something."

"What?"

Claude stopped the car at the front step.

"I don't want you to feel guilty for finding pleasure, or be embarrassed because you found it with me."

She stared at him, hanging on his words as if he were reciting a lover's poem.

He continued. "What we did was wonderful. Every moment was bliss. But the experience was private between you and me and no one, I repeat, no one, will ever know what we did back here."

"Really?"

"I'm not going to tell them. You're not going to tell them." He cupped her cheek in his hand. "And if you can manage not to blush every time I look at you, no one will ever guess."

She leaned into his palm, a trusting gesture he treasured. "I'll try."

"That's good." She looked so relieved, he couldn't help adding, "Next time, I promise we'll do something worth being embarrassed about."

He should have been sorry to make her blush again, but damn it. He was suffering, and how was he going to get out of this car with his trousers looking like a one-man tent? "You look lovely." He pushed her hair out of her face. "Philippe's right. You're going to be the hit of the party. Women are going to want to be you and men are going to simply . . . want you."

"I guess that's true." She put the lipstick away. "This outfit worked with you."

He sighed. "I wish that was all there was to it." Because right now, even in her couch upholstery dress, she could lead him anywhere, into any danger.

Claude discreetly knocked on the door. Obviously the chauffeur had a suspicion what had been going on in the backseat.

Aaron unlocked the door and opened it. "Please assist Dr. Hall," he instructed.

Claude held the umbrella and offered his hand to Rosamund. As she slid her legs out, Claude very carefully didn't look at her.

Smart man.

Taking a breath, Aaron calmed his rampaging body, then joined her at the bottom of the long sweep of steps.

"How was the champagne, sir?" Claude asked.

"I can unequivocally say it was the best I've ever had." Aaron smiled, a slash of savage humor. Taking Rosamund's arm, he walked with her up the stairs.

Aaron had been in a lot of grand houses in Paris, but not Fournier's home. The seventeenth-century château had been constructed of pale marble by one of Louis XIV's nobles. A cacophony of elaborate towers, spires, and mansard roofs, surrounded by a sizable park planted in mazes and formal gardens, the place was a monument to Louis Fournier, the financier, and his rise to riches. Even more telling was the string of limousines that snaked down the drive, waiting to deliver noble and affluent guests to the home of a man who had risen from the deepest poverty to the greatest heights . . . by any means possible.

Fournier had a reputation as a son of a bitch with shady connections to the underworld and a ruthless streak that didn't shrink at blackmail. He was also a well-known old goat with a reputation for buying enviably beautiful mistresses, using them for a time, and discarding them. All in all, the kind of man Aaron took care to avoid.

Yet for all that, Fournier was well-known in the antiquities world for his library of ancient manuscripts and his collection of ancient art.

So here they were. Rosamund would be beautiful and fashionable and provide a distraction. Aaron would find the manuscript and steal it. Together, they would work as a team, and if all went well, after tonight they would return to New York City with the knowledge that would assist the Chosen Ones in their battle.

If only she were more worldly, he would feel better about leaving her to fend for herself.

"Listen," he said in an undertone. "The people at this party are rich and decadent. They come to these parties to see and be seen. They have no employment, they drink too much, they experiment with drugs, they revel in every kind of sexual excess."

"I understand. This is the Roman Empire at its most decayed." She nodded.

"Exactly." He could speak her language. "And Louis Fournier is Caligula."

"Insane?"

"No. Corrupt. The ultimate debaucher of innocents." Aaron swallowed. *Innocents like Rosamund.* The top of the stairway grew closer and closer. He had too little time to properly warn her, and he talked faster. "At some point, I'll have to leave you to get my hands on the manuscript—"

"You're going to coerce some poor employee to show you the manuscript," she corrected.

She really did think he was the Godfather.

How cool was that?

"It has to be done," he reminded her. "There's no other way. Now listen. Be careful who you talk to and what you say. Don't go into any unoccupied rooms with anyone. Drink only bottled water with the top still screwed on—"

"All right. I've got it. Avoid date rape and date rape drugs." She placed her hand on his arm. "I'll be wary."

"Yes. Good." She could never be wary enough to satisfy him. After all, *he* knew she was wearing a garter belt and a lace thong.

As they reached the top and the lights of the château reached out to encompass them, she glanced at him. Once. Twice. "You've got my lipstick all over your mouth," she whispered frantically.

Of course he did. How could he not?

Pulling out his handkerchief, he wiped at his lips.

At once the scents of fine champagne and Rosamund's pussy filled his head, and if retrieving this manuscript were not a matter of crucial importance, he would have picked her up and carried her off into the night to have his way with her. Instead, he tucked his handkerchief back into his pocket, and swore that for the pure pleasure of knowing his touch had brought her to completion, he would never wash the fine scrap of linen again. Turning his face to hers, he asked, "Better?"

"Yes. Yes. I'm fine. Stop asking me!" She wrung her hands in distress. "I'm not that much of an idiot. I know men and women do what we did all the time. I'm okay!"

So. She was feeling a little high-strung.

He looked into her eyes, and enunciated clearly. "Did I wipe off all the lipstick?"

"Oh. Oh, I thought . . ." She didn't seem to know whether to look at him or not, but he waited patiently, and finally she steeled herself and looked into his face. "There's a little . . . you missed a place. . . ." Swiftly, she used her thumb to wipe his lower lip.

Swiftly, he caught her thumb between his teeth and bit.

She caught her breath. Jerked her hand back. Looked up at the open door where the butler stood waiting. Looked down toward the town car below that discharged another couple, handsome and sophisticated and French. "Don't *do* that."

Taking her hand, he kissed her thumb. "Or what will you do?"

"I'll tell everyone you're an enforcer."

"That's fine, but most of these people have been acquainted with me for years." He felt that prickling at the base of his neck, the one that meant he was being watched. He scanned the cars coming behind them, looked at the open door ahead. "They wouldn't be-lieve you, and if they did, they'd be thrilled at the idea of knowing a real enforcer."

"Really?"

"Really. I told you. They're corrupt and useless. Well, most of them are, anyway." He made a lightning-swift decision. She needed to be warned. "Some of them are merely venal—and one of them has put a price on my head."

Chapter 25

———⟨◇⟩———

"*What?*" Rosamund pushed her glasses up on her nose and shoved her hair out of her eyes.

"I removed something from his possession that he had stolen from its owner. He took it badly, and Fujimoto Akihiro has sworn to remove me from this life." They walked through the front door of Louis Fournier's home, and stood waiting, a little apart.

"Fujimoto Akihiro? I met him. He's a well-respected Japanese businessman. He made a donation to the library."

"He buys stolen art, or if the piece he wants is not on the market, he commissions his people to steal it." The little creep. Aaron detested Fujimoto, detested the kind of ruthless conceit that demanded he have everything he ever desired regardless of who the owner might be. He thought he was something special, but to Aaron, who actually was something special, Fujimoto was nothing but a man with no morals and far too much money.

Aaron examined the grandiose entry, the security team, the guests milling not far away . . . and Rosamund.

Together, they had managed to restore her makeup and clothing to the same condition they had been in when Philippe had tucked them in his limo. Yet at the same time, she looked different.

In some undefinable way, she looked well-loved.

In his effort to make her believe in her beauty . . . All right. No use lying to himself, at least. In his effort to get between her legs, he had made her even more . . . well. Just even more.

It was going to be a very long night.

"Is he here tonight?" she whispered.

"Fujimoto? Probably not. I've been underground for months. Philippe contacted Fournier's people this afternoon and informed them that *we* would be using the invitations, and even with the best sources of information, I doubt Fujimoto could react that quickly." Although Aaron was assuming the little asshole wanted to be in on the kill. If Fujimoto sent in his assassins, Aaron could be dead before the evening was old.

Again he surveyed the guests, but saw nothing amiss, nothing out of place, nothing obvious to worry about.

Two security people approached Rosamund and Aaron and asked their names, checked them off the list, then politely begged their pardon and thoroughly frisked them for weapons. When they were cleared, they were each handed a glass of champagne and escorted into the public part of the château.

"Aaron." Rosamund tugged at his sleeve, looking at him as if she wanted to say something, but didn't know how.

Probably she was remembering that time in the limo, was too shy to speak. Placing his hand protectively at the base of her spine, he asked, "What is it?"

"If I see the right manuscript, how do you want me to tell you?"

She wasn't thinking of sex. She was thinking of Sacmis's journal.

Damn it.

"If you find the right manuscript, probably a few quiet words should alert me," he said.

She smoothed her skirt. "Then I'm ready. Let's go."

He had been thoroughly put in his place, and by a woman who didn't even know she had done it.

Standing at the top of the stairs, looking down at the huge ballroom, Rosamund breathed, "Fascinating."

"It is, isn't it?"

The château had been stripped of its original seventeenth-century stylings and transformed into a stark black-and-white modernist showcase for Louis Fournier's antiques. The pieces were displayed in glass cases set randomly around the room. A spotlight shone on each piece of art, electronic security sparkled warningly, and beside each case, a beefy security guard had been placed to stop anyone foolish enough to try to touch.

Aaron knew Fournier kept the manuscripts in his private library, and no one saw them without an invitation—which meant no one except his staff had seen them for years.

Colorfully dressed guests swirled around the cases, looking, admiring, drinking too much and eating too little.

"With this kind of security, even if you threaten the

right person, how will you be able to take the manuscript?" Rosamund gripped Aaron's arm in alarm.

He enjoyed her concern a little too much. "I have talents you don't know about," he said in understatement. "Don't worry. All you have to do is circulate."

As they descended the stairs, the guests were starting to notice them, glancing up and then doing the same double take Aaron had done in the salon.

As a distraction, Rosamund was perfect.

Unfortunately, as they reached the ballroom, every man in the place took a step closer.

She was a distraction for more than just the guests— Aaron couldn't concentrate worth a damn.

Rosamund jabbed Aaron in the arm with her fist. "Look. Look! Have you ever seen anything like that?"

Aaron looked in the direction of her gaze, and saw him. DeMonte D'Alessandri, playboy and industrialist. Of course she would gush about him. Any woman would. The guy was handsome and wealthy, he knew it all too well, and he was headed right for Rosamund. He stopped before her, struck his best pose, and in his suave Italian accent, he said, "Aaron, introduce me to the lovely signorina."

No. I don't want to. "D'Alessandri. Good to see you. This is Dr. Rosamund Hall, daughter of the antiquities expert Dr. Elijah Hall and an antiquities expert in her own right." Those credentials should be boring enough to send DeMonte fleeing.

Instead, DeMonte lifted her hand and kissed her fingers with all the elegance of his noble Florentine background. "Tell me I have met you in time. Tell me you are unwed."

"No. No, I'm not married." She tugged her hand free and pointed at the first spotlighted glass case. "Do you know what that is?"

Knocked off-balance by her blatant disinterest, D'Alessandri looked over his shoulder. "No. What?"

"It's an Andrei Rublev Russian icon, fourteenth century, one of the finest I've ever seen." Rosamund stepped around DeMonte and rushed toward the case. "I wonder how Mr. Fournier acquired it."

Aaron chuckled at the sight of D'Alessandri's face as Rosamund walked away from him without a backward glance. *That* would put the Italian Lothario firmly in his place.

Instead D'Alessandri hurried after her like a dog in heat. Aaron followed and arrived in time to hear him say, "It is a wonderful piece. Perhaps you could tell me what you know about it."

Rosamund launched into a description of the Russian culture, the significance of the icons in Russian religion, and the meaning of this particular piece.

In normal circumstances, D'Alessandri would have fallen over in a stupor. Instead, he stood beside her, stared at her bosom, and made interested noises.

No. No, this wasn't possible. Rosamund couldn't be so enticing that shallow, frivolous DeMonte was willing to be bored to death for a chance at her.

It got worse. Three other guys—two married, one single, all horny bastards who couldn't keep their hands to themselves—joined Rosamund and D'Alessandri at the case. Damn it all to hell. Rosamund was fulfilling every boy's dream of uptight-and-sexy-as-hell librarian.

Thank God she was oblivious.

As she hurried from case to case, expounding on the antiquities she saw beneath the spotlights, Aaron knew he should be slipping into Fournier's library, finding the manuscript, and "borrowing" it for the evening.

But the silly, vain, I'm-living-on-Daddy's-money, worthless and wealthy society boys were listening to Rosamund. As if they were interested. When Aaron knew for a fact they were fighting to remain awake. If he left Rosamund alone, one of them would suggest that he knew where more antiquities were located. He'd lure her into some dark bedroom and try to . . . try to do what Aaron had tried to do on the drive over.

And she hadn't finished with her orgasm! She was primed, ready for sex as provided by the right man.

Aaron was that man, damn it.

She used her clutch purse to gesture at her captive audience, then impatiently placed it on top of the case and kept talking.

It wasn't her travel pack. It wasn't hooked around her waist. She was going to forget about it. She was going to—

Just as he'd predicted, she wandered to the next case, leaving the purse behind.

He started forward, ready to leap to the rescue.

D'Alessandri beat him to it. He picked up the purse, pushed his way to Rosamund's side, and offered it to her.

She took it, absently thanked him, and tucked it under her arm.

D'Alessandri laughed and spoke, then lifted his hand toward the lock of her hair that draped over her eye—and without knowing how he did it, Aaron had crossed the room and had D'Alessandri's wrist in his hand. He locked eyes with the Italian and said, "Don't . . . touch . . . her."

He must have looked as if he meant business, because the Italian nodded. Just nodded. And when Aaron dropped his arm, he backed away, viewing Aaron the way a man would view a rabid grizzly bear.

Rosamund, being Rosamund, barely noticed that he'd made a royal fool of himself over her.

Taking the purse from her, he extracted the chain that served as a handle, threaded it up her arm, and rested it on her shoulder.

She frowned and pushed her hair out of her eyes again. "I'm not supposed to wear it that way because . . ." She squinted, trying to remember why.

"It'll ruin the line of your jacket," Aaron supplemented. "Better to ruin the line than to forget the purse."

"Right. Thank you." She lavished a smile on him, clutched his sleeve and asked, "Have you seen the Mycenaean knives in this case over here?"

"Very impressive. Go ahead and look." Aaron let her and the little crowd around her wander away. He started to pull his handkerchief from his pocket and wipe his face, then remembered the scent that perfumed it and feared that if he smelled that fragrance, he'd start rampaging through the ballroom, using the Mycenaean knives to cut the throat of any man who dared look at Rosamund.

"You look a little frazzled, Aaron." A warm, soft, feminine voice spoke beside him, in French, and he turned to see the model Pacquin. She was twenty-one, dressed in designer red silk, glorious in her beauty.

"Does it show?" In their way, she and Aaron were friends. They'd both had to grow up at an early age.

"You mean, did anyone notice when you leaped like a gazelle across the ballroom to forbid DeMonte to touch your woman?" She chuckled warmly. "Everyone did." Young as she was, Pacquin had done and seen everything, and now she watched Rosamund with the smile of a woman wise beyond her years. "She's almost pulsating with innocent sexuality, and it's like a magnet. Every man here thinks he's the only one who can break through that innocence and mate her."

"How do they *know*?"

"Men are almost doglike in their instincts. Except you, Aaron." She placed her hand on his chest over his heart. "You're pulsating, too, but it's dangerous. Wolf-like. Attractive, especially when you watch her like that. It tempts a woman to see if she can turn your attention to . . . other matters."

He looked at her, so slim, so gorgeous, so young, so knowledgeable. He knew that if he said the word, she would take him into a bedroom, unzip his pants, and relieve him of this persistent hard-on.

A month ago he would have accepted the invitation, and gladly.

Now he didn't give a damn whether he had sex with her. One woman and one woman only had his attention.

Rosamund.

Pacquin knew, of course. She smiled and removed her hand. "If I were you, I wouldn't worry about De-

Monte getting to her. I'd be more concerned about Louis Fournier." She nodded toward the crowd around the case.

Fournier, one of the wealthiest men in the world, a disgusting old lecher, and a man renowned for his conquests, was holding a Egyptian clay clock vessel in his gloved hands and pointing out the markings to Aaron's own personal librarian—while Rosamund was looking dazzled and enticed.

Dear God. Fournier wanted Rosamund, and he had figured out the one way to seduce her.

Aaron started forward just as Fournier replaced the piece in the case, took Rosamund's arm, and walked toward the velvet rope that separated the ballroom from his private quarters.

Every person at the party watched with avid excitement.

Aaron tried to follow.

The security guard, a man of impressive bulk and mean little eyes, stopped him with a fist in his tuxedo jacket. "Not without an invitation."

"Rosamund!" Aaron yelled.

Rosamund glanced back and saw him. "He's my friend," she told Fournier.

Fournier made a lazy gesture that allowed Aaron to come through. "If he is your friend, he can stay . . . in the corridor."

Chapter 26

Rosamund waited while Louis tapped in a security code that would allow them into his personal library, and while she did, she tossed a conspiratorial smile at Aaron. She'd done it! She'd managed to gain access to Fournier's collection. Aaron didn't have to threaten and intimidate some poor employee into letting him in to steal the prophetess's journal. Best of all, Rosamund had managed this based on one conversation about Egyptian antiquities with a fellow enthusiast. Aaron had to be happy.

But he didn't look happy. He looked like he wanted to grab her and—

Then he did—grabbed her arms and pulled her close, so close they stood chest to chest, so close she breathed in his scent.

Her heart beat faster. Her breath quickened. "What are you doing?" she asked.

She understood her own reaction. She really did. In

the limo they had been intimate as she'd never been intimate before. Of course his closeness affected her.

But to recognize his scent . . . how had he managed that? Was that some kind of sexual branding?

"What am I doing? What are you doing?" he whispered furiously.

She took a deep breath. Yes, sexual branding was the correct term, because she now unwittingly displayed all the signs of arousal. Her nipples pressed hard against the inside of her bra, her skin felt hot and too tight, and between her legs . . .

"Rosamund?" He shook her slightly.

She focused on him. He smelled great, but he looked grumpy. About what? She had done what they had desperately needed her to do. "Louis invited me to look over his manuscripts."

Aaron cast a guarded glance at the older man's back. "Or his etchings."

"What? Wh-what do you mean?" Aaron was being very odd. "Is he also a collector of etchings?"

Louis opened the door and turned back to them. "I assure you, Mr. Eagle, that I'm not so unimaginative as to show Dr. Hall any etchings, nor would she be seduced by anything so pedestrian. As she explained, I intend to show her my . . . manuscripts." He smiled at her.

She smiled back.

Louis Fournier was not a handsome man. Probably he never had been, for he was short, no more than Rosamund's height, and naturally slender, with narrow shoulders and no excess flesh to round out his form. Now he was old, stooped, bony. His thin face sagged like a basset hound's, his ears stuck out, his faded brown eyes were world-weary, and his thin lips had disappeared with the march of time.

But he had something. Charm or charisma or power that made Rosamund realize that the man, even now, would be hard to resist. "Louis assured me the journal he has purchased isn't something transcribed for Sacmis, but her actual writings in her own hand. It allegedly came with her from Casablanca to her place in the French court, and she left it behind when she fled the city during the storming of the Bastille."

"Quite right. Are you ready, my dear?" Louis indicated a small vestibule beyond the door where lights blinked in a dazzling security array.

"Yes." She yanked at her arms. "If Mr. Eagle will let go of me."

Without warning, Aaron wrapped his arms around her and kissed her, a soft, slow, explicit exploration of her mouth that cared nothing about their audience—and after thirty seconds, she didn't care, either.

He tasted of passion and champagne, smelled of luxury and leather, and the memory of those moments in the limo rose like an irresistible tide, making her forget Louis and the security guard and the prophetess of Casablanca. There was merely Aaron, invading her heart and mind, feeding her carnal pleasure until her knees collapsed and only his embrace kept her on her feet.

Unhurriedly he released her, steadied her, and when she opened her eyes, he was watching her with such sensuality she wanted nothing more than to take him by the hand and lead him somewhere dark and warm, where they could—

"Now are you ready, my dear?" With a suave smile, Louis offered his arm.

She took it.

As they stepped inside a small, bare access room, Louis said, "Mr. Eagle, you have lipstick on your mouth."

Aaron locked gazes with Louis. Removing his hand-kerchief from his pocket, he wiped his lips, took a deep breath—and smiled.

Louis swung the heavy door shut behind them with a solid thud, leaving Aaron behind.

"What was that all about?" she asked the air.

But Louis apparently thought she was really asking him. "I believe most people would call that a pissing match. I should have won." He glanced at her swollen mouth. "But I did not."

In exasperation, she said, "I don't understand men."

"That's obvious." Louis placed his hand on a screen. A blue light scanned his palm, and a beep sounded. "But you're a librarian. Have you ever considered re-searching the gender?"

"Yes. I suppose I could. But there are so many more interesting subjects waiting for me to delve into!"

Louis gave a bellow of laughter. "Indeed. Why would you bother?"

Was he offended? She didn't think so. He had laughed. But as they had both agreed, she didn't un-derstand men.

She observed as Louis leaned forward, placed his eye at a peephole, and allowed a red light to scan it.

This vestibule was obviously filled with the latest in security. They'd come in one door. They would enter the library through another.

"Your Mr. Eagle has a very impressive résumé," Louis said.

"He does?"

"He's the best fine antiquities thief in the world."

"No, he's not." Fresh air puffed over her, removing dust and lint. "He's an enforcer, like the Godfather."

"Really." Fournier's voice was cool. "That's not what my research revealed."

Taken aback, she asked, "You have researched him?"

"I had him researched," he corrected. "All of my guests are researched, some more extensively than others. I don't like to be surprised."

"If you thought he was a thief, why would you let him in?"

"Because he was bringing an interesting date with him." Louis inclined his head to her.

"You had *me* researched?" Her voice squeaked with astonishment. "Before the party?"

As Louis performed his security checks, numbers beside the inner door began to illuminate in a random pattern. "Only the tiniest bit, but it was enough to intrigue me. You see, my dear, I worship at the altar of knowledge, and you have fascinating credentials. I wanted to meet you, to see why you were dating a . . . thief."

"Honestly, he's not a thief. He's an enforcer. I'm not happy about it," she assured him, concentrating on the numbers, catching glimpses of some intricate pattern that was forming. "But we're trying to track down the prophetess of Casablanca, so he's the enforcer I need."

"No. You need me." Cynicism etched every line of Louis's face. "But I suppose you know that." Stepping back, he studied the numbers at the door; then in rapid succession, he pushed the next three numbers.

The lock on the door to the library released with a slow whoosh.

"It's a sequence," he told her. "It changes every time I come in. I wrote the program myself, and not even the finest computer created today can see the progression within the required time—and only a few people in the world have the brain to put the numbers together."

"You're one of them."

He gave a little bow.

"What happens if you don't succeed?"

"The doors are locked and whoever's within is electrocuted."

She laughed.

He didn't.

With great precision, he placed his hand on one spot on the unlocked door and pushed it open.

Stepping into the imposing chamber, she gave a gasp.

Irving Shea's collection had been impressive, with relics and antiquities and manuscripts, but with the layman's disregard for their age and fragile nature, he left them on open shelves in full light.

Louis Fournier concentrated his attention on documents, and when it came to the preservation of those documents, his library compared favorably to the Vatican's.

"The glass over the shelves is bulletproof and air-locked. The lighting is low, the lowest limit to preserve the ink. We handle everything with gloved hands, and I've got the most modern equipment to verify the authenticity of the documents." Louis watched in open delight as she walked reverently toward the shelves containing the scrolls. "This is my passion. And yours."

The first title she read raised goose bumps on her skin. "You have a copy of the Seventh Gospel? Is it real? No, it can't be. They were all destroyed in the sack of Rome by the Visigoths."

"Why don't you look at it and see what you think?" Fournier handed her a pair of gloves.

She couldn't believe he was serious, but he pressed a series of electronic buttons by the case, and with a whoosh, the vacuum that protected the scrolls was released.

"Please." He indicated the scroll.

She put down her purse and donned the gloves, opened the case and lifted the tray that contained the text. She visually examined the edges of the paper, the gilding on the roller, the splotches left by time and water.

Fournier indicated the microscope. "Go ahead and unroll it. I keep the best restoration team in the world on retainer, and they have done marvelous work with this gospel."

With the instruments at hand, she peeled back the edges and examined them, then slid the document under the microscope. The media was parchment, a *volumen* of great age. As the Latin words came into focus, she realized Louis was right. He had an authentic copy of the Seventh Gospel.

She looked up, troubled. "This is not just rare. This is a legend. No one knows that it really exists, yet you have it. It deserves to be studied, translated, a gift to the modern world."

"How very Indiana Jones of you. You think it should be in a museum." He was openly amused.

"Or a library."

"Do you know how much I spent on keeping the manuscripts and scrolls in my possession preserved? This system, with its vacuum seal, its special lighting, its perfect climate control, cost me over six hundred and fifty million dollars. How much does the Arthur W. Nelson Fine Arts Library spend to protect its collection?"

She shook her head. "Nothing even close."

"In the last five years, I've paid the team who does my restoration over seventy-five million to work in my library."

"Seventy-five million? That's absurd. How big is your team?"

"Eight people, the best in the world. But I don't pay that much for their work. I pay for their silence." Louis rested his hand on one of the marble bookends carved into the shape of a gargoyle's head. "Have you heard any rumor of the Seventh Gospel?"

"No." She searched her memory. "Not even in restoration circles."

He inclined his head.

"But I did hear that you'd purchased the prophetess of Casablanca's journal."

"I bought it at a private auction. Others were involved. The seller. The other buyers." He shrugged with Gallic fatalism. "Those people cannot be silenced, at least not without bloodletting. And while the prophetess manuscript is of interest to collectors like me, it's not that valuable."

"Why not?"

"It's indecipherable. Some people say it's a hoax, that the prophetess was not literate."

"Or that she wasn't a real prophetess," Rosamund reminded him.

"Ah, but I believe that the prophetess wrote in the language of her tribe, an obscure script that has proved impossible to translate—and believe me, I've had the best linguists here to try."

"You didn't have me," she said.

He cast her a sharp glance. "Good for you. I like a woman who knows her value."

But one detail had caught her attention. "How did you know I worked at the Arthur W. Nelson Fine Arts Library?"

"I was watching you on the security monitor, realized I was not only interested in your background as a linguist but also in you as a woman, and had you investigated."

"You said you had me investigated before the party!"

"Not as thoroughly as I would have liked."

"So you've made more inquiries about me *since* I got to the party?" His gall took her breath away.

"Great wealth does have its advantages."

She stared at him, for the first time seeing beyond the charm. He was a man with too much power, used to having his own way, no matter what the means, and with a jolt, she remembered the warnings Aaron had given her as they walked up the stairs to the château.

He had warned her about Louis Fournier, called him Caligula, the ultimate debaucher of innocents.

She was a librarian, a talented one, but a librarian nevertheless. What was she doing in Paris at a high society party? Why were men suddenly surrounding her, flattering her, wanting to whisk her away into a corner?

Why had Aaron done everything in his power to seduce her in the back of the limousine?

She knew the answer—because she wore a designer outfit, had her hair styled by a professional, wore makeup applied by an expert.

With abrupt uneasiness, she realized—she was out of place, an imposter. *This was not who she was.*

With the perspicacity that made Louis who he was, he observed her sudden wariness and said, "You're not in danger. You can't find a man who has more respect for a paleographer of your talent than me."

True. And perhaps he could be a danger to her, but she was young and strong. He wouldn't easily subdue her.

And anyway . . . it wasn't Louis Fournier who put her on edge.

It was Aaron. Something about Aaron, about the way he'd found her in the library, about how easily he had coerced her to leave with him and never go back . . . It was as if he had hypnotized her. And the way he brought her whatever texts she needed . . . She had accused him of being an enforcer, and he hadn't denied that. But how did any man get through security like at the Arthur W. Nelson Fine Arts Library? Or the university library in Casablanca? His skills were *spooky*.

Aaron wanted her, yes. In the limo, he had seduced her with passion and intensity . . . now that she looked like he wanted her to look. Now that she'd left the real Rosamund far behind.

Then like a burst of light, she remembered Lance. Lance, who wanted her when she was working in the library. Lance, who liked her as she truly was, plain and unadorned.

She wasn't afraid that Lance would disrupt her life and make her feel things she didn't want to feel, like . . . like out-of-control passion in the back of a limousine. Lance didn't look deep into her eyes, trying to see into her soul, and he never made her want to expose the fear with which she'd grown up.

Lance was dressed in normal clothes. No tuxedos for him. No silk ties or shoes polished to a high gleam. Sure, he was handsome, even more handsome than Aaron, but he wore jeans and a golf shirt. He was merely a normal guy.

"Do you have a restroom in here?" As she looked around, she was proud of her assumption of ease. "It's been a long evening and I've had a lot of . . . champagne." She willed herself to meet Louis's gaze and not blush, and she must have convinced him—or maybe it was a subject he didn't want to argue—because he waved her toward a closed door.

"Thanks." She headed toward the lavatory and locked the door after her. She turned on the water, pulled out her phone, typed in, *Paris is lovely, party at Louis Fournier's, wish u were here*, and sent it winging its way to New York City and Lance.

And collapsed against the sink and burst into tears, half afraid she'd been stupid beyond measure—because she was falling in love with Aaron Eagle.

*   *   *

In New York City, in Osgood's office, Lance looked up at the man who owned his soul. "She's at Louis Fournier's. Do you have men in position there?"

"I have men in position everywhere." Osgood picked up his phone and spoke into the receiver. "Louis Fournier. Rosamund Hall. Aaron Eagle. Make it look good."

Chapter 27

Aaron paced the darkened corridor outside Fournier's library, wondering if he should break in and save Rosamund from that licentious old man. Sure, she was strong and healthy; Fournier was old and weak. But look at the way D'Alessandri and the other men had trailed her, wanted her, listened to her when Aaron knew she must be boring the shit out of them because they were too dumb to comprehend her conversation and the breadth of her knowledge.

Aaron knew her. Aaron understood her interests, because those were his interests, too. But had he ever really told her how fascinating he found her?

No, of course not. He hadn't realized she was going to run into Louis Fournier.

She wouldn't bore Fournier; Fournier would actually be interested in what she had to say, and Aaron knew how seductive a smidgen of knowledge and a little true interest could be to his librarian. Not to men-

tion Fournier had that reputation as being irresistible
to women, even women who should know better, even
women who were miles more worldly than Rosamund,
even women who were wealthy in their own right.

Aaron should break in. He should.

But if Rosamund was actually reading the journal of the prophetess of Casablanca, she would be
furious at him for interrupting. And if he suddenly
materialized in the library, he'd be busted, not only
with Fournier and the rest of the art world, but with
Rosamund.

She didn't believe in the Chosen Ones. She insisted
they could not exist, probably because, for whatever
reason, her old man had been so adamantly against the
possibility of the paranormal. So in New York, at Irving's, she'd been oblivious to the proof that had been
right before her face. And when she found out Aaron
was a member of that all-too-exclusive group . . . well.
He feared she wasn't going to take it well.

No. He had to trust her to do her work, and he had
to do his. When working a house, he always made sure
to discover an alternate escape route . . . just in case
things went sour.

He glanced toward the velvet rope that marked the
boundary between the ballroom, with its music and fri-
volity, and Fournier's world, quiet, dark and elegant.
The goon who guarded the boundary stood placidly,
seemingly without a thought in his well-muscled head.
Yet Aaron wasn't dumb enough to believe that Fournier
employed anyone who wasn't fast on his feet and de-
ceptively intelligent. Casually he wandered close, and
when the cruel little eyes had fixed themselves on him,

he looked at the goon's name tag and asked, "Marcus, is there a bathroom somewhere back here?"

"Sure. Right in there." Marcus nodded toward a door down the corridor.

Aaron headed toward it, counting doors as he walked, glancing inside the rooms, figuring which passages led out and which passages led deeper into the château. If this place was like most European noble homes, it was a rabbit warren of rooms. That could be an advantage or a disadvantage; it all depended on him.

The bathroom was a very nice powder room, windowless, and apparently without any survey equipment.

Aaron didn't believe that for a minute.

He used the facilities, washed his hands; then for the benefit of whoever was watching, he pressed on the bruises on his face and winced. Then he fussed with his hair.

There was something about a man fussing with his hair that made him appear harmless, and Aaron very badly wanted to appear harmless.

When he had finished, he walked out and back to the goon. "Marcus, is there somewhere I can sit and wait until Fournier comes out with my girlfriend?"

"Let me find out." Marcus opened the narrow door behind him and asked, "Is there somewhere the guy with the pretty hair can wait until Mr. Fournier is done with his girlfriend?"

Aaron had just learned two things: There was video in the bathroom, and he wanted to kick Marcus until he screamed like a little girl. But that would get Aaron thrown out onto the street or into the gutter or, if the rumors were true, into the deepest coalpit in Europe.

So instead he slipped past the goon and into the security room.

"Hey!" Marcus grabbed for his arm and should have had it, but Aaron tried a trick—he let his flesh dissolve so the goon's hand passed right through it.

Usually that maneuver didn't work worth a damn. Tonight, it worked like a dream. Something was happening to him since he'd met Rosamund, something powerful and pervasive. He was gaining perfect control over his gift.

Inside the narrow room, two uniformed security pinheads sat in front of a bank of monitors. Each monitor scanned a corridor or a room; each was carefully labeled.

Marcus made another grab for Aaron; this time Aaron caught the guard's hand and broke his finger. Because it wouldn't be wise to do that fade trick too often. Someone might notice. And to pay him back for that jibe about Rosamund.

To Aaron's intense enjoyment, Marcus did indeed scream like a little girl. Lifting his hand, he looked at the broken joint incredulously. "You American pig. I'm going to throw you so far out of here, you'll bounce like a rubber ball."

Without looking away from the wall of monitors before him, Pinhead Number One said, "Let him stay. If he's planning on robbing Mr. Fournier, he might as well see what he's up against."

"I'm not on the list of guests who are thieves, am I?" Aaron asked mildly.

"You look like a guy who has aspirations."

That was not an answer.

Pinhead Number One glanced at Marcus. "Get out. Man the rope."

With a resentful glance at Aaron, the guard took his crooked finger out and shut the door behind him.

"Not much of a fighter," Aaron observed.

"That's why he's in charge of the rope. We don't need much there except for the ability to string words together and if necessary, mix it up with a few drunk guests," Pinhead Number One said.

The château's floor plan was on one big monitor on the wall. Aaron moved closer and stared. The ballroom was full of red dots that moved—the guests.

"Infrared?" Aaron asked.

"That's right." Pinhead Number One was apparently the chatty one.

Pinhead Number Two didn't move, didn't speak; yet somehow he seemed aware, like a crocodile waiting for his victim to move close.

As Aaron walked to the wall of room monitors, he gave Number Two a wide berth.

One guest had wandered into the upstairs, tripping a silent alarm. Pinhead Number One spoke into a microphone. "Remove Mr. Wilson." As Aaron watched, a uniformed security pinhead walked out of a bedroom, apprehended Mr. Wilson, and after a brief scuffle, escorted him out the back door and to his car.

"Reporter. He thought we didn't know. But we know everything." Pinhead Number Two turned his reptilian head and looked at Aaron, his cold eyes satisfied with his demonstration. "He could have stayed if he had behaved." Still staring at Aaron, he spoke into the microphone. "Escort the lady with Mr. Wilson to their car."

On the floor of the ballroom, two men converged on a well-dressed woman holding an animated conversation with the French president. A few words from the guards and she was gone.

"Very efficient," Aaron approved blandly. "Every room is monitored?"

"Every room," the pinheads confirmed in unison.

"Not Mr. Fournier's private library." Because Aaron had examined each monitor, looking for a glimpse of Fournier and Rosamund, but he saw nothing.

"It is, most carefully, but not when Mr. Fournier is inside. He prefers not to be observed with his . . . books." The reptilian head turned toward Aaron again, and its tongue flickered out.

Shit. The guy was gay. Not like Philippe his fashion designer was gay, but I'm-the-head-prisoner-and-I'm-going-to-make-you-my-bitch gay.

Dangerous. This room and these men were very dangerous.

But it was too damned late to worry about that. For now, he could only pretend to be oblivious. "The bathrooms are monitored?"

"*Every* room," Pinhead Number One reiterated.

Mentally Aaron counted up the doors down the corridor. Maybe every room, but not every space. One door was unaccounted for. Fournier's private can? A closet? A passage out? A stairway down? Or up? Aaron intended to find out.

"Thanks, guys, I appreciate the tour. It's boring out there in the hall waiting for Dr. Hall to finish translating for Mr. Fournier." Aaron eased toward the door, careful not to make eye contact with the crocodile, not to make any sudden moves. "I'll see you around."

"Every time you piss," said Pinhead Number Two.

Aaron flinched. "Yeah." He cast one more glance at the screen that monitored the corridor outside Fournier's private library—still empty—opened the door and headed out.

He was safer with an angry, broken Marcus than with the crocodile.

Chapter 28

Rosamund splashed water on her face, dried it, and stepped briskly out of the restroom. "All right. May I see the prophetess journal"

"Direct and to the point." Louis's sharp gaze may have recognized the signs of tears but, wise man, he didn't address the issue.

"I need to translate the text. Time is not on our side." Aaron was probably pacing the corridor, and if he decided to try to break in here, he would certainly be arrested, possibly electrocuted. "May I see it now?"

"Of course." Louis offered gloves, then removed the journal from an unlocked display case—a sign of its lesser value. He brought it to the table and offered it without any obvious worry as to its frailty. "It was found recently in a box in the attic of a private home in Paris. It's in very good condition."

The book was a slim volume of no more than two

dozen pages, bound in leather richly decorated with African tribal symbols etched in gold, and until the moment she recognized them, she hadn't truly dared believe they had finally found Sacmis's journal.

But she knew these symbols, had come in contact with them on an African safari she'd taken with her parents, and now she traced them with her gloved fingertip. "No wonder the family hid it in their attic. These are not praises or good wishes."

"You know what they say?"

"The prophetess put a hex on those who sold her, on those who kept her in slavery, and on all those who hold the spirit of her words." Rosamund looked at the older man. "If you believe in curses, you might want to unload this."

"I don't." Then he laughed. "Shall I give it to *you*?"

She drew back, instinctively repulsed. "No!"

"Why, Dr. Hall, it would appear *you* believe in curses." He leaned forward, his gaze fixed to hers.

"Coincidence, my father said, but lately . . ." Lately, so many odd things had happened, she no longer believed the world was safe, easily explained, and logical. "Lately, I have doubts."

"Are you speaking of your mother's death?"

Jolted by how much Louis knew, she shrugged and nodded. "And my father's."

"Another mysterious death."

"Yes, and I fear—" She stopped. "Do you believe that someone could be bad luck?"

"No. I've seen people who constantly fall down stairs or off curbs, but they're merely clumsy. I've seen people who fail at their endeavors time after time, but they're either careless or gamblers who play regardless of the odds. Believe me, you make your own luck, good or bad."

"I suppose you're right. To believe otherwise is superstition."

"And your father taught you to despise superstition."

She froze, and tried to remember if she'd told him that. But no. She hadn't. So how had he known such a trivial detail?

Louis leaned back and sighed. "I should not have pried into your life. I see that now. But I assure you, I meant nothing by it. I had to know that you were genuine before I let you into my library, and more important, I am old. I haven't the time to get to know someone at a leisurely pace."

She tested the thick paper and examined the binding. "But to gobble up all the knowledge about another person—that removes the pleasure of a growing friendship."

"You seem so young and fresh, almost childlike in your enthusiasm, yet in your way, you're wiser than many an old man." He grimaced. "You're right. In addition, I have an unfair advantage over you, and it makes you uneasy. I wouldn't wish that to come between us. I believe we *can* be friends."

Louis knew more about her than any person alive . . . except Aaron, and she'd been telling him stuff because he'd acted interested. And why? Why would he suddenly be interested when no other man had ever bothered?

For her linguistic skills, of course. But what was so

important about this prophecy that he needed to be nice to her?

She glanced at her purse, wondering if Lance had texted her back yet, then looked up into Louis's eyes. "I'd like to be friends. In fact, I think we already are."

"Good." He sounded brisk as he opened the book for her. "Now—can you comprehend any of the script?"

"It's very odd—part tribal, part hieroglyphics." Placing the book on the table beneath the light, she turned the pages slowly, picking out a phrase here, a word there, but finding the text, for the most part, disappointingly indecipherable. "I think this is derived from an ancient language that has completely died off."

"Yes, so my people say."

Excitement began to bubble in her. "But perhaps there is a way to read this." She reached for her purse. "If you would allow me?"

"Of course."

She pulled out the reading glass Irving had given her, and stroked it for the pure sensual pleasure of its touch. "This supposedly translates any text into a readable script. I know it sounds too good to be true, but it can be effective."

The rounded dome glowed with all the colors of the rainbow; the surface felt slick and surprisingly warm, as if it had been sitting in the sun, and the flat bottom was perfectly smooth.

Louis started as if he'd been stuck with a needle. "Where did you get that?"

His tone contained such suppressed excitement, she looked at the old man. His eyes sparkled; his expression was rapt. "From Irving Shea of New York City. Do you know him?"

"He has a reputation among collectors." Louis reached out a hand as if in longing, then yanked it back. "I see that it's true."

"Yes, his collection is fascinating. He called this Bala's Glass—"

"Bala's *Glass*? Really?"

She placed the flat side over the lettering on the page. "It's reputed to translate the most indecipherable text. . . ." She looked up sheepishly. "I suppose that's absurd, that there's some trick to it. This glass would have to be magical to do that, wouldn't it?"

"If you believe in curses, then you can believe in magic," Louis said.

She stirred uncomfortably. She didn't want to believe in curses or magic, for if she did, the world became a much more perilous place, where not even the library was safe. "I've carried the glass with me, but until now, I haven't come upon anything I couldn't translate. I'm fascinated to see if this works." She leaned over and stared through the glass. Nothing happened, and she sighed with disappointment. "Of course, it is a hoax. It doesn't work."

"Don't give up yet," Louis urged.

As he spoke, the colors of the glass picked up the symbols and rearranged them. Bit by bit, she began to comprehend, and in a soft, slow voice, she read, "'I, Sacmis, descendant of Isis, prophetess to the great/Do wish to write of the visions I have seen/And the tragedy I foretell. . . .'"

Louis rolled a chair close to Rosamund and urged

her to sit down, then seated himself beside her. "May I see through the reading glass?"

She turned the book toward him, and he stared at the page, glancing between the bare, unreadable script and the cogent writing beneath the dome. "I've never seen anything like this. This manuscript has baffled the best translators in the world, and with the help of Bala's Glass, even I can read it."

"Can you? I am so glad that it's not just me."

"Bala's Glass chooses its friends."

"If you believe an inanimate object can make choices." She laughed. "I suspect the answer is somewhat easier than that. Reading is clarified through the glass, but only for someone who is trained in linguistics like you or me."

"My dear." He placed his fingers over hers. "I am barely literate even in French."

She looked up, startled.

He waved a hand around at his magnificent library. "Why else would I worship at the altar of so many great works of the ages?"

"Oh." That made sense. "But how do you run your businesses?"

"I hire the best, I put the fear of God in them, and usually, they don't betray me. It does not end well for those who do. I can smell a lie a mile away." For the first time, he looked cold and ruthless.

This was the man about whom Aaron had warned her.

Yet she liked him. She wasn't sure she believed him about his literate abilities, but she recognized a kindred spirit, a man who loved the learning imprisoned in the stones and the manuscripts of the past.

Then Louis's face again assumed its curiosity. He returned the book to her and said eagerly, "Go on. What else did she say?"

"'The traders who sold me, the family who bought me/They will live to suffer/As their children die before their eyes/Boils cover their bodies in seeping agony/And all their worldly gold is lost....'" Rosamund stopped, and swallowed in consternation. "She's almost biblical in her desire for vengeance."

"Perhaps the curse is worth worrying about, heh?" Louis might have been joking. But perhaps not.

Rosamund returned to the manuscript. She hurried through it, reading aloud the prophetess's praise for herself and predictions of doom for any who had displeased her. At one point, Rosamund interrupted herself. "It might behoove you to discover how much of this came true. In Casablanca, people didn't want to talk about her, or even acknowledge she had been there . . . not even for profit."

For the first time, Louis appeared to be uncomfortable with his purchase. "There are other collectors who would like this book. Perhaps I *will* sell it," he conceded.

Finally, on the last page, Rosamund read, "'I go now from this Casablanca/To this place of Paris to be a gift to the queen Antoinette, wife of the king Louis/Yet already I see his death and hers, the downfall of his family, the delight of his nation.'" A chill went up Rosamund's spine, and she stopped. "She did foresee the French Revolution. And she wasn't even in France yet."

Louis was leaning back in his chair, arms crossed

over his chest, listening with his eyes half closed. "I think you may have to cease doubting and believe in magic."

She thought of Aaron, of her suspicions, and rubbed her hands up her arms.

"Is that all she has to say?"

"I wish," Rosamund muttered. " 'When the mothers rise to feed their children/Tear down the bastions of oppression/Sharp blades end all tyranny/Then will I go to the Sacred Cave/There to write my final prophecy/And pass into the gentle hands of the god of the blue-flamed eyes.' " Abruptly, her revulsion became too much. She snatched the glass off the page and slammed the book shut. "To the devil? She wants to go to *Satan*?"

" 'The god of the blue-flamed eyes,' " Louis repeated. "Yes, traditionally, that is the devil. After reading this diatribe, that can't surprise you." Picking up the book between two fingers, he carried it to the shelf from which he had retrieved it. "I changed my mind. I'm not going to sell it. It's going in the fire."

"Good." Rosamund cast an apprehensive glance at the manuscript, half worried it had heard and would take action.

Then she dropped her head into her hands.

This wasn't the end of the quest for the prophetess. She and Aaron would have to travel on, to the Sacred Cave where Sacmis had died, and see what they would find there. Rosamund knew she should be disappointed at this failure. She should be anxious to return to her job in the antiquities department of the library. But except for her desire to examine the stone

tablet left by her mother, she couldn't think of one reason to go back. She ought to want to see Lance again,
but instead, she couldn't wait to continue this adventure . . . with Aaron. Aaron. Handsome, knowledgeable, sexy Aaron with the great, dark eyes that saw
into her soul. Tough, adventurous, enforcer Aaron,
whom she loved with every fiber of her staid librarian body.

She was in such trouble.

And perhaps . . . he was, too?

Louis returned to her side. "Now. I have shown
you my library, believed I could trust you to keep
my treasures secret and safe. May I see your looking
glass?"

She hesitated. Irving had told her to keep it in her
possession. But Louis was right. He had trusted her
with so much. Surely she could trust him in return.

He put out his hand. His palm was pale with age,
deeply lined, and the old calluses had turned a trans-
parent yellow.

She slid the glass into his outstretched hand.

"I've dreamed about this my whole life. To hold
something that proves there is more to life than what
we see on this mortal plain." He cradled it, stroked it
with a look of amazement and exhilaration. "While in
India, I heard an obscure legend about a reading glass
that translates indecipherable texts, but it wasn't called
Bala's Glass. It was called Bala's *Stone*." He was very
intense.

She answered gently, "I suspect there are all kinds of
stones reputed to be formed from Bala's bones."

"Ah, but Bala's *Stone* holds the power of the gods

within, for it is not merely a gemstone, but a diamond of absolute purity."

He looked at her, waiting for her to come to some realization. . . .

"I already had this conversation with Irving Shea." She stated the obvious. "This isn't a diamond. Diamonds this large always have inclusions and defects. Diamonds are the hardest natural mineral in the world. This glass—stone—isn't cut into facets that sparkle, but rather is rounded and flattened. Do you know how hard it would be to shape a diamond of this size into a dome? Even with modern techniques, it would require other diamonds as polishing agents and years of work. If this was truly created before machinery, the polishing would take *centuries*."

"The legend declares that the king of the gods laid claim to the largest diamond created by Bala's bones, and pressed it and shaped it like clay until it imprisoned all the colors of the rainbow, then used it to learn to read the writings of the ancients."

"It's a legend. A very obscure legend." Louis had to be pulling her leg. He had to be.

But he looked so grave, so concerned. "Legends mask truths, and, my dear girl, there is one thing I know. In this world, throughout all eternity, when a man holds wealth and power, he can hire or intimidate or buy the best craftsmen to do whatever he desires. Case in point." Louis waved a revealing hand around at his exquisite library. "Face the facts, Rosamund. This is Bala's Stone, the largest uncut diamond in the world."

"It can't be. Irving just *handed* it to me." Panic stirred

in her. "If it was a diamond, it would be worth millions, and I've been carrying it in my *purse!*"

"The value of a diamond is influenced greatly by its history." Louis weighed it in his hand. "This one isn't famous among gem collectors, so I would estimate its street value at a hundred thousand a carat, and it's probably five hundred carats."

"That's five million dollars." Her voice was nothing but a dry croak.

His serious expression softened into a smile. "You forgot to carry a zero. It's fifty million dollars."

"No," she moaned.

"What worries me is that those who study the occult would kill for it." Louis pressed Bala's Stone back into her hand.

She put it carefully on the table.

"You don't need to worry about dropping it. The table would be dented, not the diamond."

She didn't care. She couldn't stand the thought of holding that thing. "What was Irving thinking?"

"I suppose he thought you would need it, and ignorance would provide protection. But should anyone recognize that as a diamond, and especially that diamond . . . I beg you, friend, to keep this magical thing secret."

"I'll leave it with you. It will be safe here."

"Yet I think you'll leave here and go to the Sacred Cave, and there you'll need it."

She chewed on her knuckles and stared at the stone. "Yes. I suppose. But I thought the Sacred Cave was in Central America. Surely Sacmis didn't go so far to . . . to write her final prophecy and die."

"In the literature of western Europe, the Sacred Cave is reputed to be in the French Alps near the village of Sacre Barbare."

"I suppose more than one culture could have imagined the idea of a Sacred Cave." Gingerly she picked up Bala's Stone, put it in her purse, and flipped the latch.

"Or . . . there is only one Sacred Cave that exists in specific places of power and sanctity."

"You're kidding." She laughed.

He shook his head. "The idea is espoused in the Seventh Gospel."

She sobered, and said slowly, "I suppose if you believe in a Sacred Cave where God or the devil reigns and the real world is only a dream, it could be anywhere, anytime."

"That's it." Louis put his hand on her shoulder. "You have a brilliant mind, but some figure of authority drew a line around it and told you never to think beyond. It's an artificial line, Rosamund, not a real boundary. Release yourself."

She stared at him, this old man born in the Paris gutters who had wrung his fortune from the bitch of Destiny, and his wisdom sank into her like a balm. "After my mother died, my father insisted I go to school, study hard, learn to be like . . . think like other people."

"He was a fool."

"He was afraid." Rosamund had never allowed herself to realize it before, but now the words had popped out and she knew it was the truth. "He was afraid that I would end up like my mother, killed by my passion for exploration and adventure."

She considered how much she had enjoyed this trip—exploring Casablanca, exploring Paris, bartering, eating, listening, reading. This whole quest had been a change from her stale life, glorious from the start. Even falling in love with Aaron, painful and stupid though she knew it to be, had touched off sparks in her soul that she had never imagined.

"My father passed his fear on to me." The child she had been had sought an explanation for her mother's death. She had learned the hard way that she could no longer run to her father for comfort or joy. Elijah Hall had changed toward her when her mother died, becoming cold and controlling, full of admonitions to stay safe. She absorbed his caution. She had come to see life as a risk. And she had come to the logical conclusions—her father no longer loved her because somehow, she was responsible for her mother's death.

Louis scrutinized her and the dawning of realization on her face. "Better to die free than to live in a cage."

And if she was responsible for her mother's death, was she not also responsible for her father's? Did everyone she loved have to die?

Here, in Louis's library, surrounded by the greatest works of the ages and sitting beside a man whose wisdom she had come to respect, she could see clearly. She might not know how or why they had died, but it wasn't her fault.

She had lived cautiously, in the cage Louis so cleverly saw she had built around herself.

From this moment, she would swing wide the cage door and embrace the world—and Aaron.

"You're right." She kissed Louis on the cheek. "You are my wise old man."

His face twisted as if she'd stuck a knife in his gut. "That is not the role I relish with a pretty girl. But with you, who have that young man waiting outside this door, I suppose it will have to do." Standing, he held out his hand. "Come on. Let's go relieve his worry."

Chapter 29

Rosamund was so excited, she almost danced out the door of the library.

Louis followed, holding her purse.

Aaron grabbed her—man, he was a grabby sort—held her before him and looked her over. "Are you all right?" His voice was deep, harsh, like a man under deep duress.

"Of course I am." She beamed. "And do you know why?"

Aaron glanced at Louis, hostility radiating from every line. "No. Why?"

"Because I found where we need to go next."

"Next." Aaron sagged. "I had hoped this was the end of the line."

"No. But it is the next to the last on the line. Sacmis left Paris and traveled to the small village of Sacre Barbare in the French Alps. Do you know why? Do you know what 'Sacre Barbare' means?"

"Sacred and . . . barbaric?"

"Roughly. And do you know what's there?" She couldn't wait for him to answer. "The Sacred Cave."

Aaron let go of her arms and stepped back. "The Sacred Cave. *What* Sacred Cave?"

"The one where Sacmis wrote out her final prophecy!"

Aaron looked between Rosamund and Louis. "The Sacred Cave is here. In France. In the Alps."

"According to the legend that Louis explained to me, the Sacred Cave is one place that exists in different locales that are specific to it. Sacre Barbare has always been an outlet to the Sacred Cave."

In the dim light here in the private corridor of Louis's home, with the noise of the party hushed by the walls that separated them from the people, the conversation, the music, Aaron looked almost pale to her. Probably he was distressed, as she had been, that she hadn't found the prophecy in Louis's book.

Hastily, she reassured him. "The Sacred Cave is where Sacmis went to die, so that *is* the prophecy we're looking for. I read it in a book. Her book." Taking his arm, she lowered her voice and looked at him meaningfully. "Bala's Glass helped me read it." Putting her finger on his lips, she shushed him. "I'll tell you about that later. But for right now, Louis has promised to help us."

"Why would Louis help us?" Aaron sounded so suspicious, she wanted to hit him.

So she did, a good hard punch on the arm. "Stop that! He's been wonderful. Haven't you, Louis?"

"I agree. I have." As he watched them, a cynical fold creased his cheek. "I'll arrange for you to take one of my cars into the mountains with all the equipment you will need to enter the Sacred Cave. I'll have it brought around to the north entrance for you. No, Mr. Eagle, don't thank me. It's my pleasure."

Aaron flushed, a deep red staining his cheeks and making him look every inch an American Indian warrior.

"Now about your clothes . . ." Louis ran his gaze over them both, and as he looked at Rosamund, his expression softened and grew avid.

She wanted to laugh. She could read Louis now. He was trying to annoy Aaron, pretending to be attracted to her.

From the expression on Aaron's face, he was succeeding.

Louis continued. "Sacre Barbare is very high, very windy, and cold even in the middle of summer. You'll need coats and boots. Come with me." He set off down the corridor, walking past the velvet rope without a glance at the ballroom buzzing with guests and music. He stopped at a closed door and, with a grand gesture, opened it. "This is the closet containing garments for my guests."

Rosamund peeked inside. The closet smelled of cedar and sizing. Coats and jackets hung on poles and lined the walls on either side. The shelves above were thick with gloves and hats. A chest of drawers was built into one wall, and a straight-backed wooden chair sat in the corner; boots and overshoes of every size and description were scattered on the floor around it.

"Mr. Eagle, you'll find many new down-filled jackets. Help yourself. Rosamund, my dear." Taking her hand, Louis smiled into her eyes. "Take your choice from among the furs. There's a particularly fine Russian sable that would contrast beautifully with your violet eyes."

Aghast, she pressed his fingers and answered firmly, "Thank you. You are so kind. But I can't wear fur."

For one moment, he looked startled. Then he sighed. "What a foolish old man I am. You are, of course, concerned for animal rights, and opposed to furs. Very well. Take one of the down-filled coats. And for both of you—hiking boots. The path to the cave is reputed to be challenging. I would not have you fall to your deaths, not when at last you're so close to your goal."

"Oh, me, too." Aaron couldn't have sounded more sarcastic.

For all the attention Louis paid to him, Aaron might not have existed. Taking Rosamund's hand, Louis held it warmly, lifted it to his lips, and kissed it. "If you were twenty years older, or I was forty years younger . . ."

She laughed, hugged him hard, caught his face between her hands, and kissed him on his wrinkled lips. "You are very sweet, and I love you dearly."

He sighed and handed her her purse. "Twenty years older," he muttered. "Forty years younger . . ."

She stood watching him as he turned away and headed for his library. "I think I made a wonderful new friend. He gave me his private phone number. He's going to visit me the next time he's in New York City. He is such a dear man," she said to Aaron.

"A dear man?" Aaron grabbed her hand. "A dear man?" He dragged her into the coat closet, slammed the door after them, and backed her up against the far wall. "Did that old lecher do something to you?"

"No! The old lecher is a sweetheart—which I can't say about you!" She struggled in his grasp.

He handled her all too easily, and his brown eyes blazed into hers. "What the hell does that mean?"

"It means I can't figure out . . . I just . . ." Doubt reared its ugly head. "Why are you interested in me?"

"Oh, honey. You can't be that innocent." He kissed her, a full-throttle kiss that took her from angry to passionate in a single leap.

She shouldn't be passionate with him. She'd already been passionate with him, and the experience had thrown her into a quicksand of worry that totally messed with her normal good sense. Usually she could focus on the task at hand, especially when she was thrown into a library composed of manuscripts and codices. Tonight she'd been in a library of *treasures*, and she hadn't been able to fully concentrate. Instead she'd cried in the lavatory for a love she believed to be futile. Impossible.

Then she remembered . . . *Better to die free than to live in a cage.*

"Right." She spoke to Louis, to her father, to the ghost of her former, repressed, librarian self.

Better to die free than to live in a cage.

Grabbing Aaron's lapels, she pulled him as close as she could and kissed him back, thrusting her tongue into his mouth.

He paused in astonishment; then his whole body hardened against hers. He held her against the wall and kissed her back. She could feel the passion in him gather strength, like a storm taking shape against the mountains. "You are in so much trouble," he muttered.

She pushed his coat off his shoulders, and declared, "I think so, too. But when I'm done with you, I won't be in trouble alone."

Chapter 30

Aaron took her purse and tossed it aside. He grabbed a handful of down coats off the rack and threw them to the floor.

A bed. He'd made them a bed.

Rosamund kicked off her shoes, peeled off her jacket, and used both her hands to unzip her skirt.

A deep indrawn breath from Aaron stopped her.

She looked up.

With her hands behind her, her pale breasts swelled above the pure white lace that skimmed her nipples. She inferred from his fixed stare and frozen stance he could see nothing else.

"That bra is all you had on under the jacket?" he asked.

"Philippe said otherwise I'd be hot." Apparently she *was* hot. Who knew? "Why?"

"I'm going to kill him." Aaron's voice was furious, guttural. "Or . . . no, I'm going to kill him."

"Do you . . . like this?" She waved a hand over the area covered with lace. From the way he was acting, she wasn't sure.

"Right now, all I want to do is push that bra out of the way, take your nipples in my mouth and make you crazy."

He did like it, and just talking about his reaction made her wet. "I'd like that."

"Rosamund." The way he looked at her, in absolute frustration, gave her a jolt of pleasure. The way he said her name, with absolute agony, brought a smile to her face.

Being with Aaron had fed her heretofore unsuspected capacity for cruelty.

She dropped her skirt and stepped out, then checked to see if the sight of her in that wretchedly uncomfortable thong and the frilly garter belt riveted him to the same degree.

She had never been confident in herself as a sexual creature. Men and makeup were always too much hassle, and the rewards, as far as she could tell, were ephemeral at best.

But seeing Aaron as he stood frozen in place, staring at her as if she were Little Red Riding Hood and he were the big bad wolf . . . well.

She leaned against the wall, put one hand behind her, and used the other to push the hair off her forehead.

Eating Little Red Riding Hood took on a whole new meaning. "Are you going to stand there all night?" she asked.

He took a breath, apparently the first one in quite a

while, and came to life. Grabbing a coat off the rack, he stuffed the crack under the door so no light could seep through. He placed the straight-backed chair under the door handle. "That'll keep the bastards out," he said with satisfaction, and with a flick of the switch, he turned off the lights.

She blinked as her eyes tried to adjust, but the dark was absolute. "What . . . ? Why did you . . . ?"

"There are security cameras all over this château."

"In here?" She looked around as if she could see an eye gleaming at her from some high corner.

"I scouted it out," he said, and she jumped.

He stood a lot closer than she expected.

He continued. "The guards don't have an eye in here, but I don't trust Louis Fournier any farther than I can throw him."

And while she couldn't see a thing, Aaron's hands landed unerringly on her cheeks. He removed her glasses and placed them . . . somewhere. On the shelf above them, she supposed.

"What we are doing is not for the entertainment of some lascivious old man. This is for us." Picking up one hand, then the other, Aaron kissed her fingers. "It is my privilege to be your lover."

"I like you, too," she blurted, and then wished she hadn't. Why couldn't she be as smooth, as sophisticated as he was? "Are we going to . . . I'd love to . . . now . . ."

"I swear to you, if the ice age comes and plows down this château, and we are the only two people left alive on earth, tonight we will finish this thing." It was as if he were merely a passionate voice and two hands that stroked her collarbones, her ribs, her stomach.

Blindly she put her hands out toward him . . . and touched bare skin. Warm, naked, smooth skin that heated under her touch. Her hands shyly wandered across his shoulders and lower, down his chest to his belly and around his hips. After he turned off the light he must have stripped completely.

It was worth noting that when he had a goal, he moved very quickly and with great certainty.

Somehow knowing that made her breath come more quickly.

She had thought the dark would lessen the experience of lovemaking, but the deprivation of sight made her more aware of the calluses on his hands, and the indefinable power that pulsed from him to surround her.

His hands slid up to hold her breasts. His fingers explored the dips and curves of the lace, never quite touching her bare skin. Her breasts swelled into his hands, her nipples tightened, and she gradually pulled him close so only an inch separated their bodies. The air grew heated between them, and the scent of his cloves and citrus soap filled her head, intoxicating her. His breath caressed her face. He kissed her mouth, warm and soft, filling her with the essence of sex and heat and Aaron.

In the silence of the closet, she could hear nothing but the beat of her own heart, and when he opened the clasp of her bra, the snap sounded like liberty. When without warning his lips swooped to suckle at her nipple, she hissed at the shock of his warm, wet tongue, the sharp edge of his teeth, the suction that fired her need and her passion. "Aaron." She supported herself against the wall.

His mouth moved to the other nipple.

"Aaron," she said again. She stroked his bottom, cheeks hollow and taut, then his thighs, athletic and sturdy.

His hand reached between her legs. His fingers pushed the thong aside and explored her, touching places only she—and he—had touched before.

She would do for him what he did for her.

She stroked his belly, taking pleasure in each muscular ripple. She cupped his testicles, marveling at the texture and the weight. Finally, as he stood frozen beneath her touch, she found his penis, silky, heated, with ridges and veins she wished she could see. He filled her hands, filled her fantasy of how he would ride her—with determination, and patience, and fire.

Taking her down to the floor, he rolled her under him. The down-filled coats crinkled beneath them. He pushed her panties down her legs, freed her from the garter belt and stockings. He opened her thighs, and kissed her as he had done in the limo—deeply, using his tongue to penetrate her body, rolling her clit between his lips like a piece of hard candy. The sensations she had experienced earlier with such caution and wonder hovered close to the surface, and having discovered them once, the ache of passion returned easily, bringing her heartbeat up, wringing small moans from her throat.

"Now . . . I'm going to satisfy you in a way no other

man could ever do." His low, husky, confident tone made her toes curl with anticipation.

Then somehow, everything changed.

He changed.

He was no longer a weight on her, no longer a mouth that tasted her, no longer hands that caressed her.

Instead, he was over her. He was around her. He kissed her lips, her throat, her fingers, her toes. His embrace was a breeze, stroking her belly, her shoulders, her thighs, her spine, so lightly that every nerve clenched in response. He molded her breasts, tasted her nipples, her navel, her clit. He brushed her hair away from her face and slid subtle fingers around the shell of her ear. Blindly she tried to grasp him, to hold him, but he was everywhere, and he was nowhere. He lifted her legs and slid between them, smooth as silk and warm as water, and as he did, sensation flowed along her bottom and between her buttocks, then surged into her passage as smoothly as a spring torrent. As the heat and strength of him touched the deepest part of her womb, she couldn't restrain her small cries of desperation and pleasure, nor the movements of her hips as her body demanded to be filled. He grew inside her, longer, thicker, stretching her, making her wild and damp with need. She pressed her hands behind her head and against the closet wall, in suspense, desperate, straining to have more—more heat, more passion, more . . . him.

"Rosamund." His voice sounded deep and rich in her ears. "Give yourself. Give everything. Move for me. Breathe for me. Be part of me . . . forever."

His urging was all she needed to push her over the

edge. Her blood thundered in her veins. Her orgasm caught her, lifted her, gasping, struggling, in anguish and in joy.

And suddenly, Aaron was there, a man's weight on top of her: muscles and sweat and need. He moved forcefully on her, thrusting deep, groaning with need, and through the glory of her orgasm, she felt the power and the pain of this man inside her. She cried out, startled, but he held her hips and moved her with him, and her next climax roared through her, sweeping away the last remnants of her innocence.

He groaned in magnificient agony, caught in the glory of her body, his body, clasped in the primitive embrace that welded them into one.

Wrapping her legs around him, she lifted herself, opened herself, gave herself to him in every way possible.

This was it. This was unity. This was love.

This was all she had ever dreamed of, hoped for, imagined.

As he finished, subsided, and slipped beside her to hold her in his arms, somewhere in the depths of the closet, her phone rang.

A text message.

He grew tense in her embrace. "What is it?"

Without a single thought, she lied. "It's my alarm. I can't figure out how to reset it."

He chuckled and relaxed. "I'll do it for you . . . later." He lightly kissed her forehead, her cheek, her lips.

"Much, much later," she murmured, and kissed him back.

Before she slipped into slumber, she thought about

Lance, and how unfair she had been to him, and that she would have to tell him the truth about loving Aaron.

But she would worry about that much, much later, too.

Because right now, all that mattered to her was Aaron. Being with Aaron. Holding Aaron. Loving Aaron.

Chapter 31

A aron and Rosamund slept, huddled together in a stack of coats in Louis Fournier's closet, and when Aaron woke, he smiled into the darkness. Perhaps this hadn't been the most elegant of lovemakings, and certainly it wasn't the most comfortable, but as long as he lived, he would treasure these moments with Rosamund. Here, in the deepest dark, he had become his other self, his dark mist. He had caressed her everywhere at once, given her pleasure inside and out, until the moment when his climax swept all control away, and he became a man once more.

Now he gently woke her. "Rosamund. We have to go."

She moaned and stretched as sensuously as a cat. She kissed his shoulders and murmured, "I just went to sleep."

"Two hours ago. It's past midnight. We need to go."

"No. Not yet. I want you again."

"You, my little virgin, are through for the evening." But he knew that in the dark, he wore a stupid grin. She was warm and satisfied, and he had done that. He had made her first time good. "Besides, we have a prophecy to chase."

"Oh. No. Darling." Her fingers slid through his hair at the back of his neck. "Another few hours won't hurt anything."

He helped her sit up. "We're not going to get another few hours in Louis Fournier's guest closet. Somebody's going to find us." Remembering Pinhead Number Two's reptilian looks provided Aaron with a shot of adrenaline. He covered her and stood up. "In fact, we're running on borrowed time now." He groped his way to the door. "Close your eyes. I'm going to turn on the light."

"Okay." She sounded sulky.

He flicked the switch and glanced her way. She was nothing but a tumble of carrot-colored hair peeking out of a pile of coats.

Good. She was concealed.

In a series of rapid forays through the chest of drawers, he found them both jeans, tops, and socks. He managed to locate a pair of boyleg panties he thought would fit her—although it went against his inclination to let her wear underwear at all—and after flipping through a bunch of bras and realizing he couldn't begin to guess what would be comfortable, he grabbed an exercise bra that involved no snaps or cups, just pure elastic that pulled over the head.

"What are you doing?" She peeked at him from beneath the coats.

"Being a guy. I mean, I understand about sizes, but how do you women know which bra to use when?" He tossed her the clothes. "Do you think you can dress without showing any skin?"

"Sure. It's like camping in Alaska. Duck under the covers and rumble around. It simply has to be done with care."

He dressed, found a pair of boots that fit and laced them on, and all the while he watched as the coats rose and fell, twisted and flipped, and when she rose, Rosamund had once more been transformed. No longer the prim librarian, no longer the oblivious man-trap, she was now Rosamund, the adventurer, and she fit this role as easily as the others. The first time he'd seen her, he'd placed her in the niche of a dreamer. Then he'd seen the sadness she used as a barrier between her and the world, and he wondered what had broken her spirit.

Now the sadness was vanquished; her face was alight with eagerness for life, with passion for him, with love as yet undeclared.

Helpless to stop himself, he strode across the closet and kissed her.

And when he did, the lights blinked out.

They pulled apart, startled.

"Did you do that?" she asked.

"No." More important, rich men like Fournier owned generators and power companies. They didn't have power outages, and he didn't like what this might portend.

"Stay here." As he walked to the door, his mind leaped from one scenario to another.

Fujimoto had found him.

Louis was playing games.

The closet was monitored by the Pinhead Security Team, and they were moving in for the kill.

The Others had tracked them down.

Shoving the coat away from the bottom of the door, he knelt and listened, straining to hear what was happening beyond the closet. He heard distant screams from the ballroom. Running feet. Men shouting.

"Oh, no." She had heard them, too.

"Rosamund, I don't care how, but find some boots that fit and a coat, and put them on." He knocked out orders like a general. "I'm going out to reconnoiter."

She comprehended the urgency in his voice all too well. They had lingered when they should have gone.

But God, how sweet this interlude had been.

She fumbled for her glasses, found them on a shelf above the coatrack and put them on, then groped her way toward the pile of shoes on the floor. "I'll find gloves and hats for us both, too. Did you find a coat?"

He didn't answer.

The lights blinked on again.

She glanced around. Stared.

He was gone.

"Aaron?" She hadn't heard him open the door and shut it behind him. Had she really been so focused on those boots? "Aaron . . ." Apparently he'd somehow slipped away.

Very well. She would wait for him, and question him later.

Meanwhile, the light made it easier to find her shoe size, and within a few minutes she was ready to go, and had put aside down-filled coats for them both. She found a travel pack, too, similar to the one she'd worn from New York to Casablanca and then to Paris, and she transferred Bala's Stone from her purse to the pack. She was strapping it around her waist when there was a light tap on the door.

She took a quick, frightened breath.

Aaron stepped in and shut the door behind him. She'd never seen him look so bleak, but before she could question him, he said in clipped tones, "We're going to make a run for the car Fournier left us. The house must be running on a generator, or maybe there's a fire somewhere, because the light out there is misty and dark."

"Okay. That's weird." She was referring to the fact that he wasn't telling her what they were screaming about out there.

Aaron misunderstood her. "The smoke or whatever it is makes it hard to see, and we want to get out as quickly as possible. Walk in front of me. Don't talk to anyone. The people are panicked—they won't notice us at all."

"I hope not." Something awful had happened, and Aaron wanted them out of here.

"We're heading for the north entrance. Remember, I'll be directly behind you." He smiled at her, but it was a lopsided smile that only slightly eased the severity of his expression. "Listen to my instructions, and we'll get through all right. Are you ready?"

"Yes." And scared, but now wasn't the time to admit it.

He stepped behind her. "Open the door now, and remember—walk steadily, don't talk to anyone, and don't look around at me."

She put her hand on the knob and opened the door. As soon as she did, it was exactly as he said. A mist covered her vision, and it was as if she were looking through a screen or walking through smoke.

Aaron spoke directly into her ear. "To the right."

It felt as if he was all around her, touching her everywhere as he had done when they made love. But now, he hurried her along as she walked down the corridor, away from the commotion in the ballroom. In grim silence, guards were running toward the noise. One guy, ugly and cold in a way that made the hair lift on her neck, walked along shouting, "Shut down the house. Shut down the house!" Guests had broken through the velvet rope, and were streaming away from the ballroom, babbling, "They say he's dead." "He is dead." "They're going to kill us all."

Rosamund walked more quickly.

Then, coming toward them, she saw Fujimoto Akihiro, flanked by four men who looked tough and fast.

She took a frightened breath.

Fujimoto's head turned. He stared right at them. Right through them.

She froze.

Aaron pushed her, and in a calm, quiet tone, he instructed, "Don't say anything. Just walk."

She stumbled along, watching Fujimoto, expecting at any moment to hear him shout and point, for the men around him to pull out guns and knives and kill Aaron.

But although Fujimoto's eyes narrowed as if trying to read in low light, he seemed not to see them at all. Finally he turned away, and in a rapid burst of Japanese and with a wide gesture, he sent his men fanning out toward the ballroom.

"Why . . . ? How . . . ?" She didn't understand. She and Aaron seemed to be invisible.

"It's hard to discern things in this light." Aaron's voice was soothing. "No one will see us. Now—turn here. We're going to go down those stairs."

She and Aaron reached the basement level without incident, and as Aaron promised, no one looked at them. No one noticed them at all.

"The servants' quarters," he said. "This is where it gets tricky. We have to go through the kitchen to get outside, but we don't want to call attention to ourselves. So wait for the door to open . . . Now!"

He pushed her in past the butler who rushed out, and then steered her around the caterers and waitstaff. Without warning, one of the cooks turned toward them, a bubbling pot in her hands. She bumped—into Aaron?—bounced away, and screamed. Backed away and screamed again.

Aaron hissed as if in pain.

But when Rosamund tried to turn and look, he whispered, "No. Keep walking. A few more minutes and we'll be outside."

The staff raced to the aid of the shrieking cook; they acted as if Aaron and Rosamund weren't even there.

"His ghost!" the cook screeched. "I saw the master's ghost!"

Rosamund didn't know how or why, but the woman behaved just as Fujimoto had—as if Aaron and Rosamund were invisible.

As they reached the door, Aaron spoke in her ear again. "Open it."

She did. Fresh night air washed around them. From somewhere in the front of the château, she heard sirens wailing.

Inside the kitchen, the cook's screaming redoubled, and other voices joined hers.

Aaron paid no attention. "The car is right outside. Just go up the stairs and we're there."

The BMW M6 coupe was small and fast, and waiting with the keys on the console. Aaron opened the passenger door for her, then ran around and entered by the driver's door. "Put on your seat belt," he said, and started the car. The engine roared to life.

He put the gas pedal to the floor.

The Beemer spit gravel. The tires gripped the road. He whipped down the service drive like a bat out of hell, ending up on a narrow road that took them north and east.

When she knew they had escaped, and the road to the Alps stretched before them, she turned to Aaron and said, "All right. Tell me now. Who's dead?"

"I'm sorry, Rosamund." Aaron placed a comforting hand on her shoulder. "Louis Fournier was found murdered in his private library, his skull smashed with a marble bookend."

Chapter 32

The narrow road wound through alpine passes blistered by winds. Aaron gripped the wheel, held the BMW steady, and wished he could assure Rosamund everything would be all right. But their escape from the château last night had rendered her silent and thoughtful. She was more determined than he had ever seen her, for the murder of Louis Fournier had again raised the barrier of sadness in her eyes.

She would find the Sacred Cave and read the prophetess's last words. Nothing Aaron said had changed her mind. As far as she was concerned, she owed it to her friend Louis.

They had driven all night on tiny, winding roads, and at last a small sign announced the crest of the pass. He steered around a corner, and saw it—the village of Sacre Barbare. A dozen small, quaint homes and businesses nestled into a valley surrounded by rocky peaks.

Deliberately, he broke the silence. "There it is."

She looked behind them, then looked ahead. "If we can get on the path right away, we'll be at the Sacred Cave before the sun sets."

"We should wait until morning." Or not go at all.

She looked at him. "I can't wait. Tomorrow might never come."

He hated that she was right. If they didn't get this prophecy, tomorrow *might* never come.

Since they had fled Fournier's, the wounds that had so miraculously healed now returned to pain Aaron full force. His bruises ached, his finger hurt, his ribs burned, the muscles of his thigh felt like hamburger that had been ground too long. Worse, as he and Rosamund made their escape through Fournier's kitchen, the silly cook had branded him with her pot of boiling water.

He was not so foolish as to disregard the ill omen, or imagine it was an accident that the burn on his arm smoldered like an ember of hell.

He parked the car on the outskirts of Sacre Barbare, but then neither of them moved. They sat there in silence until she heaved a sigh and put her hand on the door handle.

"Do you remember what my father texted me?" she asked.

Far too well. "Run."

"Do you know where he was going when he left me?"

"Into Guatemala, back to the cenote where your mother died."

"That's right. Do you know what the village where

we stayed was called?" When he shook his head, she said, "*Hogar Sagrado.*"

"Sacred Home," he translated. He followed her logic with no trouble. "You think the cenote was an entrance to the Sacred Cave?"

"I don't know." She stared out the windshield. "But I do think Father knew someone would come after me and once again, someone I loved would die."

She was taking responsibility for Fournier's death, and what was worse, it was possible she was right.

They'd seen Fujimoto and his henchmen at the party, but it seemed unlikely *he* would have the motivation to kill Fournier. No, he had been looking for Aaron. He had utilized the chaos surrounding Fournier's death to search the mansion.

So who *had* killed Fournier?

The Others had tried to capture Rosamund in New York, and been thwarted. They wanted her and the prophecy, or at least they wanted to be sure she didn't give the prophecy to the Chosen Ones. Somehow, the Others had followed them to Casablanca and tried to kill him, Rosamund's protector. Then, despite his best efforts at secrecy, they'd tailed them to Paris and killed the man who had helped Rosamund with her quest. How were the bastards finding them? When this was over, he swore he would find out.

"It's not that I think someone you love will die." Aaron chose his words carefully. "My fear is that you're the next victim."

"I don't care. It's not death that frightens me. It's being forever alone." She turned and looked at him, eyes shocked as if her own words had surprised her.

"We are all afraid of that."

"Yes, I suppose. But why does everyone I love die?" It was the cry of a seven-year-old girl who had lost her mother. Reaching across to him, she squeezed his arm. "For the love of God, Aaron, I need you to go with me to the Sacred Cave, and I know that you're strong and versed in mountain lore, but *be careful*." Then, avoiding his eyes, she opened the door and stepped out on the road.

Did she mean she loved him?

He stepped out of the car, too.

Or did she refer to their lovemaking last night?

He wanted to ask her, but she stood with her jaw clenched and her head high, and when he joined her she didn't wait, but headed into the village square.

He followed close on her heels.

Time had left this place behind. The houses were two stories, brightly decorated with gingerbread trim. Signs swung outside the doors of the pub, the *boulangerie*, the souvenir shop. "This looks like the Hollywood set for the filming of *Heidi*," Aaron said.

"Yes, except—where are the people?" Rosamund wondered.

As if to answer her question, a woman left the tiny shop holding a squat loaf of bread and a bottle of dark red wine, and walked toward them. She nodded to them pleasantly, and said, "*Bonjour. Je suis Dr. Servais. Puis-je vous aider?*"

Aaron put on his best smile and his best French, and said, "*Merci*, Dr. Servais. Could you tell us how to find the path to the Sacred Cave?"

The female's geniality vanished as if it had never been. In harshly accented English, she said, "I don't know how these rumors get started among you tourists. There is no such thing as this Sacred Cave. Go away!" She walked away, offense in every line of her dumpy figure.

"Wow. That didn't go well. Maybe you should let me try." Rosamund headed into the tap house.

Aaron followed, and as they entered, the aroma of bacon and garlic wafted past. Aaron had had nothing since the hors d'oeuvres the night before, and his stomach rumbled. "We need to eat."

"We don't have time!"

"Trust me." He took her arm. "An army doesn't march on an empty stomach. If we're going to climb to the Sacred Cave, we're going to have to eat."

She didn't argue more. She had to be hungry, too.

A burly man stood behind the tiny bar, serving a bowl of onion soup to one man, a glass of wine to his wife, while listening with obvious boredom to their quarrel. High on the wall in the corner, a television was turned on the news and muted, with a scrawl at the bottom to read the information. The proprietor's face lit up at the sight of Rosamund and Aaron, and eagerly he gestured toward a table.

They sat, ordered onion soup, bread, and two glasses of red wine, and when the proprietor put the food on the table, Rosamund smiled and in her halting French asked, "Monsieur, can you tell us how to find the Sacred Cave?"

The man's head jerked back as if Rosamund had slapped him. His lip curled in a sneer such as only a Frenchman can perform. "I can't understand you. Your French is execrable. Go to the next village. Perhaps they will understand you, you . . . Americans." Turning on one toe like a robust ballerina, he stormed back to the bar, where he leaned forward and hissed in French at his other customers.

Rosamund turned to Aaron. "Talk to him. Tell him—"

"It's not your accent." Aaron dipped his spoon into the soup and took a taste. It was perfect peasant fare— caramelized onions swimming in a beef broth with melted Gruyère cheese on the top. "They're not going to talk to us."

"But why? All we want—"

"Honey, all we want is to go to the place that made this village infamous." Picking up her spoon, he put it into her hand and made eating motions. "They're not going to tell us where that is. Whenever someone goes up there, they've got a disaster on their hands."

"How do you know that?" She put the first spoonful of soup in her mouth, and paused as if in worship, then got serious about eating.

Thank heavens, because they'd had disasters enough—he didn't need her to faint. "Because I've been in the Sacred Cave, and I've seen the death it deals out."

She stared at him, breathing hard. "That's ridiculous. It's not an entity. It's a cave, a physical formation in the earth with no personality, no feelings, no malice."

"Then why did Sacmis choose to come here to write her prophecy and die?" He tore the crusty bread apart.

"She was an ignorant savage." Crumbs flew as Rosamund devoured a piece.

He threw back his head and laughed. "As am I, my dear."

"I . . . I didn't mean . . ." She looked abashed and embarrassed.

"I know you didn't." Taking her hand, he held it for a moment, cherishing her very normalcy, and wishing she could stay like this forever. "I can lead you to the Sacred Cave."

She drew back. "You've never been here before."

"I can hear it calling me."

He could tell by the expression on her face she didn't believe him. But what she believed didn't matter. All his life, no matter where he was in the world, the siren call of the cave sang in his head, and here in the village of Sacre Barbare, the melody was louder, sweeter, more seductive.

It called him to his death.

"I suppose because of your years in the mountains, you know how to find your way. . . ." Her voice faded. She stared over his shoulder. Something had distracted her, and he turned to look where she looked.

Video was playing on the muted television, and there was Pinhead Number Two—the name listed was Joscelin Deschanel—staring at the camera, his small eyes deadly. As his lips moved, the text across the bottom read, *I saw this person hit Fournier with a bookend. He fell, his skull crushed. . . .*

A photo of Rosamund taken at the party flashed on-screen.

She dropped her spoon. It clattered on the table, bringing the attention of the customers and proprietor to them.

Thank heavens, because Aaron didn't need them looking at the television. With a smile, he called, "This soup is wonderful, but we have to get on our way." He put an exorbitant amount in euros on the table, rose, and took Rosamund's arm. "Come on. Let's get our coats and the caving gear."

They left the tap house and headed for the car.

In shock and horror, Rosamund said, "He said I did it. He said I smashed Louis's skull. Why would he say that?"

"Because he did it." Aaron put her in the car, got in the driver's seat, and headed out of the village. "Someone very powerful wanted Fournier dead, and he hired the right man to take care of the matter." He was sick at the thought. He and Rosamund had made love in a closet in Fournier's house while men hunted and killed. They had been as helpless as it was possible for two people to be, and if they'd been found . . . "If we had stayed, we'd be dead, too."

"I don't want to be accused of murder. How did all this happen?" She truly didn't understand.

"Because fate marches on, demanding we find our destinies." He parked the car at the base of a cliff and turned to her. "Me, I'm done resisting." He cupped her cheek and smiled. "Come on. I'll carry the coil of rope."

He had, of course, located the head of the path.

As they strapped on their gear, a flock of sheep came around the mountain and surrounded them. Blue dabs of paint colored their wool, identifying their owner, and a shepherd followed them, whistling sharply. When he caught sight of Aaron and Rosamund, he stopped and stared. "You can't park there," he said in perfect English.

Aaron looked around for a sign. "Why not? We're not in anyone's way."

"The path—it's unsafe. We don't let tourists go that direction." The shepherd was young, muscled, and he watched them with the kind of hostility usually reserved for muggers in Central Park.

"This is the way to the Sacred Cave, and we have business there," Rosamund said.

His antagonism grew. "We guard the Sacred Cave from half-wits."

"So this *is* the way." She nodded, pleased to have trapped him into a betrayal.

"Didn't you believe me?" Aaron wanted to laugh at the chagrin on the shepherd's face, and at Rosamund's satisfaction.

"I don't understand how you know," she said.

Aaron looked at the shepherd. "I know."

The shepherd ran toward one of his sheep as it teetered on the crest of a rocky incline. Waving his stick, he drove it back into the herd. Facing Aaron, he said, "Sheep are foolish. They dash toward a fall on the rocks and I drive them back. But sometimes they won't be stopped, and if they must die to be taught their lesson, then they die."

"Sometimes there's no choice but to take the fall," Aaron told him.

"There's always a choice," the shepherd answered.

"Sometimes the choice is between dying with honor, or living with shame." Aaron tightened his grip on the coil of rope he had slung over his shoulder.

Rosamund had been looking between them. Now she said, "You're not a sheep, and you are not going to die. I won't let you." She spoke intensely, staring into his eyes, like a kindergarten teacher with a recalcitrant boy.

"Believe me. It's not my intention," he assured her.

"Good. Now come on. We haven't got much time." She headed for the trail and began the climb.

Aaron saluted the shepherd.

The shepherd spit on the ground to indicate his disgust.

Aaron followed Rosamund.

At first, the path was wide and smooth, cut into the bones of the mountain. They walked through meadows of flowers and groves of trees that dappled the ground with shadow. The sun shone warm, a breeze blew softly, and here they didn't need their heavy down coats, their caps, or their gloves.

Rosamund looked down at the village of Sacre Barbare. "It's pretty here. Peaceful."

The wound on Aaron's thigh was hot and infected. The burn on his arm throbbed more insistently. He slowed.

"What's wrong?" she asked.

"I need to rest for a moment." He leaned against a rock. "These mountains are like the Sawtooth Mountains where I lived when I was young. Yet they're not. The flowers are different. The rocks are different. The air is different. But I could live here. . . ." Except that the call of the cave was growing harsher, more insistent.

That was why he had finally run from the bleak life to which he had sentenced himself and into a life of luxury and elegance. If he had stayed, he would have eventually gone mad, and gone into the Sacred Cave. And he would never have come out.

"Come on. I'll help you." She put her hand under his arm.

He looked at her.

"Look. We haven't any time. You know we haven't. The French police are after me. Fujimoto would love to eliminate you. Irving Shea needs this prophecy ASAP—"

"I know. I know." He pushed himself up. "And you want to avenge Fournier's death."

"Yes," she said simply.

Rounding the corner, they stepped into the shadow of the mountain. Warmth faded. Their view of the village vanished. The path fell away under their feet, dropping into an abyss a thousand feet deep.

"Oh, yeah," he said. "This is the way." As they inched their way up the mountain, the wind began to blow, softly at first, then harder, raking their exposed faces with cold so harsh Aaron's cheeks felt stiff and his lips cracked. They put on their coats, their hats, their gloves. Aaron helped Rosamund across the narrow places, gripping her wrist with both hands, knowing full well the mountain would toss her into the valley out of sheer spite and indifference.

The path spiraled down, then up, into a notch in the mountain.

By some freak of location, here the sun shone, warming the stones, and the angle of the mountain blocked the wind. The path was broad, with low boulders that rested against the side of the mountain, inviting the pilgrims to sit, to rest, to rethink . . . to turn back.

For around the corner, there it was—the entrance to the cave.

The small dark hole was exactly the same shape, the same size as the Sacred Cave in the mountains of his birth. He approached cautiously, listening to the whisper of the cave that had haunted his soul since the day he was born.

You are mine. You were born here, and you will die here.

He turned to Rosamund. "We need to go back."

"But we made it. We're here." She looked at the sky. "If we go in and find the prophecy right away, we can go back to Sacre Barbare and drive away before it gets dark."

"It's not that easy." Taking her hand, he dragged her away, around the corner to the single spot of sunshine. Here the wind whistled harmlessly past, but couldn't touch them, and he could hardly hear the summons of the cave.

Lifting her, he placed her on a sun-warmed boulder, then clambered after her. They sat, shoulder to shoulder, looking out over the Alps that climbed, one after the other, toward the sky, until on the farthest horizon they faded to blue and vanished like a dream.

"What is it?" she asked.

"The cave is dangerous." Vicious. Deadly. Cruel. He'd seen what the cave could do. He'd witnessed its vengeance, and now he feared . . . he feared for himself. He feared for her. Most of all, he feared what would happen if they didn't succeed, and that torment tore at him.

She, of course, settled into a lecture that told him everything she knew about caves. "Caves are dangerous, mostly because they're unregulated by any kind of international agency, which is surprising considering the number of caves scattered throughout the world and the injuries possible when exploring caves. The predominant rock that forms this area appears to be basalt, and very stable, so unless a tremor should disturb the earth, I think this will be a safe caving experience."

"No." He put his arm around her. "The Sacred Cave is dangerous because it chooses whom it wishes to enter and whom it wishes to keep out. It demands sacrifices and extracts payments. It is ancient. It is malevolent. It is—"

"Are you claustrophobic? Is that what this is about?" Her wide violet eyes were concerned for him.

Shaking his head, he tried to explain, knowing that she was anxious to go forward, to continue her adventure. She obviously believed if she did the right thing, her life would return to normal.

He knew nothing could ever be normal again. "You translated the journal of the prophetess how?"

"With Bala's Gl— Stone."

"And how does Bala's Stone work?" He answered for her. "It's an ancient magic. Just because you don't believe in it doesn't mean it's not true. You're a librarian who looks at the facts. So look at them now. Bala's Stone is real, and the Sacred Cave is sacred for a reason."

"My father would have told you that was nonsense." She lifted her hand when he would argue. "But even if it's not, even if the Sacred Cave is waiting to chomp us into bits, we need to try, because we need that prophecy."

She was right, and yet . . . the old fear cramped his stomach and turned his mouth dry. "Come back with me, down the mountain to the village, and we'll drink wine and have dinner, and later we'll make love."

"What if the police recognize us?"

He ignored her. "In the morning when the sun is high and reigning over the sky, we'll come back and do what has to be done."

"What if it rains?"

He had no answer.

"What if it snows? It feels cold enough to snow, even in August. What if we can't get up here again for days, and the time we lose enables the police to find me and take me away? What if Fujimoto finds you and kills us both?" She was relentless. "Right now, this is our chance, maybe our only chance, to read the final prophecy and do some good in the world. Aaron, let's not run away!"

Once again, she confounded him with her bravery and her good sense. Worse, she was right. They had to go on.

Besides, the cave wanted him. Only him. She would be safe.

"Kiss me once for luck," he said.

Sliding her arms around his shoulders, she kissed him so sweetly, so generously, he realized the truth.

He loved her. He had never loved before, but he did love her.

Perhaps, together, they could triumph.

Chapter 33

Rosamund blocked the entrance of the Sacred Cave, faced Aaron, and planted her feet. "I'm going in by myself."

"That's not possible." Here the wind blasted them, urging them toward the cave.

Lifting her fingers, she counted down the reasons why. "First—I'm not claustrophobic."

"Neither am I."

"I assumed—"

He grinned and crossed his arms. "After what we did in the closet, you assumed I was claustrophobic?"

Her face softened. "But there's a difference between a nice, safe closet and a spooky, bat-ridden cave."

"Trust me. There are no bats—bats aren't crazy enough to live in the Sacred Cave—and I'm not claustrophobic."

"All right. I believe you." She counted down another reason. "Second—my parents were all over the Petén in Mexico and Guatemala, in cenotes and caves, and

I grew up having cave safety drilled into me. I know what I'm doing."

"That is good to know."

"And if I'm reading you right, you avoid caves like the plague."

He shrugged and nodded.

"So you don't need a *man-chomping* cave. You could get hurt out of sheer ignorance of proper caving procedure."

"The cave is safe when it wants to be."

"You've never been here before and . . . oh, never mind." She lifted another finger. "Third—I don't believe the Sacred Cave can hurt me."

Capturing her hand, he folded it into a fist. "Perhaps the Sacred Cave doesn't care what you believe."

"Perhaps not, but for some reason you believe it has a vendetta against you. Maybe you're right. Maybe it wants to kill you. But it doesn't want to kill me. Consider this—if the Sacred Cave wants to murder you, and I'm with you, I'm going to be hurt in the fallout."

As her words hit home, he jerked and turned away.

She followed, knowing she had him. "So I'll go in alone, you can sit right here outside the entrance, and if I need you, I'll call. I promise."

A compromise. He could compromise. "I'll come with you into the cave, sit by the entrance, and if you need me, I can respond immediately." She started to argue, but he put his hand over her mouth. "Take it or leave it. I wait for you inside, or I go with you to find the prophecy."

She nodded.

He took his hand away, lightly kissed her lips; then

lying on his belly, he shoved the coil of rope forward and crawled into the cave.

As soon as his head breached the cave, that familiar sense of otherworldliness surrounded him.

It was exactly as he remembered it. Light leaked in behind him, and the Sacred Cave itself glowed with a diffused light that seeped from the stone. The walls were alive with cave drawings that worshipped the magic cave, words written in languages long vanished, and here and there, the desperate scratches made by a dying soul. The ceiling near the entrance was low, but gradually sloped up and back, extending into darkness. The floor sloped down and back, into the darkness at the center of the earth, or the home of the gods, or heaven, or hell. No one knew. No one who had followed the cave down had ever returned.

The fire pit was there, too, hollowed out of the hard rock.

His father, Cripple Eagle, would have scolded him for failing to bring wood to build a fire and appease the gods.

But Aaron knew the gods would not be appeased until his own blood stained the rocks.

Rosamund followed close on his heels. He heard the intake of her breath, the soft whisper of her voice. "This is magnificent. It is . . ." She searched for the word.

"Holy," he said.

"Yes."

Even through his sense of incipient disaster, he had to smile at the awe and excitement she wore so easily. There was nothing of artifice in Rosamund; she saw the cave, the writings, the light that came from some mysterious source, and she worshipped the sight.

If the cave was indeed sentient, it must bask in her admiration.

She walked toward the pictures of dancing antelope drawn in ocher on the wall. "I've never seen anything like this. In a *National Geographic* layout, of course, but not in real life. These must have been drawn forty thousand years ago."

"When the world was young," he said.

The cave was quiet. Waiting.

"The art close to the entrance is the oldest. The farther we go in the cave, the newer the work." Eyes glued to the walls, she walked along the smooth floor, heading for the back where the floor fell away into darkness.

"Rosamund."

She stopped and looked back inquiringly.

"Watch where you place your feet."

She glanced around, focused, and nodded. "Right."

"Look for the prophecy."

She swept the walls with her gaze, found what she was looking for, and knelt on the floor in front of a scrawl that extended for two lines, one on top of the other, for a six-foot length. "This is it." Brow furrowed, she studied the symbols.

As she did, a soft tremor shook the earth. The grinding of one rock against another made him look up toward the ceiling; sunshine now shone through jagged cracks above. His heart began a slow, deep thumping. "Did you feel that?"

"Yes. I'm sure it's fine," she said absently.

As if her words commanded it, the earth stilled.

In a voice he kept deliberately low and casual, he asked, "Can you read the prophecy?"

"No . . ."

"Use Bala's Stone."

She turned her head and looked at him, and he clearly saw the misery in her eyes. "I want to be able to read it myself."

"Because you want to *prove* it wasn't the stone that translated the symbols in her journal?"

A steady wind sprang up from nowhere, and went nowhere, ruffling Aaron's hair, then moving to Rosamund and brushing one lock from her shoulder.

The cave was taunting him. Mocking him. *Threatening her.*

The tension in him ratcheted up another notch. "We need to leave as quickly as possible. Please. Use the stone."

She stared again at the script, squinting, tilting her head, trying everything to force sense out of the prophecy. Just when he was ready to shout with frustration, she opened the travel pack at her waist and brought out the stone. The rock wall zigged and zagged, a natural surface that made her job difficult. She held the stone an inch above the plane where Sacmis had written her final words, and skimmed the script, right to left, then down to the next line, and right to left again.

She frowned. Shook her head. Did it again.

"What's wrong?" he asked. "If you still can't read it, it doesn't matter. You've tried your best, and it's time to leave."

"It's not that. I can read it. I can comprehend it perfectly." Rosamund stared at him with concern. "According to her writing, she knew we were coming after her. She speaks directly to us."

"What are you talking about?" He took two steps into the cave.

Rosamund read, " 'Greetings, woman of books and man of mist. . . .' " Rosamund faltered.

"That sounds like us, all right." Two more steps into the cave.

Rosamund kept her head turned away from him, and continued. " 'I foresaw the day you would come after me/Seeking knowledge.' "

"She saw a vision of us chasing her for her prophecy."

"That's what she says, but I can't believe . . ." Rosamund took a breath. " 'With my last breath/I led you astray/Clues placed like bread crumbs/In a trail that leads into the trap.' "

Two more steps. Danger humming in his ears. "Rosamund, let's go."

She didn't budge. " 'Who would do such a thing/in malice aforethought?/I, Sacmis, descendant of Isis, prophetess to the great/have done this/The Others are my brothers/The Others are my sisters/The battle is joined and we have won.' "

The trap set two hundred and fifty years ago had been sprung. "Rosamund. Leave. Now."

"I misread everything." Rosamund wrung her hands. "Sacmis says she's one of the Others, and every bit of research I've performed, every translation I have made, is wrong."

"Shit happens. Especially when we're dealing with

the Others." With all the emphasis of a man on the edge, he said, "Rosamund, we need to leave."

Impatient and upset, she raised her voice. "If you're afraid, Aaron, leave. I need to stay until I understand what's happening here. How could someone who lived two hundred and fifty years ago see us coming?"

"How can a cave, a hole in the earth, be sacred? How can it demand sacrifices, deem who could live or die?"

"It can't. It *doesn't!*" Rosamund came to her feet, fists clenched.

At last, at long last, he lost patience. "Yes . . . it . . . does. I was born in the Sacred Cave, abandoned by a mother who left me to die as the gods wished, but my foster father stole me away, and for that insolence he paid with his leg. The cave smashed it, trapping him, so he cut off his own leg with his knife."

Rosamund took a horrified breath.

Aaron didn't care about her horror. Not now. Not while he remembered. "I knew the story. I was raised on the story. But when I reached adolescence, I wanted to go to the Sacred Cave, to see the place where I had been born, to beg the gods to let me live a long and full life free from fear. My father warned me the gods were never lenient. But I was young. I was confident. I thought I could interfere in the eternal battle between good and evil, and escape unscathed." He took a harsh breath. "My father insisted on coming with me. I had to carry him most of the way. The cave—" Aaron waved a hand around. "This is the cave I saw that day. We burned new wood in the fire pit, sprinkled the logs with herbs and flowers, and I spoke to the cave, to the gods, whoever they were, telling them who I was and asking humbly for my life."

She watched him, violet eyes wary. "What happened?"

"The Sacred Cave doesn't give a damn about humble. It wants blood, and that day, it wanted mine. The cave creaked and groaned. My father told me to get out. But the rocks were falling all around me, and I couldn't make it to the entrance. I didn't see how either of us was going to survive. It was impossible to survive. But I wanted so badly to be out of that place, and then . . . I was. I didn't know how, but I was. I waited for him to follow. That was the first time that I . . . turned . . ."

"Turned what?"

He found himself staring at the spot where he had last seen his father, at the rocks still stained with his blood and brains.

Rosamund's insistent voice broke into his reverie. "Aaron? What happened to your father?"

"He couldn't follow me. A rock had fallen and smashed his head." In a rage of anguish at the memory, Aaron grasped the neck of his shirt and tore the material. "He rescued me. He raised me. He loved me. And I killed him."

"You didn't kill him. The cave killed him." She realized what she'd said, and caught herself. "I mean, if the Sacred Cave could be said to kill someone, that killed him."

"I wandered the forest for years afterward, alone, surviving the most bitter of winters, the briefest of summers. I hunted. I planted. I starved. I was looking for death, but no matter how hard I looked, I never went back to the Sacred Cave." He looked around. "And yet . . . here I am. I should have known—I could never fight destiny."

"But that story doesn't make sense," she said gently. "Why would the cave want your blood? Why wouldn't it be satisfied with the sacrifice of your father?"

"Because of this." Stripping his shirt off his shoulders, Aaron turned and bared his back to her. He knew what she saw—a tattoolike mark on his back that looked like two crumpled wings on either side of his spine. "I was abandoned by my mother, and when that happened, I was given this mark, and a gift." Pulling his torn shirt back on, he faced her and told her the truth. "I am one of the Abandoned Ones."

At last, he had shocked her into listening, into the first stages of belief.

But still she fought.

She shook her head in denial. She backed away from him. Backed away as if he were something unclean. "No. That's a myth."

Relentlessly, he followed, determined to make her see the truth at last. "More than that, I am one of the Chosen Ones."

A small rock gave way beneath her foot. She stumbled and sat down hard.

"If the cave claims me, my power is part of it forever," he said.

Still she shook her head. "That's impossible. My father didn't believe in stories about the Abandoned Ones."

"Didn't he? Didn't he really? I think he did. I think he more than believed. I think he was married to one of the Abandoned Ones."

"What do you mean?" She sprang onto her knees. "What are you saying?"

"You don't know your maternal grandparents, do you?"

"My mother was an orphan. So what?" Rosamund looked up at him, her violet eyes half bewildered, half enraged, on the verge of a revelation she didn't want to face.

"She had tattoos on her fingers. She didn't know who her parents were. She was gifted, making leaps in the translation of ancient languages that were almost magical." Like a sprinter in a race, Aaron crouched on the balls of his feet with his fingers touching the rocky floor. He looked into her eyes. "Her parents abandoned her as my parents abandoned me, and at that moment, she was given a gift . . . the kind of gift that could get her killed."

"She was *not* one of the Chosen Ones." Rosamund rose to her feet, and her eyes shone hot beneath her glasses.

"No. Not that. But she was pursuing a prophecy, died unexpectedly, and whatever she had learned died with her."

"I don't care. I don't believe it." Rosamund pushed her hair back and glared. "I don't know why you're lying to me. I don't know why you're condemning yourself. Father said it would be dangerous if I believed any of those wild legends."

"You are ignoring the truth with all your might." Aaron waved a hand toward the west, toward New York. "Who do you think the people at Irving's house are? What do you think is happening, with people chasing us, men being murdered in our wake, and a trail of bloody prophecies before us?" Striding forward, he picked up Bala's Stone and shoved it under her nose. "This is a diamond, and it is magic. I am one of the Chosen Ones, and I have a gift."

"You're an enforcer. You force people to do what you want."

"No. I'm a thief, because I can do this." As she watched, he dissolved into his other self, into a dark mist that blended into the shadows.

She stood frozen, staring at the place he had been.

He moved behind her, touched her hair. "I'm here," he said.

She whirled in a circle, hands outstretched. "Where?"

He moved in front of her, touched her cheek. "Here."

"Aaron? Where are you?" Her voice shook. Tears rose in her eyes. "You're frightening me."

He took his human form again. "Good. You should be frightened. I am Chosen, you and I are in more danger than you can possibly imagine, and we *need to get out of this cave.*" Grabbing her wrist, he tried to drag her toward the entrance.

She fought him, wrestled herself free, and cried hotly, "So you're one of *them.* You found me in the library, not by accident, I'm sure. You lured me to Irving's mansion, you traveled the world with me, and you made love to me. You made love to me as a dark mist! Didn't you?"

"Yes! And my dear, I didn't need to see you to know you enjoyed it!" He caught her arms. "Mine. I made you mine, and more important—you gave yourself to me, and you made me yours."

She yielded. Just for a moment, but she did yield, softening against him, and he thought he'd won. Then that logical brain kicked in, backed by her father's strictures and her father's last warning, and she pushed herself away. "How do I know you're one of the good guys? How do I know you're Chosen?"

He couldn't believe it. He couldn't believe her. He felt as if she had stabbed him through the heart. After all they'd said and not said, all they'd done and not done—and she doubted him? "You don't believe me? You think I'm lying to you? That I'm one of the Others?"

"You've convinced me. My mother died because of her work with prophecies. Probably my father died because of that, too, and he warned me. Texted me. *Run.*" Her pale skin flushed with fury. "Yet you want me to trust you? After you've lied to me about who you are?"

She was furious? Well, so was he. He had given her himself, his true self, and she rejected him. He wrapped his arm around her waist, pulled her close, and bent her backward. "I'll leave, if that is what you truly want. But you'll never forget me. Never." And he kissed her. Kissed her in despair, in torment, because the woman he loved didn't love him back, and never again in this world or the next would he have a chance to make her feel the truth and believe in him.

"Damn you, Rosamund Hall. Damn you for doing this to me." He strode toward the entrance, intent on one thing, getting out of here and leaving Rosamund to her research and her prophecies and the safety of knowing he was gone and she could be alone.

Beneath his feet, the ground trembled. The movement intensified, deepened, made the earth groan in anguish.

He turned, and as he watched, the ceiling shivered and began to collapse over Rosamund.

Then he knew the truth.

If the Sacred Cave could not have him, it would take his love.

Chapter 34

———⟨⟨⟨⟨⟩⟩⟩⟩———

Aaron threw himself at Rosamund.

She yelped in surprise.

He knocked her off her feet, slammed her to the ground. Her head smacked the rocky floor. She saw stars, and when she cleared her head, his body was gone and she was again seeing through a dark mist. *Through* Aaron. He had wrapped himself around her to hide her while they escaped Fournier's mansion.

Now he wrapped himself around her to protect her.

Rocks as big as basketballs slammed down, aimed for her head, her chest, her hips.

She threw her arms over her face.

She heard Aaron grunt. She felt the compression as the rocks struck him. But nothing touched her. The stones hit the mist that was Aaron and rolled away.

His voice sounded in her ear. "All right?"

"Yes. Aaron, I—"

But before she could apologize, tell him the truth,

tell him she loved him, she heard a strident scraping, like the sound of gigantic fingernails on a cosmic blackboard.

Aaron's voice was tight with pain. "Brace yourself."

She looked up—and screamed.

With a rain of stones and a roar, the ceiling of the Sacred Cave collapsed.

She must have blacked out, because when she came to consciousness, she heard nothing but a deadly quiet, and the sound of something dripping beside her ear.

Her eyes sprang open.

The ceiling was gone. The front wall was gone. The late-afternoon sun streamed in, illuminating the dancing molecules of dust.

Aaron was in human form again, sprawled on top of her.

"Aaron. Come on." In a panic to get away, she shook him. "We have to get out of here."

He didn't move.

"It's dangerous. We have to get out of here." She shook him again.

Still he didn't move.

Again something dripped beside her ear.

She pushed her glasses up on her nose. She turned her head and looked.

Blood pooled on the floor, and as she watched, another dark red drop splashed into the puddle.

Then she knew. She knew. *She knew.*

"No." Grasping Aaron's shoulders, she rolled him

off of her, onto his back, onto the rocks. "No. Aaron. No."

Beneath the smears of blood, his tanned, proud, Indian face was pale as parchment. His eyes were half closed. His head lolled on his neck.

She pressed her fingers to his neck over his carotid artery, trying to find a pulse.

Nothing.

She picked up his wrist.

No pulse.

Putting her head onto his chest, she listened for his heart.

No sound at all.

"Not you. Not you. Please, I never meant for you to become one of my . . . I'm sorry." She stroked his hair back from his face. "God, don't let this be true."

Desperate and determined, she dragged him into the one place where rocks had not landed—in the spot where she had lain, where he had protected her. She cleared his air passage, then began CPR, compressing his chest, blowing in his mouth, compressing his chest, blowing in his mouth. . . .

Panting from the effort of slamming her fist to his chest, she kept doing the CPR long past the time she knew the truth.

He smelled like Aaron. He looked like Aaron.

But the flavor of his blood touched her lips, and she knew this wasn't Aaron.

Aaron was gone.

This couldn't be true. It could not be true.

She collapsed onto the floor beside him. She put her forehead onto his chest. And tried, oh God, tried to hold off the emptiness she knew would claw itself up from inside her, expand, take her over and leave her with . . . nothing. Because Aaron was gone. *Gone*.

The last thing she'd done was fight with Aaron, yell at Aaron, reject Aaron for what he was. She had told him to go away, and now the man she loved was dead.

They had traveled across the world, chasing a prophecy she had cheerfully assumed she would find. But instead she had failed miserably, and the man she loved was dead.

She would have to go back to New York, tell Aaron's friends the truth, that Aaron had flung himself on her to protect her, and for that brave deed, the man she loved was dead.

Lifting her head, she looked into his face, stroked his hair off his forehead, kissed his lips. "Please," she whispered. "Don't leave me."

The cave creaked ominously.

But she wasn't afraid. She was mad. "You stupid gods. You are so proud of your stupid Sacred Cave. You think this is about you." She stood and lifted her fists toward the blue sky where the rock ceiling had once been. "A sacrifice? You wanted a sacrifice? Well, you can't have him!"

The cave groaned again, the sound coming from the back where the floor sloped down into the hole that funneled deep into the earth.

"No. I will have his body, at least." Grabbing Aaron under his arms, she strained with all her might. He moved a few inches, the rubble from the collapse rolling under his prostrate body. With another heave, she turned him, dragged him around the boulders, through the place where the entrance had been, and out onto the path.

There she placed him in the warmth and let the sunshine bathe his proud, high cheekbones, narrow nose, and broad, stubborn chin. Even battered as he was, he was handsome. He had been strong and brave, with hair so black it shone with blue light. He had been an Indian warrior, knowing full well the Sacred Cave and all its cruelties, yet returning to do what had to be done for the Chosen Ones, and for her.

Kneeling next to him, she gathered him into her arms and held him. Just held him, and pretended he was still with her. The old grief at her mother's death, and the new grief at her father's, came at her in a wave. Her anger at her father built on that; if he had told her the truth, she wouldn't have been caught unprepared. She wouldn't have been naïve.

At the same time . . . her father had always known what predators stalked them, and everything he'd done—the way he'd raised her, the cool discouragement with which he had greeted her eager interest in her mother's studies, even hiding the stela from her—it had all been to protect her. In the end, he had returned to find out the truth about his wife's cruel demise, and for that, he paid with his life.

And he had told her to . . . *run.*

She heard the sigh of her father's voice.

Run.

"No. I won't. Daddy, I won't. I can't leave him." Something clear splashed onto Aaron's still face. Another something. Another. She put her hand to her face and found it wet with tears. "Oh, God. What have I done?" She wiped Aaron's face with the edge of her jacket, then pulled his still body close and rocked him in her arms. "What have I done?"

Chapter 35

Rosamund didn't know how long she sat there, but the sun had started to set behind the mountains when the older lady they'd met in Sacre Barbare came hiking up the path. Men with stretchers followed her. The woman knelt beside Rosamund, put her hand on her shoulder. "Do you remember me?"

"Of course. You're Dr. Servais." Why wouldn't Rosamund remember? They'd met only a few hours ago.

"Good. You are still sane and in possession of your faculties." Dr. Servais put her hand on Aaron's forehead, and sighed. "You can let go of him now. We'll take care of him."

Rosamund nodded and with agonizing slowness released Aaron to their care. Her arms ached from his weight, her knees hurt from sitting with her legs crossed, but she didn't cry for herself. The tears that trickled down her cheeks were for the loss of the man who held her heart.

As the men placed his body on the stretcher, the doctor returned to kneel beside Rosamund. "You're smeared with blood. Are you injured?"

"No. Not at all." Rosamund never took her gaze away from Aaron's body. "He was by the door. He was leaving. Then the cave cracked. Stones started to rain down. And he ran at me. He knocked me down. He covered me with his body." The men with the stretchers stopped and stared at her, and she realized her voice had grown louder and more shrill. She stopped. She took hard breaths, trying to get herself under control. More quietly, she said, "Aaron sacrificed himself for me."

"Did he?" Dr. Servais looked at Aaron, too. "When the time comes for a man's life and actions to be weighed, a sacrifice like that is a very great thing."

"The cave doesn't deserve him." Rosamund didn't deserve him.

"I promise you. The cave does not always win."

Rosamund didn't understand what Dr. Servais meant, or why she wore that expression of resolve. Rosamund didn't care, either. Instead, she viewed the wreckage where the cave had been. Huge boulders were strewn down the side of the mountain. The damned thing had been obliterated—except for the hole that stared like a black eye of hell. "Promise me you'll send someone back up here to roll one of these boulders over the entrance to the cave. Then it can't ruin anyone else's life. At least I would have that comfort."

"It can't be blocked." Dr. Servais stood. "This area has been an outlet for the Sacred Cave since the world was young. Soon someone else will walk a path through the mountains outside our village and once more find the cave exactly as it was, with the fire pit for sacrifices, the writings on the walls, and the entrance to the land of the dead."

"What do you mean?" Rosamund tried to stand, but one leg collapsed beneath her. "The cave comes back? It heals itself?"

"It's the Sacred Cave." Dr. Servais seemed to think that explained everything. Putting her hand under Rosamund's arm, she said, "Come. Let me see you walk and know that you're really not hurt."

With her help, Rosamund did stand, and she did walk, and when the men carried Aaron's body down the mountain, she followed and mourned like his widow.

They took him into the tap house, and there at the door, Dr. Servais turned to face Rosamund. "Why don't you go home?"

"But . . . I want to sit with him. . . ."

"No. It's your destiny to find the prophecy."

"The prophecy? How do you know about the . . . ?" Rosamund took a step back.

The Chosen. The Others.

Aaron's words echoed in her mind, and now she believed.

So who was this woman?

Dr. Servais spoke slowly, quietly. "I, too, have visited the Sacred Cave. I, too, barely escaped with my life. I know what's in there, and I know you didn't find your prophecy. I also know you won't find it sitting beside a dead man. Go home, I tell you. Go home." Something about Dr. Servais's compelling green eyes made Rosamund remember her father's text message.

Run.

So she did. She walked through the village, looking from side to side, behind and in front. The houses, so oddly quaint, looked sinister now, and the empty streets reminded her of a medieval plague village. She moved slowly at first, then more and more quickly, finally fleeing toward the car.

No one was chasing her, but all the while, she could hear her father's voice.

Run.

She got into the driver's seat. She sat and looked at the controls. She had never driven in her life, but she'd seen Aaron start the car. So step by step, she went through the process. The engine turned over. She put it in gear. And she ran away from Sacre Barbare, leaving her love behind.

Rosamund walked into the Arthur W. Nelson Fine Arts Library and past the desk where Jessica worked.

As soon as Jessica saw her, she started chatting as fast as she could. "Rosamund, where have you been? It's been over a week!"

Rosamund waved a limp hand.

Jessica kept talking. "I asked about you, and Mr. Perez from the board of directors said you were on leave, but you left your stuff out on the table and that guy was with you when you walked out, and I knew that wasn't like you. . . ."

Rosamund went through the ritual of identification without saying a word.

Jessica didn't notice. "Rosamund? Are you all right? You look different."

Rosamund stared at her. "I know. Glamorous, huh?" She kept walking.

"Glamorous? Sure. Glamorous. A little, um, tired, though."

Jessica's voice faded as Rosamund took the elevator, and let herself into the basement of the library. She trudged down the long, shadowy rows of books toward the back and into the nook where her father had worked, where she worked. . . . She was so glad to get here at last. All the way home, she had dreamed of her little corner of the library, longed to be in the familiar sanctuary. To be safe.

She had done what her father had urged her to do.

She had run.

With a sigh, she flipped on the light.

Nothing had changed. The rows of dusty books were the same. The desk chair with the torn seat and the wobbly wheel was the same. She uncovered the library table and found it stacked with more books, notebooks, and her mother's pre-Columbian stela.

Yet everything was different. Because she was different.

For one thing, she was wanted for the murder of Louis Fournier. Her picture had been everywhere in Europe, but on her trip home, no one had even noticed her. Even the ticket agent in the Paris airport had taken one look at her passport, then at her tearstained face, and he couldn't wait to get her on the plane and out of there.

Thank God for men who were afraid of weeping women.

She dropped her backpack and sagged into the chair. Leaning her elbows on the table, she gave up the effort to hold herself together, and wept.

She wanted to go back to her ordinary life, to her research in the library, to being the kind of woman no man cared about. She wanted to be the kind of woman who didn't notice men, especially men with dark hair, tanned skin, and a long, silent stride. She wanted to stop expecting Aaron to appear, jacket slung over his shoulder, voice deep and sure, to kiss her. She wanted to have succeeded in doing the one thing he had asked her to do—find the prophecy.

He never had a chance to tell her why the Chosen Ones required it, but knowing what she knew about myth and legend, she suspected the need for the prophecy was urgent. Someone else would die if she didn't find it.

So instead of sitting here missing Aaron, dropping tears on her mother's untranslated stone tablet and feeling sorry for herself, she needed once more to become the language and prophecy expert who could somehow, somewhere, solve this terrible mystery of the prophecy. Then she would give the prophecy to the Chosen Ones as reparation for Aaron's death, and maybe she would be worthy of the sacrifice he'd made of himself for her.

She opened her eyes. She reached for a tissue. She blew her nose and wiped her cheeks and as she did, she found herself staring at the pre-Columbian stone tablet. With sudden, desperate energy she blotted the tears off the stela, pulled out the mink brush and whisked it clean.

As Aaron had said, that first day when he'd come in here, the language chiseled into the stone was logosyllabic, an Epi-Olmec script that to the untrained eye looked similar to Egyptian hieroglyphics. While Rosamund was not proficient, because of her mother she had always had more than a passing interest.

Her hand paused, the brush held immobile above the symbol that caught her eye.

Otoch. The Mayan word for . . .

House.

Not just one word. Two words.

Otoch. Sak. The Mayan words for . . .

House. White.

She straightened.

White house.

She and Aaron had been looking for a black female slave who was a prophetess and lived in a white house.

In Spanish, white house was *casa blanca.*

In Mayan, white house was *otoch sak.*

Rosamund calmed herself. While searching for the prophecy, she had already jumped to conclusions once, and with disastrous results. She had dragged Aaron to Casablanca, to Paris, to the French Alps, and to his death. So this time she would be careful. She would be sure. She needed more than two words to get excited. She needed a word like—

The Mayan symbol for "slave" jumped out at her.

Slave. Yes. That was one of the words.

Female. Was the Mayan symbol for "female" on this stone?

Feverishly she looked for the symbols that made up the word.

Female slave.

There it was. There they were, both symbols, together.

And there was more.

Slave of dark skin.

Probably not a black woman, for this stone tablet predated the import of African slaves into the New World.

Who could she be?

For a half hour, Rosamund tried, *tried* to translate using her mother's notes and her own notes, but her skills weren't quite good enough. She couldn't find the thread that told the slave's story.

Then she remembered Bala's Stone. With a murmur of disgust at her own foolishness, she opened the travel pack at her waist, pulled out the impossibly large diamond, and placed it on the stela. Once again, before her eyes, the words took shape, and she read the text.

A woman of a rival tribe had been taken in war from her people. She who had once been great now worked the fields, the sun in its anger burning her, turning her skin dark, until one day in a delirium of fever, she spoke a prophecy. Her master brought her to the priests in the white stone house of the sun god, and here her words are recorded for all time.

The prophecy had been right before Rosamund's eyes the whole time.

Without taking her gaze away from the stela, Rosamund groped on the table, found a notebook. With

Bala's Stone in one hand and a pen in the other, she started copying every word.

In the distance, she heard the library door open and close once. Twice.

But she paid no attention.

Chapter 36

———⟨≋⟩———

S omeone cleared his throat.

Rosamund looked up, surprised at the interruption.

Lance Mathews leaned against the end of a row of metal shelving, his arms crossed over his chest, his eyebrow cocked rakishly.

Oh, no. *Lance Mathews.* How had he managed to get in?

Rosamund sighed. She supposed he had smiled at Jessica. Jessica, who was so shallow she could be manipulated by a guy with blond hair, blue eyes, and a physique so very developed and easy on the eyes.

Rosamund remembered feeling that way about him, too. Now she didn't care at all. The only emotion she felt was impatience. She'd been working for a long time translating the prophecy. An hour. Maybe two. But couldn't he have waited *ten more minutes*? She was almost done.

She straightened, rotating her stiff shoulders. "Hi, Lance. I didn't expect to see you here."

He strolled forward, a big, handsome, conceited guy with a smile gleaming with an obscene number of white teeth. Making a fist, he pretended to clip her under the chin. "Naughty girl. You didn't let me know you were back from Europe."

"I just got back, and, um, I was going to text you." If she'd thought about him, which she hadn't, she would have hoped he'd forget her. "I'm afraid I'm not going to be able to continue our relationship. Not that it's a relationship, but . . . I met another man and I fell in love." Her voice wobbled.

"Where is he?" Lance looked around.

She could hardly bear the pain, but she had to speak the words aloud sometime. "He's dead."

"Really? Aaron's dead?" Lance grinned. "Now that's just good news."

She didn't know what to say. She was shocked. Horrified. How could this man be so unfeeling, so cold? "Lance, that's an unconscionable attitude. I hoped that we could be friends, but not after that. Not when you care so little for my feelings, and even less for the death of a good man."

"Honey, I don't want to be your friend. I don't want to be your boyfriend." Lance held out his hands. "I just want that prophecy."

She stared at him, and it was as if she saw him for the first time.

He wasn't Sir Lancelot. He was a user, a grabber, someone from another organization chasing the same prophecy as Aaron. A fiery tattoo marked his chest. He was . . . "You're one of the Others," she blurted.

His grin disappeared. "And you're too smart for your own good."

"I always have been." Although not good about keeping her mouth shut.

"I'm here for the prophecy. So cough it up."

"I didn't get the prophecy." Which was true.

"You know, they tell me your mother said exactly the same thing. And look how it turned out for her."

Rosamund's hands and feet went cold. Her cheeks went hot. Her face went blank. "My mother? You didn't know my mother."

"No, I admit, I never had the privilege. But I know the people who questioned her. I know the people who finished her off."

Rosamund had suffered over her mother's death. She had mourned. She had imagined every scenario, both dramatic and mundane, and now, this guy said—"Are you *admitting* she was killed?"

"Of course she was killed. Your father knew it. I'm surprised he never warned you."

Run. "I guess he did." *Run.*

"Now, when it comes to your father's case, I had a direct hand in his demise. I can personally assure you it didn't go well for him when *he* tried to tell us he didn't know where the prophecy was. I mean, I would have given him the benefit of the doubt. By the time we were done with him, he was pretty crazy with the pain, and he was still saying no, he didn't know where the prophecy was. But orders are orders, and once we figured out where you were, we figured it would be kindest to put him out of his misery." Lance smiled charmingly. "So be a good girl, save yourself a lot of agony, and give me the prophecy."

"No."

He leaped forward. "So you've got it!"

She leaped back. "Perhaps. But I wouldn't spill a glass of water on you if you were on fire."

"On fire? That's very close to the truth. Look at me." He unbuttoned his shirt and pointed to the colorful flames that marked his chest. "Look at me! Do you know who I am?"

"You're the son of a bitch who killed my father."

"That's right, honey, and if you don't give me that prophecy, I'm going to kill you, too."

"Remember what you said. You said I'm too smart for my own good."

"So?"

"So I know you're going to kill me anyway."

His mouth worked as he glared furiously at her. "You *are* smart. Now see how much those brains protect you from this." Opening his arms wide, he gave off an unearthly glow, then sent a blast of light and heat toward her.

She covered her eyes, but too late.

He had blinded her.

She staggered back, bumping into the wall, banging into the gray metal filing cabinet.

"Give me the prophecy." He blasted her again.

This time she managed to cover her face, but she smelled hair singeing—her own. Her clothes were smoking, and her skin hurt as if she had a sunburn.

But when she could see, she followed her father's final instructions.

She ran.

She dodged around the library table, and when Lance dashed toward her, she crawled under and into the stacks, fleeing down one long row of metal shelves lined with books, hearing the thump of Lance's shoes behind her. There was a gap between this row of shelves and the next. She wiggled through and into another row, and had the satisfaction of hearing him curse as he tried to follow. She ran toward the door, wanting to get out.

But Lance backed out of the gap. She heard his shirt tear, heard him yell, "You bitch. You're going to fry!" He sent a blast of fire toward the shelving between them.

The heat sent her staggering sideways. Books, precious codices, rare manuscripts, began to smolder.

She hated Lance Mathews. Somehow, she was going to make him pay. For the books. For Louis. For her mother. For her father. Most of all, for Aaron. He was going to pay for what the Others did to Aaron.

She picked up speed. She was almost there—

And Lance rounded the corner in front of her, cutting off her escape. He looked different. Wild, angry, his face contorted and his hands like outstretched claws. "Give me the prophecy!"

She backed up. "No. I'm not helping the murderous bunch of devils who killed my parents, and I will not betray the love of my life."

A shadow coalesced behind Lance and took form as a man: a man with hair so black it shone with blue highlights, with proud, high cheekbones, narrow nose, and broad, stubborn chin.

"Aaron," she whispered.

He leaped on Lance's back, sending him staggering.

"Are you talking about me?" As Aaron hooked his elbow under Lance's chin and jerked, his voice echoed down the aisle. "Am *I* the love of your life? Because if that's the truth, you've made me the happiest man in the world."

Chapter 37

———◆❈◆———

Rosamund stood frozen, staring.

Aaron clung to Lance's back as Lance careened around the room, choking, gasping, trying to dislodge him.

Was Aaron a ghost? He seemed real enough. He fought like a man, and a man who was aiming to win.

Lance clawed at his arm.

Aaron jerked his arm against Lance's throat.

Lance gagged. His color changed from pale to bright red, and his eyes grew bloodshot and wild.

He staggered backward, slamming Aaron into the metal bookshelves.

In a surprising lack of stamina, Aaron dropped like a rock and hit the floor.

Then she realized—this was a trick by the Others. They would do anything to make her betray her knowledge, including bringing the dead to life. In a fury, she pelted back toward her table, back toward the precious notebook. She would hide it. She would throw it away.

Somehow, she would keep it out of the greedy, sleazy hands of the Others.

And she would not hope, would not believe, would not love that man who fought Lance for her.

Behind her, Lance gave chase. His voice was no more than a croak. "You bitch, you said he was dead!"

"He is!" she shouted. "Don't pretend otherwise."

In the next row, she saw Aaron running beside her. "Come through at the next crossover," he said.

Yeah, right. She picked up speed, burst into her work area. She ran for the table, her eyes fixed on her open notebook. Behind her, she heard the men collide. She snatched up the notebook and turned in time to see Lance throw out his arms and blast Aaron with heat and light.

Aaron stumbled back toward the stacks, his fingers over his eyes, smoke rising from his hair and clothes. Livid bruises extended along the side of his head and over his forehead. Bruises discolored his hands. This man had been badly hurt, beaten by rocks that slammed him with all the force of a cave's malevolence.

No. No matter how they tricked her, she would not believe he was alive.

Lance backed toward her, grinning at Aaron. "I'll see you dead. I'll send you to hell." He blasted him again.

Rosamund couldn't believe Aaron had returned to life. She had been there when he died. She had held him while his body cooled.

Yet if he was one of the Others, why was Lance trying to kill him?

How could Aaron be alive?

From the corner of her eye, she saw something move on the left. Two men, men she recognized. She had passed them in the corridor as she and Aaron had escaped from Louis's château. They had walked with Fujimoto Akihiro. They were his assassins.

From the right, she caught another movement. Two more assassins, and behind them, Fujimoto Akihiro himself.

Rosamund could think of only one reason why Fujimoto Akihiro and his assassins had arrived in the basement of the Arthur W. Nelson Fine Arts Library in her antiquities department.

They were following Aaron . . . to kill him.

They believed he was alive.

Hope, ridiculous, meaningless, irresistible hope bloomed in her heart.

The memory of Dr. Servais popped into Rosamund's mind. The look in the woman's eyes when Rosamund said, "Aaron sacrificed himself for me." And Dr. Servais had replied, "When the time comes for a man's life and actions to be weighed, a sacrifice like that is a very great thing."

Could it be? Was it possible?

Yes. Somehow, a miracle had happened. Aaron was alive.

Rosamund dropped the notebook on the library table.

Lance lifted his arms to blast Aaron.

She picked up the heaviest thing she could find— her mother's stone tablet. A thousand years of history and fifty pounds of weight gave it heft, and she felt every ounce as she heaved it over her head. She yelled, "Lance, Aaron's not that easy to kill!"

In a fury, Lance turned, arms outstretched, ready to fry her.

She swung the stela right at his head and smashed his pretty face.

The stela shattered, then disintegrated. With the horror of a trained antiquities librarian and the anguish of a daughter, she grabbed for the dust as it flew through the air. "No. Oh, no!"

But the stela was gone, the writing vanished.

And all because of Lance.

With loathing, she looked down at him and realized—even if she had known what would happen, she still would have hit him—for Aaron. She kicked him and in a harsh whisper said, "You don't get to win here. This is *my* Sacred Cave."

Chapter 38

The four assassins circled Aaron.

Rosamund shouted, "Look out!"

Aaron pulled his hands away from his eyes.

She leaped to help.

And something huge, heavy and alive hit her from the side and slammed her face down onto the table. Someone grabbed her arms in brutish hands and twisted them behind her.

Her knees collapsed, the joints in her shoulders and elbows on fire from the strain. She screamed in agony and rage.

Someone bent close, put his head on the table beside her, and breathed garlic and rot in her face. "This is just the beginning, pretty girl," he said, and jerked her arms again.

It was Louis Fournier's security guard, Joscelin Deschanel, the guy with the cold, cruel face, the brute who had publicly accused her of Louis's murder.

"You!" She could scarcely speak for the pain. "What are you doing here?"

"I came in with them." He jerked his neck toward the fight she could hear going on behind them.

"You work for Fujimoto Akihiro?"

"No. But I was sent along to make sure nothing goes wrong this time. No matter what happens, I'm to clean up the mess." And he smiled.

His smile was horrible.

He was going to make sure they all died.

"You want to watch?" He swung her off the table and, still holding her arms, dropped her to her knees.

She closed her eyes, battled the pain, then opened them. Because she did want to watch. She couldn't stand not to watch.

Aaron fought. He climbed the bookshelves, reached the top, and shoved against the next bookshelf until it fell with a roar that scattered books and slammed two of the assassins to the floor.

Fujimoto screamed curses at his men.

Deschanel chuckled to hear them shriek in pain. "Smart. Good fighter," he said to her. "Too bad about him."

"You can't kill Aaron," she said. *Oh, God, please make it true.*

"I can kill anyone." Deschanel spoke English, but with a harsh accent, and he had no inflection in his voice. He might as well have been discussing accounting.

She knew she shouldn't bring it up. She was afraid an accusation might anger him. But she had to say it. "You killed Louis."

"I did. I was ordered to do so. I'm going to kill

you, too. More orders. But with you, I can take my time."

She couldn't think of that. And she wanted to know—"Who gives you your orders?"

"I don't know." After a thoughtful pause, he added, "But I'm scared of him."

"Scared of him." Who, or what, could ever scare this monster?

Still in that reflective tone, Deschanel said, "Your boy's hurt. As soon as they can get their hands on him, he's done. There. See?"

One assassin caught Aaron as he tried to climb another bookshelf, and jerked him to the ground.

The impact made Aaron go limp for a crucial second.

The other assassin followed up with a kick to the ribs.

Aaron caught his foot and flipped him.

The assassin rolled, came to his feet, and tackled Aaron.

Then they had him. He groaned as they hauled him up to a standing position, and gasped as they punched his belly, over and over, heavy motions that drove deep.

Rosamund flinched as each blow landed, then stared as Fujimoto ran forward, yelling like a samurai warrior.

A wave of fetid breath once more washed over her as Deschanel said, "Watch this. The Jap has got one great revenge planned."

With a flourish, Fujimoto opened his trench coat. From a specially built pocket inside the lining, he pulled an eighteen-inch samurai sword.

Rosamund was appalled. "Is he crazy? He can't use a sword here in the library. He can't—" *He can't kill Aaron before my eyes.* She tried to spring forward.

Deschanel laughed and moved her arms higher.

She felt her shoulder dislocate; the bone came out of the socket in one slow, torturous movement. Red spots swam before her eyes; she thought she was going to throw up.

All the while, that hateful voice droned. "Fujimoto has a thing about being a samurai—fat chance he could ever be one. He's short and weak, and refuses to practice his self-defense. But samurai beheaded their enemies, and he thinks that's cool."

Rosamund was barely hanging on to consciousness.

She suffered such agony. She wrestled with such fear. The tension, the anguish and the pain made her want to scream, and scream, and scream. But she couldn't. She didn't dare. Aaron was totally focused on Fujimoto and the sword, and if he could even have a chance of getting away, she couldn't distract him.

Aaron didn't look worried. He stood insolently, laughing a little as he said, "A little dramatic, aren't you, Fujimoto?"

Fujimoto responded with a rapid spate of Japanese, and although Rosamund understood little of the language, she understood the tone—not complimentary, and very smug.

Then he barked out a series of commands.

The assassins bowed to him, then forced Aaron to his knees. One of them grabbed his hair and stretched his neck out.

"They can't kill him. They can't kill him." Rosamund

repeated the mantra over and over, but she didn't believe it.

Her eyes were dry as she stared, and stared. She had already seen Aaron die once to save her. Then he'd returned to her and before she could touch him, hold him, know that he was Aaron and truly alive . . . he would die again, and in her defense.

She couldn't stand this.

This was her fault.

Fujimoto lifted the sword above his head with both hands. The blade glistened in the light.

Rosamund braced herself for the anguish she knew would follow.

The sword whistled as it descended . . . and as the edge reached Aaron's neck, he turned to smoke.

The blade passed through him.

Then he was human again. Human . . . and unharmed.

Rosamund collapsed in relief, and at last the tears came, rolling down her face, relief made real.

In unison, the assassins released him and backed off, their hands held out as if they feared having touched him.

In that dreadful monotone, Deschanel said, "Neat trick."

Fujimoto stared at Aaron, examined the blade as if somehow it had malfunctioned, then stared at Aaron again.

Slowly Aaron got to his feet, his gaze fixed on Fujimoto.

"Your guy is pissed. If the Jap was smart, he would run," Deschanel said.

Instead, Aaron hit Fujimoto with a lightning-fast right cross to the gut.

Fujimoto flailed backward, stumbled over the piles of fallen library books, and before he landed, Aaron grabbed him by the collar, stood him up, and hit him between the eyes.

Fujimoto's head snapped back, and Rosamund saw his consciousness shatter.

The guy slammed into the floor. He was out.

The assassins—the two who were conscious—turned tail and ran.

The shelves behind Aaron were tilted sideways. Books were scattered across the floor. The other assassins sprawled beneath Aaron's feet, unmoving.

Aaron turned to face Rosamund and Deschanel. His eyes were cold and deadly. "Come on."

Deschanel dropped Rosamund to the floor.

She collapsed, her arms numb, her elbows burning, and the dislocated shoulder . . . oh, God. The pain came at her in waves, each wave bigger than the next. Yet she couldn't do anything except roll into a ball under the table and make herself as small as possible.

"Don't be stupid. I've got a pistol." Reaching into his pocket, Deschanel pulled out a handgun and pointed it at Aaron.

To Rosamund's inexperienced eyes, the pistol looked like a cannon.

Aaron seemed unimpressed. "Use it or shut up."

Deschanel laughed, and when he did, he boomed like Jabba the Hutt. "I like you. But you knew that."

"I don't like you," Aaron replied. "So I guess I'm going to have to kill you."

Deschanel laughed again, a slow merriment that sat so gracelessly on his flat, cruel face. He placed the pistol on the table, and flexed his fists. "I will enjoy everything I do to you." He took a step. "You won't."

Aaron watched Deschanel lumber toward him, step by step, a giant who lived to create pain and death, and Aaron's face was calm, certain. He looked as if he were waiting.

When Deschanel was four feet away from the table, Aaron leaned down to the unconscious assassin at his feet. He opened the assassin's coat and quick as lightning pulled the handgun out of its holster. Straightening, he emptied six shots, one after the other, into Joscelin Deschanel.

The noise was tremendous, six sharp reports, and Rosamund never saw it coming.

Apparently, neither did Deschanel.

For a second, nothing changed. He kept walking.

Rosamund thought that somehow, Aaron had missed.

Then, like a giant redwood, Deschanel tilted, staggered, and slowly toppled to the floor, slamming into the linoleum hard enough to rattle the table.

He wore an expression of surprise.

Aaron leaped Deschanel's body, pulling his cell phone from his pocket, and ran to Rosamund's side. He knelt, not touching her. "What did he do to you?"

"Dislocated my shoulder." Woozy as she was, sick with pain and the trauma of seeing men fight, fall, die, she could only stare at Aaron with her hungry gaze, observing the tilt of his chin, the shining black hair, the bones of his face, so masculine and sculpted, the dark, dark eyes that scrutinized her anxiously.

"You're going into shock." He removed his coat and placed it over her shivering body, then dialed nine-one-one, gave the location, demanded immediate assistance.

With a measured moan of distress, Rosamund worked herself into a sitting position. Tears of pain welled in her eyes and rolled down her face.

"What are you doing?" Aaron tried to help her.

Slowly, painfully, she leaned her broken body into him. "I saw you hit by all those rocks. I held your cold body in my arms." She kissed him, breathed his scent, and soaked in his comfort. "And I don't care . . . if this isn't really you. I don't care if the Others are playing a trick. For right now, you're mine, and I don't dare ask for eternity."

Chapter 39

"**H**ey, Samuel, did you bust them out of jail?" Charisma stood in the kitchen in Irving's mansion and hopped on one foot, nuclear with excitement.

"With the help of Irving's crack law team, yes, I did." Samuel stepped aside to allow Aaron and Rosamund to step in. "Here you go. Here are the reprobates."

Through the hubbub that broke out, no one listened to Samuel as he said, "I suppose we're required to have a group hug?"

Aaron grinned at his friends around the long table: Irving, getting to his feet with Caleb's help; Jacqueline, sporting a new diamond engagement ring; Isabelle, glowing with refined happiness at the sight of them; Charisma rushing at him, arms wide. "No!" He stopped her with his hands outstretched. "We were not just in jail. We were in jail in the *hospital*."

Charisma took a slow step forward and embraced him gingerly, then with an eye on Rosamund's sling, embraced her just as gingerly. "You guys do look a little rough."

Rosamund smiled at his friends. "I'm so glad to be here."

"Yes, being here with us beats being handcuffed to a hospital bed," Samuel said.

"Charming as always, Samuel." Isabelle tapped her fingernails on the table, more ruffled by Samuel's blunt speaking than Aaron thought was warranted.

Rosamund didn't seem offended. "Having my shoulder dislocated is not an experience I want to repeat. Neither is having it put back in its socket."

Samuel pulled out a chair for her. "Sit down before you fall down."

She thanked him and sank into the chair so gratefully, Aaron said, "You need to go to bed."

"No. Please." She relaxed with a sigh. "I'm simply tired from the trip home, and now I want to sit here and enjoy my friends."

Irving seated himself again—at the head of the table, of course. "I'm pleased you consider this your home."

Isabelle said, "I'm pleased you consider us your friends."

Aaron took the bench next to her, and he relaxed, too.

The kitchen was working its magic.

Irving's mansion was pristine, filled with delicate antiques, polished hardwood floors, and fringed velvet drapes held back with gold cords. So of course, with the possible exception of Isabelle, the Chosen Ones felt woefully out of place.

Consequently they'd moved their group meetings

to the kitchen, a huge, warm, cavernous room on the bottom floor of the mansion, where they could easily access the refrigerator for Cokes, the freezer for Popsicles, and the stove for toasted cheese sandwiches. The floor was below ground level, the ceiling above, and when they sat around the massive, heavy table, they saw the legs of pedestrians as they walked by.

McKenna and Martha hated having the Chosen invade their domain.

The Chosen loved it, especially when McKenna and Martha did as they were doing now and rushed to create food for the triumphant homecoming.

In a suitably deferential voice, McKenna asked, "Would Mr. Eagle and Dr. Hall like a beverage? I would be pleased to serve our returning heroes."

By that, everyone else knew they would have to serve themselves. They hurried to grab something to drink; then chairs scraped as they found their places around the table.

Aaron accepted a cup of coffee, took a long breath of air scented with freshly baked bread and a beef roast cooking in the oven, and knew a vast gratitude that he had returned to his friends, and more important, that he had returned at all.

When the Chosen Ones were settled, Caleb asked, "What happened? Sam, how did you get them out?"

"By the time I got to police headquarters, the cops had fingerprinted two of the guys on the floor and found out they were known assassins. That helped. It also helped that Fujimoto Akihiro was there, with his fingerprints all over a priceless samurai sword stolen last night from a collector here in New York City, and that Fujimoto had been at Louis Fournier's party. So the investigators had already deduced that Fujimoto, not Rosamund, had ordered Fournier's murder." Samuel smirked. "At least, it didn't take much prompting from me for them to have already deduced it."

"Very slick." Caleb approved.

Isabelle nodded, and for the merest second, Aaron thought he saw pride on her face.

"Tell them about Lance Mathews," Aaron said. "Now *that's* a story."

"Lance Mathews? The Other who wanted a date with Rosamund?" Jacqueline asked.

"He's the one. He managed to track us through Casablanca and Paris with the slimy little trick of having Rosamund text him her agenda," Aaron told them.

"I'm *sorry*." Rosamund spread her hands in apology.

"Not your fault." Aaron had no excuse for that kind of carelessness, and he knew it. "I should have thought to ask you about him, instead of assuming that you'd be focused only on me."

"Ego will get you every time." Samuel laughed shortly. "Apparently, in the library while Lance Mathews was getting ready to fry Aaron, Rosamund decked him with something called a stela—"

"An irreplaceable pre-Columbian stone tablet," Aaron filled in. "She knocked him out cold and ruined his pretty face."

"All right, sister!" Charisma offered a high five.

With her good arm, Rosamund clumsily slapped Charisma's hand. It was probably the first high five she'd actually exchanged in her whole restricted life.

"When Lance woke up, he was on the library floor,

and the police were taking us away in cuffs. Nobody was paying a bit of attention to him, and he staggered to his feet and came running at Rosamund, screaming that he'd get her." It was a sight Aaron would never forget—that bloodied, broken face contorted with rage, the police so complacent about the crime scene they didn't react in time. "He was reaching for her. I thought he had her." Aaron looked around expectantly.

"And?" Isabelle prompted.

"And he dropped dead at her feet."

"Why?" Caleb asked.

"Heart attack," Aaron said.

"Really." Irving didn't sound as if he believed it.

Aaron didn't believe it either. It was too convenient for the Others. The guy who had screwed up his mission was gone.

But possibly it wasn't a bad thing, either. Unless the Others already had someone lined up to take Lance's place, they were now down a man, too. Six Chosen against six Others. Aaron liked the odds balanced.

Taking care not to touch her sling or her shoulder, he embraced Rosamund. "I have asked Rosamund to marry me."

"Yay!" Charisma threw her arms in the air and bounced in her chair. "I knew it would happen. I knew it!"

"I recognized the way you were watching her— frustrated and hungry." Caleb cuddled Jacqueline to his side. "I know the feeling."

"You were never frustrated," Jacqueline retorted. "And if you were, it was your own fault."

"No wonder you look like shit, Aaron." Samuel

looked amused. "Any sensible woman should beat you up for suggesting she spend her life with you."

"She hasn't agreed." In fact, Rosamund had looked horrified when he asked. "But I'm confident I can convince her." Although first he had to figure out why, when she said she loved him, she was balking about making vows.

Personally, pinning her down with marriage was all he could think about.

"Aaron and Rosamund," Irving began, "I feel as if I speak for everyone here, Jacqueline and Caleb, Isabelle, Charisma and Samuel, McKenna and Martha, and of course myself, in saying that we're delighted that you've returned to us relatively unharmed and without a felony record. It's moments like this that make me proud to be part of the Chosen Ones support group." Without pause, he snapped, "Mr. Faa, please stop rolling your eyes."

Samuel scrunched down in his chair like a scolded child.

Apparently the list of Chosen present set off a lightbulb in Rosamund's brain. She looked around the kitchen, then asked, "Excuse me, Irving, but where's Aleksandr?"

"Aleksandr has been spending a lot of time at the university. I believe he's getting quite a reputation for successfully tutoring students in calculus. Now." Impatience almost steamed off Irving's lean form. "May I continue?"

Aaron leaned close to Rosamund. "He gets cranky when we interrupt his speeches."

"I noticed," she murmured back.

Clearly irritated, Irving asked, "Aaron! Rosamund! Is it possible to get a report on your success in searching for the prophecy?"

Aaron hated to announce the bad news. "No prophecy. We were chasing the wrong black slave prophetess from the wrong white house."

Faces fell around the table.

"But I saw her," Jacqueline insisted. "I saw her. She was dark-skinned. She worked in the fields. There were jungles all around. She had a vision, and they took her in chains to a tall white house. . . ." Her voice trailed off as she tried to pin down the details.

"What went wrong?" Irving asked.

Aaron took Rosamund's hand, and held it, and together they led the Chosen Ones step-by-step through Casablanca, through Paris, and finally to the Sacred Cave in the French Alps.

"The cave was as it always was, glowing, speaking in the voice of the wind, and greedy for my blood." As Aaron spoke, the memories grew vivid—of the glowing rocks, the breeze that taunted and danced, and the giant boulders that would have taken Rosamund's life. He broke out in a cold sweat.

Now Rosamund grasped his hand tightly. "We entered. I used Bala's Stone to read the prophecy, and the prophetess said she had seen us coming and deliberately led us astray, knowing that would put us in danger—because she was one of the Others."

No one moved.

Then Charisma said, "What a hag."

"Not the word I would have used," Aaron said.

"I know, but Irving doesn't like me to use vulgar

language. He thinks women who have purple hair and dog collars need to have a care what they say." Charisma seemed totally unoffended. "He's probably right."

Irving accepted a cup of coffee from McKenna and toasted Charisma.

"But what happened to you two?" Caleb asked. "You didn't get those bruises from finding the wrong prophecy."

"You're going to have to get the rest of the story from Rosamund, because the last thing I remember"— the fear for Rosamund and the anguish of knowing he could not save her were burned onto Aaron's memory—"is seeing the cave collapse."

Every head turned to Rosamund.

"He was killed protecting me."

Every head turned back to Aaron.

Isabelle sat on the other side of Aaron. Leaning over, she picked up his wrist. "He looks a little pale," she told Rosamund. "But he seems to have a pulse."

"He was dead." Rosamund sounded calm, interested, like a scientist reciting the results of an experiment. "I am sure. I held his body while it grew cold."

Everyone in the kitchen shifted uncomfortably.

Still in that calm voice, Rosamund continued. "The paramedics, or whoever they are in France, must have felt the rumbling in the earth. Or maybe they always expect disaster when someone finds the cave, but they showed up with stretchers, one for him and, I guess, one for me."

"You weren't hurt at all?" Isabelle leaned around Aaron to watch Rosamund with a worried frown.

Aaron thought he knew what it was. During Rosamund's sojourn in Irving's library, the women had grown to know her. Now something about her had changed. Her expressive, mobile face seemed more mature. She no longer waved her hands to punctuate her points, and maybe that was because her shoulder hurt, but he didn't think so. Rosamund had changed. Sometime between the beginning of their journey to Casablanca and this moment, she seemed to have lost something precious—her unquestioning trust that something wonderful was about to occur.

"No. Aaron protected me with his body, or rather with the dark mist he becomes when he"—Rosamund caught her breath as if remembering that time in the closet—"when he works."

Aaron picked up her hand. Her fingers were cold, almost as if she had died, too.

"Dr. Servais confirmed Aaron had died of his injuries—"

Irving interrupted. "Servais? Female, short, broad in the beam, abrupt in manner?"

"Yes, that's her," Rosamund confirmed. "Although she wasn't abrupt right then. She was very kind about Aaron, and very firm about me needing to return here."

Irving exchanged a look with Martha. "She's a former Chosen, very gifted in healing, but argumentative and assertive."

"For a woman, you mean?" Jacqueline asked coolly.

Irving didn't seem to catch her point. Maybe he really didn't. Maybe he figured that at his age, he could be a chauvinist if he chose. "Servais was very unfeminine. She returned to France—she disagreed with my insistence that we keep on budget—and we haven't heard from her in years. I wonder what she's up to."

"She has become a doctor, an amazing doctor," Aaron told him. "And . . . well, I don't know what else she is. As you say, she is very gifted."

Rosamund turned to Aaron, and again with that scientific note of inquiry in her voice, she asked, "Can you tell us what happened?"

Aaron spoke to her and her alone, weighing her reactions, trying to understand her. "I . . . my being . . . was in the depths of the Sacred Cave." He heard her inhale sharply, saw her face twist with . . . what? Anguish? Guilt?

Then her face smoothed again, and she became Rosamund, the analytical listener. "How did you know you were in the depths of the Sacred Cave? Have you been there before?"

"No, but my first breath was taken in the Sacred Cave, and I recognized the smell of molten rock and death. I remembered a death and I knew it was me who had died. I was stretched out on my back. I couldn't open my eyes. Outside the chamber, I could hear this horrible gibbering and howling." His mouth dried with remembered fear. "I was afraid of whatever that was, wherever it was. It wanted me, and I was helpless." He glanced around.

Charisma's eyes were full of tears. Jacqueline had both fists up to her mouth. Isabelle had her head turned away as if she wanted to escape, and the men were pale.

Rosamund was stoic.

"Inside the chamber with me, I could hear this woman arguing in French. I'm not sure who she was—someone very brave to have accompanied me so far."

"Was it Dr. Servais?" Rosamund asked.

"Maybe. But the chamber was huge. Her voice echoed and rolled." He shook his head. "I can't be sure."

"I think it must have been her." Rosamund sounded thoughtful, logical. "Because . . . well, please finish, Aaron."

"Thank you." When had Rosamund grown so serenely polite? "I don't know who the woman was arguing with, because I never heard anyone answer, but she was giving him hell." He winced at his own idiom. "She said the sacrifice had been made, the terms of the deal satisfied, but the sacrifice of my life for Rosamund's had to be weighed in the balance. No one answered, at least not that I heard, but finally, she said, *'Bon! C'est fini.'* And I opened my eyes, and I was in this room over the top of the tap house at Sacre Barbare, with Dr. Servais leaning over me giving me—" He stopped himself. "She was haranguing me for going up to the Sacred Cave when she had told me not to. She said lots of people managed to ignore the call of the cave until the end of their lives, and she said it would be wise if I stayed out of the deep places of the earth from now on."

"Amen, brother," Samuel said.

Aaron continued. "She told me to be careful, because I'd been hurt badly, but that she had worked on my case, and I was better now."

"Did you tell her you'd been dead?" Isabelle asked.

"I couldn't talk about it then. It was too soon, too close." Aaron cleared his throat and admitted, "I was still terrified."

Around the table, heads nodded.

"Then she arranged for me to come home. She said I *needed* to come home because there were things I *needed* to do. Of course, she was right." Aaron touched Rosamund's face and smiled at her.

Her skin was cool. Her eyes were cool.

"It is all very weird," Aaron concluded, but he was no longer talking about his own death.

"I'll give you weird on that one." Samuel shuddered as if spooked.

"I've never heard of such a thing." Irving stroked his coffee cup and stared, narrow-eyed, at Aaron. Raising his voice, he asked, "Martha, have you?"

"No, sir. Most Chosen just die, or they don't. Or they're injured like poor Gary White, and lie there in a coma for years." Martha placed a broad wooden board on the table, filled with freshly cut hot bread. "But to come back to life . . ." She shook her head.

McKenna brought small plates of olive oil and pesto, salami and pepperoncini, grapes and cheese.

"How do you feel?" Isabelle stroked the bruise on Aaron's face, the cut on his ear.

Samuel tensed.

Aaron didn't care if Samuel was jealous. Isabelle was their empath, their healer, and her light touch spread strength through his body, and that strength pooled in the places where he'd been most injured—in his head, his hand, his shoulder, his thigh.

Isabelle answered her own question. "You're a little achy, and you're delicate, but with a little rest, you'll be fine."

"The fight today was rough," he said. "If I'd been one hundred percent, I would have performed better. But nothing on me got seriously injured. It was Rosamund who was tortured."

Isabelle stood and came to Rosamund, and ran her hand over her shoulder. "That really hurts. Did they give you something for the pain?"

"Yes, but you've made it feel better than drugs ever could." Rosamund did look better; she had color in her face, and she sipped her tea with more enthusiasm. Quietly she added, "I guess empathic healing is your gift then."

Isabelle nodded.

At the same time, Rosamund looked at Aaron consideringly. "I saw you die, and now I wonder—will you get to remain on this earth?"

"Oh . . ." That was why she was offhand. That was why she'd refused to marry him. She'd suffered so much with his first death—embarrassing as it was to admit, he hoped she had suffered—she was afraid he was going to make her a widow again soon. "Do I get another get-out-of-jail-free card? I would guess not."

No. Her lips moved, but nothing came out.

She *had* loved him. She *had* suffered. He was sure of it now, and sure, too, that when she was over this shock, she would become the old, enthusiastic Rosamund once more. He injected heartiness in his voice. "Hopefully I'll be here until I die a natural death of old age."

Maybe a little too much heartiness, for she once

again assumed that mask of . . . of . . . not indifference. Surely it couldn't be indifference.

"Sure. You'll die a natural death of old age—if you don't get rubbed out by the Others first," Samuel said.

Rosamund's fingernails suddenly bit into Aaron's hand.

Aaron heard a hard thump from under the table.

Samuel jumped.

Another hard thump.

He jumped again. "That hurt!" He glared at Isabelle on one side of him, at Charisma across the table.

"Whatever is wrong, Samuel?" Isabelle asked with gentle innocence.

"Yeah, Sam, whatever is wrong?" Charisma flashed her leather bracelets with the stainless steel studs.

Jacqueline muttered, "I wish I was sitting closer."

Caleb leaned back in his chair and crossed his arms. "That's our Sam. Making friends everywhere he goes."

"Fine," Samuel snapped. "He'll survive. We'll all survive—but not without the damned prophecy!"

"Samuel." Martha put a plate of antipasti in front of him. "Fill your mouth with something besides words. Eat something."

"If the prophecy is all it takes for you to survive, then we're in good shape," Rosamund said.

"How do you figure?" Samuel asked.

Rosamund's lips curved in the slightest and most superior of smiles. "I found the prophecy in my own library."

Chapter 40

A babble broke out around the table, but Rosamund could only hear Aaron's voice saying, "Well done, my darling. Well done." He placed his palm against her cheek and kissed her.

She kissed him back, of course. She couldn't not. But she held a precious piece of herself in reserve, and when he drew back with a frown, she knew he had tasted the distance between them.

He wanted to ask. She could see that. He was ready to ask.

Then Samuel, bigmouthed, caustic, hard-nosed lawyer Samuel, interrupted. "So, Rosamund, what is it? What did you find?"

"Be quiet, Samuel. Let them have their moment." Isabelle watched them with a kind of stark loneliness on her lovely face.

Rosamund straightened away from Aaron. "No. It's fine. We were done." Clearly, Aaron was not done with *her*, but she thankfully escaped into her report. "The prophecy was given by a lady captured in war, enslaved by the Mayans, worked until she was black from sun, and when she revealed her visions, she was taken to the white temple. The priests didn't believe in her. Then she proved her skill, over and over, and so at last they wrote down her guiding vision on the stone tablet my mother recovered from a cenote in Guatemala."

Martha filled more plates. McKenna passed them around.

The Chosen Ones listened more intently than anyone had ever listened to Rosamund before.

"The Mayan language is not my specialty—my father didn't encourage my interest, and now I know it was because my mother was murdered in pursuit of this prophecy." The urge to cry caught Rosamund by the throat, squeezing with sorrow's fingers.

She shook it off. She took a long, slow breath to contain her tears.

"Did Bala's Stone help you?" Irving nibbled on a piece of crusty bread, and a shower of crumbs dusted the table before him.

She turned to him at once, grateful to be dragged back away from the chasm of grief that yawned at her feet. If she concentrated on what she had to say, on her desire for vengeance against the Others for the deaths of her parents, for the death of Louis, for the death of . . .

Her gaze flew to Aaron.

Aaron *was* alive. He was watching her, and he was alive, and she had no reason to feel as if her composure hung on the sharpest point of a blade.

Tearing her attention from him, she pushed aside the small plate McKenna placed before her—she couldn't force food down her tight throat—and with the brisk efficiency she lent to her reports to the library board, she said, "Very much. I couldn't have done so much translation in so short a time without it. Unfortunately, the police wouldn't let me take my notebook with me. And there's one other thing. When the stela disintegrated—"

"Disintegrated? How did it disintegrate?" Caleb asked.

"It broke apart and turned to sand when I hit Lance's face with it." Even now she could remember the feel of the dry grit in her hands, and feel the moment of heartbreak at the destruction of the historical object Elizabeth Hall had died to retrieve. "My mother found the stela in a water-filled cenote, so it was soaking for a thousand years. When it was brought up, it should have been cared for, but my mother was dead and I think . . . that is, I realize now my father was angry and anxious. He apparently couldn't bring himself to destroy the stela, so he cleaned it up and put it away in his library, where it would be safe."

"But it should have been kept in water to preserve the stone." Irving wasn't guessing; he knew his way around ancient artifacts.

"Exactly. I was lucky Father placed it on a board. When I pulled it out of the drawer, it was supported, and I didn't realize how fragile it had become. I *should* have realized. . . ." She shook her head at her own foolishness. "I would have if I'd had more time. I was simply so thrilled to have found this precious thing that held a piece of my mother's heart, I wanted to examine it immediately. Then Lance and Aaron came in, and then—" She caught herself. Then Lance and Aaron came in, both to ask about a prophecy; her safe world was broken and reshaped into a place of mystical terror.

"Can you remember the details of the prophecy?" Aaron asked. "Or should I go to the library and steal your notebook?"

Her heart leaped, then beat like a Kentucky Derby racer. "No! Don't . . . steal . . . anything. Don't . . ." She held up a hand, realized it was shaking, and tucked it into her lap. "I remember everything I read. It's very simple, very forthright. The prophetess of *Otoch Sak* said that when the Chosen Ones had taken the wrong path and vanished from this earth, leaving only the infant Chosen to defend the weak, then each of those Chosen must find their true love and sacrifice the greatest thing for that love. When they did that, they would receive their full powers." She said apologetically, "I don't know why she said the Chosen Ones had taken the wrong path, but the Mayans were great with calendars, and she placed the date on the day that the Gypsy Travel Agency was destroyed."

"Whew." Even Samuel was impressed enough to stop eating.

"That's deep." Charisma poured a puddle of olive oil onto her plate and dipped her bread. "What happened to the prophetess?"

"The priests killed her," Rosamund said.

"They ripped her heart out?" Isabelle didn't seem surprised, and when Rosamund nodded, Isabelle said,

"So to give us this prophecy, she did sacrifice her greatest thing—her life."

Samuel didn't seem impressed. "So we have to find true love and sacrifice the greatest thing. *What* thing? Do we have to do like the prophetess, and get axed?"

"I don't know," Rosamund said. "Those were the prophetess's words."

"That's helpful," he said. "Are you sure you interpreted her correctly?"

"Yes." Rosamund decided she not only did not like Samuel; she did not like having her expertise questioned. "I wouldn't make false claims and lead you astray. These Others killed my parents. I have at least as great an interest in the Others' extinction as you do."

"Fair enough." Samuel nodded gruffly. "So how do we know if we've found our true love, et cetera?"

"The proof that you've succeeded is you get another mark or tattoo, or the one you have is enhanced," Rosamund answered.

Jacqueline looked at her palms.

"But all seven of you must succeed before the next cycle of the Chosen—" Rosamund began.

"We've got seven years, kids." Charisma grinned. "We can do it!"

Rosamund continued. "Or you lose your gifts and the Others are triumphant, able to wreak their havoc without anything or anyone to stop them."

"Oh, good. There's nothing to it." Now Isabelle sounded as sarcastic as Samuel.

"No, it'll work!" Aaron sprang to his feet. "I mean, it *does* work. Listen—I was born in the Sacred Cave, and left there by a mother who leaped to her death for the shame of having me. I was meant to be a sacrifice to the cruel old gods, but my foster father saved me, and ever since, I have been running away from that cave, knowing that if it could take me, it would, and keep me there in the depths of the earth for all eternity. Every day of my life, I've heard the call of the Sacred Cave, and fought against it. Then the gods, or fate, or mere chance put Rosamund into my life, and from that moment on, my feet were inexorably on the path to the Sacred Cave. I thought once it had me in its clutches, I would die. But no. That was too easy. It gave me a choice. The cave would either kill me, or it would kill my love."

Anguish rose in Rosamund, a hundred times as harsh as the anguish she had felt at her mother's death, at her father's death. *He doesn't mean that. He never said that before.*

"When the ceiling collapsed, I had a split second to decide—leave and live, forever alone, or stay and die, for Rosamund. I stayed. I died. I didn't like it." He smiled painfully around at his friends, then down at Rosamund.

I can't do this. I can't stand this.

"I made my choice. I allowed the cave to crush my life from my body." His voice was vibrant.

His friends watched him, riveted by his intensity.

"But the cave couldn't keep me because I had sacrificed my life to save Rosamund. And look! My powers have grown beyond anything I've ever imagined." He turned to Rosamund. "Before you, I could dissolve my body, become a dark mist, and without ever being seen, retrieve stolen objects of art. And I made a good living at it, too. But as wonderful as that was, that was all I could do. Worse, that ability had started to fail me."

Rosamund saw Samuel nod. "My gift has been getting a little chancy for me, too," he said.

Aaron continued to gaze at Rosamund as if she were truly the Fair Rosamund of ages past. "But once I found you, once I learned to admire your strengths, and love your weaknesses, I could create myself into different forms. I could dissolve my body and make it a shell to protect that person who is most precious to me. When Fujimoto tried to execute me, I could pass that sword through my neck without harm. Most wonderful, I could make love to my Rosamund and touch her everywhere at once." Before her eyes, he dissolved and wrapped himself around her, and surrounded her with a warmth and tenderness she could breathe into her lungs and feel on every pore of her skin.

Dimly she heard Charisma say, "That's golden."

Luckily, before Rosamund allowed herself to relax into him, to allow him to care for her, Aaron snapped back into his human form, leaving her feeling chilled and abandoned.

It was a feeling she remembered all too well.

"But this is the most telling." Aaron stripped off his shirt the same way he had stripped it off in the cave. "The mark of the Chosen on my back has expanded. It used to be these tiny, crumpled wings, mere outlines in black. But look at them now!" On either side of his spine, he had developed a true representation of angel wings, each feather large and colorful, covering his back from his shoulder blades to his waist.

"Awesome!" Charisma said.

Rosamund didn't know what to say. What to think. She didn't want to be stricken with wonder at the sight of his muscled back and the glorious decoration he wore so proudly, but she was. She didn't want to lust at the sight of his bare body, but white-hot lust filled her.

She didn't want to love him . . . but she didn't know how to stop.

Proudly, he finished. "I've succeeded in finding my true love. I made my sacrifice, and now I have complete control of my gift."

"Me, too. Look!" Jacqueline showed them the palms of her hand, and the two black, stylized eyes there. "I used to have an eye on *one* hand. Then, when I sought a vision I desperately feared, and did so to protect Caleb, I got the second eye. Plus, I can access my visions at will!"

While the Chosen who had still to fulfill the terms of the prophecy exchanged pained and doubtful looks, Rosamund tried to understand what Aaron meant. "Are you trying to say I'm your true love?"

Aaron pulled on his shirt. He sat down next to her and fastened the buttons. "Of course you are. It didn't take a pair of wings and an enhanced gift to tell me that."

She stammered, "B-but you only wanted me when I was made pretty."

Aaron's jaw dropped open, and he looked foolish and confused. "What are you talking about?"

"I'm talking about you. You barely noticed me before Philippe did a makeover."

Aaron's mouth moved soundlessly.

She pushed her glasses up on her nose. "That's not who I am. I'm Rosamund, the plain librarian. Everyone thinks so, and I know you do, too."

Everybody did, too. The uncomfortable silence that fell over the table said it all.

Somewhere, a door slammed.

"Rosamund." Aaron tried to take her hands.

Angrily, she snatched them away. Angrily, because being angry with him beat thinking about, dealing with, the fear, the grief, and the love that shadowed her every thought, her every move.

Footsteps ran down the stairs outside the kitchen. Aleksandr walked in and dropped his backpack on the floor. Seeing the food, seeing Aaron and Rosamund, he dove toward the table and said, "Hey, you two, you're back. Did I miss anything?"

An awkward laughter rippled through the room.

"Not much." Jacqueline nibbled on grapes and cheese. "Just that Rosamund found the prophecy."

"All right!" Aleksandr tried to high-five her.

She shook her head, too disheartened to pretend joy.

"All right," he said in a totally different tone. "What is the prophecy?"

"The Chosen Ones, all *seven* of us, have got to find and fall in love with our soul mates before our seven years are up or—" Samuel made a slitting-his-own-throat gesture.

Aleksandr straddled a chair. "Except for the fact there are only six of us, that shouldn't be too hard."

"Shouldn't be too hard? How random is this? Find your true love, hope to hell you've got the right one, and somehow make her fall in love with you?" Samuel's eyes narrowed on Aleksandr. "Wait a minute. What do you mean, shouldn't be too hard?" He turned to the group. "We were right. He *is* in love with someone!"

"No!" Aleksandr jumped up, went to the refrigerator, opened it, and stared inside as if expecting to find a treasure of jewels and pearls.

Finally, Martha said in her most annoyed voice, "Would you get what you want and shut the refrigerator?"

"Okay. Geez." Grabbing a Coke, he turned back to the room, and found every eye on him. *"What?"*

Rosamund knew the truth, knew he wanted to keep his girlfriend a secret, and why not? He was young, and a man who didn't believe in kiss-and-tell. She respected his ethics even if no one else did.

So she diverted them. In a voice pitched a little too loud, she said, "I didn't get to read the *whole* prophecy."

Chapter 41

In unison, the Chosen Ones turned to stare at Rosamund.

She gritted her teeth and tried to smile.

"What do you mean, you didn't get to read the whole prophecy?" Samuel asked in a chilly voice.

"I was trying to tell you. I hadn't finished my translation when the fight broke out."

"And the stela disintegrated in your hands." Jacqueline leaned back in her chair. "Of course. It would be too easy if we knew everything we needed to know."

"Everything we needed to know. You are kidding!" Samuel leaped to his feet and paced across the kitchen. "We each have to find our true love—our true love, for Pete's sake! Have any of you ever been involved in a messy divorce? *True love.* Honestly."

"I've found true love, Samuel." Caleb was the last person Rosamund expected to say such a thing. He was lean, tough, laconic. Yet as he looked at Jacqueline, his eyes shone with an inner light that set a treacherous envy burning in her chest.

"Tell me that in seven years when we're all broke because we can't work at our regular jobs, and we're crushed by the burdens of our duties, and maybe I'll believe you then." Samuel showed his true colors now. "Right now, you guys are doing the horizontal mambo every chance you get. What you feel isn't true love. It's infatuation."

"You're a fool, Samuel." But Caleb didn't seem in the slightest bit worried.

Samuel wasn't done ripping up the prophecy. "Oh, oh, and after finding our true love, we have to romance her or him, fall deeply in love ourselves, and I assume mate for life. Not a problem!"

Charisma leaned across the table toward Rosamund. "He's magnificent when he's in lawyer mode, isn't he?"

He was, really. Rosamund nodded, unable to take her eyes off the Rom with the flashing eyes.

Isabelle, too, watched him as if she couldn't look away, but her mockery was bright and sharp as a blade. "He's right. For who is ever going to love Samuel Faa?"

Samuel stopped pacing and glared, and the heat between them blazed like fire. At that moment, if the kitchen hadn't been full of other people, Rosamund would have feared for Isabelle's life . . . or virtue.

"She's not tactful, but she's right," Jacqueline said.

Samuel swung on her.

Jacqueline laughed in his face. "Oh, sit down, Faa. You're making an ass of yourself. And you're right, too. Why couldn't the prophecy be that we needed to find the Temple of Doom, or the Lost Ark?"

"Because none of us is Indiana Jones?" Caleb suggested.

Samuel went back to his chair, seated himself, crossed his arms over his chest, and in his normal tone of voice said, "By the way, has anyone noticed there aren't seven of us? Another tiny bump in the road to fulfilling the prophecy *which isn't complete.*"

"Rosamund? Now that you know so much of the prophecy, can you find corroboration in another form elsewhere?" Irving spoke with the voice of reason.

She nodded. He knew his stuff. "Possibly. I intend to search, and with Bala's Stone, I may be successful."

"You might want to start *now*," Samuel said.

"She can't start now." A warm, rich, man's voice spoke from the deepest shadows of the kitchen.

Rosamund jumped in surprise.

Aaron leaned close to her ear. "That's Vidar Davidov. He's, uh . . . he brews beer."

"Okay," she whispered, and strained to see this Davidov.

But still he hung in the shadows, and his voice was tense and commanding. "There's a situation in New Jersey, a two-year-old girl at an orphanage with a very interesting mark on her shoulder blade that looks like a unicorn. One of the day-care workers is convinced its eyes open and close, and watch, and she told her boyfriend, who has sold the child to the Others. They are coming to take possession, and—"

Chairs scraped on the stone floor as everyone jumped to their feet.

Rosamund knew what this meant. The Chosen Ones would go into danger, into battle, to rescue the little girl.

Aaron would go into danger.

Her artificial calm began to crumble.

With cool authority, Isabelle assumed command. "Samuel, get whatever information Davidov has for us. Jacqueline, anything you can see would be helpful. Caleb, you're in charge of organizing the attack or diversion. Charisma and I will rescue the child. Irving, Martha, McKenna, I don't know where to place the child when we rescue her, but you do. Please, if those places are still safe—"

Martha and McKenna both nodded.

Rosamund stood there, embarrassed at her uselessness and wanting desperately to forbid them to go into danger.

I can't stand to lose the people I consider my friends. I don't want to lose Aaron.

I can't lose Aaron.

But she could. She already had.

Yet Isabelle looked at Aaron and shook her head. "We've probably got too many people working this anyway, but since it's our first operation, I'd rather be safe than sorry. Please stay here and try to recover from—"

"Your death," Samuel filled in.

"Thank you, Samuel," Isabelle snapped.

Rosamund felt a glimmer of hope. "Can he stay here? If you need someone, I could go in his place."

"Sure. Bring the antiquities librarian with the arm in a sling in place of the former dead guy," Samuel said.

"Samuel, shut up," Charisma commanded.

"Samuel, I'm not bringing either one of them." Isabelle turned to Rosamund. "Thank you, but the reason there are seven Chosen—or rather six right now—and a support team is so we have a variety of skills we can draw on. Your job is to heal as quickly as possible, then go looking for any information that can help us recover the future."

"But Aaron's not going with you." Rosamund wanted that confirmation.

"As much as I would like to help, right now I'm afraid I'd be a hindrance," Aaron told her gently. "Besides, this is Isabelle's decision to make, and she said no."

"That's right. We can't use a dead guy, or even an almost dead guy," Samuel said.

Isabelle turned on him and pointed toward the shadows. "Information from Davidov. Now."

"No. First—group hug!" Charisma extended her arms.

Isabelle hesitated, then nodded decisively. "Yes. First, we need a group hug."

Samuel turned back and looked at her. Just looked at her.

"Just this once, I will explain." Isabelle spoke right to him, then to everyone. "We're breaking down. We're complaining about Aleksandr drinking milk out of the jug, Samuel leaving water rings on the wooden tables, every guy here leaving the toilet paper unchanged, Charisma's shoes thrown on the floor, my papers scattered everywhere. We need to rebuild our unity and remember who has our backs."

Samuel sighed loudly, with exasperation, but when he spoke, it almost sounded like humor. "I knew there would be a group hug. There's never any getting out of it."

The Chosen Ones, and Irving, and McKenna, and Martha, moved quickly to stand in a circle in the middle of the kitchen. When Rosamund shook her head, they called her until she had no choice but to join them. Then Aaron joined them, too, taking his place beside Rosamund.

"Mr. Davidov?" Isabelle looked toward the shadows with a shy smile.

"No. Thank you." The voice was so distinctive, Rosamund knew she would recognize it anywhere. "I am not one of your group."

Rosamund still couldn't see Davidov, but she knew from the slight relaxation of Aaron's body that he was relieved.

On the other side of her, Jacqueline wrapped her arm around Rosamund's waist, and Rosamund did the same with her. Like a braid, the Chosen and their friends joined together, shoulder to shoulder, arms intertwined. They looked in one another's eyes. They nodded as if exchanging words unspoken yet understood.

And to Rosamund's astonishment, something zapped them, flashing through the circle. It was an electrical current, hot and bright, or maybe a feeling so strong and vibrant they felt it in unison.

Everybody jumped.

Rosamund cried out in shock.

Aaron laughed.

Charisma nodded her head over and over. "That's

what I'm tellin' ya. Rosamund is the right choice, and we've got our feet on the right path."

Rosamund looked from one to another, bewildered by the flash and confused by their reaction. "What *was* that?"

"It's approval," Irving told her. "As Charisma said, this is the right group, and we've got our feet on the right path."

"Now," Isabelle said, "let's go rescue the child."

Chapter 42

At once, the atmosphere in the kitchen grew somber. Samuel joined Davidov. Caleb, Jacqueline, Aleksandr, and McKenna strode toward the stairs. Martha disappeared into the darkest corner of the kitchen, and Rosamund heard a door open and shut.

Aaron put his hand in the small of Rosamund's back. "Let's go. I have to show you something."

She stumbled along under his guidance, feeling miserable and wishing she were someone else, somewhere else, hoping they could make love one more time before she had to leave him, knowing he suspected a problem and would never let her get away with evading his questions.

Leading her to the bathroom off the kitchen, he flipped on the light. He looked into her eyes and said, "You say I don't love you unless you're pretty. Well, here." He pushed her in front of the mirror.

"Oh." Surprised and dismayed, Rosamund stared at

her reflection: windblown hair, dust-smudged cheek, mascara rings beneath the eyes. "But . . . I don't understand. Philippe told me the makeup was waterproof and resistant to wear."

Aaron grinned, then hastily straightened his face into gravity. "I don't know a lot about makeup, but I can say with a great deal of certainty that 'resistant' doesn't mean it's going to stay in place for more than forty-eight hours."

"When . . . when did the Paris magic disappear?" In the coat closet? In the Sacred Cave? On the airplane on the flight back to New York?

Yet Aaron said he loved her. . . .

Over her head, he watched her knowingly.

He was sculpted and bronzed, handsome even with bruises and cuts, and the contrast with her made her miserably aware that he was so debonair and urbane, and she was so not. She had to make herself clear. "The thing is, I liked being pretty, but it took hours. It was okay to do once, but it's not me. I mean, of course, I put on lipstick. . . ." She almost said *every day*, but she couldn't lie. "I do put on lipstick every once in a while and I comb my hair every day."

She didn't know why, but he chuckled.

Dauntless, she plowed on. "But this is the real me." She pointed at her reflection in the mirror.

He turned her to face him. "This is exactly the woman I want—intense, intelligent, fascinating, and not at all pretty."

She stiffened. She knew it was true, that she wasn't pretty, but he didn't have to say so.

She knew that he wanted her, too, but what they had could never work . . . because she was a coward.

Capturing her chin with his cupped hand, he lifted her face to his. "You are the most *beautiful* woman I've ever seen, and all I want is to spend the rest of my life with you." Sliding his arm around her waist, he pulled her close and kissed her with such passion and heat, she forgot her qualms, her fears. With his lips on hers, she thought of only one thing. Having him. Mating with him. Giving him pleasure, learning passion from him.

But as soon as he stopped kissing her, the truth came flooding back. *I can't do this.*

And he knew. He scrutinized with those deep, dark eyes, and he just knew. "What's wrong?"

She shook her head, not wanting to ruin this moment.

"No. Don't pretend with me. You loved me, I know you did, and I'm just a guy with no sensitivity, but you're on the verge of crying." He used his thumb to catch the tear that spilled over and trickled down her cheek. "After the fight in your library, you said you loved me, but ever since Samuel got us out of the hospital, you've been . . . distant. Why? Did I say something wrong?"

"Say something wrong?" She tore herself out of his arms, wrapped her good arm around her stomach, tried to contain the agony that bubbled inside her. "It's not what you said. It's what you did."

"What did I do?" He tried to embrace her.

"You *died*." She evaded him.

As if he were startled, he laughed a little. "But I'm

okay!" He spread his arms as if to show her. "You heard what I said in the kitchen. I'm more than okay. I'm great!"

"No. No! It doesn't matter. I don't love you anymore."

"Hm." He took her hands, uncurled her clenched fingers, and held them. "You know, I just don't believe you."

"It's true." He *had* to believe her, because she was going to make herself believe it.

"All right. Why don't you tell why you don't love me anymore?" He walked her toward the stairway that led to the mansion's impressive foyer.

"I told you. You died." She grabbed for her composure again, and found it, never mind that it rocked like an ice floe on the arctic waters. "I have too much experience with that kind of loss. I lost my mother when I was a girl, but I was a kid. I didn't understand then. I thought that somehow, someday, I'd see her again, hear her voice, somehow touch her spirit. Or something! I didn't understand forever, the emptiness that weighs more than love, that like a glacier grinds you a different path so that you become someone who doesn't dare hope. Because hopes are destined to be dashed. My father's gone now, too. Both of my parents gone . . . because they were scholars seeking knowledge, and the Others . . . the Others wanted to hoard the knowledge for themselves."

They reached the foyer, and Aaron turned her. "I would understand if you declared you didn't love the Others. But your parents' deaths are not my fault."

"I know that."

"You haven't told me why you don't love me."

She didn't want to face him while she talked. She didn't want to meet his eyes. She pulled away from him, turned her back, stood before a Queen Anne antique side table graced with a green porcelain vase. With her finger, she traced the design cut into the smooth wood. "In a lesser way, I loved Louis, and a few hours after I met him, he was dead."

"The fact you knew and loved him didn't make him a target for death." As Aaron spoke, he moved to one side of her.

"I know that. I mean, when I was a kid, I thought I must have been the cause of my mother's death. It was the only reason I could imagine that my father would suddenly dislike me so." She looked up, and realized she faced into a mirror, and Aaron had changed positions so he could observe the expressions that chased across her face. "Okay. I thought that all the way up to the time when Lance admitted he'd killed my father. Then I realized both my parents were killed for knowing too much and poking their noses into a dangerous business."

Aaron still watched her.

So she still talked. "In a weird way, it was okay to lose my parents. Not good. Not easy. I loved my mother, I loved my father, but my parents were always supposed to die before me. You—I fell in love with you. I didn't want to. I just couldn't help it. You were strong and smart. And competent! You handled everything in the world so easily. You could get a cab. You could find my purse. You could fight off a dozen attackers. You could hide me in plain sight to get me out of Fournier's château. You could make love so beautifully." She put her hand over her aching heart.

He stood very still, very quiet, his dark eyes intent on her. "Honey, you're talking about me in the past tense. I am still here. I am still that man."

"But don't you see?" She faced him, leaned against the table, said, "You could die again."

"Yes. That's true." He captured her hand, kissed the back of her fingers. "Darling, I'm so sorry. I'm so sorry you're afraid, but what comfort can I offer you?"

She tried to yank her hand back.

He wouldn't release her. "Listen to me. I'm one of the Chosen Ones. The mark on my back—it's a gift."

"A gift you have to pay for."

"I don't *have* to. I admit, I had to be blackmailed into joining the Chosen Ones. But when the Gypsy Travel Agency exploded, and so many people were killed, and I realized there was only us, seven people who didn't know what they were doing . . . well, six now . . . It means I'm someone who has a job to do, and that job is dangerous." He used his grip on her hands to gather her close to him. "The mark on my back is a target, and when I do what I must do, I'm going to be in peril."

She smelled the scent of him, felt his warmth, listened to his voice, and all the time, she knew she only had this moment with him. She could not depend on tomorrow. "I don't want to be in love with a man who could die again. The first time . . . the first time almost killed me. I sat there in the ruins of that collapsed cave and held you in my arms, and I knew your spirit had gone from me. You were gone, and I was alone. Forever."

"Darling . . ." He tried to kiss her.

She fended him off. "No. If you're going to go off and steal things, to embrace danger, I don't want to know. If you're going to be one of the Chosen Ones, I don't want to be here. I can't be here. I cannot love a hero." Her eyes filled with tears. Her voice wobbled.

In a flat tone, he said, "If I can, you can."

"What?" *Huh? What? Had he lost his mind?*

"You have spent the last week dashing across oceans and up mountains in search of a prophecy. You faced off with men who counterfeit antiques and with assassins and murderous security men. You dealt with hostile French villagers and the collapse of the Sacred Cave." He held her close and shook her, then wrapped his arms around her shoulders and pulled her closer, into his chest. "Most terrifying, you emerged triumphant from the dreaded fashion makeover. You beat every challenge—and today, you told Irving you were going to explore a way to corroborate the prophecy you found."

"I'm not brave. That's just research."

"That you could be killed for conducting." When she would have objected, he added, "As your parents were killed. So don't tell me you fear my death and the loneliness that would follow, because if you died in the quest for a prophecy that I asked you to find . . . I would never forgive myself." His voice shook. He put his face into her hair and took a long breath, and said, "Rosamund, I love you. I can't live without you. Living with you, for no matter how much time is given us, is better than living an eternity without you."

"Oh. You had to say *that*." He was so completely

logical, she was forced to be logical in her turn, and face the fact he was right. The pain of losing him would be nothing compared to the pain of never being with him again.

"I trust you to have a care for yourself," he said. "Won't you do the same with me? I'm good at what I do, and getting better all the time. Do you believe that?"

"Yes. I do." She'd been witness to his skills and his gift. "You are very competent. Even . . . brilliant."

"Good. I'm glad we agree." He muffled his laugh in her hair. "So stay with me, and we'll be brave together, and if one of us has to pass on before the other, we'll know that someday, we'll be together again."

She stood in his embrace, trying to think, to understand what had happened that she, the ordinary, too-smart, bookish librarian, should inspire this kind of devotion from Aaron Eagle, the man who fought, stole antiques, hailed cabs, and made love, all with unparalleled proficiency. Still, she tried to protect herself. "All right. I want to try with you for a while."

"How long a while?" He leaned back and looked into her face.

"A year?"

"I have a better idea. I think we'd be better off starting with fifty."

"Fifty what?"

"Fifty years. That way we'd really know if we could handle this situation with aplomb."

"Aaron. That isn't funny."

"I assure you, funny is the last thing I'm trying to be." In fact, he looked utterly serious. "Rosamund Fair,

I want to marry you. I want to live with you forever, and when I die, I want to die in your arms. I don't know if I can live without you, but I know I don't want to try. Take a chance with me. Say yes."

She thought about the things he'd said, but more than that, she thought about who he was—a man of honor, a man of valor, a man who loved her so completely he had died to save her life, then put his life on the line again to save her again. "Yes. I'll marry you."

He laughed again, this time a lighthearted laugh that made her smile in her turn. "Do you still love me?" he asked.

"No matter how hard I try, no matter how long I live, I will never stop." Even though she was opening herself up to so much pain . . . and so many sweet rewards.

He lifted her gently and spun in a circle of exultation. "I love you, too, Rosamund, all the way through this world and into the next."

As they circled, her heel caught on the edge of the table.

The green vase teetered toward the marble floor.

She squeaked with dismay.

He dropped her to her feet, lunged, and caught the fragile porcelain. Looking up at her, his eyes horrified, he said, "Ming dynasty. Chrysanthemum styled."

"Priceless?" she asked.

He nodded and carefully placed the vase back on the table. "McKenna would have killed us."

"That would have ended our quandary." For the first time in days, she laughed.

He listened to her merriment, a half smile on his

face, and said, "Now, *that* is priceless." Putting his arm around her, he said, "We have got to find someplace private."

As he hustled her up the stairs, she smiled at him, besotted by his intent, chiseled, severe face. "You know, we'll always have Paris."

"To hell with Paris." He opened his bedroom door and ushered her inside. "Wait until you see what we can do in New York City."

Chapter 43

Aaron and Rosamund were upstairs. The Chosen Ones had left for their first mission. Martha had gone to establish a place for the rescued child. Mc-Kenna was monitoring the rescue operation from afar. In the kitchen, Irving and Davidov stood together.

Irving turned to Davidov. "You couldn't have left them alone a little longer."

Davidov moved out of the shadows. He didn't look a day older than the last time Irving had seen him, teeth gleaming, blond hair glowing with vitality, mus-cled body hard—and that was forty years ago.

But his eyes were tired.

"You couldn't have let them be safe." Since the mo-ment Davidov had spoken, Irving's hands had been knotted. Now he rubbed them together trying to ease the ache.

"Irving, you're an old man." Davidov shoved a chair toward him. "The Chosen Ones aren't supposed to be safe. They're meant to be out there, fighting the good fight."

"They haven't got training. They haven't got backup. They're the most inexperienced Chosen since—"

"Since the world was young, and the twins went out to fight for good and evil." Davidov seated himself on a low stool. "Isabelle's got a good head on her shoulders. Caleb is a bodyguard, and he trained Jacqueline to fight. Give them a chance."

"Thanks to you, I don't have a choice." Irving didn't want to sit, didn't want Davidov to know his weakness. He'd had never liked the man, with his deep secrets and his dark warnings and the way he showed up whenever he pleased and disappeared just as quickly. Davidov wasn't a company man. He wasn't even . . . Well, Irving didn't know what he was or wasn't, but he knew Davidov couldn't be controlled. He knew Davidov was dangerous.

Yet Irving's knees were shaking from tension, and he eased himself into the chair.

Davidov leaned his arms on his knees, gazed at Irving, and in a reasonable tone that set his teeth on edge, said, "Listen. Six Chosen is bad luck. You know that. You need to get that seventh Chosen."

"I don't believe in bad luck. The records have been destroyed. I don't know who to get." Irving recited every excuse without expecting Davidov to listen or care.

"There are past Chosen out there who would respond to an appeal."

"If they weren't at the Gypsy Travel Agency during the Choosing, then they're renegades."

"You mean they're Chosen you can't control." Davidov slapped his hand on the massive table—and it quivered from the shock. "Irving, this isn't about you and your position as CEO of the Gypsy Travel Agency. Yes, when you stepped into the position fifty years ago, the whole organization was in a mess, and you fixed it. You incorporated, you made the Gypsy Travel Agency financially secure, and the Chosen Ones were able to do their jobs without worrying about how to fund their missions. But what you did was—" He hesitated.

"What I did was . . . what?" Irving fixed his eyes on this man, this thing that had always been his nemesis.

"You saved them," Davidov said simply. "And condemned them."

The two men stared at each other, challenging each other, saying more than words.

Irving's gaze dropped first, to his gnarled, aching, spotted old hands that gripped the armrests on his chair. "I retired because I was old."

"It was already too late."

Something jingled in the pantry.

Davidov turned his head. "What's that?"

"It's the doorbell. It rings down here, and it rings on McKenna's pager. He'll get it."

Like a dog worrying a bone, Davidov returned to the issue at hand. "The seventh Chosen. You are missing an integral component to this team. You need a gift of raw power."

"I know."

"Why didn't you pick one in the first place? Then perhaps now you wouldn't have your cock in a wringer."

"Because of what happened last time. And because he's still the only Chosen of power we've had for a century. He didn't finish his seven years because he . . ." Irving shook his head at the memory. "You scoff at control, but John Powell cannot be trusted to control *himself*."

"If you don't get someone in here with experience, someone who can provide guidance and *protection* to those fragile human beings who just walked out the door, they will die. The Others have prepared for this for years, and you know—Irving, you *know*—what is driving them."

"The devil himself."

"Him, too. But that's not what I'm talking about. I'm talking about a deep, bloodthirsty desire for vengeance—and you know who will have that revenge, and why."

Irving knew Davidov was right—but he was right, too. John could not be trusted.

Davidov, of course, could read his reluctance. "I don't care what you *think*. Get that seventh Chosen in here." He had power in his voice, and he used it to try to bend Irving to his will.

Irving would not yield to such tricks. "I will make this decision when I see the need."

Davidov slowly stood, glorious in his masculinity, his strength, his resolve.

In that moment, Irving knew he faced death—and he was not resigned. He was surprised how much he wanted to remain on this earth, to see the drama of these days played out; yet he would not be reduced to obedience. He would do as he had always done—what he thought best for the Chosen Ones. He stood also, prepared to have his neck snapped.

Then Davidov turned his head in the attitude of listening. "I don't believe it," he whispered.

"Believe what?" Irving listened, too. He knew the sound of McKenna's footsteps. But he had someone with him. Someone who walked a little off-kilter, dragging one foot behind him.

Davidov seemed to know who it was.

Irving didn't have a clue.

McKenna stepped through the door, his eyes bright, his posture sprightly. Irving had never seen him like this; he was the epitome of hope.

"What is it, McKenna?" Irving asked.

McKenna straightened his lapels, and in a sonorous voice announced, "Mr. Gary White."

And the man Irving had only two weeks ago seen in the depths of a coma walked in the door.

Don't miss *New York Times* bestselling author Christina Dodd's triumphant return to historical romance with this brand-new, sexy, sweeping adventure . . .

IN BED WITH THE DUKE

Coming from Signet in March 2010

Moricadia, 1849

The four-piece ensemble ceased playing, and with exquisite timing, Comte Cloutier delivered the line sure to command the attention of all the guests within earshot. "Have you heard, Lady Lettice, of the ghost who rides in the night?"

Certainly, he commanded the attention of the Englishman Michael Durant, heir apparent to the duke of Nevitt. There had been very little to interest him at Lord Thibault's exclusive ball. The musicians had played, the guests had danced, the food was exquisite, and the gambling room was full. But of gossip, there had been nothing . . . until now. And now, Michael knew, only because Cloutier failed to comprehend the seriousness of his faux pas. He failed to comprehend that by tomorrow, he would be gone, traveling back to France and cursing his penchant for gossip.

With every evidence of interest, Michael strolled closer, to stand near the group of suitors surrounding Lady Lettice Surtees.

"A ghost?" Lady Lettice gave a high-pitched squeak, worthy of a young girl's alarm. "No! Pray tell, what does this ghost do?" Before Cloutier could answer she swung around to her paid companion, a girl of perhaps twenty who stood at her left shoulder, and snapped, "Make yourself useful, girl! Fan me! Dancing with so many admirers is quite fatiguing."

The girl, a poor, downtrodden wisp of a thing, nodded mutely. From the large reticule she wore attached to her waist, she withdrew an ivory-and-lace fan to cool the abruptly flushed and sweating Lady Lettice.

Lord Escobar hovered at Lettice's left elbow. "Indeed, senorita, it is an unseasonably warm summer evening."

It was a gross flattery to call Lady Lettice "senorita"— she was a widow in her early forties, with the beginnings of the jowls that would plague her old age. But her bosoms were impressive and displayed to advantage by her immodestly low-cut, ruffled bodice, and more important, she was wealthy, and the half dozen impoverished men around her wooed her for her fortune.

"So, Cloutier, tell me about this ghost." Lady Lettice withdrew a white cotton handkerchief from between her breasts and blotted her damp upper lip.

"This ghost—he rides at night, in utter silence, a massive white figure in fluttering rags atop a giant white horse. His skin is death, his clothes are rags, and where his eyes should be, there are only black holes.

A terrifying apparition, yet the peasants whisper he is the specter of the last king of Moricadian blood."

"Peasants," Lady Lettice said contemptuously.

"Exactly." Cloutier's lip curled with scorn. "But others who have come to this fair city to take the waters and enjoy the gaming tables have seen him, too, and if you are unlucky enough to see this fearsome ghoul, you should flee at once, for this fearsome phantom"—Cloutier lowered his voice in pitch and volume—"is a sign of impending death."

Michael snorted, the sound breaking the shocked silence.

At once, Lady Lettice fixed him with her gaze. "You're impertinent. Do you know who this man is?" She gestured to Cloutier.

Her mouse of a paid companion made a small warning noise and flapped the fan harder.

Lady Lettice paid no heed. "He is Comte Cloutier, of one of the finest noble families in France. One does not *snort* when he speaks."

"One does if one is Michael Durant, the heir to the Nevitt dukedom." Cloutier bowed to Michael.

"Oh." Lady Lettice extended her hand. "My lord. Your grace."

Cloutier did the honors. "Lady Lettice Surtees, this is Lord—"

"Please." Michael held up a hand. "In England, my name is old and honored. In Moricadia, I am nothing but a political prisoner, a nonentity, a man who has vanished from the world due to the oppression of the ruling family. Call me Durant. It is the only decent title for a disgrace such as me, and even my family name is too honorable." His voice was a low rasp, one that played into the tragedy he projected with a sure hand.

"A political prisoner?" Lady Lettice said. "I am shocked! How is this possible?"

"The only ghost in Moricadia is me, my lady, for until I was allowed out for this one night, my existence has been no more than a rumor." Michael bowed and strolled away.

"The poor man." Lady Lettice spoke in a whisper so high as to pierce ears. "What did he do?"

Michael paused behind a marble pillar to hear the answer.

No one replied at first; then Escobar reluctantly said, "Durant fell foul of the de Guignards. They accused him of assisting the rebels and undermining their position as rulers of Moricadia, and for these two years, he was believed dead. Only recently has it come to light that he is being held prisoner by Lord and Lady Fanchere, trusted allies of Prince Sandre."

"But I don't understand," Lady Lettice insisted. "How do the de Guignards dare to hold an English nobleman against his will?"

"In the case of Moricadia, the de Guignards overthrew King Reynaldo and won"—Escobar waved his hands toward the window where brightly lit villas, gambling houses, and spas decorated the peaks of the Pyrenees— "all this. But we dare not talk of it. Prince Sandre has spies everywhere, and he does not tolerate dissension in his country." Escobar bowed. "Now, if you'll excuse me . . ."

Michael nodded to the man as he hurried past. Wise Escobar. He would seek another wealthy widow, one not at the epicenter of a possible upheaval.

A well-dressed youth of twenty-two stepped into Escobar's place. He paid no attention to the companion still vigorously fanning Lady Lettice's neck. Nor did any of the other suitors.

Fools. The girl appeared to be no more than eighteen, nervous as a rabbit. The drab gray wool of her plain dress did nothing to complement her pale complexion, and the cut completely obscured what appeared to be a shapely, if too thin, figure. She had typical English features, and might have been pretty, but she kept her eyes down and her shoulders hunched as if expecting at any moment a slap across the cheek.

In Michael's opinion, the lords and gentlemen who fought to capture Lady Lettice in wedded bliss would be well-advised to look to her cowed companion.

The young man jockeyed for position, and the result was disaster—for the companion. They bumped arms. The fan smacked the back of Lady Lettice's head, making the curls over her ears bounce. Turning on the girl, she bellowed, "You stupid thing, how *dare* you hit me?"

"I didn't mean—" The girl's voice matched her demeanor, low and timid, and it trembled.

In a flurry, Lady Lettice adjusted her hairpins. "I should throw you out on the street right now. I should!"

"No, ma'am, please. It won't happen again." The girl looked around at the men, seeking help where there was none. "I beg you. Let me stay in your service."

"She isn't really sorry," Lady Lettice told the others. "She only says that because she's an orphan, the daughter of a Yorkshire vicar who left her with nothing, and she would starve without my kindness. Wouldn't you, Emma?"

"Yes, ma'am." Emma adjusted Lady Lettice's shawl across her shoulders.

"All right, fine, stop." Lady Lettice pushed her away. "You're annoying me. I'll keep you on, but if you ever hit me again—"

"I won't! Thank you!" Emma curtsied, and curtsied again.

Poor Emma. If Michael weren't in such a mess himself, he would see what he could do for her. But as it was . . .

"Actually . . ." Lady Lettice stared at her handkerchief, and Michael could see the spark of some dreadful mischief start in her brain. "I'd like this dampened. Go to the ladies' convenience and do so."

"As you wish, Lady Lettice." Emma took the handkerchief and scurried away.

"Watch, gentlemen," Lady Lettice said. "The stupid girl has no sense of direction. She turns right when she should turn left, goes north when she should go south. The ladies' convenience is to the right, so she'll turn left."

Emma walked to the door, hesitated, and as promised, turned left.

Lady Lettice tittered. "Would you gentlemen care to wager how long it will take my stupid companion to find her way back to me?"

"Good sport," said Bedingfield. "I wager your handkerchief will still be dry!"

Michael, ever the fool for the underdog, quietly went to rescue the girl from her own folly.

Emma was lost. She stood in the garden and looked back at the château. From here, she could hear the music from the ballroom, see the light spilling from the windows. Surely, if she studied the location, she could find her way back.

But then what? She still wouldn't have accomplished her mission, and she knew very well the price of disobeying Lady Lettice's commands.

As she stood there under the stars, staring at the splashing fountain, she wished she was rich, noble, and beautiful instead of poor, common, and well educated. What good did common sense and a sharp intelligence do for a woman when her main duty was to fan a perspiring beast? But as Emma's father had always said she might be a timid child, but she had an analytical brain, and that was a gift from God she should utilize to make her life, and the lives of others, better and more fruitful.

So walking to the fountain, she dipped Lady Lettice's handkerchief into the pool—and heard a warm, rasping chuckle behind her. Dropping the handkerchief, she turned to face Michael Durant.

"I came out to direct you to the ladies' convenience, but I see you found a better solution." He nodded toward the fountain.

"It's not what you think." He would report her to the beast. She was going to be thrown onto the street in a strange country with nowhere to turn. She was going to die a slow death. "I didn't come out here on purpose—"

He held up one hand. "Please. Lady Lettice made

clear your amazing ability to get lost. She didn't realize your ability to improvise. Miss . . . ?"

"Chegwidden." She curtsied. "Emma Chegwidden."

In the ballroom, she had watched him and thought him a handsome brute, big-boned, tall, and raw. His hair was red. His eyes were bright, piercing blue. His black suit was well made, yet the clothes didn't fit well: The formal black jacket was tight across his shoulders and loose at his waist, and the ensemble gave him the appearance of a warhorse dressed in a gentleman's clothing.

"A pleasure, Miss Chegwidden." He bowed. "Shall I help you retrieve the handkerchief?"

In the ballroom, she had thought him a phony, another nobleman flirting with tragedy for the outpouring of sympathy and the residual gossip.

Out here, he seemed different, sympathetic to her plight. Yet he saw too much, and he had a quality of stillness about him, like a tiger lying in wait for its prey. So she must step carefully. Durant could be every bit as nasty as the other gentlemen, and a good deal more dangerous.

Glancing down into the clear water, she saw the white square floating just below the surface. "Thank you. I can do it." Without turning her back to him, she caught it in her fingertips, and wrung it out over the pool. "So she did this to humiliate me."

"She is not a gentlewoman, I believe. Nor a particularly pleasant woman." He walked up the steps and looked back at her. "Shall we go back in?"

By that, she assumed he meant to guide her to the ballroom, and cautiously she followed him.

"This way." He gestured down the corridor, and as they walked, he said, "I recall Lady Lettice was the only daughter of a manufacturing family, married for her fortune to Baron Surtees, and after a mere twenty-some years of hellish married life, Surtees escaped wedlock by dropping dead."

"You are uncharitable, my lord." Emma took a breath to avoid laughing while she spoke, and when she had herself under control, she said, "But yes. After his unfortunate death, Lady Lettice took his title and her fortune, and has lately been touring Europe in hopes of meeting her next, er, husband."

His height made her uncomfortable, and as they walked, she watched his hands. Big hands. Big bones. Big knuckles. Broad palms. Hands weathered by fighting experience. And she was walking alone with him. "Gentlemen of the Continent have a sophisticated attitude toward women of her age and wealth."

"I can imagine. This way." He took a twisting route leading down corridors lined with closed doors.

"Are you sure?" She could have sworn they were headed back to the garden.

"I never get lost." He sounded so sure of himself.

Irksome man. He might not get lost, but he was certainly in trouble. With more sharpness than she intended, she asked, "What did you do to get yourself arrested as a political prisoner?"

He stopped walking.

She stopped walking.

"In Moricadia, it doesn't do to poke your nose into local troubles." He tapped her nose with his finger. "Remember that."

Affronted by his presumption, she said, "I certainly would not do something so stupid."

His eyebrow lifted quizzically. "Of course not. You're supremely sensible."

The way he spoke made her realize—she'd just called him stupid. "My lord, I didn't mean—"

"Not at all. You're quite right. Now." He opened a door to his right.

At once, the sound of music and laughter filtered through, and peeking in, Emma saw the dining hall, and beyond that, the ballroom.

"Do you still have Lady Lettice's handkerchief?" he asked.

"I don't lose things, my lord." She showed it to him, still twisted between her palms. "I only lose myself."

"And now you are found. I'll leave you to make your own way to Lady Lettice's side." He bowed. "It's been a pleasure, Miss Chegwidden."

She curtsied. "My lord, my heartfelt thanks." She watched him walk away, then hurried past the long dining table and stepped into the ballroom.

She found herself standing behind Lady Lettice and her admirers, and opposite where she thought she should be. But she was back, the handkerchief was wet, and Lady Lettice and her nasty game had gone awry.

As Emma walked up behind the group of suitors, she heard Cloutier say, "She must arrive within the next minute, or I lose!"

"Lose what, my lord?" Emma stepped into the circle.

Lady Lettice jumped. Her skin turned ruddy with displeasure, all the way down to her amply displayed breasts, and she snapped, "Where did you come from, girl?"

"The ladies' convenience, as you commanded." Emma extended the handkerchief.

Lady Lettice plucked it out of her palm. "It's wadded up, and too wet. You stupid girl, can't you do anything right? Must I instruct you in every nuance? To think that you are the best the Distinguished Academy of Governesses had to offer is simply—" With a flip of the wrist, she opened the handkerchief.

And a tiny, still-wiggling goldfish slipped out and down her cleavage.

She screamed. Leaped to her feet, slapping at her chest. Screamed again.

The dancing stuttered to a stop.

The men around her backed away and burst into hearty laughter.

And a horrified Emma Chegwidden backed away, murmuring, "I am ruined."